the Geneva Option

the Geneva Option

A Yael Azoulay Novel

Adam LeBor

BOURBON STREET BOOKS
An Imprint of HarperCollinsPublishers
www.harpercollins.com

FIRST EDITION

Designed by Michael Correy

Library of Congress Cataloging-in-Publication Data is available upon request.

ISBN 978-0-06-220855-2

13 14 15 16 17 OV/RRD 10 9 8 7 6 5 4 3 2

For Kati

Most blessed among women is Yael

Judges V, the Song of Deborah, verse 24.

Acknowledgments

This book is dedicated to my wife, Kati. She and our children, Danny and Hannah, provided all the love, energy, and inspiration a writer could wish for, and more. My special thanks go to Elizabeth Sheinkman, my brilliant agent at William Morris Endeavor. Her belief in *The Geneva Option*, and in Yael Azoulay, never wavered. But a novel also needs an ardent editor or two: Claire Wachtel at HarperCollins in New York and Lynn Gaspard at Telegram were enthusiastic overseers, encouraging, excising, and skillfully honing where needed. Thanks also to Matthew Patin for his diligent copy editing, to Elizabeth Perrella for keeping the show on the road, to Michael Correy for his elegant design, and to Jo Rodgers, who guided me through the geography of New York bar culture.

The seed for *The Geneva Option* was planted in July 1992 when I flew into besieged Sarajevo on a United Nations airplane while on assignment for *The Times* of London. The memories of my time in the former Yugoslavia, and the friendships I made there, are as vital as ever. I am grateful to John Kulka, formerly of Yale University Press, who commissioned and published *Complicity with Evil*, my nonfiction work about the United Nations' response to genocide and to Robert Baldock at YUP in London. Special thanks to Andrew Tuck, Steve Bloomfield, and Tyler Brûlé of *Monocle* magazine, who have sent me to all sorts of interesting places, assignments that helped inspire this book. My thanks also go to my colleagues at the *Economist*—Fiammetta Rocco, Emily Bobrow, and Lucy Farmer for providing me with thrillers to review; and to Edward Lucas, John Peet, Tom Nuttall, and the late, much missed Peter David. Over the years, I have met and interviewed numerous senior UN officials and diplomats. Many prefer to remain anonymous but I am especially grateful to Michael Williams, David Harland, the late Richard Holbrooke, Samir Sanbar, Mo Sacirbey, Mukesh Kapila, David Hannay, and Diego Arria for sharing their insight, as did James Bone, a veteran former UN correspondent.

In New York there are no hosts more gracious and welcoming than Peter Green, Bob Green, and Babette Audant. Peter also generously shared his expert knowledge of the United Nations and guided me through the intricacies of life in Manhattan. Sam Loewenberg was an enthusiastic guide to Geneva at night and showed me parts of the city that tourists do not usually get to see. In Budapest Erik D'Amato provided me with welcome company and a room of my own that proved the most creative of incubators. Olen Steinhauer, Michael Miller, and Andrew Miller cast an expert eye over the manuscript. George Szirtes and Charles Cumming helped along the way. Justin Leighton and Roger Boyes were there when needed with advice and encouragement while Joshua Freeman kept my website updated. Alan Furst has always been a source of inspiration. I am especially grateful to Laura Longrigg, my former agent, who helped me get this far. My mother, Brenda LeBor, gave me an artist's eye for detail and my brother Jason has always been there for me. My late and very much missed father, Maurice LeBor, always encouraged my writing career and would have been thrilled to see this book.

In September 2012 I took an early draft of *The Geneva Option* to an Arvon residential writing course at Totleigh Barton. I benefited greatly from the feedback of my fellow students and our tutors Andrew Miller and Monique Roffey, while Oliver Meek and Claire Berliner were warm and welcoming hosts. Special thanks to Annika Savill, my former colleague at *The Independent*, who first encouraged me to become a foreign correspondent, for her insight and wisdom over the years. When inspiration flagged, Miles Davis, John Coltrane, Harold Budd, and the Cocteau Twins set synapses crackling once more. Csaba Toldi at Anahita Yoga helped keep me in shape. Last, but by no means least, a tip of the hat to my good friend Z., a deft guide to the world of shadows.

Prologue

The wind rose and fell through the airshaft, roaring so loudly it seemed the building was breathing.

Olivia de Souza held her right hand out over the void. Her fingers were steady as she felt the draft rush up against her palm, whisking the smoke from her cigarette away. She loved the still of the early morning, standing on the narrow maintenance balcony, staring into the darkness below, where dust and secrets gathered. The United Nations secretary-general's staff meeting started in two hours, at 9:00 a.m. Until then, this was her special time, shared with no one.

But today her sanctuary on the 38th floor brought her no peace. She picked a sliver of rust off the railing, flicked it over the edge, and watched it vanish, her lips pressed tight with worry. She had sat up half the night, lighting one cigarette after another and staring into the gray haze as she turned things over and over in her mind. She had to talk to somebody, but there was only one person she could trust—a colleague, perhaps even a friend now, who was on mission but due back tomorrow. She could wait one more day.

Like many middle-aged women working in the Secretariat building, Olivia was a UN widow. After twenty years she was still addicted to the adrenaline rush, the glamour, and proximity to power, and all for the cause of humanity's greater good. She would have liked to have been a diplomat herself and, of course, to have had a family of her own. But there were few enough opportunities for an orphan from the slums of Managua. She had made her choices and a good life for herself. Even her detractors, the ones who whispered to each other that the world's most powerful diplomat should have his affairs arranged by someone more, as they said, "presentable," than a short, dark, Nicaraguan spinster, admitted she was loyal, dedicated, and supremely efficient.

A light switched on and off in one of the rooms nearby and she turned around to look. Who was wandering around the 38th floor at this time in the morning, she wondered. It must be one of the cleaners. Nobody else from the SG's office came in this early. He had not continued his Korean predecessor's habit of starting the workday at 8:00 a.m.

The building itself was slowly waking up. Olivia shivered and pulled her coat around her as the heating system hissed and sputtered. The UN's New York headquarters was of pensionable age and showing it. Condensation dripped off the inner windows, which were crusted with decades' worth of dirt. The airshaft's panels were peeling away, revealing gray slabs of asbestos underneath. The concrete was fissured with tiny cracks. The balcony gently vibrated as the service lift stopped and she stepped away from the edge. A notice on the low railing declared, "Maintenance Staff Only: Do Not Gather or Loiter."

She stifled a yawn and tried to put her worries aside, thinking instead about her dinner date last night, the second in a week, and how hopeful his eyes had looked as his hand slid across the table to hers. It had been a long time, such a very long time. He had asked her to keep their rendezvous secret for now, which made it even more romantic. What did he see in her when he could have his pick of his department, if not the building? He even promised to come to the Latino orphanage on 155th Street with her this weekend to help deliver toys and food. His fingers were long and slim, and it was all she could do not to grip them as hard as she could.

The door to the balcony opened. Olivia turned, smiling with pleasure and surprise, her heart pounding at the sight of him.

He stared at her, his eyes alive with excitement as he walked toward her. "I can't sleep. I can't eat. I can't stop thinking about you."

She trembled like a teenager on a first date. "Me too."

"I am so happy to see you," he said, his voice warm and reassuring. He moved closer, and she breathed in the familiar smell of his lemon cologne.

Her smile wilted as she began to ask, "But how did you know I—"

"Shhh," he said, and she felt the latex glove hard against her lips.

He slammed her against the railing, his hand clamped over her mouth. She jammed the burning cigarette end into the base of his neck. He gasped and gritted his teeth with the pain, knocking her hand away and trying to punch her in the stomach. She swerved sideways and the blow glanced off her rib cage as she flailed wildly at his face, raking her nails across the base of his neck, jabbing at his eyes.

She kicked his shin, digging her heel into the bone and scraping it hard down his leg. He yelped in pain, swore, and she felt his grip loosen. She slipped out from under him and tried to grab the door but he snatched her arm again and held his hand flat against her face, pushing her hard against the railing with his body. He gripped her wrists together with one hand, grunting as he forced his weight on her and clamped her mouth and nose shut with his thumb and forefinger, twisting the cartilage, bending her backward at the waist. The metal bar of the railing dug into her spine and the pain lanced like knives through her.

The sky spun, the walls rushed back and forth, and the terror soared inside her. She tried to cry out but she could barely breathe. He worked diligently until suddenly she was flying, and there was nothing left to fight against.

Goma and New York

ONE

Yael Azoulay tapped her pencil on the cover of the blue plastic file and slid it across the coffee table. "Game over, Professor," she said.

Jean-Pierre Hakizimani smiled and picked up the bottle of Johnnie Walker Gold Label whisky. "And if I say otherwise?"

Yael slowly shook her head. "There is no otherwise."

Hakizimani poured himself a generous measure and picked up the folder. He glanced at the United Nations logo on the cover and opened the file, flipping through the pages as though examining an essay by an especially tiresome student. He slowly tore the sheets into pieces, dropped the shreds into an overflowing ashtray, and reached for the heavy silver cigarette lighter on the table in front of him. He pressed the lighter gently and touched the flame to the scraps. The papers began to burn.

Yael leaned forward, picked up the bottle and upended it over the ashtray. The flames smoked and sputtered. The tawny liquid slopped over the sides, the ash and cigarette ends swirling in the puddle as it spread over the table. The stink of alcohol filled the room. Yael put the whisky back down. She picked out a scrap—sodden, charred at the edges, and emblazoned with the logo of the International Criminal Tribunal for Rwanda. She placed it in front of him. She then extracted another piece from the wet mess on which Hakizimani's photograph and the word "genocide" were clearly visible.

"Shall I continue?" she asked.

"What do you want?" he said, his voice bored.

"You to stop."

"Stop what? Smoking cigarettes? Wasting my time in meetings like this?"

Yael spoke clearly and methodically, as though to an errant child. The puddle had spread to the edge of the table and began to drip over the side, taking the ash and cigarette ends with it.

"You stop killing Tutsis. You stop your raids into Rwanda. You disband the Rwandan Liberation Front, send your Hutu militiamen home, and close your bases in Congo. You sign a peace treaty with Rwanda and the new government here. You surrender to the UN tribunal."

Hakizimani laughed. "Absurd. Go back to New York or wherever you came from."

"Prison, or a life on the run, Professor. You choose."

"That does not sound like much of a choice," he said.

She pulled the chair close and looked into his eyes. They were a startling shade of turquoise. "It's more than your victims had."

"That's true," he said, smiling.

He raised his glass to her and proffered the bottle. What Yael wanted most of all was not whisky, but some fresh air. Even with the windows open, the presidential suite at the Hotel Goma smelled of bodies, stale tobacco smoke, and the half-eaten plate of goat curry sitting on the room-service trolley. The new Italian furniture was pockmarked with cigarette burns. The air conditioner rattled and shook to very little effect. The sweat ran in rivulets down her back and down her forehead, into her eyes. A fan stood on the floor, slowly churning the fumes.

Yael wiped her face, nodded, and the president of the Rwandan Liberation Front passed her the bottle. She poured herself a small measure. She had read Hakizimani's UN file so often that she knew every line by heart: born in 1955 to two schoolteachers, educated by Belgian nuns in a Catholic school in Kigali, a scholarship to the Sorbonne to study medicine, a master's degree from Harvard, and then marriage to a daughter of Rwanda's most powerful Hutu dynasty. This former chairman of the medical school at Kigali University in the Rwandan capital had once been marked out by London, Paris, and Washington, DC, as one of the new generation of African leaders, a generation that would lead the continent to stability, prosperity, and open markets for the world's multinationals.

By early 1994 Hakizimani was minister of health—until a car bomb in Kigali killed his wife and three children. He had decided to walk to work that day and lent them the car to go shopping. Tutsi extremists had been blamed, but nobody had ever been charged with the crime. The genocide started two weeks later, although the planeloads of machetes had been ordered from China long before. In three months the government's militias had slaughtered 800,000 of their Tutsi countrymen, most of them by hand, along with any voices of Hutu moderation.

Hakizimani was the ideologue of slaughter, the Goebbels of Rwanda, whose theory of "Hutu Power" demanded the complete extermination of the Tutsis. He had broadcast on the state station day after day, hour after hour, urging his compatriots to stamp on, squash, kill, and exterminate the "cockroaches." He had even used his medical expertise to give instructions on how to slash the femoral artery in the upper thigh so that the Genocidaires could conserve their energy and dispatch their victims with a single blow.

Hakizimani looked at Yael and shrugged. "Why would I surrender to anybody? I am quite safe here in Goma," he said, clinking his glass against hers. "*À votre santé.*"

Yael nodded. "Thank you. And to yours. For now, maybe, yes, you are safe in eastern Congo. But nothing is forever, especially in Africa. The new government will make sure of that."

He stared hard at her. "There are no elections due here for three years."

Yael held his gaze as she spoke, her legs resting against the brown leather bag on the floor between her feet. "There will be a new government in Congo in three months, Professor."

She paused and sipped her whisky. "It will not be your friend. "

Yael had waited a long time for this moment, to meet the

man dubbed "The Butcher of Kigali." Reading his file was one thing. To see him in the flesh, quite another. Unusual for a Hutu, Hakizimani was tall and slim, like his Tutsi enemies. His face was narrow, almost triangular. Dressed in a black corduroy jacket, blue shirt, and jeans, and wearing designer rectangular metal-framed glasses, he still looked like a university professor. Yael had been worried that her emotions would betray her. A memory flashed through her mind: she was seven years old in Central Park, sitting on her big brother David's shoulders, giggling loudly as he pretended to be a giant, striding between the trees. She looked at Hakizimani's throat: soft, exposed, in easy reach. She gripped her pencil and mentally measured the distance across the table. The pencil's point was sharp against her skin. Her heart started thumping. She silently calmed herself and controlled her breathing. Not now. Not here.

Yael's face and voice showed nothing of what she felt inside. She was calm and in control, a professional UN official on a delicate assignment. She opened her hand and let the pencil fall on the table. She leaned toward Hakizimani, her manner confiding. "Professor, please, face reality. You are wanted by the International Criminal Tribunal for Rwanda for genocide. All UN member states are required to arrest you on sight. Your capture is merely a matter of time. You can no longer travel. You have to live in the jungle. Your friend, General Akunda, also thought he was invulnerable. He is now in a cell in The Hague. His indictment was sealed, so he was quite surprised to be arrested while he was buying chocolates in Brussels for his wives."

She picked up her drink and slowly inhaled its aroma. "It's very good, the Gold Label. Much more complex than the black. There's no whisky at The Hague's detention center, of course. General Akunda's trial starts next week. He is facing a life sentence. Would you like me to take him a message from you?" she asked, smiling brightly. Hakizimani did not answer.

Her voice turned cold. "Professor. Be sensible. We know where your bases are, how many soldiers you have, where the mines are, and which airstrips you use to move the shipments out. We know who your business partners are in Kigali and Kinshasa, Paris, and Geneva. We can easily leak this information to the hundreds of journalists who cover the UN. The French and Swiss governments will feel obliged to take action. We even know who your bodyguards are and that you are increasingly worried about their loyalty. Which is why you just fired your security chief and appointed your cousin instead. Good move."

She nodded thoughtfully. "Or maybe not. You might like to ask your cousin how he paid for his new 1,600-square-foot apartment in the 6th arrondissement in Paris. But your more immediate problem is that President Freshwater is taking a special interest in your case."

Hakizimani sat up straight. "Why?"

"It seems it's personal. She is an old hand at African crises—a former US ambassador to the United Nations and assistant secretary of state for Africa. President Freshwater was a junior Rwanda desk officer at the State Department during the genocide. She wrote lots of long and detailed memos calling for US intervention. Nobody took any notice of her. But now, they do."

Yael paused. She had Hakizimani's full attention now. "I can help you."

"I don't need your help. I have read your so-called indictment," he replied confidently, sitting back and crossing one leg over the other, as though he were holding a tutorial. "It is based on the incident at the Belgian Mission School in Kigali. The only one when UN aid workers were killed—by Tutsis of course, who then tried to blame us. The school was surrounded for hours. They were panicking inside, sending faxes, making telephone calls to the UN in Kigali, in New York, Geneva. Everyone knew they were dead men if they weren't rescued. CNN and the BBC were reporting outside the gates. A dozen peacekeepers could have saved them. But they never arrived."

Hakizimani sat silently for a moment, staring into space as he drew on his cigarette. His eyes narrowed, his breathing deepened and sped up. Yael sat up, alert now. Her sixth sense—an acute sensitivity to other people's moods—was in full flow. She could feel the memories coursing through his head. She sensed anger and indignation, the lies and denial blending and mutating into a righteous rage, one that could turn violent. Her adrenaline kicked in as she scoped the room. The door was several yards away and Hakizimani's men were standing guard outside. His rage was surging and the window was too high to escape from.

Hakizimani had insisted that Yael's bodyguard, Joe-Don Pabst, a US Special Forces veteran, remained in the hotel reception area. Pabst agreed, on the condition that he could check the room for hidden weapons and frisk Hakizimani. Both were clean and Yael knew how to defend herself. But if the situation turned really nasty, even with Pabst on her side, there were just two of them against several SUV-loads of Hakizimani's heavily armed militiamen. There was an escape protocol, of course, but even if Pabst radioed for help the UN helicopter would take several minutes to get there.

Hakizimani stood up, his face twisted in anger. He lifted his hand and swept the ashtray off the table, together with the spilled whisky, ash, and cigarette ends. Yael flinched as the ashtray slammed into the wall and shattered, sending charred scraps of paper all over the floor. She visualized her possible moves as she eyed the ceramic fragments. They were thick and jagged and in easy reach. And she still had the pencil.

Hakizimani sat back again and picked up his drink. "So put your UN on trial. Not me."

Yael felt his rage begin to dissipate. This was theater, all part of his negotiation.

He gulped his drink, almost emptying the glass. "Explain to me what is so special about those UN workers? Hundreds of thousands of Africans are slaughtered here and the world does nothing. Renee Freshwater sent some memos. But when six Europeans get caught up in something they can never understand, then, *then*, we must have justice." His voice was heavy with sarcasm.

"Nine. Not six. Nine," she said, calmly. She leaned down and picked up a shard of the broken ashtray.

He laughed out loud. "Nine people. Blood flows here like

a river and now the UN wants justice for nine people. Who is going to arrest me? You? The Congolese police? You think they don't know I am here?"

According to his indictment from the UN's Rwanda tribunal, Hakizimani had organized competitions among his militiamen to see who could kill the most Tutsi prisoners with their machetes, while he and his commanders drank beer and placed bets on the outcome. Or they made their prisoners kill each other for sport. Fathers were forced to fight their own sons, brothers made to murder one another.

But the Hutu kingdom of death was short-lived. By the summer of 1994 the Tutsis had invaded from Uganda and recaptured the country. The Hutu Genocidaires fled over the border to Congo's refugee camps and jungles. Fed, housed, and protected by the UN and other aid agencies—who studiously ignored Rwanda's protests—the Genocidaires regrouped, rearmed, and formed the Rwandan Liberation Front and carried on hunting and killing Tutsis.

The fighting had continued ever since, as each side launched raids and reprisals back and forth across the border. The slaughter had reached new heights that month. More than two hundred Tutsis had been found dead, many floating in Lake Kivu, hacked to death. Then the word had come down from the superpowers on the UN Security Council to Fareed Hussein, the UN secretary-general: make this stop. Which was why Yael was sitting here negotiating with one of the world's worst mass murderers.

Hakizimani stood up and beckoned her to the window. She rose and walked over to him. He moved closer to her.

Yael smelled the sharp tang of his sweat, the whisky, and cigarettes. Eau de Warlord, she thought, the same the world over.

Hakizimani gestured at the view. "Look. Even the UN cannot change geography."

The room looked out over Lake Kivu. The water shone azure under the morning sun, its surface ruffled by the autumn breeze. Two Scandinavian aid workers in bikinis sunbathed on the beach, looking up as a Jet Ski roared past. The border crossing was a few hundred yards away. A line of SUVs and white UN Jeeps was backed up on the Congolese side, behind two red and white metal poles that reached across the middle of the road. Soldiers wandered back and forth, smoking and chatting. The blue, gold, and green flag of Rwanda sagged in the heat.

The SUVs were emblazoned with aid organizations' colorful logos. The vehicles slowly inched forward, their giant radio antennae wobbling as they bumped over the slabs of dried lava that still coated the road after Mount Nyiragongo had erupted years earlier. Some days it took five minutes to cross, others five hours. Goma had grown rich on the aid industry and was a long way from the capital Kinshasa. Visas, letters of introduction, and government permissions counted for nothing here. Whisky, cigarettes, and US dollar large-denomination bills did.

Hakizimani spoke softly into her ear. "There it is. My homeland," he said, gesturing at the frontier post. "Next time we will finish the job."

Two

Yael stepped away from the window. Hakizimani was beginning to take control. That was OK to a point, but now it was time for her to assert herself.

"Understand this, Professor, if nothing else," she said, her voice cold now. "There will be no next time." Only the deep lines around his eyes and the neatly trimmed black hair that was graying at the temple and sides showed his age. He could even be described as handsome, she thought. She softened her tone. "Professor, how long can you carry on living in the jungle? You are a graduate of the Sorbonne."

He smirked. "Yes."

"What exactly did they teach you there?"

They sat back down, facing each other across the table. Hakizimani lit a cigarette, leaned back, and let the smoke trail through his nostrils. It was a posture of confident superiority. "Do you know what my family name means?"

Yael shook her head.

"'God saves.' But God does not save. Hate saves. That is what I learned. The power of hate," he said calmly.

Yael ignored the provocation and moved toward him, as if confiding some especially sensitive news. "Surrender, Professor, and you will take part in lengthy—very lengthy—peace negotiations under special UN license. You will live in five-star hotels. In Geneva or more likely, New York. It will be very pleasant. You will have a suite. Room service. A per diem. You can bring one or two advisers. A female secretary, some bodyguards. The negotiations will doubtless last several months, a year, perhaps more. Nobody will be in a hurry."

"And after?" he asked, rubbing his chin thoughtfully.

"You will be given a month's notice, and then you will be arrested and put on trial. The charge of genocide will be reduced to crimes against humanity. There will be insufficient evidence that you ordered all the slaughter to take place. There will be problems with showing a chain of direct command and control leading back to you. A charge of genocide is hard to prove. There needs to be evidence of intent to exterminate."

"But that was our intent," he replied, his voice matter of fact, as though ordering a pizza.

"It doesn't matter," she said reassuringly. "There will be insufficient evidence. You will blame your subordinates, whose excesses you tried to rein in."

"I did?" he said, raising his eyebrows. "That was good of me, *non*? And how long would I serve for being such a good man?"

Yael began to relax and poured him some more whisky. When the target party queried the personal cost of a hypothetical compliance scenario, it meant progress was being made. It was a small step from "what if" to "when." She saw Hakizimani's body language change. He was leaning forward now, his hands resting together on the table with his fingers entwined. He was moving into her space, his eyes on her. That meant progress.

She held his gaze, subtly harmonized her breathing with his, and mimicked his posture, moving toward him before she spoke. Their hands were just a few inches apart. "You will be sentenced to six years. There will be an international outcry, demands for a retrial, new charges to be brought. CNN and the BBC will broadcast extensive footage of the 1994 genocide, Tutsi survivors will demonstrate in Paris and Brussels, Rwanda will threaten to remove its soldiers from UN peacekeeping operations, the talking heads and analysts will pontificate. The UN Human Rights Commission will convene an emergency session in Geneva. America and Britain will ensure that the Commission passes a resolution condemning your weak sentence. France will abstain and the African and Arab states will vote against the resolution. All this will last about thirty-six, perhaps forty-eight, hours, we estimate, before the news circus moves on. It will certainly continue for longer in Africa, but that doesn't really matter."

Yael paused and raised her glass to his. They clinked and she drank the whisky, feeling its warmth trickle down inside her, willing the alcohol to wash away her resentment. The scenario she outlined had been carefully planned out and forecasted by the SG's staff, in conjunction with the P5, and was bound to be accurate. Everywhere else—Iraq, Afghanistan, Sudan, all the world's hellholes—had so far followed the script drawn up in the SG's suite on the 38th floor of the UN building on First Avenue. Congo would be no different. What was it the UN and the P5 diplomats called these planning sessions? "Gaming"—that was the word. Gaming the world.

Yael was thirty-five years old and had worked for the United Nations for twelve years. She had brokered ceasefires in East Timor and Darfur, charmed Taliban fighters in Afghanistan, and sweet-talked Shia insurgents in Iraq. She had once persuaded a teenage suicide bomber, caught by the Israelis at the Rafah/Gaza checkpoint, to disarm his bomb and surrender. But she had started as an administrative assistant in the Department of Peacekeeping Operations, ensuring that officials' reports and briefings followed the departmental line, were properly written in grammatical English, and were distributed on time to the relevant committees, department managers, and the Security Council.

This demanded more than a good command of English. Like every organization, the DPKO was riven by turf wars, but in this case the stakes were the highest of all: superpower interests demanding war or peace. Passions ran high on the 37th floor, where decisions were made to send troops to battle and sometimes, inevitably, to die. There was grief and recrimination, often bitter. Quentin Braithwaite, a former British army officer on reassignment from the Ministry of Defense, had soon noticed Yael's uncanny ability to defuse office departmental crises. Her sixth sense allowed her to see through to the heart of the matter and mediate between her

UN colleagues, easing diplomatic tensions and even satisfying the honor of prickly male egos.

From there she had been promoted to the operations room, the department's nerve center, and soon started going out on field missions. In Afghanistan she caught the eye of Fareed Hussein, the secretary-general, who had made her his protégé, causing admiration and jealousy in equal measure among her colleagues. Her UN ID card said she was a political adviser to the UN High Commissioner for Refugees. Her actual job had no title. Officially, it did not even exist. But it was known, where it needed to be, that she spoke for the SG, and that her word was as good as his. And that meant she also spoke for the P5, the permanent members of the UN Security Council: Britain, the United States, Russia, China, and France. She was the most powerful woman on the planet, as long as she stuck to the script. And once again, standing next to Hakizimani, she felt a familiar mix of triumph and self-disgust.

She heard her voice outlining the terms of the deal to Hakizimani, but the words seemed to come out on autopilot. "You will only serve half of your sentence because of your remorse and your good behavior. In a Western prison—Paris, if you like. You will have your own cell, with a shower and an internet connection. Day release after a year. After which, relocation to America, France, or wherever you want. You can remarry, start a new family. You will have a house, a car, school fees paid for your children. You may even be able to come back here, if the peace holds."

Hakizimani nodded thoughtfully. "Anything else?"

Yael reached down, picked up the leather bag, and placed it on the coffee table. Hakizimani reached for it but she pulled it back, out of his reach. She opened the zip and allowed him to look inside. His eyes opened wide at what he saw.

"That will buy a lot of Gold Label," said Yael, putting the bag back under the table.

A low rumbling sound filled the room as Yael stopped talking.

Hakizimani raised his head. "The volcano is angry. Show me your UN card, please."

She reached into her pocket and handed it to him.

"Azoulay," he said, frowning. "Where is your family from?"

"Córdoba."

He looked at her face. "You are too tall and too pale for a Spaniard. And you have green eyes."

"The Azoulays left Spain in 1492, on a boat to Salonika in Greece. They moved to Baghdad in the nineteenth century. My father was born there, but by then Jews were not welcome anymore. They left for Israel when my father was a child."

"You were born in Israel?"

"No, in New York. My mother is American. Her family was Hungarian. They left after the war. My father met her in New York and moved there, but they divorced when I was twelve and he went back to Israel. I lived with my father for a while. Then I came back to New York and studied at Columbia."

"And you speak?"

"English, Arabic, French, Spanish, and Hebrew. Some Hungarian."

Hakizimani looked at Yael with interest. "A one-woman United Nations. How do you think of yourself?"

Yael smiled wryly. "As a human being."

"Did you serve in the Israeli army?"

She nodded. "I did my military service, yes."

"Which branch?"

"I was a PA to a general," she replied smoothly, still surprised at how easily the lie came.

Hakizimani walked to the window and looked out over the lake. "I had three daughters."

"Tell me about them," said Yael. Everyone loved to talk about their family. The human connection was the best lubricant for difficult negotiations.

He took out his wallet and showed Yael a worn photograph, covered in sticky plastic film. Three bright and happy young faces grinned at the camera in their best dresses. "This is the only picture I have left. It was taken in March 1994 at Abigail's sixth birthday party. They were clever girls. Abigail wanted to be a teacher. Fleur was eight. Fleur wanted to be a doctor. Valentina was eleven. A real idealist. She wanted to work for the United Nations, to save the world. Like you. Valentina survived for a few hours. She would be thirty now. Perhaps I would be a grandfather." He looked away, his face twisted in anguish.

Yael suddenly felt ashamed. "I am sorry for your loss."

"So am I." Hakizimani carefully returned the photograph to his wallet. "Do you know Menachem Stein?" he asked, composed once again.

She hesitated for a second before she answered. "No."

He looked at her in surprise. "You work for the UN and you don't know the head of Efrat Global Solutions? Stein was a general in the Israeli army. A war hero. Now he runs the world's biggest private military contractor."

"I said I don't know him. Not that I had never heard of him. Is he working for you?"

Hakizimani laughed. "You don't expect me to answer that. Come," he said, standing up.

She followed him out of the room and down to the lobby, out into the landscaped gardens. Yael's tall, slim figure and long auburn hair immediately attracted the stares of a group of South African businessmen at the check-in desk. She ignored their shouted invitations for a drink. The air smelled of orchids and cut grass. She breathed deeply, relishing the breeze blowing in over the water as they walked down to the lakeside. A cormorant soared, wheeled, and dived, riding the air currents. Aid workers lay on sun loungers, soft drinks or cold beers in their hands. Uniformed hotel staff, all African, picked up cigarette butts, swept the paths, and watered the plants. A manicured lawn reached down to the beach, which was dotted with palm trees. Mount Nyiragongo loomed over the lake in the distance, spilling smoke and steam. The volcano had recently covered much of the city in lava. Most of it was still there. Locals even built their homes out of lava. The volcano could blow again at any moment.

They stood together. Hakizimani pulled out a pack of Marlboros and offered the box to Yael. She took a cigarette and he leaned over and lit it for her. His eyes were startling, like molten sapphire. She drew deeply on the cigarette, pulling the smoke into her lungs, feeling the instant nicotine buzz.

"So why the rush?" he asked. "I have been on the wanted list for years. Then the messages start arriving. Then the intermediaries, and now the envoy herself, in person."

There were times to tell the truth, Yael knew. This was one of them. She said: "Coltan."

He nodded. "*Bien sûr.* Give me your telephone please."

Yael handed it to him. He cradled the shiny handset. "You know they use children to mine coltan? They are small—they can fit in confined spaces. They eat less. They are paid almost nothing. Some food perhaps. They often have no parents. What does it matter what happens to such children? Nobody knows if they are alive or dead. Sometimes the tunnels collapse, and the children cannot get out. But as long as you can call your friends, Yael, who cares?"

She did not reply. Everything he said was true. Coltan was the world's most coveted mineral, essential for mobile telephones and computers. Yael had read a seventy-page UN document on the plane from Paris to Kinshasa: "Report of the Panel of Experts on the Illegal Exploitation of Natural Resources and Other Forms of Wealth of the Democratic Republic of Congo." The report had been commissioned by the Security Council a decade ago and was publicly available. It was a detailed, thorough account. It revealed the front companies that processed the mines' profits; the airlines whose rickety Soviet-era jets shipped the coltan out from remote landing strips in Congo, Rwanda, and Uganda; the warlords and businesspeople who organized the trade; the banks that facilitated it; and the role of Congo's neighbors and the shadowy international gangs who built their empires on the mineral.

The UN document had lain unread in ministries and company headquarters across the world.

Hakizimani handed Yael her telephone back. "Your proposal is interesting. But I have a better offer."

"Which is?"

They reached the edge of the lake. She watched a white UN helicopter fly low overhead, deep into Congo, the roar of its rotor blades churning the lake.

Hakizimani smiled at her. "I always admired Yael. Your biblical namesake. The Hebrew spy who seduced Sisera, the enemy general, seven times, and lulled him to sleep. And rammed a tent peg through his head. You joined the UN to make the world a better place, *non?*"

Yael nodded warily.

"Maybe you are right. Imagine how much of a better place this part of the world would be if there was a peace agreement here. Thousands, tens of thousands of lives saved. Stability. Education, economic growth. Mobile telephones for all."

Hakizimani bent down and took a handful of soil. "This land is rich, not just with coltan, but with gold, diamonds, the wealth of the world. Eastern Congo could be a shining example for the new Africa. All because of you, Yael."

He let the earth run through his fingers and took Yael's hand. He stared at her face: "Your eyes are beautiful. Like a cat's."

He stepped closer. "I am older now. I cannot promise seven times. But I will do my best."

Three

Sami Boustani leaned back in his chair and stared up at the ceiling, his head in his hands, his feet on his desk. The damp patch had spread along the grubby white plastic tiles. The electric cable poking through the dividers was drooping even lower and was covered in condensation. The neon tube buzzed and flickered. Despite his repeated calls to building maintenance, nobody had turned up to fix it. Sami was increasingly irritated at both the decrepitude and the size of his office. It was ten feet by ten, cold in the winter and a sweatbox in the summer. The reporters who worked at shared desks in the overcrowded press center considered him lucky to have any office. Instead, his workspace reminded him of the old joke about the two Jewish ladies on holiday in the Catskill Mountains: "The food here is terrible," says one. "Yes, and such small portions," her friend replies.

Sami did not think himself to be an arrogant person. When he offered his thick, white business card—embossed with his name, the words "United Nations Correspondent" and the logo of the *New York Times*—to new contacts, he still felt the same thrill as when he joined the Gray Lady as a trainee a decade ago, fresh from Columbia University's post-graduate journalism program. Still, modesty aside, surely the world's most famous newspaper deserved something better than a tiny room in a distant annex of the press center, with a single cracked window that opened onto a ventilation shaft.

Sami sat up and gulped some coffee. He had started work early today, and was sitting at his desk by 8:30 a.m. He wanted to dig deeper into the recent announcement that next year was to be the UN's "Year of Africa." The UN dedicated years for good causes as often as the fashion industry raised and dropped hemlines and usually with about as much effect. So far Sami had witnessed the years of water, education, and rice. Most people on the planet still lacked enough of all three. But there was something brewing in, or around, Africa, especially central Africa, he sensed. He opened a new browser window, pulling up the story he had written for today's paper: "Genocide Suspect Offered Shorter Sentence, Insider's Memo Alleges."

He read it again and then jumped to the UN website, biting into his bacon-and-egg sandwich while reading the publicly available sections of the SG's diary. As usual, the staff meeting was scheduled for 9:00 a.m. Sami guessed that Yael must have been called in to see the SG first thing this morning, or even last night when his story went up on the website. There was no doubt that the SG would have gone ballistic.

Sami had worked as a reporter covering Congress in Washington and Parliament in London, but he had never known anywhere like the United Nations' New York headquarters. It was a journalist's heaven, a modern-day fusion of the court of the Borgias and the last days of the Roman Empire, all conveniently hosted in a thirty-eight-story skyscraper in midtown Manhattan. It was the single most important building in the world, where wars were started, peace treaties brokered, and the fate of the planet decided—a lumbering, uncoordinated, bureaucratic machine fueled by intrigue, lubricated by betrayal, staffed by spies, sycophants, a handful of idealists, and sinecured relatives of Third World potentates. And it leaked like the proverbial sieve.

Sami looked like a bright but absentminded postgraduate student. Most days he wore a standard outfit of Gap khaki trousers, a long-sleeved shirt over a T-shirt, and sneakers. His mop of curly, dark-brown hair needed a trim, and his black eyes gleamed with intelligence and a ready smile. This façade served him well. The building was full of diplomats and UN officials who had been disarmed by Sami's warm and apparently disorganized manner into revealing far more than they had ever intended.

Official department spokespeople, employed to speak to the press, had four levels of attribution: on the record, meaning they could be quoted by name and so would say nothing quotable; as a "department source," meaning they would open up a little, but only warily, because colleagues might trace the information back to them; as a "UN source," when they would speak more freely, because that term encompassed about sixty thousand employees; or, every official's favorite, "deep background," which meant that the information could be reported but not attributed to anyone at the UN, even though it was obvious that it originated there. The really wily operators started a discussion with the words "I'm going to tell you this, but you cannot use it" as a means of simultaneously flattering the journalist and stopping information being printed. As soon as Sami heard that phrase he immediately stopped the conversation. Whichever level of sourcing they chose, rival factions and departments continuously briefed, leaked, and counterbriefed against each other.

Had it always been like this? Sami wondered. Probably. Despite the burst of idealism that created the UN in 1945, countless wars and political disasters have ensued. Not even half of its 192 member states could be described as any kind of democracy. Many, especially from the developing world, were stuck in a 1960s mind-set, as though they were still fighting wars of liberation against their colonial overlords.

Perhaps they still were. Certainly to walk into the Secretariat building was to enter a time capsule. The UN complex was a period piece, modernist and functional, and much of the décor and furniture still dated from the 1960s and 1970s. The walls were bedecked in peace murals, maps of the world (without borders, so as not to offend the squabbling member states), and pictures of doves being released. Ancient cultural artifacts were displayed in glass cases in every corner. Diplomats, sleek and cordial, prowled the corridors and bars, murmuring and plotting. It was like being stuck on the set of *The Man from U.N.C.L.E.*

And yet, despite all this, Sami still felt a thrill each morning when he crossed First Avenue and walked into the lobby, a feeling that he was walking in history's footsteps. Here Nikita Khrushchev had banged his shoe on the podium, declaring to the United States, "We will bury you"; here the American and Russian ambassadors had debated and eventually defused the Cuban Missile Crisis; and here Colin Powell had demanded action against Iraq's weapons of mass destruction, triggering the 2003 invasion. Information, or rather, misinformation, had triggered the Iraq War, and information, not money, was the UN's most valuable currency. Every exchange was a transaction. The building manager, a surly Russian called Yuri, had twice dropped unsubtle hints to Sami about his reporting. Yuri had not exactly said that brighter articles would get him a brighter office, but the message had been clear enough. After today Sami would probably be moved to a desk in the corridor.

A loud buzzing filled the room again, interrupting his thoughts. The neon tube flickered violently. He threw an apple core at the light. It bounced off, and the noise stopped. Sami normally had a healthy appetite, but despite his triumph, and congratulatory e-mails from both his editor and the publisher, he was not enjoying his breakfast. The food was dry in his mouth and he could barely swallow it. The two laudatory notes and his front-page story had exacted a high price: burning the best UN contact he ever had, and the dream, perhaps even the prospect, of something more personal. But once the e-mail had landed in his inbox, he had no choice except to use it. One part of him thought she would never speak to him again, another that she would storm in any moment and slap him. He would prefer the latter.

Sami opened up his e-mail inbox and scrolled through their brief correspondence, surprised at how nostalgic he suddenly felt. Yael always wrote to him from her Gmail account, and never, obviously, from her UN e-mail address. There were only a handful of messages, mostly brisk thank-you notes for the coffees he had bought her, and a longer one after he took her for lunch at Byblos, a Lebanese diner just off Union Square, where she had charmed the owner with her Iraqi-English-accented Arabic. Sami had recently tentatively suggested going for dinner at a superb Syrian restaurant he knew in Brooklyn. Yael had given him a searching look, trying to figure out if this was a ploy for extra inside information, or something different. Sami was fairly sure he was asking for the latter, but he was not very experienced with women. He had blushed and blurted out that he was not "trying to hit on her, or anything like that." Yael had said she would think about it. He put his sandwich down and touched the screen where she had signed off her last e-mail: "Yael, xxx."

It was time, he told himself sternly, to stop mooning around and start working. He closed his inbox and looked at the pile of papers balanced perilously on the edge of his desk. The UN spewed out documents by the truckload every day: briefings, press releases, addenda, amendments, reports, revisions, new reports about the progress of earlier reports, drafts of revisions, and proposals for the next tranche of reports. Perpetual motion did exist, in the self-propelling UN bureaucracy, and this was just the New York headquarters. Throw in the organization's regional headquarters in Vienna, Geneva, Nairobi, and Bangkok and the vast constellations of satellite organizations like the World Health Organization, and it was clear, if not scandalous, that an organization supposedly committed to the environment was pulping too many trees, especially in the digital age.

Wasn't that a story? He grabbed a pen and scribbled a couple of lines in his reporter's notebook—*Story idea: How many forests die in thickets of UN bureaucracy?*—before picking up a two-page press release from the Vienna office. He scanned the headline, barely paying attention. "Secretary-General Appoints Akbar Kareem-Zafreedi as the Director of Office for Outer Space Affairs." He blinked, frowned, and reread it slowly. *Outer Space?*

The door swung open and Sami's heart raced.

Yael stopped walking and stared at the woman clasping her elbow. She was trying to steer Yael down a badly lit, narrow side corridor to a part of the 38th floor of the UN headquarters Yael had never seen, away from the SG's office.

"Have we met?" Yael demanded, looking her escort up and down.

The woman shook her head. She had blue eyes and sharp features that were made more pointed by the onset of middle age. Her short, dark-blond hair was expensively cut, and she was well dressed in a navy two-piece business suit, cream blouse, and a simple gold necklace. She was brusque, almost hostile, but Yael also sensed a definite undercurrent of uncertainty. She could work with that.

"No, we have not," her escort replied with a strong French accent.

Yael removed the woman's hand from her elbow. "Then don't touch my arm. Who are you?"

She stared at Yael angrily and wiped her hand on her skirt. "Yvonne Dubois. I have just been reassigned to the secretary-general's office, helping with his diary and appointments. He would like you to wait in here," she said, opening a gray metal door.

"Reassigned by whom?" asked Yael, turning to face her as the warm, stale air seeped out.

"The French foreign ministry," she said, gesturing inside.

Yael did not move. "And where is Olivia?"

"Ms. de Souza is not available."

"Why not? It's eight o'clock in the morning. She is usually in by now. I had arranged to meet her today."

"Eight o'clock in the morning or eight o'clock in the evening. It makes no difference. Ms. de Souza is not available," said Dubois briskly.

Yael watched Dubois carefully as she spoke. She looked away and blinked several times. Her voice was tight. There was something wrong here. Yael asked, "Where is Mahesh?"

Mahesh Kapoor was the SG's chief of staff and had worked with him for the last twenty years. Kapoor was a Delhi Brahmin in his midsixties, extremely handsome, and unmarried. His eyelashes were the envy of every woman in the building. His bachelor status had caused much speculation about his personal life, but he always brushed away questions, claiming that he was "married to the UN, the most demanding wife of all." Kapoor had helped Yael out behind the scenes several times, defusing potential crises and providing her with discreet support.

Dubois ignored Yael's question and walked into the room. "Please wait in here, and the secretary-general will see you when he is ready."

Yael stood her ground. "Madame Dubois. I have just spent twenty-four hours on airplanes and in airports, flying from Goma to Kinshasa, Kinshasa to Paris—where I was stuck for five hours—and Paris to JFK. I had just got home when I got a message that the SG needed to see me immediately. I don't understand what could be so important that it could not wait until I had a shower and even some sleep, but I came straight out again, and so here I am, jetlagged, dazed, sweaty, and starting to get pissed. What is wrong with my office, and why can't I wait there?"

Dubois gave her a blank look. "There's a problem with the lock."

"Why don't you call building maintenance?"

"We have. It's best if you wait in here. You can rest."

"Best for whom?"

"You will be called when the SG is ready." Dubois turned and walked out of the room.

Yael was too tired to argue any more. She sat down on a lumpy, beige, fake-leather sofa and looked around her. The room was a small space, about fourteen feet square, with faded cream walls and a window overlooking the East River. A neon bulb flickered overhead, and a low coffee table stood by the sofa. The only decoration was a large framed photograph of Fareed Hussein and a cheap plastic wall clock. The Indian-born secretary-general was wearing his trademark Nehru jacket and white collarless shirt, his hands resting comfortably on his expansive stomach, his gray eyes looking out benevolently at the world.

She pulled that day's *New York Times* out of her purse, glad that she'd grabbed it off her doorstep during her brief stop at home, and scanned three articles. The first story reported that leaks from members of the Congressional committee investigating President Renee Freshwater suggested she could be impeached for misuse of office and corruption. The second article detailed how the International Criminal Court had just found the president of Sudan not guilty of genocide, war crimes, and crimes against humanity. Judges had declared a mistrial after UN investigators were found to have fabricated evidence. Spontaneous celebrations had erupted across the Arab world, while the Arab League and Organization of African States had demanded the court be disbanded immediately and had pledged to withdraw all cooperation from it, demands echoed by Republican politicians in the United States. Fareed Hussein had declared that the ICC had suffered a "serious blow to its credibility" and that the organization's future would have to be "examined." The third recounted how a high-level UN envoy in Congo had offered a secret deal to a notorious Rwandan warlord who was wanted for genocide, promising him a short prison sentence in exchange for signing a peace deal. The SG's spokesman, Henrik Schneidermann, had denied any knowledge of the deal, calling it "malicious nonsense."

Suddenly, everything was clear. The story in the *New York Times* not only quoted at length from the memo Yael had sent to Hussein after her meeting with Hakizimani in Goma, but sourced it to her by name. It described her as a "senior UN official close to the secretary-general." Yael, the report said, was a "glamorous" figure with a mysterious background, who was charged with negotiating behind-the-scenes deals for the SG in the most dangerous and unstable conflict zones, including Iraq and Afghanistan. Glamorous was nice, she thought—the level of detail not.

The article outlined how Yael was nominally rotated through different UN departments, but always worked for and reported directly to the SG. It was completely accurate, and recounted her offer to Hakizimani almost word for word. Who had told him? She had sent the memo as an encrypted e-mail to the SG's private address. How had Sami Boustani got hold of it?

Yael dropped the newspaper on the floor and called Olivia: voice mail. She tried Mahesh Kapoor with the same result. She took a fountain pen from her bag, unscrewed the bottom half, and inserted the hidden 64-gigabyte memory stick into her UN laptop. She downloaded all the computer's files and repeated the procedure with her mobile telephone, copying numbers and text messages. The process complete, she put the pen back in her bag and walked over to the window. A garbage scow chugged slowly along the gray waters, its cargo spilling over the side and leaving a trail of detritus in its wake. She tried to open the window for some air, but it was jammed closed.

Her UN career was over. She felt angry and betrayed. Not just by whoever had leaked her memo and career history to Sami, but, to her surprise, she felt betrayed by Sami. She thought of him as one of the best reporters in the building:

sharp, conscientious, and diligent. She enjoyed his company and recently had found herself looking forward to their meetings. What an idiot she had been. The only thing he'd wanted was the information she could provide.

Yael reached into her pocket and took out a pack of Marlboro Lights. She lit a cigarette and inhaled. It tasted awful, and the tobacco made her dizzy. She sat down heavily, stubbing the cigarette out on her shoe and dropping the end on the table. Her mouth was dry, and she was exhausted and thirsty. And now she was being treated only slightly better than a criminal.

She closed her eyes for a minute, gathering her thoughts. She stood abruptly and picked up her bag as she walked out into the corridor and toward Olivia's door. Olivia was a serious smoker, with a taste for rough, unfiltered cigarettes from around the world. Yael always brought her back a carton of the local variety, and Kivu brand was about as rough as they came. Even if Olivia was not in, she could leave the cigarettes on her desk.

Yael knocked twice and the door opened. "Yes?" asked Yvonne Dubois.

"These are for Olivia," said Yael, handing the carton of Kivu to her.

Dubois stepped back, looked at the cigarettes, and then at Yael. She sniffed and wrinkled her face in distaste. "Smoking is forbidden in the building. As are gifts of more than a ten-dollar value."

"It's a carton of cigarettes. It cost five dollars. I am not smoking them. I want to give them to Olivia." Yael closed her eyes for several seconds, breathed slowly and evenly, and forced herself to damp down her rising irritation. "Could I have some tea, please?" she asked politely. "I am tired and very dehydrated. There are a kettle and teabags in my office."

In a building—and a city—that ran on coffee, Yael was regarded as an eccentric for preferring tea, a habit she had picked up while living in London with her father. She favored a high-caffeine blend she called her "builder's brew": a mix of Kenyan and Assam, steeped until thick and black, topped with milk, and sweetened with plentiful amounts of sugar.

Dubois looked at Yael as though she had asked her to strip naked and sing the "Marseillaise." "Your office is closed. There is a problem with the lock." She turned on her heel and stepped back into her office. "I told you, I will call you when the secretary-general is ready," she said over her shoulder, and closed her door behind her.

Yael walked back to the dingy room and threw the cigarettes against the wall. She sat on the sofa, a sour cocktail of anger and anxiety curdling inside her. And where was Olivia?

Still, Yael thought, she was an autonomous human being. She was not a prisoner. She could leave. The SG's 9:00 a.m. staff meeting was set in stone; there was no point in trying to start a meaningful discussion with him now at 8:35. She had once seen Olivia ask President Freshwater to please call back in an hour when the White House telephoned during the staff meeting, even though a Russian nuclear submarine was stranded in US waters and leaking fuel. But walking out, she knew, would change nothing, merely delay the verdict.

She began to doze off when Dubois walked in and beckoned her forward to the SG's suite. "The secretary-general can see you now. You have twelve minutes."

Four

Reinhardt Daintner sat back comfortably in the black leather seat, sipped his mineral water—Apollinaris, he noticed appreciatively—and stared out of the window as the stretch limousine crossed the George Washington Bridge at West 178th Street, drove down the Henry Hudson Parkway, and turned onto Riverside Drive. The Hudson River sparkled in the morning sunshine, and even the once-grand apartment buildings of Washington Heights seemed to glow anew with promise. The driver pulled up at a stoplight, and Daintner watched a group of Dominican men in their twenties, muscles straining against tight T-shirts despite the autumn cool, smoking and staring enviously at the car before he sped away.

Daintner knocked on the chauffeur's window and asked him to take Broadway. It would be slower, but he wanted to see the city. Compared to the sprawl of Berlin, his hometown, Manhattan was tiny. But Daintner still felt a frisson of anticipation as the vehicle sped downtown. For what Manhattan lacked in geographical size it more than made up for in opportunity. Nowhere more than at Daintner's destination, the thirty-eight-floor skyscraper and neighboring complex at First Avenue between 42nd and 47th Streets.

The communications director of the KZX Corporation picked up the folder of papers resting on his knees. Despite the nine-hour flight from Geneva, he felt rested and awake. After a dinner of filet mignon, accompanied by a superb claret, he had slept most of the way across the Atlantic in a full-length bed in a private cabin on KZX's corporate jet, a Bombardier Global Express. Everything had gone smoothly at Teterboro, a small airport across the river in New Jersey favored by corporate travelers. He had been whisked through the VIP channel and straight to the limousine.

Daintner was tall and rake thin, with a slight stoop at his shoulders. Dressed in his customary handmade gray silk suit, white shirt, and slim, black knitted tie, he was almost feline in his elegance. He was a near-albino, with white-blond hair in a widow's peak, matching eyebrows, pale lips, and a penetrating gaze. Confronted with unwelcome news or events, he had the unsettling habit of licking his lips with a long tongue, like a lizard contemplating an especially juicy insect. But when the occasion demanded, he made whomever he was talking to feel like the most important person in the world. Daintner flicked through the papers and contemplated his schedule. Three days solid of meetings, meetings, and more meetings, with the one television appearance he had agreed to.

A lot of reporters wanted to talk to KZX, one of the world's largest media and communications conglomerates.

The German company had recently moved its headquarters from Berlin to Geneva. After the collapse of communism in eastern Europe, KZX had branched out from its core business of pharmaceuticals into media, and its growth in the last twenty years was unprecedented. It now owned almost every newspaper and television station from the Baltic coast to the Balkans and was making rapid inroads in Russia, China, and Brazil. Daintner sat on the company board, where he was charged with overseeing KZX's image and rebranding, especially after some recent unpleasantness with the Romany people in eastern Europe.

He watched the Upper West Side glide by. The car stopped at a traffic light at West 72nd Street. Daintner smiled as an elegant, silver-haired matron watched her dog, a tiny terrier, lay a stool on the pavement. She pulled on rubber gloves to wrap the dog mess in newspaper, added them both to another bag, and placed the whole lot in a dedicated garbage can before wiping her hands with antiseptic tissues. Nowadays everyone had a conscience, he thought.

But conscience was apparently ephemeral. The media had forgotten about KZX's development of drugs used to sterilize Romany women. A series of all-expenses-paid press trips for reporters from every continent to celebrate the launch of KZX's publishing company, which would pay unheard-of advances to academics and journalists specializing in aid and development, had shifted the news cycle. The buzz about KZX now was its "corporate citizenship." In just over a year, under Daintner's direction, KZX had endowed chairs in business ethics at the London School of

Economics and Nairobi and Delhi Universities; launched a global trainee program for underprivileged urban youth at company headquarters in Berlin, London, and New York; and hosted a series of all-expenses-paid seminars on poverty and development at UN headquarters in New York, Geneva, Bangkok, and Nairobi.

Daintner was proudest of the new UN-KZX Innovation in Development Prize, worth $500,000 for the winner and $100,000 for the five runners-up. Total cost of KZX's "Department for Corporate Social Responsibility": 0.34 percent of the company's annual turnover. Estimated value of good PR: incalculable. And now, his most ambitious project yet was coming to fruition.

Yael watched Charles Bonnet stride out of the SG's office. The newly appointed UN Special Representative for Africa's Great Lakes region was the scion of a powerful family of French industrialists with extensive business interests across the continent. After a short stint in the French Foreign Legion and a decade working at the Bonnet Group's headquarters in Geneva, he had joined the Department of Peacekeeping Operations as a desk officer during the Rwandan genocide and had risen to assistant secretary-general, in charge of African operations.

Bonnet was immaculately dressed in a navy pinstriped Savile Row suit, a white shirt, and a French regimental tie, an ensemble tastefully offset by a Patek Philippe watch and plain gold cuff links. At first glance he appeared strikingly handsome, in his early fifties, with dark wavy hair streaked with gray, hazel eyes, a mahogany perma-tan, and a military bearing. But his face and neck were dusted with face powder to cover large pores and the deep scars of childhood acne. The makeup seemed especially thick today, Yael thought. She watched him scratch his neck.

The Frenchman was, as usual, charm itself. "Yael, what a pleasure to see you," he gushed, air-kissing her on both cheeks and smiling broadly. His face turned serious, as though suddenly remembering the *New York Times* stories. He looked down at the floor and shook his head. "It is a disgrace. An absolute disgrace. Shocking and outrageous that your private correspondence with the SG was leaked. We will thoroughly investigate this."

Yael smiled, despite herself. Even by Bonnet's standards this was a bravura performance. At first, when Yael started work at the DPKO, Bonnet had patronized her. When he realized that her star was rising, he became almost sycophantic. He had asked her out to dinner at least six times. Each time she refused he declared he would never take no for an answer, his eyes glinting with annoyance. He dropped frequent, obvious hints that he could help her career. As the SG's special representative Bonnet was enormously influential, the most senior UN official in his African region, able to both make and implement policy. His appointment had triggered numerous protests from human-rights groups concerned about rumors of child labor in the Bonnet Group's mineral mines in Congo. The SG himself had reassured the press corps that there was no conflict of interest. Bonnet, he said, had resigned all his positions with the Bonnet Group and sold his shares.

Before Yael could answer, Dubois stepped closer. "Nine minutes. And counting," she said, gesturing at her to enter the SG's office.

The sight of Najwa al-Sameera slowed Sami's heart a fraction. The UN correspondent for Al-Jazeera, the most popular independent Arab television channel in the world, was a niece of the King of Morocco. Schooled in Switzerland, educated at Oxford and Yale, she spoke five languages and had recently caused a minor scandal across the Arab world by modeling a line of evening wear for one of New York's more avant-garde designers.

Najwa moved aside a pile of papers and sat on the edge of Sami's desk, her long legs swinging slowly back and forth, encased in a pair of black patent-leather boots. "How is the star of the UN press corps this morning?" she asked, fixing him with her large brown eyes.

"Fine," he replied, watching her warily. "Seen this?" he asked, holding the press release about the Office of Outer Space Affairs. "A Saudi physicist is going to run outer space for the UN. That's a great story for you."

"*Shukran*, thanks, *habibi*. We also get UN press releases."

"So, Najwa, what can I do for you today?" Sami asked brightly.

"I wanted to congratulate you, Sami. *Elf mabrouk*, a thousand congratulations!" she replied, smiling broadly, her full lips opening over two rows of perfect white teeth.

He nodded. "*Shukran*. Can I help you with anything else?" It was highly unlikely Najwa dropped by just to pass on well wishes to a major competitor. Sami waited expectantly.

Najwa paused, considering her next move. "Yes, Sami. You can. Your front-page lead today. My editors are very excited about it. The SG's secret envoy doing deals with genocidal African warlords. And she is an Israeli. How perfect is that?"

"She is also an American citizen. Her father was born in Iraq. So she's almost an Arab," he replied, intentionally keeping his sentences short. Najwa made even the most self-possessed men babble, and her skin-tight blue cashmere sweater did not help his concentration.

"Clever Sami. I knew you would have all the details. That's even better. So are you going to share her memo with me?" she asked, smiling sweetly.

"My editor says I cannot. So, no. Sorry," he said, not sounding very sorry at all.

Najwa slid closer across the desk. "Are you sure this is just work between you and Yael, Sami? Perhaps you have some personal feelings that are clouding your judgment. She is very attractive. She certainly charmed the owner of Byblos."

Sami found himself blushing. How did Najwa know about that? "No. I don't. You could ask your editor-in-chief to ask mine. Maybe he would authorize it."

Najwa laughed. "Authorize. You are funny. Do you always obey the rules, Sami?" she asked, slowly smoothing her thick, shoulder-length jet-black hair away from her face. "We could help each other. I could find space for you in our office. We have a huge corner suite. We even have a spare room. You could use it."

She looked around Sami's tiny office with distaste. "The world's most important newspaper deserves better than this. And we could see each other every day."

"I'm not sure that's such a good idea, Najwa. And the *Times* would never share space with another news organization."

Najwa tilted her head to one side. "No? What a shame. Maybe we could have dinner one evening. My fiancé is away for a while. I don't even know when he is coming back," she said demurely. She picked up the half-eaten sandwich, held it between two manicured fingers, and shook her head. "*Haram*, Sami. You shouldn't be eating bacon."

"Why not? I'm a Christian."

Najwa looked down, embarrassed. "Of course, I forgot. I apologize."

Sami watched a flush spread under her olive skin. It was surprisingly satisfying to be in control of any situation involving Najwa, no matter how briefly. The Boustanis were Christian Palestinians originally from Gaza and had arrived in America twenty years ago. He had repeatedly suggested to Najwa that Al-Jazeera cover the worsening situation of the rapidly shrinking Arab-Christian minorities and their persecution by radical Islamists, especially in Gaza. He had even given her some names of friends and relatives there who were ready to talk about life under Hamas's rule, but nothing had come of it.

"There is nothing to apologize for. Speaking of Christians, how's Al-Jazeera's investigation into life in Gaza going?" he asked innocently.

Najwa sat up and stood next to Sami, enveloping him in a cloud of perfume. "We are planning a twenty-five-minute special on how one of the oldest religious communities in the world is being driven from their ancient homeland by a new generation of Islamist fanatics."

"Planning is good," Sami said, toying with his keyboard. "Broadcasting is better."

"A credit as associate producer is best of all. Especially for a newspaper reporter with no television experience," said Najwa, raising her eyebrows and looking straight at him.

Sami had grown up around Arab women. He knew when to surrender. He opened a window on his laptop, quickly typed on the keyboard, and pressed a button. A page spilled out of the printer marked in large bold type—HIGHLY RESTRICTED: SG EYES ONLY. GOMA/HAKIZIMANI—followed by three more sheets.

Najwa stared hungrily at the papers. Sami said, "This program will happen?"

She nodded determinedly. "Sami, *habibi*, we are not in the *souk*. Yes. I give you my word."

He handed her the papers. She scanned them briskly, her eyes shining with excitement. "Thank you. Now I have something for you. Call extension 7068."

Sami picked up his telephone and pressed the number. "Olivia de Souza. It's on voice mail."

"Now call the SG's office and ask for her. Ask when she will be back."

Sami followed her instructions. He listened and put the handset down. "They say she is not available. They don't know when she is coming in. What's this about?"

Najwa moved nearer. "Olivia is dead. It happened this morning, here in the building."

Sami started with surprise and opened his mouth to speak when Najwa's iPhone trilled. She looked at the number. "Sorry, Sami, I have to take this," she said, and walked out.

He watched Najwa depart. How did she know that? And was it true? There was no reason for her to make it up. Sami knew and had liked Olivia, and felt genuine sadness at the prospect of her death. But his reporter's instincts crept up, and he put his feelings aside. A few beers a couple of months ago with one of the building's telephone technicians had elicited the information that all UN voice mail boxes had an override code. The seven-figure number accessed any voice mail up to assistant-secretary-general level and allowed the listener to hear the messages. A hundred-dollar bill had bought him the code.

If Olivia were dead, UN security and who knows who else would be monitoring her telephone line. By calling to ask for her he'd probably just alerted them to his interest. But Internet telephone calls weren't placed through a telephone number and could not be traced. He logged into Skype on his laptop, brought up the call record console, and dialed Olivia's number. When he heard her voice he pressed the record button, moved his cursor to the application's keypad, and tapped out the seven-digit code.

Five

Yael said good-bye to Bonnet and walked into the inner sanctum. The SG's suite encompassed the entire width of the 38th floor of the Secretariat building and a good part of its length. The back windows looked out over the East River, the Queens shoreline, and an enormous billboard for Pepsi-Cola. The front windows had a breathtaking view of Manhattan, its skyscrapers glinting silver in the morning sunshine. The walls of the office were decorated with pictures of the SG shaking hands with various world officials and the presidents of the P5, as well as numerous actors and pop stars who had been made honorary UN ambassadors, Hussein being notorious for his love of glamour and celebrity. The SG was sitting at his gargantuan black desk, made from environmentally certified Brazilian hardwood. A small leather sofa, a coffee table, and two leather armchairs stood on the other side of the room. That was where the SG usually met with his trusted confidants in a more relaxed atmosphere. Sometimes he even insisted on making tea and coffee himself in the en-suite kitchen and bringing it to the gatherings.

Yael moved to sit down on the sofa. The SG shook his head. He beckoned her to one of the chairs in front of his desk. The seat was hard and positioned just low enough so that she had to look up at him. The desk was bare apart from a small pile of documents and papers and two silver-framed photographs. One showed a smiling Indian boy about five years old, the other a pretty young Indian woman in a graduation gown. Yael saw that her memo to Hussein was on top of the papers, together with a copy of that day's *New York Times*.

The eighth secretary-general of the United Nations was Indian, the son of a Muslim father and Hindu mother. Born in Delhi in 1940 to an upper-class family and educated by private English teachers, Hussein still used the idioms of the 1930s and 1940s, an affectation that he carefully cultivated. The family's mixed heritage meant they were targeted by extremists on both sides during partition in 1947. Hussein and his parents fled in the violence, and lost everything they owned. A photo of his younger brother Omar sat on his desk next to a framed half of a postcard of the Taj Mahal that had been torn in two. The brothers had pledged to keep their halves for life if they were ever separated.

Omar had been ripped away in the chaos at the Delhi railway station and never heard from again. The family had resettled in London, where Fareed Hussein studied at the London School of Economics and worked as an investment banker before moving to Frankfurt and New York. His appointment as finance director of the office of the UN High

Commissioner for Refugees had surprised many. The fact that he had no experience with the UN or indeed any humanitarian, development, or public-policy organization caused considerable resentment. But one by one his opponents had retired or been put out to pasture, and Hussein had climbed steadily up the ladder, moving from finance to policymaking and an assistant-secretary-general position in the Department of Political Affairs. Even by UN standards he was notorious for being an arch-conciliator, whose main concern was keeping the P5 ambassadors happy. So as Yugoslavia collapsed into war, and Rwanda slid toward genocide in the early 1990s, the P5 judged Hussein to be the perfect candidate for chief of the Department of Peacekeeping Operations, even though he had no military or peacekeeping expertise, and they ensured he got the post.

"Yael, what a pleasure to see you," Hussein said, his voice brittle and terse. "Terribly sorry to keep you waiting so long. I'm rather overloaded at the moment. And you must be so very tired after your long journey. When did you get home?"

She sat for a few seconds, trying to disentangle the emotions she could feel coming off Hussein in waves. A febrile indignation, even anger, but it somehow felt manufactured. There was no passion. And an undercurrent of something else, uncertainty, even foreboding.

Yael said, "Fifty-five minutes ago. As you know. Your office called me. They said you urgently needed to see me."

Hussein nodded, steepling his hands as he spoke. "Indeed I do. I received your memo."

"Good. Because we really need to talk about Hakizimani."

Hussein looked down at his desk and slid the newspaper toward her. "We do. It seems the *New York Times* also received your memo."

Yael slid the newspaper back across Hussein's desk. "I had nothing to do with the story in the *New York Times.* And you know that," she said, keeping steady eye contact.

The SG briefly held her gaze, flushed, and looked down. He picked up the newspaper, and held it in his hand. "I find that rather hard to believe. Allow me to read you an extract from the article: 'General Jean-Pierre Hakizimani is one of the world's most wanted men, a mass murderer of the first order, who has been indicted by the UN's own tribunal for Rwanda. Yet we have cut a deal with this killer and are allowing him to escape justice for tawdry reasons of realpolitik and commercial interests.' That is an accurate quote from your memo to me?"

Yael nodded at Hussein's question. "Yes, that is an accurate quote from my memo to you, but so what? That doesn't mean I sent it," she said, momentarily distracted by a large new photograph on the wall of Hussein and the willowy blond actress Lucy Tremlett surrounded by smiling, barefoot children in a refugee camp in Darfur. Tremlett's recent Oscar win made her a hot property in Hollywood, and her law degree from Cambridge added a little gravitas to her celebrity. Hussein had just appointed her ambassador-at-large for UNICEF.

Yael continued: "The question is how did the *New York Times* get the memo? It was encrypted and sent to you personally. Nobody else could have seen it. Nobody else could even open it."

She leaned back in her chair. "Maybe you leaked it yourself."

Hussein shook his head and spoke softly, his voice full of regret. "Yael, I can only say how disappointed I am that it has come to this, that after all our years together, you seek to resolve your differences with us, not in person but through the news media. "

Your differences with us. The words echoed in her brain. Any hope that she could salvage the situation died. Her UN career was now over, she realized, but she kept control over her emotions. "Why would I do that?" she asked, her voice calm and reasonable.

Hussein said, "Because, as you say, you are disgusted by this deal. By leaking it to the *New York Times*, you put the arrangement in jeopardy."

"Hakizimani should be in prison. Instead he is booked into a suite at the Millennium UN Plaza." The Plaza, a five-star palace of luxury, was a block away from the UN complex on First Avenue and was the favored billet of VIPs, diplomats, and visiting officials. It even had its own tennis court.

Hussein nodded. "Indeed he is. The price of peace and saving future lives means that sometimes, bad men go free. You have personally ensured that bad men went free in Iraq, Gaza, Darfur . . . shall I go on? But always for the greater good. As indeed is the case here. Why are you so vexed about Hakizimani?"

Hussein's reply hit home, angering her. The words were out before Yael could stop them. "Because you let Rwanda happen!" But even as she spoke, she admitted to herself that she was just trying to provoke him. Hussein's complicity had very little to do with the real reason for her obsession with the Rwandan warlord.

Hussein stiffened and his eyes glittered with anger. Rwanda, genocide, and the DPKO's actions—or lack thereof—during the slaughter were currently the most sensitive topics on the 38th floor. At first, Hussein had dismissed his own peacekeepers' increasingly frantic reports of the mounting slaughter in the spring of 1994. When the evidence, in the form of piles of mutilated corpses, was broadcast on CNN and the BBC, the DPKO refused repeated requests by the Canadian UN battalion in Kigali to intervene and open fire on the Genocidaires—even after the massacre at the Belgian Mission School. Hussein later blamed the P5 for prevaricating and preventing him from authorizing effective action against the Genocidaires. That autumn he was awarded the Légion d'honneur by France for services to world peace.

The principle of nonintervention was firmly established. The UN's neutrality was now more important than the lives of those it was supposedly protecting. The following July Dutch peacekeepers had handed over almost eight thousand Bosnian Muslim men and boys to the Bosnian Serb army after the fall of Srebrenica. The UN commander even forced almost two hundred terrified civilians out of the UN base where they had taken refuge, into the waiting arms of the Bosnian Serbs to be slaughtered. All this time Hussein was on holiday in the Seychelles, as a guest of its president. By the time he returned to New York more than eight thousand prisoners were dead.

But backed by the P5, Hussein rode out the storm and

refused the calls for his resignation. He continued his slow and steady advance, never confronting, but always bending and flowing with the wishes of the great powers. Hussein's commitment to the ideals of the UN was unshakable, he explained to visiting officials, and was he himself not proof of the possibilities of coexistence between different religions and cultures?

Hussein was a survivor and had not risen to the SG's position by being provoked. His eyes were cold, but his voice was calm. "This is the United Nations, Yael. It is a diplomatic arena, neutral and impartial. It is not a private army on call for the world's humanitarians. Nobody 'let anything happen' in Rwanda. It was a terrible confluence of events. Personalizing it does not help anyone, least of all those trying to understand how this house may learn from the tragedy. The DPKO was completely exonerated in the UN's own commission of inquiry. Once again your predilection for emotional outbursts shows your lack of professional judgment."

Yael looked away and read the message scrawled on the photograph of Hussein and Lucy Tremlett. The SG had his arm around her shoulder and was grinning excitedly. The big, loopy letters read, "Fareed, thanks for everything. We are doing so much good. Lucy, XXX."

Yael closed her eyes and tried to control her rising anger. Hussein was right. She was being unprofessional, too sensitive, and not sufficiently impartial. She was not *neutral* enough. But she had already lost her job. She felt her emotions surge through her like a physical force. "Either you or one of your staff leaked the memo. They will be furious in Kigali about this. I am sure that the prosecutor for the Rwanda War Crimes Tribunal is already drafting a statement condemning the deal. And so he should."

Yael watched the SG stand up and walk over to the window. He was stooped and moved slowly. His clothes, all of which were handmade, were hanging off him. She thought he had aged five years in as many weeks. What was going on? Olivia had told her several times how worried she was about him. Was he sick? Hussein looked out over the East River. A helicopter flew by, on its way to the 34th Street heliport.

He said, "The facts are these: Firstly, it seems the prosecutor for the Rwanda tribunal has been tampering with evidence. He has been suspended on full pay while an independent investigation proceeds into how the tribunal is working. It may be connected to the scandal at the International Criminal Court. It will almost certainly affect Hakizimani's indictment. And secondly, there is no evidence of any deal. Only a memo to me from a junior UN employee."

Yael jumped out of her seat and strode over to the window. "*What?* The evidence of the deal with Hakizimani is your instructions to me. I did precisely what you told me to."

"Do you have something in writing?" Hussein asked, calmly.

Yael was incredulous. "Something in writing? No, of course not. You never put your instructions in writing. You explained that to me when I started this job. The evidence of your instructions is that they are working. The UN military observers are already reporting that the RLF is pulling back and disarming. A day after I met with Hakizimani. And when did I become a *junior UN employee*?" she demanded, her voice tight with anger. "Was I a junior employee in Kabul when I arranged for American defense contractors to secretly guard the Taliban's poppy fields in exchange for them not blowing up President Freshwater's new gas pipeline?

She stood so close to Hussein that she could smell his coconut hair lotion. "Or maybe I was a *junior employee* in Baghdad, handing over a suitcase full of used hundred-dollar bills to the Shiite insurgents in exchange for your nephew, who, despite being twenty-one years old and fresh out of college with no experience whatsoever, had somehow landed a senior job with the UN Development Program, and who had refused to attend his security training, and whose driver, a father of three, was killed when he was kidnapped? And as for the Rwanda prosecutor, you know as well as I do that he is one of the most honest, hardworking people you could ever meet."

"Apparently not. Anyway, he is not your concern this morning."

"Where is Olivia?" Yael demanded.

Hussein returned to his desk. "No longer with us," he said, his voice reverential.

Yael stood in front of him, her arms folded. "Has she been sacked as well?"

Hussein shook his head slowly. "A tragic accident. Truly tragic."

She stared at Hussein, the hollow feeling in her stomach spreading rapidly. "What are you talking about?"

"Olivia was in the habit of smoking on the maintenance balcony on the 38th floor every morning. Such practices are strictly forbidden. Some time ago I instructed the health and safety department to post notices on each one, reminding staff of this. The health and safety of UN staff has always been of the utmost priority for me. The notices were put up, just two weeks ago."

Yael nodded impatiently. "And?"

"The railing was loose and she slipped over."

Six

Yael sat back down, trying to absorb the news that Olivia was dead. Shock, then a wave of sadness coursed through her. She and Olivia had spoken just a couple of days ago and made plans for a dinner at Le Perigord, an upmarket French restaurant a few blocks away, to catch up and gossip. Olivia was not yet a close friend but could have become one. She was fun, vivacious, and, unlike most at the UN, could be trusted to keep a secret.

Yael tried to put her sadness aside. Olivia was dead. Someone had leaked her memo and she was about to be sacked. Too much had happened this morning. *Think*. "When?"

"Yesterday morning," Hussein said.

"When did Dubois start work?"

"Yesterday afternoon."

"Who decided that Olivia's replacement would be reassigned from the French foreign ministry?"

"We, the UN, did. France is a founding member and sits on the Security Council."

"And you had Dubois all lined up and ready to go. How convenient."

Hussein picked up a photograph of a young woman from his desk and stared at it. "The best memorial Olivia could have is for us to build on the fine work she did for us and carry on our mission. We plan to launch a scholarship in her name."

"Wonderful. Why isn't this in the news? I did not see anything in the *New York Times*."

"Thankfully, there are some people working in this house who can keep confidences when necessary. We will release the information this afternoon."

Yael ignored his sarcasm. Something did not fit here. Beneath Hussein's bluster she felt uncertainty. "When is Olivia's funeral?"

"Next week."

"I will see you there."

"Unfortunately not."

"Olivia worked for you for ten years, died here, and you aren't going to her funeral?"

"I will be at the summit on global warming and sea-change levels. As I said, the best memorial for her is to build on her achievements."

"At a five-star hotel in Mauritius?"

"Wherever my work takes me."

Yael stared at him with disdain. "Rina is right. You are a pious hypocrite who cares about nothing except his own self-advancement."

Hussein's eyes blazed with anger. "*Enough*."

His voice turned icy. "It was a mistake to ever involve you in my family affairs."

The photograph of the young woman rattled against the desk as he placed it facedown. "I have consulted senior colleagues. The feeling in this house—"

Yael closed her eyes and breathed deeply before she spoke but could barely control her temper. "The feeling in this house? Whose feelings? Yours? Or the P5's? You know full well that I did not leak my memo to the *New York Times*. But I knew that sooner or later, something would leak out. I remember sitting in this office the day you asked me to do this job. You guaranteed that you would stand by me. 'Whatever happens, I will protect you.' That is what you said. You gave me your word. So why aren't you protecting me?"

Hussein looked at the wall of celebrity photographs as he spoke. "Yael, as of now you are on indefinite paid leave. An internal investigation has been launched into the circumstances in which your memo to me appeared on the front page of the *New York Times*. It will also be looking into claims that you engaged in inappropriate personal behavior with local staff while on mission in Kandahar. *If* it finds no grounds for action, we can discuss your future with the UN at a later date, when we are all calmer."

Kandahar. Her resistance collapsed. She stood up to leave.

Hussein leaned forward, twirling a pencil in his hands. "Please wait. Yael, you know the details of many of the most sensitive events in which the UN has been involved. I would remind you of the confidentiality agreement you signed when you joined us. Specifically of the potential criminal penalties, which have universal jurisdiction among member states, if you breach its terms. And please hand in your UN passport, telephone, and laptop to Madame Dubois."

"Is there anything else?"

Hussein nodded. "Yes. Your name, face, and personal details are known to numerous governments and non-state actors with whom we are forced to deal."

"Meaning?"

Hussein waited for a moment before he spoke, bending the pencil between his fingers. "Regrettably, despite our best efforts, some of them have questionable human-rights records. And long arms. Very long. But as long as you remain under our . . . imprimatur, as it were, they will respect your personal security."

Yael asked, "And if I do not?"

The pencil snapped.

Sami pressed stop and saved the sound file of the messages on Olivia's voice mail. He transferred them to a USB memory stick attached to his key ring and wiped the file off his laptop with a government-security-level erasure program. Later, when he was off the UN's network, he would back the messages up on the encrypted storage database site where he stored sensitive information. He printed out the other information he had found. A Google and database search of Olivia's name turned up numerous photographs of her standing by the SG's side over the last year: in Astana, Kazakhstan; on a visit to UNESCO; in Washington, DC, Jerusalem, Paris, and Beijing.

The most recent photograph and brief article showed her with the SG, a couple of weeks earlier, visiting the Goma refugee camp. There were numerous photographs of the visit on the UN Development Program website, several of which showed Hussein deep in conversation with a tall, thin European man with pale skin and snow-white hair. Sami had never seen such a man inside the building. Who was he?

Yael opened the door of the SG's office to find Yvette Dubois and two UN policemen standing outside. She handed the Frenchwoman her passport, laptop, and mobile telephone. Dubois placed them in a cardboard box, turned on her heel, and left without saying thank you or good-bye, her high heels clattering on the polished wooden floor.

The younger officer loomed over Yael with a soldier's ramrod posture and haircut. The other was middle-aged and overweight, his paunch hanging over a belt laden with a gun, handcuffs, flashlight, and pepper spray. The policemen escorted Yael down the familiar beige corridor toward her office. The walls were lined with posters and photographs showing smiling, multiethnic children, many promoting the "Year of Africa." The size and proximity of each workplace to the SG's suite was carefully delineated according to its occupant's rank and seniority. Yael's was six doors away, and she merited both a window and a two-seater sofa, which placed her high in the pecking order.

The 38th floor was usually a hive of activity, crowded with secretaries, advisers, and assistants buzzing around self-importantly. This morning it was silent and still, and every door was closed, except Mahesh Kapoor's. She heard a voice call her name as she walked past, and the SG's chief of staff appeared, dressed in his trademark black turtleneck sweater and black linen suit. His mane of thick dark hair was tied back in a bundled ponytail, with a single streak of gray on one side. He looked even more like a Bollywood film star than usual, Yael thought.

Kapoor stood in front of Yael and placed a hand on each of her arms. He shook his head as he spoke. "Yael, I am sure this is all a huge misunderstanding. I am going to sort it all out. You will be back in your office in a few days and we will be saving the world together again."

The officers stood watching her, irritated at the delay, but unwilling to interrupt the SG's chief of staff. Yael looked at him, enjoying the presence of a friendly face. "I don't think so, Mahesh. Not after that memo in the *New York Times*. The SG has made up his mind."

Mahesh walked closer. She smelled soap and chewing gum. "I will tell you something," he said, smiling mischievously as he whispered in her ear. "Sometimes the SG needs to have his mind made up for him. This may be one of them."

He stepped back. "Now that is between the two of us. Our little secret," he said, his fingers lightly brushing her arm as he left.

The younger officer stepped forward. "Mr. Kapoor, we have to escort Ms. Azoulay from the building," he said as he took hold of Yael's arm.

Mahesh instantly swiveled on his foot and turned to face him, taking the policeman's hand away from Yael's arm and dropping it. "Your orders are to escort Ms. Azoulay, officer. Not manhandle her," Mahesh said indignantly. He rested his hand again on Yael's arm. "Don't worry, I am going to sort this out. You had better go now."

The officer looked at his elder counterpart, a question on his face. "Leave it," the senior officer said. Yael thanked Mahesh and walked a few doors away to her office. The senior officer opened the door, which was unlocked, told her to wait outside, and directed the other to search the room. The younger policeman methodically and enthusiastically went through Yael's shelves and desk drawers. He gathered up her battered UN rucksack, a pair of walkie-talkies, and a blue peacekeeper's beret she had been given in Afghanistan.

"Can I keep the beret?" she asked the senior officer.

He shook his head.

"Why not?"

"UN property, ma'am." He gestured at Yael to go inside.

She opened her filing cabinet. It had been emptied. "Where are my papers?" she asked.

He shrugged. "UN property."

Yael reached for a DPKO coffee mug and looked again for the officer's approval. He shook his head.

"Yes, I know," said Yael as she put the mug back down on her desk.

The policemen watched carefully as she gathered her personal belongings: photographs and postcards, two filigreed porcelain teacups from Kandahar, a bottle of throat-searing *slivovitz* she had picked up in the Balkans, a small Iraqi prayer rug, and several airport thrillers.

The senior officer said, "Please turn your purse inside out and turn out your pockets onto your desk, ma'am."

"Is this really necessary?" Yael asked.

"Just do as I ask, please, ma'am. Then we can all go about our business," the policeman said. "Are you in possession of any items or information, confidential or otherwise, belonging or relating to the work of the United Nations or any of its subsidiary or allied organizations?"

"No. I am not," said Yael.

She pulled her bag inside out and emptied her trouser pockets as instructed: they yielded a set of keys to her apartment, a crumpled pack of Marlboro Lights, a Zippo lighter, tissues, chewing gum, a wallet, a half-eaten apple, and her pen. The younger officer riffled through her possessions, trying the lighter, and looking through her wallet. Yael watched, her face expressionless as he picked up the pen.

The officer weighed it in his hand. "Heavy," he said.

"It's a fountain pen. I like to write with ink," said Yael.

The young policeman looked at her disbelievingly.

"Go ahead. Take a look."

He unscrewed the top. Black ink spurted out from the nib, staining his hand. He pulled a face and put the pen down. He nodded at Yael. "OK, they are all yours."

Yael said, "Yes. I know."

She put her things inside her shoulder bag. The policemen took her to the elevator.

The door opened and a tall, ruddy-faced Englishman in a tweed jacket grinned at her for a second until he registered the scene in front of him. Colonel Quentin Braithwaite was now under-secretary-general, or chief, of the DPKO. He purposefully cultivated the mien of a public schoolboy about to put jam in his housemaster's shoes. In fact, he was one of the most adroit UN operators Yael knew, and she liked and admired him. The British army officer had served in Bosnia, Kashmir, and Afghanistan. He was the undeclared leader of the UN's interventionist faction, who thought that a fleet of attack helicopters and several companies of well-armed peacekeepers would quickly teach most troublesome warlords the error of their ways.

Braithwaite looked at Yael, and at the two policemen, taking in the situation. She saw surprise and then anger flicker in his pale blue eyes.

The DPKO chief nodded at Yael. "We'll talk as soon as I find out what's going on."

Yael thanked Braithwaite. To her amazement, the Englishman stepped forward and hugged her. He smelled of lime cologne. "Don't worry. We are going to sort all this out," he said as he walked down the corridor.

The DPKO chief turned as he entered the SG's anteroom. "Call me, Yael. Anytime," he bellowed.

Yael stepped into the elevator, the policemen on either side of her. It seemed to stop on every floor. As soon as the door opened, the lively babble from those waiting outside immediately ceased. Numerous colleagues from the DPA and DPKO with whom Yael had worked got in as the elevator made its way downstairs. One or two greeted her warily but most fell silent as soon as they saw the policemen and quickly edged away. A space soon appeared around her as though she had a contagious disease, which, in UN terms, she did. None asked her what was going on or if she needed any help.

Leila, an Egyptian secretary from the Department of Information, got in on the 14th floor. Yael had recently spent an evening with Leila advising her how to fend off the advances of her Brazilian boss and keep her job. Leila had promised to cook her an Egyptian dinner in return. She said nothing to Yael but stood staring at her with her mouth open, until Yael put a finger under her chin and gently pressed upward. Leila closed her mouth and turned bright red. Thanh, a new junior assistant at the DPKO, got in on the 8th floor. Still young, in her early twenties, and finding her way at the UN, Thanh Ly was French-Vietnamese and head-turningly beautiful. Her desk was a magnet for the male members of the department. Yael had several times rescued her from their attentions.

Thanh walked straight over to Yael. She took Yael's hand and squeezed it.

"Can I help?" she asked.

Yael shook her head. "No, but thanks for asking," she replied, and meant it.

Eventually the elevator reached the ground floor and the policemen escorted her past the newsagent and candy store, through the turnstiles, and into the public lobby. It was crowded with tourists and visitors waiting for their passes at the security desk. Almost everyone turned to look at the spectacle of Yael and her escorts. The policemen walked her through an exhibition of gruesome photographs commemorating the Rwandan genocide. A large banner proclaimed "Never Again," and a floor-to-ceiling poster for a charity called Africa Child Rescue displayed a photograph of near-naked children laboring in a mine. A bank of flat-screen televisions covering most of a wall showed Fareed Hussein nodding gravely as he was interviewed by UN television, and promising that the UN had learned the lessons of the 1990s. Africa Child Rescue, he intoned, was a new initiative, a unique program that would be at the heart of the UN's Year of Africa, combining the resources and dynamism of the corporate world with the knowledge and experience of the UN.

They stopped at the security tent. The chubby senior officer patted her down slowly, drawing out the process as long as he could. The young officer put her bag through the X-ray machine and guided her through the metal detector. Finally, the policemen walked her past the hordes of gawking tourists, down the steps, through the black metal fence, and onto the sidewalk at First Avenue.

"You are now free to go, ma'am," said the junior officer regretfully.

Yael smiled. "Yes. I know. This is New York. You have no jurisdiction here."

"I'll remember that on your next visit to the UN, ma'am," he replied, stone-faced.

Yael pointed at his hand. The policeman looked down at his palm, stained with ink from her fountain pen.

"It's indelible. It doesn't come off," she said, smiling sweetly. "Ever."

His face twisted with anger, and he stepped toward her.

Yael nodded. "Be my guest. Because if you take one step closer, officer, I will call the NYPD and have you charged with assault."

The senior officer put his hand on his colleague's arm. "Leave it. We're done," he said, shaking his head as they walked back into the security tent.

Yael stood still for a moment, her bravado evaporating as she tried to process what had happened to her. It was a crisp autumn day, the kind New York did well. A cold breeze blew in hard from the East River; the sun was shining in a bright blue sky dotted with white clouds. Sirens howled in the distance, traffic honked and stalled, and the air smelled of coffee and exhaust fumes. Everything looked exactly the same as usual. The giant sculpture of a revolver with a twisted barrel was perched on its plinth, the lines at the security tent snaked down to the pavement, and the flags of the member states were a blaze of color, flapping in the wind. The new American UN mission loomed over the corner of East 44th Street and First Avenue, its cream-colored concrete façade with no windows on the lower floors still fresh and shiny. But she knew nothing would ever be the same.

Yael stepped off the sidewalk without looking. A tourist bus flew toward her, honking so loudly she jumped backward instinctively, her heart pounding as the bus thundered past. Yael shook her head, focused, and stepped into the road again, this time looking carefully as she crossed First Avenue. She turned left at the corner of 46th Street at the Turkish UN Mission, walked past the blue wooden fence around the empty lot that covered most of the block, and continued up First Avenue toward the Dag Hammarskjöld Plaza. The open space was a popular site for protests. A crowd of dozens of demonstrators was gathered, shouting and waving placards with graphic pictures of the Rwandan genocide. Two cops stood nearby chatting.

A young Indian woman waving a megaphone stood behind a large banner that declared, "No deals with murderers: put Hakizimani on trial." Her upper-class British accent sounded familiar. Yael went to take a closer look. After all, it was thanks to her that they were there at all.

Seven

The young Indian woman with the megaphone was, indeed, familiar. She was Rina, the only daughter of Fareed Hussein. Rina was enthusiastically leading the crowd in a chant: "African resources for Africa!" and "No more UN sellouts!" Rina Hussein was one of Yael's rare failures. A year or so earlier the SG sent Yael on what he called "his most delicate mission"—to try to reconcile with his estranged daughter. The two young women quickly became close. Rina was great company: sharp, fast, and possessed of a dry wit. Yael did not have many friends and found herself drawn to Rina, who certainly seemed to enjoy her company. Yael kept procrastinating over the real reason for her meetings with the SG's daughter, perhaps because she sensed the likely outcome. One evening, over dinner at a chic bistro in Harlem, Yael carefully raised the topic of Rina's father and his wish to make contact. Rina said nothing. She simply picked up her bag and walked out. She never returned Yael's calls or e-mails. Eventually Yael gave up.

Yael looked briefly and regretfully at the SG's daughter, and walked around the demonstration into Dag Hammarskjöld Plaza. The large plaza, named for the UN's second secretary-general, was one of Yael's favorite places in Manhattan. The plaza covered most of a block between First and Second Avenues on East 47th Street. Considering it was located between two of the city's busiest roads, the plaza was a surprising oasis, at least when there were no demonstrations. A row of wooden benches lined either side, under iron streetlights garlanded with flower baskets. There was a café in a greenhouse—a popular spot for diplomats who wanted to meet away from their offices—six fountains under square wrought-iron canopies, and a small garden named for the actress Katherine Hepburn, who had lived nearby. The rows of trees on either side almost touched each other, making a canopy of branches. The trees were shedding their greenery now, and the wind blew the autumn leaves across the wide open space.

Yael sat down on a bench and looked out at the nearby monument to Raoul Wallenberg. Four black pillars pointed skyward, while a briefcase lay at the bottom, signifying unfinished business. Wallenberg, like Hammarskjöld, was also a Swedish diplomat, but based in Budapest in 1944. Wallenberg had saved tens of thousands of Hungarian Jews in the closing months of the Second World War by issuing them with Swedish papers and placing them under his protection. Over the years, when Yael was plagued with doubts about the deals she had brokered, even though she knew they were the lesser of two evils, she often came here to sit and think. Wallenberg too had dealt with the devil, the Hungarian Arrow Cross Nazis, giving their murderous regime the diplomatic recognition they craved by deigning to negotiate with them. That was how he had plucked Yael's grandmother, Eva Weiss, from a lineup of Jews waiting to be shot or deported. Wallenberg had been arrested by the Soviets in Budapest in January 1945 and had never been seen again. Mystery still surrounded his fate.

There were still many questions over Hammarskjöld's death too. Hammarskjöld had died in 1961 in a plane crash in what is now Zambia while mediating between the newly independent Congolese government and secessionists in the province of Katanga. Despite three official inquiries, the cause of the crash had never been finally determined. Many in the UN still believed that Hammarskjöld was killed by Western intelligence agencies because he was about to achieve something still far out of reach: African control of its own resources.

Yael had read a lot about Congo before her trip to Goma. The chaos and continuing bloodshed were rooted in its colonial past under Belgium's brutal rule. Belgium had plundered the country's wealth and slaughtered or enslaved much of its population. Congo's declaration of independence in 1960 had enraged powerful Western business interests not just in Brussels but across Europe and the United States, especially when Patrice Lumumba, the new president, declared, to wild applause from his compatriots, "We will no longer be your monkeys." Lumumba was a handsome and charismatic figure who believed in pan-Africanism and in Africans' right to benefit first from Congo's wealth—beliefs that made him many powerful enemies. With Belgium's help, the mineral-rich province of Katanga seceded from the new state.

As Congo collapsed in civil war, Lumumba turned to the Soviet Union for political support. UN troops arrived to stabilise the country. But they had little effect on the ground, and the fighting continued between Lumumba's government and the Katangese. Aided by the CIA, Joseph Mobutu, a colonel in the army, organized a coup. Allen Dulles, the CIA chief, personally ordered Lumumba's removal from power. Despite the presence of UN troops, Lumumba was arrested and flown to Katanga, bound and gagged. Lumumba and two comrades were propped up against a tree and executed by a firing squad commanded by Belgian police officers. Lumumba's body was later dissolved in acid to prevent his grave becoming a shrine.

Had Lumumba lived, Yael and many others believed, the whole of African history would be different. Mobutu served as president until he was finally deposed in 1997. He was one of the greatest kleptomaniacs in history, embezzling an estimated $5 billion while his citizens starved. He built a runway for the Concordes that he chartered to go shopping in Paris. None of this mattered to Paris or Washington or London, because Mobutu was a staunch anti-Communist and keen friend of the mining companies. But with the end of the Cold War Mobutu was no longer needed. He had supported the Hutu extremists during the Rwandan genocide, and when two years later, in 1996, his government tried to expel Tutsis living in Congo—then known as Zaire—they rose up against him, together with Congolese opposition groups. Aided by the Tutsi government in Rwanda, the united opposition marched on Kinshasa and Mobutu went into exile, launching new rounds of wars and scrambles by Western companies for control of Congo's resources.

Yael's mind drifted back to Goma: the gaggle of street kids that greeted her with hugs and smiles when she slipped them bars of chocolate from the UN stores, Lake Kivu shimmering in the morning sun, and Hakizimani, the doctor turned mass murderer. Yael was lost in her reverie when she heard a familiar voice call her name. She turned to see Sami Boustani walking briskly down the plaza toward her and waving. He was the last person she wanted to talk to, but she was not about to run away. And she realized she did have something to say to him. She sat back on the bench, holding her bag against her chest, her emotions surging inside her once more.

Sami stopped and stood in front of her. He looked at Yael, running his fingers through his hair. A police car rushed by, its siren howling.

"Can I sit down?" he asked when the noise faded away.

Yael said nothing and stared at him.

Sami could not meet her eyes. He swallowed nervously. "I had to use it."

Yael continued watching him silently.

Sami looked down at the ground and back up at Yael. "It's my job. I can't sit on a story like that. Even for you."

Her voice was cold. "Your job. What about my job? Which I no longer have. Thanks to you. That's my reward for helping you out so many times. You didn't even give me a heads-up."

"They really fired you? I'm so sorry. I tried to contact you. You were traveling. I kept getting your voice mail."

"I checked it as soon as I got off the plane. There was nothing from you."

"Why did they let you go? It's not your fault that the story ran in the *Times*."

"No," said Yael, "it's yours."

Sami watched the wind blow her hair around her face and fought a powerful urge to brush it away from her mouth. "You are right. I should have told you it was going to run."

"It doesn't matter now. Who sent you the memo?" Yael demanded.

Sami sighed. "You know I can't tell you that."

She sensed his confusion and attraction to her and decided to push home her advantage. She stood up and stepped toward him.

"I think you owe me that much," she said, making sure to hold his gaze.

Sami smiled tentatively. "The truth is, I don't know who sent it. It's from a Gmail account. It could be anybody."

"Then forward the e-mail to me," she said, her voice friendlier now.

Sami looked relieved at the change in Yael's expression. "Can I buy you a coffee? Lunch? Dinner maybe?"

Yael looked at him. "Send me the e-mail and we can talk about it."

A stretch limousine with tinted windows and UN diplomatic plates drove past, accompanied by motorcycle outriders in front and behind. The noise of the motorcycles was so loud that conversation was impossible.

Sami waited again and shook his head. "I can't do that."

"Then at least tell me the sender's e-mail address."

Sami looked down at his feet.

"A printout?" Yael asked. "Nobody will ever know."

"I'm really sorry," he said regretfully.

Yael leaned closer and spoke into Sami's ear. "There is something you could do for me."

Sami smiled tentatively. "What?"

"Stay away from me. And don't call me ever again," she snapped.

Yael turned and marched away as fast as she could through the plaza. Her emotions burst open and her eyes misted up. She angrily brushed them away, trying to disentangle and control the feelings surging inside her. Shock, anger, sadness at Olivia's death, and a profound feeling of betrayal—betrayal by the SG, by the UN, and yes, by Sami.

She walked out onto East 47th Street, crossing Second and Third Avenues, and continued westward, her feelings ebbing and flowing with an almost physical intensity as she steered through the crowds. The movement calmed her. By the time she reached the corner of Fifth Avenue, she had slowed down and her eyes were clear. Yael turned right and walked through the hordes of tourists, past the high-end shops and boutiques, continuing a dozen blocks north, past the Plaza Hotel, the statue of General Sherman immortalized on his horse, and into Central Park.

The Hansom Cab drivers gathered at the park's entrance called out to her and she was almost tempted to hire one. What luxury it would be, she thought, to sit back in the upholstered seat and be chauffeured around the park, listening to the reassuring clip-clop of the animal's hooves, enjoying the greenery and fresh air. To let someone else take control of her life for half an hour. Most of the drivers were from Africa, and several were from Congo. She often stopped to chat with them and knew a few by sight. But today she did not feel like talking. And what would she tell them? That she had ensured that one of the continent's greatest killers would go free, so that the world could keep using its cell phones?

Instead she smiled, shook her head, and walked into the park toward her favorite bench, looking out over the Pond. The grand apartment blocks of Central Park West loomed in front of her, but the Pond was a verdant oasis, a landscaped lake ringed by trees and a curving path. The water rippled gently in the autumn sunlight, turning from olive green to khaki to gray and back again. A leaf drifted down onto the surface and the air was filled with birdsong. A raft of ducks ventured out from the bank, heading in all directions.

The setting calmed Yael. She closed her eyes and went to her favorite place. She emptied her mind and concentrated hard until she could feel the sand beneath her bare feet and the bright Mediterranean sun on her skin, hear the sound of the waves crashing against the rocks, smell the kebabs sizzling in the park nearby. She was on a small stretch of beach, exactly on the border between Tel-Aviv and Jaffa. The Ottoman seawall curved behind her, and the fishing boats bobbed out to sea on the turquoise waves. She could look right to the modern tower blocks of the Tel-Aviv seafront or left to the Jamia al-Bahr, the Mosque of the Sea, and the winding alleys of Old Jaffa. She sat on the sand in the middle, precisely located and happy. Her sixth sense—of intuition and vivid visualization—was sometimes a curse, but now it was a gift, bringing respite, no matter how brief.

A police siren howled through the park, breaking her reverie. She opened her eyes. The ducks had vanished from the pond, and the sun was now hidden behind thick, dark clouds. The wind was up and she suddenly felt cold.

It was time to take stock and deal with today's reality. Her future with the UN was over; that was clear from the manner of her departure. She had been deliberately humiliated. Hussein could just have easily arranged a discreet exit from the building; she knew there had been enough of those. Instead she had been paraded like a criminal. Dozens of staffers had witnessed the policemen escorting her through the public lobby out to First Avenue. She could imagine the breathless gossip now whizzing around the building. Doubtless Sami Bous-fucking-tani was already tapping away at another story.

So now what? Judging by her experience in the elevator, she doubted that many of her former colleagues would remain in contact. Rina would not talk to her. Olivia was dead. Perhaps Thanh would stay in touch, or maybe Quentin Braithwaite. But for how long without having the UN in common? Yael knew she was on her own now. She certainly had some very useful skills, especially for anyone wanting to disarm a suicide bomber, cut a deal with a genocidal African warlord, or arrange covert US military protection for Afghan opium fields in exchange for not blowing up gas and oil pipelines. But the confidentiality agreement she had signed meant that she could never disclose her real work to potential employers. All of whom, apart from one type of agency, would dismiss her as a fantasist. And that was a world she had no desire to reenter. Plus, judging by Hussein's pencil snapping, she would be in danger if she talked.

Maybe, she thought, it was time to forget about the whole career thing. Two young Upper East Side mothers walked by, perfectly made up and dressed in precisely coordinated designer outfits, while their Hispanic maids pushed their baby strollers several paces ahead. A pretty little girl, two or three years old, looked out from her Eskimo parka, its hood ringed with fur. She laughed and waved at her. Yael waved back, trying to ignore the sudden surge of longing and the dull ache inside her womb. She checked the date on her watch: September 25. It was exactly a year ago to the day. Fareed Hussein's timing was as impeccable as ever.

She stood up, touched her toes, stretched, and walked through the park to Central Park West. She crossed Broadway and headed uptown, past the familiar landmarks: the Greek diner with fantastic hamburgers and green plastic garden chairs; the homeless Vietnam vet who lived on the church steps by the 72nd Street subway station, to whom she gave a dollar; and Zabar's, the world's greatest delicatessen, on the corner of Broadway and West 80th Street. There she bought herself a large tub of the shop's special mix of cream cheese and smoked salmon, a sourdough loaf, a pound of mixed olives, and a tub of Ben and Jerry's Chocolate Brownie ice cream. Yael turned left when she came out of the shop, walked one block north, turned left again, and walked down 81st Street toward the Hudson River. A taxi was parked across the road from her building's entrance at the corner of 81st and

Riverside Drive. The vehicle caught Yael's attention with its tinted windows, which were unusual for a New York cab. She watched it pull away from the curb, reflexively memorizing its number plate: 7H35.

Her apartment was a good-sized one-bedroom in a 1930s apartment block with thick walls, a uniformed doorman, and a revolving door that opened onto an expansive black and gray marble foyer that looked like a Hollywood film set. Each time Yael stepped inside she half expected to see Cary Grant or Lauren Bacall come out of the elevator. Her kitchen still had the original wooden cabinets and door handles; the small bedroom had an en-suite bathroom with a deep tub and the noisiest pipes in the world; and the living room had high ceilings, huge windows overlooking the Hudson, and enough room for the three-piece art-deco furniture suite that her grandmother had shipped over from Budapest after the war.

Yael greeted the doorman, took the elevator to the 12th floor, and she was home.

Sami felt guilty, regretful, and excited. The foreign desk had ordered a 1,500-word story on the mysterious death of the SG's diary secretary and the firing of Yael Azoulay. He was the cause of Yael's unemployment, and yet he had to write about her once again. But the SG had confirmed what Sami's journalistic instincts were shouting: that something big was brewing in the UN headquarters, and he was way ahead of the pack. Sami's e-mail inbox pinged: the SG's press office announced an emergency press conference in two hours. He picked up his sandwich. It seemed his appetite was coming back.

Eight

Yael sat in the half-lotus position on her bed, and turned the piece of lava over in her hand. It was brown and pitted and surprisingly light. She lifted it to her nose and inhaled the burnt, sulphurous stink. The lava was somehow reassuring: her senses worked. It was real. Even in her current admittedly febrile emotional state, she was not imagining things. She put the lava down, paused the sound file playing on her laptop, and pushed her headphones off her ears.

It was almost 1:00 p.m. and she had been home for an hour. As soon as she'd returned she sent an e-mail to her UN address. It immediately bounced back with the message that the address was invalid. She was also locked out of the UN computer system. She had called Rina and left a message on her voice mail, but she did not expect a response. Yael unscrewed her pen and uploaded the contents of her UN computer to her personal laptop: all her files, documents, e-mails, and notes, together with all the contact numbers from her UN mobile telephone. From there they would be automatically backed up to an encrypted server, protected by a complex alphanumeric password that only she knew.

Her work done for now, Yael closed her computer and stripped down to a tank top and a pair of boxer shorts. She needed to clear her mind, and Budokan was a recent addiction. At first she had been dismissive of the sport—a mix of the tougher yoga styles and martial arts and favored by Hollywood stars. Yael already knew how to defend herself, brutally if need be. Her father had taught her Krav Maga, the street-fighting self-defense style invented in the back streets of Bratislava in the 1930s to dispense with fascists and then honed by the Israeli Army. Krav Maga was fast, vicious, and effective, using knees, fists, and elbows to attack the eyes, neck, and groin. Yael could swiftly take down two or even three assailants. But she wanted something more, exercise that left her feeling calm after a training session, instead of hyped and ready to take on the world.

Budokan's mix of the physical and mental did just that. She started the Sun Salutation, the series of yoga poses to start the day. She began slowly—bending, stretching, and holding each pose—and steadily speeded up. Each movement flowed into the next as she concentrated as hard as she could on her body, her breathing, and her protesting muscles. Slowly, the poses worked their magic. Her mind emptied as she moved into the fighting stances: kicking, blocking, punching, and lunging. After half an hour Yael was sweating, and the physical exhaustion brought a welcome and relaxing tiredness.

Until she had rechecked her e-mail and found the sound file. It was twelve minutes long and of good quality. The sender line showed an e-mail address: afriend99@gmail.com. No information there, except that the sender wanted to remain anonymous. But few people knew that buried inside each e-mail was plenty of useful information, if you knew where to look. Which was why she had pushed Sami so hard to send him the e-mail with the Goma memo. She opened the e-mail header of the message from "afriend99" that contained the message's path through the Internet, all recorded forever.

Yael wanted the IP address given to each computer that would show from where the e-mail had been sent and which Internet service provider had processed it. The IP address was recorded in the first line, next to "Received." She extracted the ten-digit number, opened a new browser window at a database website, and tapped the series of numbers into the window. The site linked to Google maps automatically. A new window opened and revealed that the mail had been routed through gratis.com, an Internet service provider located on East 43rd Street and Second Avenue that also had its own Internet café. It was two blocks from the UN.

Yael grabbed the bottle of mineral water by the bed and took a long drink before she pressed the sound file's play button again. The recording was clear and of high quality. There were four voices: Fareed Hussein, Charles Bonnet, Erin Rembaugh (the American head of the Department of Political Affairs), and a man she did not recognize (middle-aged, she thought, well-spoken, with a German or perhaps Austrian accent).

BONNET: We need at least five hundred. That will have maximum impact.

HUSSEIN: [*sounding dismayed*] No, no, that is unnecessary. It's far too much. A couple of hundred at most would be sufficient for our purposes. Less would suffice. Even a few dozen.

REMBAUGH: [*brisk and confident*] We disagree, Mr. Secretary-General. Five hundred is really the absolute minimum, if this is going to work. More, ideally.

Yael was surprised to hear Rembaugh arguing for more of anything. Rembaugh was a lanky, unmarried Texan in her early fifties. A former deputy director of the CIA and influential member of the National Security Council under President Bush, she was not known as a humanitarian. The DPA was the most powerful and influential department of the UN, essentially an extension of the Permanent Five. Its reach extended everywhere, from the backroom diplomacy that carved up Security Council resolutions long before they were presented for discussion, to deciding which country's cuisine would feature on the daily rota in the notably good UN staff cafés and restaurants.

The DPA was engaged in a perpetual turf war with the Department of Peacekeeping Operations. Peacekeeping had once been controlled by the DPA until the peacekeepers split off and formed their own empire. The DPKO was now the biggest department in the UN, with a staff of 130,000 in fifteen missions around the world and a budget nudging $8 billion—a UN standing army in all but name. The DPA had never forgiven its upstart child for going its own way. Rembaugh expended much energy trying to place her staff, almost all of whom were former or current American intelligence agents, inside local mission headquarters as "political advisers" reporting directly to her, rather than to the DPKO Operations Center on the 37th floor. So far, Quentin Braithwaite, the DPKO chief, had resisted.

HUSSEIN: [*sounding even more doubtful*] I am more and more inclined to stop the whole thing. I think—

BONNET: [*interrupting*] We understand, Mr. Secretary-General, that you have some doubts. We all do. That is only natural. Otherwise we would not be human. But you—all of us—need to think of the bigger picture. That will be our legacy—peace in Congo. Millions, not even born yet, will have a chance for a happy, productive life.

GERMAN VOICE: Yes, Mr. Secretary-General. That is what matters, surely. The bigger picture. How many people have died in the wars in Congo? Four million? Five? Nobody even knows, and, sadly, even fewer care. Now you have a chance to go down in history as the UN secretary-general who stopped the longest and bloodiest conflict since 1945. This is a small price to pay.

Yael pressed the pause button. What was a small price? To pay for what? And who was that talking? She rewound a few seconds. The man sounded both calm and supremely confident.

She pressed play: " . . . a small price to pay." Someone who had spent some time in the United States, someone who had studied or worked there. He was not a senior UN official, or at least not one she had ever met. She listened again, intently. It was a Viennese accent, with the telltale lilt of the Austrian capital.

HUSSEIN: But this . . . event goes against every founding principle of the UN.

REMBAUGH: [*her voice cold and hard*] Mr. Secretary-General, as you well know, there is a precedent for this. Srebrenica. You agreed that the Dutch peacekeepers would not defend the enclave. The Bosnian Serbs were allowed to capture Srebrenica in exchange for signing up to the Dayton Peace Accords.

HUSSEIN: [*anguished*] Capture the town, yes. Not massacre every man and boy.

REMBAUGH: Knowing the Bosnian Serbs' history, after three years of war, that was entirely predictable. And indeed was predicted by your own UN military observers. Fareed [*her voice softer now*], you know as well as I do that it's all a numbers game. It always has been and always will be. Eight thousand lost at Srebrenica to end the Bosnian war, which was about to set half of Europe ablaze and open the door to Al-Qaeda. Yes, it was horrible, for all of us. But how many lives were saved? Hundreds of thousands. And we brought peace to the Balkans, a peace that still holds. Believe me, Fareed, we all wish we did not have to do this. But it is the only way to clear the path to the peace accord. Like Charles says, we need to see the bigger picture here. Hakizimani has agreed to everything. His people on the ground are ready, as soon as they get the uniforms. But that deal simply will not happen under the current DPKO leadership. This is the only way to ensure the right people take control of the department. It's a means to an end. He has to go.

HUSSEIN: Why not simply sack him? This is a high price to pay to rid the UN of one man.

BONNET: We, the world, will pay a much higher price if he

stays. This is not about one man. Braithwaite not only has to go, he and his whole approach to peacekeeping must be completely discredited, together with his senior staff and as soon as possible. He can have no future in this house after what he has done to the DPKO. The department must be rebuilt, from the bottom up. Remember, Mr. Secretary-General, how he humiliated you in Bosnia, how he tramped on the most basic values of the United Nations. It was an outrage, an offense against our most important tenet: impartiality, no matter how extreme the provocation. He has UN soldiers actually fighting battles.

There were several seconds of silence. Yael could almost see Hussein nodding righteously to himself as he pondered Braithwaite's damage to the sacred neutrality of the UN. Braithwaite had gained fame at home and notoriety at the UN headquarters while commanding a battalion of peacekeepers in Bosnia in the early 1990s during the Yugoslav wars. Bosnian Serb soldiers at a checkpoint outside Sarajevo had attempted to arrest the British officer together with a British Foreign Office minister and his SAS bodyguards as they crossed the front lines and passed into government-controlled territory.

The usual UN practice was to open negotiations, which would last hours and lead nowhere. Braithwaite simply drove his armored fighting vehicle through the checkpoint, smashing the barricade into pieces and scattering the Bosnian Serb troops in every direction. A furious Fareed Hussein had summoned the UN press corps to protest this violation of the UN's neutrality. He described the incident as "reckless, foolhardy, and setting a dangerous precedent that would draw peacekeepers into the conflicts they were supposedly defusing." Braithwaite had responded by inviting Hussein to visit Sarajevo for himself. The invitation was not taken up.

Backed by the French, Russians, and the Chinese, Hussein had fought hard to prevent Braithwaite's appointment as peacekeeping chief, but for once London stood firm. UN peacekeepers around the world now shot back when attacked, with serious firepower. DPKO missions were equipped with satellite communications, high-tech weaponry including attack helicopters, and privileged access to NATO and US intelligence. There would be no Srebrenicas on his watch, Braithwaite declared, further infuriating Fareed Hussein.

Yael knew that the DPKO chief had made no secret of his contempt for the UN's covert contacts with Hakizimani and the Rwandan Liberation Front, nor did he bother to disguise his distaste for Bonnet and Rembaugh. Unforum, a gossipy insider's website, had even reported that Braithwaite had leaked what he knew of the UN's contacts with the RLF to the Rwandan embassy. Braithwaite had declined to comment on the article.

The Rwandan ambassador, a former colleague of Hakizimani's at Kigali University, who had lost sixty-seven relatives in the genocide, was at first disbelieving, then furious. She was demanding assurances that the RLF and the Genocidaires would have no role in any future regional peace agreements. At the same time, Braithwaite was also pushing for new rules of engagement for UN troops in the Goma region, allowing them to engage RLF troops on sight and to shoot to kill. The pressure was on the SG and the 38th floor, from several directions.

REMBAUGH: *Après* Braithwaite, *le déluge*. We need to clean out the DPKO.

BONNET: Absolutely. And our friend in Goma?

REMBAUGH: [*laughing*] Just try and stop him. He was pushing for five or ten thousand. I told him that it would take too long. He assured me otherwise. We settled on five hundred. But he is crucial. He still has power because of 1994, but a younger generation is rising, snapping at his heels. Hakizimani is the only one that can hold this together. Our guys on the ground are clear: without him this will not work. His people will do what has to be done.

After Braithwaite had blocked Rembaugh's move to take over DPKO field operations, she had simply stepped around him and built her own global empire. The DPA now ran what it called "Good Offices Missions" in the world's most volatile and strategically important regions: Africa, Central and South Asia, and the Middle East. The GOMs were supposedly charged with conflict prevention, peace building, and post-conflict resolution, working in conjunction with the DPKO. In fact, their main purpose, as directed by Rembaugh, was not to promote peace but to fight a war—with the DPKO. Around the world, the GOMs were steadily slicing away at its mandates and power base until Rembaugh could take full political control of the peacekeeping empire. The new DPA GOM in Goma was one of the UN's largest.

VIENNESE VOICE: [*brusquely*] Where and when?

Rembaugh: At the Tutsi refugee camp outside Goma. And soon, while Hakizimani is in New York, negotiating the peace accord. That way he cannot be blamed.

Bonnet: Are the uniforms ready?

Rembaugh: [*reassuringly*] Everything is in place. They all have been distributed.

Hussein: [*plaintively*] I am sure you all understand how difficult this is for me. I have devoted my whole life to the ideals of the United Nations—

Austrian voice: [*interrupting*] Mr. Secretary-General, we all appreciate your many years of hard work for the most noble of causes. But we need to know that this decision is made.

Rembaugh: [*conciliatory*] Fareed, like Charles said, just keep the big picture in mind. You know it's the right thing to do. History will vindicate us.

Hussein: [*reluctantly, after several seconds*] Yes. The decision is made. We go ahead.

The sound file ended and Yael pressed the stop button. She had heard correctly. The UN secretary-general and two of his most senior officials—together with an unknown Austrian—were plotting to discredit the DPKO, force the resignation of Quentin Braithwaite, and return UN peacekeeping operations to the passive approach of the 1990s, which would allow the warlords to take over again. Five hundred people were about to die —because of the deal she had brokered with Hakizimani. She had instigated a massacre.

Nine

The special press conference was standing room only, the atmosphere electric. Hundreds of correspondents were accredited at the UN New York headquarters, and it seemed every one of them was here, all talking in a babel of languages. Sami heard French, Russian, Chinese, German, Portuguese, and Urdu, and that was just nearby. Rumors had swirled through the building all day: that the SG was about to resign, that his secretary had been found dead in his office, that Olivia had been murdered in a crime of passion.

Sami counted TV crews from Reuters, the BBC, Al-Jazeera, Bloomberg News, Associated Press, Russia Today, China's Xinhua agency, and CNN in the first row of cameras, and there were two more rows behind them. A tangle of thick cables snaked across the floor. Sound men lined up their microphones on the long wooden desk, jostling for the best position, and correspondents directed their cameramen to get the best shots. Sami spotted Najwa bossing her crew around and caught her eye. She waved enthusiastically at him and he waved back.

Sami stood away from the crowd at the side of the room, browsing the Internet via his smartphone as he waited for the proceedings to start at 4:00 p.m. Jonathan Beaufort, the tall, languid, and extremely sharp correspondent for the *Times* of London wandered over. Beaufort, the doyen of the UN press corps, had been based there for more than two decades, outlasting several SGs. The *Times* of London, as the Americans referred to the newspaper, and the *New York Times* were fierce rivals, but the usual rules of engagement were that once a story was in print, details and contacts might be shared or, more often, exchanged.

He and Sami shook hands. "Sami, brilliant work. Well done," said Beaufort. He leaned forward conspiratorially. "A copy of the Goma memo gets you lunch at the Delegates Dining Room," he murmured. Aside from the SG's private dining suite, the Delegates Dining Room had the best food in the UN building. Its excellent buffet and spectacular views of the East River and the Manhattan skyline ensured it was always crowded with gossiping diplomats. The eavesdropping was of a quality just as high as the cuisine.

Sami shook his head. "Sorry, Jonathan. No can do."

Beaufort ran his hand through the hair flopping over his forehead. "I have some leads of my own. Trade? Cooperate? Nobody need know."

Sami said regretfully, "Editor's orders. Exclusive: a *New York Times* investigation."

Beaufort grinned. He knew when to retreat. "Then let battle commence. May the best man win," he said. Beaufort wandered off to talk to the new reporter from the France 24 news channel who, rumor had it, was the illegitimate daughter of the French president.

Henrik Schneidermann, the SG's spokesman, walked in and sat down behind a brown wooden desk against a backdrop of dark blue curtains emblazoned with the UN emblem. The room quieted, and the rows of journalists sat down, suddenly still and attentive. Schneidermann was Belgian—pale, podgy, and earnest, with untidy blond hair that had notably thinned out since his appointment a few months earlier. He was a former UN correspondent, but his appointment had caused deep gloom among the press corps. Schneidermann had previously worked for an obscure news agency based in Paris covering development and public health issues. Most of its output was topped and tailed versions of UN press releases, hailing the organization's latest success in combating hideous parasitical diseases.

Schneidermann tapped the microphone and the room fell silent. "I will read a statement from Fareed Hussein, the secretary-general. It concerns the events of today regarding two UN staff members: Olivia de Souza and Yael Azoulay. I will not take questions."

Yael saved and printed out the story she had just read on the *Economist* website and poured herself some more tea. The builder's brew was working nicely, clearing her head for a crash course in the Bonnet Group's history, reach, and influence. The conglomerate had been founded in 1880 by Jean-Claude Bonnet, great-great-great grandfather of Charles, a miner from Brittany who found a rich seam of gold in what was now the Democratic Republic of the Congo. From there the firm had expanded over the decades into transportation, coffee, silver and copper mining, and logging. Last year a scandal had erupted after a French Socialist MP produced documents that detailed how, during the war, the Bonnet Group had continued to trade with the Nazis through Swiss intermediaries in Geneva. The company had flatly denied the claims and stonewalled every attempt to investigate. The furor had eventually faded away, to be replaced with news of the Bonnet Group's latest charitable projects.

The *Economist* noted that turnover in the Bonnet Group's mining division, headquartered in Kinshasa, had more than doubled in the last two years. Several stories from the French press showed various members of the Bonnet family attending receptions and dinners at the Élysée Palace, the home of the French president.

Yael pulled off a piece of the sourdough loaf, slathered it with salmon and cream cheese mix, put six spicy olives on top, and chewed thoughtfully. A separate article in the *Wall Street Journal* noted that both the Bonnet Group and KZX had donated $5 million to UNICEF, the UN Childrens' Fund. Henrik Schneidermann had fulsomely praised the firms as "socially responsible corporate citizens." Yael added the printout to the growing pile of cuttings and articles now spread over her kitchen table.

She picked up the tub of ice cream, walked over to her window, and looked out over the Hudson River. The sky was dark and gray, the water choppy and flowing fast. The ice cream was delicious, thick, and rich, but provided little comfort. She watched a ferryboat chug its way across to New Jersey, the anger, resentment, and sadness surging again inside her. The shoreline across the water was lined with apartment blocks, and a patchwork of lights glimmered in the afternoon gloom. Her apartment began to shrink and close in on her. And she had an appointment downtown. As far downtown as it was possible to go.

Yael filed away her research, put on her favorite winter coat (a dark-brown vintage 1940s single-breasted wraparound), and grabbed an orange cashmere scarf and her leather backpack. She tore a small piece of paper from her printouts and walked to the door. She scrunched the paper into a tiny ball, reached up, and pressed it against the door frame to hold it in place just as she carefully closed the door. The old-fashioned tells were still the best. If someone entered her flat while she was out the scrap of paper would fall to the floor. If Yael was the first to open the door she would see it tumble.

The wind blew in cold and hard from the west, buffeting her as soon as she stepped onto the sidewalk. Yael shivered as she walked up the two blocks from Riverside Drive, along 81st Street toward Broadway. Bertrand was standing at his stall on the corner, wearing three woolly hats at once with half a dozen brightly colored scarves draped around his neck—a walking advertisement for his wares. Whatever the weather, Bertrand was there, always with a smile, a rare permanent fixture in her transitory life.

Bertrand Ogimbo was a Congolese refugee—short, round, perpetually cheerful, and full of wonder that he and his children now lived in a country where nobody would burn down his home and kill what was left of his family for belonging to the wrong ethnic group.

Yael waved hello. Bertrand greeted her with a wide grin and open arms. He gestured for her to stop for a moment and immediately unwrapped a purple scarf from his shoulders and handed it to her. "*Pour toi, chérie*," he said.

Yael smiled and shook her head. She had more scarves, winter hats, and gloves than she could ever wear, which was Bertrand's way of thanking her for using her contacts at the State Department to arrange for him, his wife, and surviving children to obtain US citizenship.

Bertrand looked downcast and beckoned her nearer. Yael surrendered and walked over to him. Bertrand pointed at her orange scarf. Yael shrugged, took it off, and handed it to him.

He held both scarves in one hand and with a few deft movements entwined them. He leaned forward, whispering in Yael's ear as he draped it around her neck. "Down there, *chérie*, a block away, there is a taxi parked on the corner of West End Avenue. Nod if you can see it."

Yael did as he said. The cab had tinted windows.

Bertrand continued in a low voice: "I see this car every day for a week now. Registration 7H35. It sits there or goes down 81st Street to your apartment building and waits there. I don't like this car. I don't like the kind of men I see around it. They bring back bad memories."

He stepped back and looked at Yael, handing her a mirror. "*C'est belle, non?*" Once again the smiling salesman.

Yael nodded.The orange and the purple went very well, a dash of color against her brown coat. She reached into her pocket for her wallet, but Bertrand waved her away, with a warm smile and a warning look.

Yael thought about what Bertrand had said as she walked down Broadway to the 79th Street subway station. It was just after 3:00 p.m., a good time to travel downtown. She loved the 1 train, which ran right through the island of Manhattan, starting at 215th Street and ending on Manhattan's southernmost tip at South Ferry, against a spectacular backdrop of the Financial District's skyscrapers. During rush hour, every car was packed solid with commuters. Now there was room to sit, breathe, even stretch her legs out.

Yael also preferred traveling at this time because it was easier to notice if she was being followed. It certainly seemed her apartment was being watched. She walked down the narrow, grimy stairway, bought a new MetroCard with cash, swiped it, and stepped through the turnstile onto the platform. It was empty. As soon as she had started working for the SG she assumed—correctly, she quickly learned—that she would immediately become a person of interest to numerous intelligence services, especially those of the P5: the CIA, MI6, France's DGSE, China's MSS, and Russia's FSB. She took it for granted that her access to high-level decision making and behind-the-scenes deals in war zones where the superpowers had economic interests meant that her telephones were tapped.

She sat down on the wooden bench and loosened her coat. The 2 train express roared past, hurtling downtown, the passengers' faces a blur. Condensation dripped down the cracked tiles, and a stale smell wafted up from a pool of stagnant water nearby. She took out a small Swiss Army knife from her bag and methodically cut her new MetroCard into small pieces.

Yael's cell phone was encrypted to military level. The encryption provided a degree of protection, for example, against Afghan warlords or Iraqi insurgents listening in, but she had no doubt that it had quickly been broken by the US National Security Agency and its foreign rivals. She didn't enjoy the knowledge that somewhere in Beijing, Moscow, or London, a technician was sitting hunched over a computer screen, listening to her calls, but it didn't bother her that much either. Her defense was transparency: she was a good soldier, obediently following the SG's orders, which were the P5's orders. There was nothing extra to discover; she was not negotiating secret deals or accommodations on the side. She did not take bribes, and she had little time for a private life.

But she drew a line at microphones in her home. Thanks to Joe-Don Pabst, she knew her flat was bugged. Joe-Don visited once a month to sweep and debug the apartment. A fresh crop always appeared soon after, but at least they, whoever they were, knew that she knew. Now, though, her life had changed. She was on her own. She needed a telephone, and one that was not traceable—one of several items she would require if she were going to really do this.

Her plan had two parts. The first part, about which she was certain, was to get information—the facts that would finally, after so many years, give her closure about the death of the person she had loved most in the world. It would be messy, difficult, and dangerous, but with skill and some luck she could probably pull it off in such a way that there would be no consequences. The second part, if she went ahead, was an act that was irrevocable. It would change her life forever. But a dark seed had been planted in her mind. Planted some time ago, she realized, and now, watered by the Hakizimani deal, it was germinating more rapidly than she could have imagined.

An angry buzz filled the press conference as though a swarm of bees had suddenly been let loose. The journalists turned to each other, incredulous and indignant that Schneidermann would not take questions.

The SG's spokesman tapped the microphone again and the room fell silent. He held a piece of paper in his hand and read slowly in his tenor voice. "Fareed Hussein and all UN staff extend their deepest condolences to the family of Olivia de Souza. She was a loyal and hardworking colleague who devoted many years of her life to advancing the values of the UN, which we all hold so dear. She will be greatly missed."

He flipped the paper over and read from the second sheet. "Yael Azoulay, a political adviser to the office of the UN High Commissioner for Refugees, is currently suspended on full pay, pending an investigation into a report in the *New York Times* that she leaked confidential and false information to that newspaper. The investigation will also look at claims of inappropriate personal behavior with local staff while on assignment in Afghanistan. Thank you."

The indignant clamor erupted afresh as the journalists shouted questions and demands for more information. Sami silently accessed a subscription-only database on his smartphone. Having obtained the information he needed, he watched the pack go into action, led this time, he could see, by Al-Jazeera.

Najwa strode up to Schneidermann, her camerawoman behind her, with a very determined look on her face. She pushed her microphone toward Schneidermann. "Can you confirm that the UN made a secret deal with Jean-Pierre Hakizimani? Is the *New York Times* story true?"

Schneidermann looked away, ignoring her as he gathered up his papers. Najwa instantly turned to her cameraman and said, "The UN spokesman refuses to answer our questions."

Jonathan Beaufort stood up. The room quietened. When Beaufort asked a question, everyone listened. "Mr. Schneidermann. Will the UN be calling in the NYPD or the FBI to investigate the death of Ms. de Souza? Or will you use the UN police? How does this death affect the UN's host-country agreement with the United States?" he demanded, referring to the complex treaty governing the UN's rules of extraterritoriality and its relations with the United States.

Schneidermann said, "As I said, I will not be taking any questions. A transcript of this press briefing will be available soon on the UN website."

"Briefing? What briefing?" demanded Beaufort. "The SG's personal secretary fell thirty-eight floors down the middle of the building today. Did she jump? Was she pushed? You read out a prepared statement and you won't take questions. What kind of press briefing is this?"

"The UN kind," one of the journalists said loudly.

The room erupted in laughter. Schneidermann's face flushed with anger. He fumbled with his folder and stood up, striding away from the posse of reporters following him out of the room.

Sami sat down and waited, doodling in his notebook as the remaining reporters packed up and drifted out. There was something Sami wanted to ask Schneidermann, but one to one, not in front of the press corps, all of whom had excellent antennae, and many of whose editors followed the *New York Times'* coverage. And certainly not in front of Jonathan Beaufort.

Ten

Yael boarded the almost empty train, sat down on the hard plastic bench, and subtly scoped the carriage. Sitting opposite her was a Chinese girl in her early twenties clutching a model's portfolio and dressed in an unseasonal short black dress and mini-denim jacket, her sleek black haircut into a geometric bob. A man in his midforties boarded the other end of the car just before the doors closed, and pulled out that day's *Wall Street Journal* as he sat down. Yael glanced up and down at him. He was tall, sallow-skinned, and had medium-length brown hair, slicked back with gel. He wore a white button-down shirt, navy tie, blue suit, and shiny black shoes. At first glance, another Identikit financier. But he had dark eyes, sharp cheekbones, and a pencil mustache that made him look a little like Johnny Depp. In fact, thought Yael, he was quite good-looking. Buy coltan, she half wanted to tell him, wondering what the commercial value of the information she held would be. Enormous, she guessed. Hakizimani was right. Peace in East Africa would trigger an economic boom.

Yael read the row of advertisements above the seats calling for passengers to enroll in community colleges, take protein supplements for a perfect physique, and call 1-800-ACCIDENT to sue for personal injury. In among the posters were three stanzas of verse, the latest offering in the city's "Poetry in Motion" campaign: "A Little Tooth" by Thomas Lux, about the birth of a daughter and her progress through life. Yael read through to the end:

"And you / your wife, get old, flyblown, and rue / nothing. You did, you loved, your feet / are sore. It's dusk. Your daughter's tall." Something pulled inside her with an almost physical intensity as she finished the poem. There were days, and this was one, when she felt very alone.

Yael was the second child of three siblings. After the death of Yael's elder brother, David, nineteen years ago, her mother had suffered a nervous breakdown. She had recovered, reverted to her maiden name, and realized that she preferred women to men and moved in with her ex-therapist in Berkeley. Yael's mother had never been especially maternal, except where David was concerned. Time, distance, and the loss of David meant that contact was now reduced to a few cursory e-mails. Yael's younger sister, Noa, had discovered religion while visiting the Western Wall in Jerusalem. An emissary from the Lubavitch sect of Judaism had persuaded her to come for a Shabbat dinner. Noa now lived in Ariel, a large settlement on the outskirts of Jerusalem, and was happily married to a full-time student of the Torah with no apparent income. They had six children, twins on the way, and were blissfully happy. If Yael called Noa, she would receive an immediate and open invitation. But Noa knew little of Yael's world and understood even less. And flying off to Israel would not solve anything.

Yael had had no contact with her father for more than a decade. She had very much wanted him to be proud of her, but he had been furious when she'd accepted a job at the UN. Yael could still hear him shouting that the UN had already taken his son, and now he had to sacrifice his daughter as well? At first Yael had been conciliatory and regularly called and e-mailed him about her adventures and to reassure him that she was safe. But he had been increasingly cold and distant. The longer she worked at the UN, the more withdrawn and uncommunicative he became, especially as promotion followed promotion. It was hurtful, of course, but she was so busy in her work that there was little time to think about it.

Curiously, Yael's father had contacted her a few days before her vetting for top-level security clearance. They had gone out for dinner and he tried to persuade Yael to leave her job yet again. He claimed to be worried about her safety and once more invoked David's memory, which annoyed her and in turn made him angry. Underneath his anger, she thought she could sense an undercurrent of something very like fear. But of what? The evening had ended badly. The following week, once Yael had received her clearance, she typed her father's name into the peacekeeping department's classified database on a whim. What she had read still haunted her. She had not spoken to him since.

The train stopped at 59th Street, Columbus Circle, and the car began to fill up with the first early escapees from West Side offices. A tall, skinny man in his late twenties with a goatee sat down opposite. On days like these Yael still missed her elder brother intensely. She had looked up to him, of course, like every younger sister does, but theirs was a special kinship. She and David had talked about everything and shared their deepest hopes and fears. As their parents' marriage fractured and their nomadic lifestyles turned from exciting to exhausting, David had been the one constant on which she could rely: always there and always ready to listen.

Until he was no longer alive. Becoming that close to someone else again would have felt like a kind of betrayal, even though she knew that the last thing David would have wanted would be for her to withdraw from intimacy because of his death. Was that the real reason for her solitariness, she sometimes wondered, or was it just an excuse? Either way the result was the same. Memories flashed through her mind as the train creaked and rattled its path under Manhattan: trips to Zabar's for bagels and lox; mornings cycling around Central Park and ice creams on Bow Bridge; riding this very subway line, downtown to the West Village to watch Satantango, a seven-hour art film from Hungary and not falling asleep once; David's breathless confession to her over her birthday lunch at the Windows on the World Restaurant in the North Tower that he was gay.

The train trundled along through midtown, past Times Square at 42nd Street, Penn Station at 34th, and down into Greenwich Village.

Yael stood up at the Canal Street station. She planned to walk from here down through the financial district to South Ferry. The man in the blue suit with the pencil mustache was still seated, absorbed in his newspaper. Yael stepped off the train, dropped the shreds of her MetroCard into a nearby trashcan, and walked into the crowd.

Sami waited until the other journalists had all left the press conference before walking to Schneidermann's office nearby. The spokesman's secretary, Francine de la Court, and her staff sat at their computers by the door, looking at him with barely disguised hostility. Only Roxana Voiculescu, Schneidermann's flirtatious Romanian deputy, gave him a welcoming smile.

"Yes?" asked de la Court. Schneidermann's gatekeeper was an immaculately dressed Haitian of a certain age, who had until recently worked as the SG's deputy protocol secretary until she had been replaced by a former Miss India.

"There's something I need to check with Mr. Schneidermann. Can I have a quick word?" Sami asked, smiling politely.

De la Court stared back, stony-faced. "The spokesman is busy."

"Too busy to include the UN's viewpoint in a *New York Times* story about the UN? OK, I can report that," he said, blithely. "And how do I spell your name?"

"Wait," said de la Court. She picked up her telephone, punched out a number, and spoke in rapid French. Sami heard his name repeatedly mentioned.

De la Court stared at him. "He will see you. For two minutes."

"Thanks," said Sami.

As he walked over to Schneidermann's door, the spokesman appeared. "I am in a teleconference with Nairobi and

Vienna, Sami. Is this urgent? We are not saying anything further about the tragic events of today."

The two men stood in the corridor as Sami scratched his mop of dark curly hair and looked puzzled. "It's not about Olivia. Or Yael Azoulay."

"Then how can I help?" asked Schneidermann, his voice brisk.

Sami gestured inside the spokesman's office. "Do we have to talk in the corridor?"

Schneidermann made a sour face and reluctantly ushered Sami inside.

Sami looked around the room. The spokesman's office was at least ten times the size of Sami's cubbyhole, with large windows overlooking the East River. Apart from a keyboard and flat-screen monitor, Schneidermann's desk was almost empty, as were the bookshelves and cork pin board. A large poster for Africa Child Rescue filled most of one wall. A screensaver showed a UN flag drifting back and forth across the monitor. A laser printer stood on a small stand in the corner of the room, blinking and whirring as it wound down, piles of stationery and different-colored envelopes carefully arranged next to it. Two sheets of freshly printed paper sat in the out-tray.

"Nice. How do I get an office like this?" asked Sami.

"Speak to the building manager. I am sure he will be happy to help," Schneidermann said in a tone that implied this would be most unlikely. He sighed loudly. "Sami, I am very busy. What do you want?"

Sami pointed at the poster for Africa Child Rescue. "This

charity that the SG is so keen on, Henrik. I'm kind of curious why the UN is endorsing it."

"Because it is doing such good work. Rescuing children from a life of slavery in mineral mines. What better cause could there be?"

"None, of course. But—"

"So we are agreed then," interrupted Schneidermann. He walked over to the printer, picked up the sheets from the tray, and glanced at them briefly. Sami could see that they seemed to be a travel itinerary of some kind. Schneidermann folded the papers and picked out a blue envelope, the color used for personal correspondence for the SG. He placed the papers in the envelope, closed it, and slid it into the breast pocket of his jacket.

Schneidermann said, "Perhaps we can even expect some supportive coverage in the *New York Times* of this important new initiative."

Sami looked at him inquiringly. "You could, perhaps, if you could tell me a little more about it. Where is the charity's money coming from?"

"From people who believe in the ideals of the United Nations, Sami, and who understand the importance of its work," replied Schneidermann, his voice clear that he did not include Sami in this august group.

Sami nodded slowly. "Isn't transparency one of those ideals?"

"Yes. And your point is?"

Sami scratched his chin. "So where is the money coming from?"

"I told you, from a group of businessmen who want to support the UN."

"Can you give me some names? Or some of the firms' details?"

"I am not currently authorized to release that information. Now if you don't have any more questions," Schneidermann said, walking toward the door.

"Just one, if you don't mind."

The spokesman nodded, not bothering to hide his exasperation.

"Last month a company called Moabi Holdings Limited was registered in Kinshasa. One of the shareholders, who owns 15 percent, is called Zeinab Hussein. So is the SG's wife. Is it the same person?"

Schneidermann turned bright red. "Please send any further questions to me by e-mail. Thank you," he said as he opened the door and ushered Sami out of his office.

Yael sat on the bench off Battery Park overlooking the river, tucked her purple and orange scarves into her coat, and pulled her legs high up to her chest. She hugged them tightly as she watched the sun set over the Jersey City skyline. Wall Street's skyscrapers loomed behind her, and the Statue of Liberty loomed in the distance over the water. The water lapped steadily at the edge of the boardwalk that marked the southernmost tip of Manhattan. The tide's calm, steady rhythm was soporific, and she felt herself relaxing as she breathed the fresh, salt-tanged air.

It helped that Joe-Don Pabst was sitting next to her. Joe-Don had sloping shoulders and the physique of an athlete whose outer layer had softened but who still had hard-packed muscle at the core. His thick gray hair was cut close, his small pale-blue eyes looked out of a pink, fleshy face, and his fingers were thick and callused. Dressed in a thick, blue woolen hat, black leather jacket, and workman's boots, a rough canvas bag over one shoulder, he looked like he was about to man a picket line at the docks and set about strikebreakers with a baseball bat.

But his squat, almost simian build belied a sharp and nuanced intelligence and an instinct for danger that was legendary at the UN. Joe-Don was a taciturn US Special Forces veteran in his midfifties. Born in Minnesota, he had worked for the UN's Department of Safety and Security for more than a decade, serving in every crisis and war zone where the UN had staff. For the last few years he had been Yael's bodyguard. He had saved Yael's life in Baghdad and Kandahar when insurgents had tried to kidnap her, and he had taken a bullet in his leg when he threw himself on top of her during a firefight in Gaza between Fatah and Hamas gunmen.

Yet despite the many dangers they had shared, and long sleepless nights marooned in numerous war zones, Yael knew very little about Joe-Don's past, except that he had worked as an instructor at the John F. Kennedy Special Warfare Center at Fort Bragg, and had spent much time in Central America during the late 1980s and 1990s. But he refused to elaborate.

Joe-Don's blunt manner and total lack of interest in self-promotion had made him numerous enemies at the UN. So had his repeated warnings that the UN compound in Baghdad was not properly secured. A long memo in 2003 to Fareed Hussein, then under-secretary-general of the Department of Political Affairs, outlined how the site needed blast walls, shatterproof windows, properly manned checkpoints at staggered perimeters, and zigzagged approach roads. Hussein had never replied to Joe-Don's memo. When a suicide bomber smashed his truck through in 2004, blowing away a whole side of the building and killing twenty-three people, Joe-Don was immediately fired for "dereliction of duty." When he'd protested, and produced written records of his warnings that the compound was vulnerable to precisely this kind of attack, he was taken off staff and made an adviser with reduced security clearance. After repeated public protests by the American ambassador—and more discreet reminders that the United States paid 25 percent of the UN's operating budget—Joe-Don was reinstated, although at a lower pay grade. Still, Washington had made it clear that Joe-Don was not to be fired. He still had carte blanche to roam wherever he liked in any UN building or mission around the world.

Joe-Don handed Yael the afternoon edition of the *New York Post*: "UN Aide in Death Plunge Horror," the headline screamed. Olivia's friendly face peered out from the front page.

Yael felt her stomach turn as she scanned the newspaper. She asked, "How?"

Joe-Don looked at her and nodded. "Murdered. I am sorry. I know she was your friend."

"Who did it?"

"I don't know. The killer knew where and when she would

be alone. Perhaps someone she knew and trusted. She fought. The railings are full of scratch marks."

Yael folded the newspaper and put it in her bag. "Why?"

Joe-Don sat silently before he spoke. "I don't know that either." He turned to Yael. "Anything you want to tell me?" he asked laconically.

Should she tell him about the sound file, she wondered? She trusted Joe-Don absolutely. He had taken a bullet for her. But she also knew him. He would tell her she was in danger, demand she leave her apartment, change her identity, move to Toronto, who knows what.

Yael watched the Staten Island Ferry slide into the South Pier terminal, the waves slapping against its sides. "No. Nothing. How's this month's haul?" she asked lightly, wondering if Joe-Don would believe her.

His look told her that he did not, but he did not reply. He reached back into his bag and took out a small metal box. He opened the lid and showed her the tangle of wires and tiny metal cubes, spheres, and discs. "The P5, Israel, India, Brazil, and a new one," he said, pulling out a black pinhead with three silver tendrils trailing from it.

He held the bug up to the light and turned it this way and that before handing it to Yael. "France, or maybe Germany. Definitely European."

"Where was it?" she asked, examining the tiny device.

"In the electricity socket by your bed. So perhaps it was the French."

She sighed and handed it back. "How long will they carry on?"

"It depends on what you do next."

Yael looked at him with a mix of affection and determination.

Joe-Don frowned. "I thought we settled this in Goma."

Yael watched a skateboarder clatter by, white wires trailing from his ears as he sped past. "I said I would think about what you said. I did and now I have made up my mind."

He stared hard at her and she held his gaze. Yael knew he would give in to her.

Joe-Don shook his head, exasperated, and put his hand in his trouser pocket. He leaned back and rummaged around until he had found what he was looking for: a small memory stick.

He then took out a thick A4 envelope from his shoulder bag. He handed Yael the envelope and the memory stick. "As requested: the hotel blueprints. And the contents of your filing cabinet."

Joe-Don reached back into his bag and took out two Nokia mobile telephones, weighing them in his hands. "Pre-paids, both charged and untraceable. Don't use any of them for more than three days. Then throw them away or, better still, take the ferry and drop them out there," he said, lifting his head toward the ocean.

He handed Yael the handsets. "Now a reminder about security. Mobile telephones are personal-tracking and listening devices. Any handset you carry records both your location to within a hundred square yards, often much less, and the period of time you spent there. That information is available to anyone who can access the phone company's records. Any handset can be turned into a long-range microphone without your knowledge, even if it is switched off. If you carry one with you, take the battery out—even if you just go to the corner shop—except when you need to talk. Take the batteries out at home as well. Take the batteries out when you throw the handsets away. Text messages are safer than talking. Or use public telephones and not the one nearest to your house. I will bring you an encrypted phone in a few days. Be careful when you use it. Encrypted calls are logged by the network providers. They set off alarms. Or just stay at home. Or communicate by carrier pigeon. Or cuneiform tablets. Or go on vacation until you forget the whole idea?"

Yael laughed and put the cell phones in her bag. A memory from the hotel in Goma flashed through her mind: Hakizimani leaning back, confidently dismissing the report of the massacre at the Belgian Mission School, sending the ashtray flying across the room. She stopped smiling. "You know I cannot do that."

Joe-Don sat staring out to sea. "Maybe Hussein is right. And Erin Rembaugh. It is all a 'numbers game.' Peace in eastern Congo would save tens of thousands of lives. Hakizimani can make it happen."

Yael turned instantly toward him. How did he know?

He looked at her. "I am responsible for your security."

She glared back. "Is there *anything* you don't know about me?"

"Yes. Why you insist on doing this. And who sent you the sound file. Come on," he said, and they walked down to the edge of the boardwalk.

She watched a seagull dive toward the water. "When does Hakizimani arrive?"

"Tomorrow."

Yael looked at Joe-Don in surprise. "So soon? I thought it was next week."

"The SG's gone into overdrive. The negotiations are to start as soon as possible. Hakizimani is booked into the Millennium Plaza under the name of Patrice Lumumba."

Yael smiled. "Are you sure?"

Joe-Don nodded. "Absolutely. Hakizimani insisted. Rembaugh was pissed at him, but couldn't do anything about it. Mr. Lumumba has agreed to everything. You did a good job."

"Did I?" She looked at him expectantly. "I haven't finished." The seagull stopped its dive, wheeled sharply, and hovered above the water.

Joe-Don took out a third phone: black, larger, and much more old-fashioned.

Yael asked, "You are not backing out?"

Joe looked unhappy. "No, I am not. If you insist on going through with this."

"I do."

"You understand the consequences?"

"Yes."

Yael drew closer to him and spoke for a couple of minutes, outlining her plans. She looked at him, a question in her eyes. He nodded and handed her the black mobile telephone.

Yael turned it in her hand. "It's heavy."

"It does the job."

The seagull plunged, then soared upward, a flash of silver in its beak. Yael said, "That's all I need."

Eleven

Sami sat in front of his computer screen and pressed the delete button again. The highlighted copy instantly vanished. He reached for the bar of dark chocolate on his desk and snapped a large chunk off. Perhaps the cocoa and sugar buzz might kick-start his article about Olivia, because nothing else seemed to be working.

Sami had never had to write about someone he knew personally, let alone someone who had died so horribly. His mind kept drifting back to a UN press trip to Darfur, Sudan's war-ravaged western province, a trip that Olivia had also been part of. Journalists were supposed to be like doctors, dealing professionally and capably with the human tragedies they witnessed. But the basic formula was simple: more misery equaled more columns in the newspaper. Still, it was his job to report accurately what he saw, so that policymakers could make better-informed decisions and so that the public could apply pressure to their leaders to do something. But even reporters were human, at least most of them, and it was impossible to remain unaffected by what he had witnessed. Especially when the UN and the press stayed in the best hotels enjoying multiple-course dinners and the hospitality of local dignitaries, while victims languished in tents nearby.

Sami had sat on the ground in a plastic UN shelter, across from a mother, perhaps in her forties, and her two teenage daughters, as they picked listlessly at some porridge in yellow plastic bowls. The mother recounted how she had watched the Janjaweed, the murderous government militia, execute her husband and fourteen-year-old son. The Janjaweed had dropped their bodies down the village well to poison the water supply so that nobody could return to the ethnically cleansed area. The mother had been raped.

Still deeply traumatized by their loss, they did not really understand who Sami was, and why he was asking so many questions. He realized after a few minutes that they thought he was a UN official. Even so, he asked for more and more details, knowing their terrible story would get plenty of space in the newspaper the next day. When the interview was over, and he stood up to leave, the mother was crying. She whispered, “Help us.” Sami passed their names to someone he knew at the State Department. The mother and daughters were eventually granted asylum in the United States and now lived in Arizona. But Sami’s sense of shame had never left him.

He chewed the chocolate slowly and stared hard at his screen. He had two articles to work on: a straightforward news story about Olivia’s death and Yael’s sacking, and a much longer, investigative piece about Africa Child Rescue and its links with the secretary-general and the upper reaches of the UN's management. The investigation, Olivia's voice mails, and the Kinshasa connection would make an explosive story. But one that needed the careful digging and cross-checking that would take a couple of days.

Sami had liked Olivia: she was bright, funny, and helpful, and had given him several useful snippets of information. Suddenly, his fingers started typing, almost of their own accord. His editors would get a proper account of her life, which was what she deserved. "With her penchant for designer shoes, matching nail varnish, and stylish jewelry, Olivia de Souza was a flash of welcome color in an organization notorious for its legions of gray bureaucrats," he started. Sami wrote fluently about Olivia's decades of service to the UN and several personal anecdotes about his encounters with her. He added a few lines at the end about Henrik Schneidermann's statement about Yael and ended on the spokesman's claim that she was suspected of "inappropriate personal behavior with a UN employee in Afghanistan."

His fingers hovered over the keyboard. Sami had heard several rumors about Yael in Kandahar, most of which seemed to boil down to the fact that on one or more occasions she may have slept with her interpreter. That was her business, he decided, ignoring the sudden pang of jealousy. There was some other stuff as well, much darker, but impossible to pin down, unless she decided to really confide in him. Judging by their brief encounter that morning in Dag Hammarskjöld Plaza, that did not seem very likely. And UN rumors were a long way from any kind of proof.

The telephone rang and Sami smiled as he answered. "Hi, Sami," a female voice said. "It's Roxana."

Yael sat down on the sofa, kicked off her shoes, and poured herself a large glass of red wine. She put her feet on the coffee table, picked up the articles she had printed out earlier that day, and began to read them again. The Bonnet Group was now the most powerful industrial conglomerate in France. Its leaders were confidants of presidents and prime ministers, its local managers often more powerful than cabinet members. Numerous stories reported on allegations of corruption and bribery—handsome bribes supposedly paid to African politicians and warlords. Several investigations reported details of child labor in its mineral mines, but nothing ever seemed to stick. The company rarely denied the reports. Instead it promised to investigate, paid copious compensation—most of which was diverted by middlemen on the way—and funded new schools and clinics. The company kept on expanding, its reach and power growing.

The shortest article was the most interesting. A news story in the *Washington Post* briefly reported that Chantal Richard, the glamorous new female French prime minister, was in Washington, DC, meeting various American officials, including Marc Rosenheim, President Freshwater's secretary of state. Ms. Richard was accompanied by a handful of French businessmen, including Henri Bonnet, elderly father of Charles, the not-so-charming UN official.

Yael put the file down and switched on the television to CNN. It was just after 8:00 p.m. and the start of the prime-time talk show *Tonight with Trevor.* Trevor was Trevor Johnson, a British former editor of a tabloid newspaper whose idea of a tough question to his celebrity interviewees was "How do you manage your busy schedule?"

To her surprise the program opened with long, panning shots of a UN refugee camp somewhere in Africa: women and children huddled in plastic shelters, families queuing for food handouts, and doctors weighing pitifully small children, their bellies swollen from malnutrition.

Yael realized that she knew where this was and had actually been there a couple of days before: the UN camp outside Goma, recently swelled by new waves of Tutsi refugees fleeing Hakizimani's militiamen.

The camera switched back to the studio and Johnson with his guests: Lucy Tremlett, the actress whose picture Yael had seen in the SG's office, and a tall, thin man in a gray suit. Tremlett looked fresh-faced, even radiant in a simple pink T-shirt and jeans. The man had white-blond hair and was so pale he looked like he would blend into the studio's white wall.

"War, famine, drought. All familiar, heartrending scenes from Goma, in eastern Congo, in the very heart of Africa," intoned Johnson gravely. "But pictures like this will soon be history if Lucy Tremlett has her way. Hollywood's hottest property has a new role, and it's far more challenging than anything the crankiest director could ever throw at her. Lucy, tell us about that, before I introduce our other guests."

The camera zoomed in on Tremlett's heart-shaped face, blue eyes, and sleek strawberry-blond hair. Yael peered at the screen. How did she do that? No spots, wrinkles, or flaws of any kind. Her hair glowed with vitality. There was barely a dusting of powder on her radiant skin.

The actress smiled warmly at the camera. "Thank you, Trevor. As you probably know, last year Fareed Hussein, the secretary-general of the United Nations, asked me to serve as an ambassador for UNICEF, and I was very pleased to accept. It's an honor and a privilege."

The camera showed a series of stills of Tremlett with Hussein in Afghanistan, Congo, and Sudan as she spoke. "I have been to places that I would never have visited and seen things I could never have imagined happening in the twenty-first century. It's only when those of us living comfortable lives with enough food, clothes, and running water realize that we are the lucky ones, that most of the world does not live like that, that anything will change," she said passionately. "And we are going to do just that: provide housing, education, water, jobs, and training. UNICEF and the UN are very excited to be working together with a new charity, Africa Child Rescue."

"Is that part of the UN, or independent?"

"Absolutely independent. It's backed by a group of businessmen from around the world who believe in anonymous philanthropy," said Tremlett, nodding earnestly. "It brings child miners out and gives them a whole new life."

"And what does Hobo think about all this?" asked Johnson. Hobo was the hottest rock star of the moment and Tremlett's fiancé. Half-Nigerian, half-Chinese and six foot three, he had been hailed by the critics as the new Prince. Hobo had recently headlined a three-day charity rock festival in Berlin.

"He is totally supportive. Actually, it looks like he . . . no,

I shouldn't be telling you this," said Tremlett, suddenly coy as she looked down at her shoes.

Johnson leaned forward. "Lucy, don't be a tease. You know you want to tell us."

The actress opened her eyes wide. "Well, all I can say is that he is really into this, and we are talking about what kind of role he could take. And I promise you, Trevor, once everything has been finalized, you will be first to know."

Johnson squirmed in his chair excitedly, as though there was a small rodent in his trousers. "Brilliant, Lucy, brilliant. Let me introduce our second guest, who is going to tell us all about this incredibly exciting new project that is going to save countless lives."

The camera panned to the pale man, who inclined his head graciously.

Johnson said, "He usually works behind the scenes. He is not a household name. You will find him at the most exclusive sessions at Davos, or in the salons of Berlin, London, and Washington, mixing with the world's movers and shakers. And tonight he is here with us: Reinhardt Daintner of the KZX corporation."

Yael put her glass down and listened carefully as Daintner spoke. She looked harder at the screen—it was one of the businessmen who had accompanied the SG to Goma a couple of weeks ago. Reinhardt Daintner was cordial and articulate as he explained that the United Nations had invited KZX to sponsor the UN Year of Africa in recognition of KZX's outstanding work in aid and development and of its corporate social responsibility, the first time that a company had been "accorded such an honor," as he put it.

Daintner outlined KZX's plans for the biggest single aid project in history, focusing on the area around Goma. The plan, known as the UN-KZX Goma Development Zone, would be a landmark: the first joint UN–private sector aid project. The corporation would provide homes, housing, education for tens of thousands of refugees, and skills training so that they could become economically independent—a mini-city in all but name. The UN would provide the staff, the expertise, and experience.

Was he the voice on the sound file? Yael asked herself. No, she decided. No Viennese lilt. Yael knew Vienna well, having visited the UN headquarters there numerous times. He spoke with a distinct German-mid-Atlantic accent. Herr Daintner had worked hard to blend in at Davos and the salons of London and Washington.

He continued, explaining that, thanks to the UN, it seemed that there would finally be peace in Congo. This was a unique opportunity to bring stability to a land that had known so much war and bloodshed, he said. "Give a man a fish and you feed him once. Teach him how to fish and you feed him for life."

Johnson nodded enthusiastically as Tremlett interrupted: "Teach a woman to fish and she will set up a training program to teach the other women in the village, and then a cooperative so they can sell the fish in the local market to raise money to build a school."

"Exactly," said Daintner. But even with the best will in the world, eastern Congo remained unstable, he continued. Which was why, in another first for the UN, KZX security guards, operating under a special UN mandate, would even protect the refugees from raids.

Yael put her glass down and listened intently. This was unprecedented.

"And what does the Congolese government say about that?" asked Johnson as he leaned forward, his face serious. "Especially after all the problems in Iraq with foreign contractors?"

Daintner lightly rocked back and forth in his chair, nodding sagely to signal his concern. "Sovereignty is a sensitive subject in Africa, and KZX absolutely understands that. We are in constant touch with the Congolese police and ministry of the interior and we are working with them. But they know, as we do, that for now, Congo's institutions are still undeveloped. Goma is 1,600 kilometers from the capital, Kinshasa, in a volatile border area. The roads are poor, government control is weak. The government recognizes that it needs help, and we are there to provide it. There can be no development or aid work without safety and security. We have already been using KZX's communication capabilities to provide the UN with real-time intelligence about events on the ground in Central Africa. But this is the ultimate expression of KZX's corporate social responsibility: we are ready to place our own staff on the line." The discussion went on until the show ended for the news.

Yael sat very still, trying to process the profound implications of what she had just heard. The UN had outsourced its intelligence gathering to a private company that was now going to provide security across conflict zones in the world's most unstable and mineral-rich country. Why had she not heard anything about this before? She was just about to switch the television off when the screen showed the CNN studio in New York. The anchor said, "Now more on the United Nations. Let's go straight to Roger Richardson at the New York headquarters."

The UN correspondent, Roger Richardson, a tall, middle-aged man with a dry sense of humor, stood in front of the Secretariat building.

Olivia's picture flashed up.

Richardson said, "The secretary-general's spokesman has just announced that the UN police will handle the investigation into Olivia de Souza's death on its own. The NYPD and the FBI will not be involved."

Yael sat up very straight, alert and listening carefully.

"Is that usual practice?" the anchor asked.

Richardson shook his head. "No, it's not. Especially in a high-profile case like this. The UN is international territory, and legally not part of the United States. So the NYPD and the FBI have no jurisdiction here. The UN police is more of a public-order force, to keep everything running smoothly and deal with security, rather than an investigative organization. But previously, when someone died in the building either the NYPD or the FBI was called in because they have a proper forensics division. So this is unusual."

"Are you hearing that this tragedy was a suicide, or are there suspicions of foul play?"

He frowned. "UN sources are suggesting that she killed herself, so that's why there is no need to bring in outside agencies. But it's puzzling. Olivia was known as a cheerful, dedicated employee and colleague here."

The screen switched back to the studio. The anchor said, "And we have some other intriguing news from the UN today, Richard?"

Olivia's picture was replaced by Yael's UN passport photograph.

Yael turned the volume up as the studio anchor interviewed the correspondent.

"Richard, who is Yael Azoulay?"

He nodded. "Until this morning she was the secretary-general's special envoy to crisis zones. The *New York Times* reported today that she has brokered a secret deal with Jean-Pierre Hakizimani, a Rwandan who is wanted on charges of genocide for the mass slaughter in 1994. But this morning she was let go and escorted from the building by the UN police."

"What kind of deal?"

"To surrender to the UN tribunal and disband his militia for a reduced sentence."

The anchor nodded sagely. "The usual murky UN trade-off. Why was she let go?"

Roger frowned, as though he too had been wondering about this all day. "Well, we are hearing from UN sources that she leaked the deal with Hakizimani to the *New York Times*."

"And did she?"

"We don't know. She has never spoken to the press. And the *Times* isn't talking. But UN sources are insistent that she leaked both the agreement and her memo criticizing it."

Yael threw her shoe at the screen. The screen wobbled and the camera returned to the studio.

The anchor said, "Thanks, Richard. And now, Congo's big cleanup. Goma struggles to cope with a volcano eruption spewing lava over a city that was already covered in it."

Yael pressed the Off button. She picked up the tiny ball of paper on the table. She had found the paper embedded in a gobbet of chewing gum and stuck to the door frame, exactly where she had left it, when she came home.

Twelve

There seemed to be no escape from Roxana Voiculescu's sky-blue eyes, and Sami was surprised to find that he was an increasingly willing prisoner. Roxana was smart, funny, attractive, and tall, with long chestnut hair, a degree in journalism from Bucharest University, and a postgraduate diploma in development studies from Oxford. They were sitting at a small corner table in Grad, an upscale vodka bar on the corner of East 10th Street and Second Avenue, watching the door for celebrities during happy hour. Page Six had just run a huge list of star patrons caught downing cocktails at the long brushed-steel bar and enjoying the faux-Moscow 1950s décor of bare wooden floors, Soviet posters, and utilitarian furniture dubbed "Retro-Irony" by the column, but none seemed to be in attendance so early in the day.

Roxana, a rare friendly face in the spokesman's office, had been flirting with Sami for several weeks, asking when he would take her for a drink, or show her some New York nightlife. Sami usually avoided such invitations from female UN officials, believing, correctly, they were only issued because of his position at the *Times*. There was a thin line between a professional relationship with UN staff and becoming too familiar—although with most of Schneidermann's people there was little danger of that. Roxana seemed different, though, and was always friendly and chatty. But Sami was not a big drinker and was always worried he would blurt out something stupid or, even worse, something important, while under the influence.

After the fiasco with Yael that morning, however, he was happy for the attention. What harm could there be in a couple of drinks with a UN contact, he asked himself when Roxana had called, virtually demanding he meet her that evening? None, he decided. The Gray Lady could buy them both a couple of vodka cocktails.

"Over there, at the bar, tall guy in a white shirt, navy suit, and blue tie, " said Roxana as she stirred her vodka and tonic with the straw, her eyes holding his as she spoke. "Brown hair, cheekbones, pencil mustache. It's Johnny Depp in disguise. Definitely."

Roxana's Chanel handbag sat on the table next to her. The bag was half-open and Sami could see the top edge of a blue envelope inside. Sami looked over to the bar and laughed. The vodka was kicking in nicely. He felt confident and relaxed. "Sure. Johnny's got a great makeup artist. Check out the Brooks Brothers outfit. Maybe he is rehearsing on Wall Street for his next role. Why don't you go and ask him?"

Roxana was easy company. It was a pleasant change to be answering questions instead of asking them. Sami realized after half an hour or so that she had extracted his entire life story: his family's arrival in the United States, the difficult early years settling in, university, his worries about his remaining relatives in Gaza, and his work with the *New York Times*. She wanted to know all about how he had got his job as UN correspondent and was incredulous that he had simply applied for the advertised opening, with no help from any contacts on the inside. For his part, Sami had found out very little about Roxana, except that she was thirty-two, born in Bucharest, and her father was Romania's finance minister. She had joined Schneidermann's office as an intern two years earlier and had quickly risen to be his deputy, although Schneidermann had not let her take any morning briefings so far. Roxana claimed to be terrified at the prospect of dealing with the UN press corps, which Sami found hard to believe.

Roxana smiled at Sami. "Go and talk to Johnny Depp? I don't know, Sami. My mother told me not to speak to strange men in bars."

Sami picked up his drink and swirled the ice cubes in the clear liquid. "Be brave. Say you are doing it for a bet. I am sure he won't mind. If you want to be a UN spokeswoman you have to learn to deal with strangers and unexpected situations."

He paused for several seconds, glancing quickly at the edge of the blue envelope. Would it work? It was certainly worth trying. "You do want to be a spokeswoman?" he asked innocently. "Actually, no, I shouldn't tell you this . . ."

Roxana sat up straight, suddenly totally focused. "Tell me what, Sami?"

Sami sipped his cocktail, drawing out the moment. "Well, I keep hearing that there is some dissatisfaction with Schneidermann on the 38th floor. That he is awkward socially, too confrontational, that he lacks the people skills a UN spokesperson needs. I have been . . . asked my opinion, about possible replacements."

Roxana did not answer but stood up and walked briskly over to the bar.

Sami knew he had a few seconds at the most. He had just raised his hand over the top of her bag when she turned on her heel and walked back. He dropped his fingers and scratched the back of his head as nonchalantly as he could.

Thankfully Roxana was focused on her career prospects. "Who says that people are unhappy with Henrik?"

Sami shook his head. "I cannot reveal my sources, Roxana, you know that. But I don't mind telling them that they should be looking for someone with a bit more . . . bar presence, maybe? Someone who can hold a room? Talk to strangers? The opinion of the *New York Times* still counts."

Roxana gave him a searching look and walked straight up to the Johnny Depp look-alike. Sami guessed Roxana would speak to him for a few seconds and would then turn and wave. He whisked out the envelope, folded it in half, and jammed it into the back pocket of his jeans. Roxana did not wave but walked straight back and sat down next to him, closer than before.

"How did I do?" she asked.

"Brilliantly, it looked like from here. You seemed very confident. Is he Johnny Depp?"

"No, of course not," said Roxana, laughing. "But he did offer to buy me a drink." Her leg brushed against his again and rested against his thigh. Her knee was surprisingly bony, he noticed. "Do I get the *New York Times* seal of approval?"

Sami nodded determinedly. "Absolutely."

They talked some more and Roxana seemed to hang on his every word, which was flattering despite how often she'd checked her watch in the last ten minutes. But when Roxana asked Sami how he got his stories and developed his contacts, the alarm bell finally went off in his head.

"We would have to know each other much better before I can reveal trade secrets," he said, keeping his voice light. "Tell me about Schneidermann. What's he like to work for?" Sami asked, smiling as he leaned in closer, the very picture of vodka-fueled camaraderie. He tried not to feel guilty. She should have closed her bag, he told himself.

Roxana moved nearer to him, as though she were about to reveal a great confidence.

"Very," she began, pausing and stirring her drink, "Belgian." She laughed. "But really, Sami, what is the secret of a good journalist? How do you persuade people to reveal their innermost confidences?"

She sat back and looked at him, her head tilted to the side. "Maybe it's your big, soulful, brown eyes that draw them in. You look so innocent, a bit disorganized. But it's all a trick. They want to help you. And then, before they even know it, they have confessed *everything*," she said, raising her eyebrows mischievously.

Sami took out an ice cube from the dregs of his cocktail and sucked on it, forcing himself to sober up now. Roxana was much smarter than he had realized. The warm weight of her leg on his was having a definite effect, despite his best efforts.

He crunched the ice cube in his mouth. So let the duel begin, he thought. "Soulful eyes? Thanks, I like that. But it's too noisy to talk properly here, Roxana. I know a great French bistro three blocks away. We can trade UN secrets over a bottle of Bordeaux."

"Sorry. Schneidermann is my boss, Sami. I cannot talk about him," she said, her voice cooler now. "I thought this was a social occasion, not an interview. And I already have dinner plans."

Sami saw that she was now intently watching the door. It opened and she immediately sat up and reached for her bag. She looked inside and her smile faded as she searched it thoroughly. She shook her head, all flirtatiousness now vanished.

"What's the matter?" asked Sami, as nonchalantly as he could, feeling the folded blue envelope in his jeans pocket pressing against his backside.

"I've lost something. It must have fallen out . . ." She looked up and stared at Sami. "Have you seen an envelope, a blue envelope?" she asked, accusingly.

Sami shook his head. "Me? No. Nothing. Wait. I'll have a look." He got off the chair and began to search under the table, trying to ignore his feelings of guilt. After a minute or so of the pantomime hunt he stood up. "Nothing."

Roxana looked almost indignant. The atmosphere was now distinctly chilly. She backed away, as though he had suddenly tried to kiss her. She looked at her watch, openly this time, and waved at someone at the bar. "Sami, I hope you don't mind, but I told a friend I would meet him here. Tell me if you find an envelope."

Sami nodded and stood up as she gathered her bag. “Sure.”

“Thanks for the drink. It was really fun. Let’s do it again soon,” Roxana said, her voice brisk and businesslike now, before giving him a chaste peck on the cheek.

“Anytime,” he said, wondering why he bothered to repeat the lie. He watched her walk over to the bar and greet a dark-haired man in his late twenties with an enthusiastic kiss on the mouth. Sami sat back down and slowly stirred his drink, the air in the booth still charged with Roxana’s energy. He was a liar—the story about dissatisfaction with Schneidermann was a complete fiction—and a thief. But he had the envelope.

Yael put the sticky paper back on the table. She sat back and watched a tugboat chugging along the Hudson river, the reflection of its lights glimmering on the waves. They were mocking her now, telling her they were watching, had been inside her flat. But Yael did not feel scared. She had Joe-Don and she had something else. She picked up a quarter from the table, reached under her chair, and levered up a loose strip of parquet floor. The wood came away easily to reveal a narrow, deep cavity. She pulled out a small, heavy package wrapped in oilcloth. She unraveled the covering and weighed the pistol in her hand: an M9, US Army standard issue. Safety catch on, one round chambered.

Yael stood with her feet apart and her legs slightly bowed, held the pistol in both hands, and sighted on an imaginary enemy. No, she was not scared, but she was angry, with a cold rage that coursed through her. Memories of Olivia ran through her head: laughing so loudly at Le Perigord that the maître d' had asked them, as politely as possible, to please be quieter; sharing a pack of throat-searing Lebanese cigarettes on the balcony on the 38th floor; swapping gossip about Charles Bonnet's latest "intern," every one of whom looked like a model from *Vogue*. They had killed her friend, and now she would take her revenge, not just for Olivia, but for David—indeed for all the other victims sacrificed, with her help, on the holy altar of realpolitik.

Yael put the gun down. She needed to be calm and smart, not hyped up and lashing out. She plugged her iPod into the speaker stand and Van Morrison's "Sweet Thing" filled the room. She switched off the light, poured herself some more red wine, lit a scented candle, and sat on her bed. She drank most of the glass just a little too fast, and the walls began to soften and blur. Van Morrison's throaty voice soared and fell, and she felt the familiar, welcome sliding. She lay back, smoking contemplatively, staring at the gray wisps as they rose toward the cracked paint on the ceiling. She pulled slowly on the gold hoop high on the side of her right ear and closed her eyes. The pain was mild at first. Waves of red and gold swirled and exploded, vanished and dissolved.

She was dancing on a snow-capped mountain, the earth cold and hard beneath her feet, the sky a sheet of solid turquoise, and the air so pure it hurt to breathe; she was sitting astride him, drenched with sweat, his body wiry beneath her as she shuddered in her orgasm. She twisted the hoop harder until she gasped with the pain, and she could see his face as though he were in the room with her: the handsomest man in Kandahar, in Afghanistan, in the whole world—skin the color of milky coffee, eyes like green laser beams, and a smile that made her knees wobble.

She rocked and gasped, the pain and pleasure fusing as the music coursed through her body. He beckoned her toward him, his eyes locked onto hers, and the hunger surged through her. He smelled of cinnamon and dust, coffee and sunshine, and his body was warm and hard. A hand slid between her legs, her back arched, and the pleasure rippled up and down; he was above her, he was inside her, and the wave built and built until it broke and she shuddered and moaned.

The music stopped and Yael lay still for a while, the sadness lighter but no less poignant. Her eyes were wet, she realized, and she wiped them dry. She glanced over at her shoulder bag on the kitchen table. A cream envelope was sticking out of the side pocket, addressed to her by hand, with no return address. She had picked the letter up from the doorman when she returned home. Yael opened the envelope. The letter inside was written in a flowing, elegant hand on thick paper; the script looked familiar. She scanned the letter: "My dear Yael," it began.

Sami took a long swig from the bottle of Brooklyn Lager and switched off his television at the end of the CNN 9:00 p.m. news show. He looked around his studio apartment on 9th Street in the East Village. It was cramped, dark, and musty. Sami had lived there for nearly two years but still had not properly unpacked his stuff. Half the room was filled with boxes of books and papers, many of them spilling out on to the floor. He kept telling himself that this was only a temporary accommodation, not worth sorting out. But at $1,500 a month it was supercheap by Manhattan standards, mainly because it belonged to his uncle, who had not used it since the 1980s. The walls were a faded cream, the floor covered with an orange acrylic carpet, and the hot water spat brown in the bathroom, but the most depressing thing was the twin bed in the corner. How could he bring a girl back here?

Still, he thought, tipping the bottle of lager up to get the last drops, that was at least a theoretical question for now. Roxana Voiculescu. What an operator. His second strikeout after Yael. But if the women thing was not going well, at least work was. The UN-KZX agreement was a huge story. He grabbed his laptop. The Department of Safety and Security, usually one of the more obscure parts of the UN, suddenly looked a whole lot more interesting.

He clicked on the DSS's website. Like every UN department, the DSS was run by an under-secretary-general. A USG was an immensely powerful position, and usually the peak of a UN career. The DSS had a new USG: Hakim Yundala. Sami stared at Yundala's photograph. He was African—short, muscular, with a wide face and small red-flecked eyes, and immensely pleased with himself. It was coming back now: Yundala was a former chief of police in Kinshasa, in charge of the investigation into the death of Aristide Belimba, the country's foremost investigative journalist, who specialized in tracking coltan shipments. He had been found locked in his car, with a rubber tube leading from his exhaust pipe to the window.

Yundala had quickly declared that the reporter had committed suicide, and was promptly promoted to interior minister. His UN appointment had caused vocal protests from Amnesty International and Human Rights Watch, and a demonstration by Congolese exiles outside the UN building. That protest, Sami now remembered, had been led by Rina Hussein, the SG's daughter—just like today's protest had been. Schneidermann, the SG's spokesman, had dismissed the objections, proclaiming that Yundala's appointment was proof of the SG's and the UN's commitment to global diversity. There was more: a three-line press release announced the SG's appointment of two new members to the Senior Management Group, the most powerful cabal of UN officials: Hakim Yundala and Charles Bonnet.

Sami put his laptop down, sat back, and picked up the blue envelope on the coffee table. There were two sheets inside, and he read them carefully once more.

Thirteen

Yael sat in a half-lotus on her bed, warmed by the midday sunshine. She had woken a couple of hours earlier. She still felt muggy-headed from the previous night's wine and cigarettes, and she was increasingly apprehensive about the evening. She had read through Hakizimani's UN file again, but something kept bothering her. The only time the Rwandan had shown his human side in Goma was when he pulled out the worn, plastic-covered photo of his three daughters. His face had twisted in genuine anguish. Yael could feel his grief, still raw after so many years. But there was something else, she sensed, a different emotion threaded into his sorrow.

The more she thought about the car bomb the less sense it made. Why would the Tutsi leadership, knowing by then that the Hutu government was preparing for civil war, if not a mass extermination, blow up the minister of health's car? If they wanted to assassinate someone, then it should have been the prime minister or the whole cabinet at once. The minister of health was not a major power broker, although Hakizimani soon became one of the most important Hutu leaders and a key architect of the genocide. It puzzled her, but the answer, if there were one, would eventually materialize of its own accord.

She walked over to the kitchen table and checked the blueprints of the 12th floor of the Millennium Plaza. Suite 3017 was the last room, at the end of the corridor, next to a fire exit staircase. Joe-Don had thought of everything, or so she hoped. Olivia's letter lay open on the table. She had reread it several times that morning, unsure when she had woken up if she had dreamed it, or if it really did exist.

But there it was, Olivia's careful, sloping handwriting, in dark blue ink, just as the nuns at the orphanage in Managua had taught her:

My dear Yael,

I very much hope that you will never read this. We always laughed about the P5 and who knows who else bugging our rooms and the SG's offices and they doubtless are. But I fear that now something much worse is happening, so if anything happens to me, I have arranged for this to be delivered to you by hand.

You know how worried I have been lately; the SG has been losing weight, his hand shakes, and he is irritable. It's my job to organize his diary, and usually I know where he is and what he is doing every minute of the day. Now hours, sometimes the whole day goes by and I have no idea what's going on, except that he is in closed-door meetings, out of the office, or unavailable. Other weird things are happening: e-mails disappear from my computer, and those I send don't always arrive. The other day I saw a document move across my desktop from one side of the monitor to another—but when I called the IT security department they just laughed and told me I had an overactive imagination.

Last night I knew I did not. I went in to the SG's office, and he was fast asleep at his desk. The figure "500" had been written on his pad several times and then crossed out with line upon line, vertically and horizontally, as though he were trying to gouge the numbers out of the paper. He was muttering, and his right hand was clenched so tightly the knuckles were white. He sat up with his eyes wide open. He stared at me, his eyes almost bulging out of their sockets, as though I was some kind of terrifying monster. But he was in a deep dream and did not see me. He cried out and dropped his head again.

The telephone rang, on his private line, the one even I cannot connect calls to. The SG murmured something but kept sleeping. You know I am under strict instructions never to touch that telephone, the "hotline" as we always used to joke. But after two or three rings I could not resist. I picked it up and said hello. Nobody answered. The line went dead immediately. I checked the SG once more. He was still asleep, so I pressed the last number redial. A woman answered and said, "Menachem Stein's office."

I hung up right away. I knew that woman's voice. She has called me several times before, asking for the SG. She always refuses to say who she is, only that it is a private and personal matter. I think I have made a terrible mistake. I am sure the UN security department monitors the SG's line, and who knows who else is listening in. Then it got even worse. The telephone rang. It must have been Stein's office calling back to check who was calling them.

I didn't know what to do. If I let it ring it would wake the SG. If I answered it again, I would have to say something. I picked up the handset, very carefully, but I was so nervous that I dropped it. It made such a crash that the SG woke up. He asked me what I was doing there and I made up some story about checking his schedule for tomorrow, but I could see he did not believe me. Yael, why is the SG getting calls from Efrat Global Solutions? We have the DPKO for all our military operations. We can call on the P5 if we need intelligence. The UN has never used private military contractors.

Now my phone rings and there is nobody there. I feel someone is watching me. I have a creepy feeling on the back of my neck. My doorman told me that people have been snooping around, asking when I get home in the evenings so they can deliver a package. When he asked them for some ID they just walked off.

Yael, I wish you were here. I wish I were not writing this letter. I hope you never read it.
Your friend,
Olivia

Yael made herself some builder's brew tea and stood by the window overlooking the Hudson River, cradling the cup in both hands. Olivia's letter had triggered a vortex of emotions: sadness at her friend's death, anger at the manner of it, and a powerful curiosity. Other feelings, stirred up by the mention of Menachem Stein, she boxed away, at least for now. At first she had thought Olivia was "afriend99@gmail.com," but presumably she would have said so in this, her final letter. For now, the identity of "afriend" could wait.

Yael grabbed her laptop and played the sound file again, listening to Hussein's feeble arguments to have less than five hundred, as though human life was a commodity to be bought, sold, and bargained for; Janet Rembaugh's cynical justification of the deaths at Srebrenica, Charles Bonnet, and the mysterious Austrian pushing the SG until he agreed to Hakizimani's involvement and settled on the final figure. She pressed the stop button and watched an NYPD police boat roar down the middle of the waterway, sending a double spray of water in its wake.

Her mobile telephone beeped several times, interrupting her reverie. She picked up the handset: a text message from a blocked number. Part of her—a large part, if she were honest with herself—hoped that Joe-Don would call or text to tell her that the plan was off, at least for tonight. She had checked her mobile for messages a dozen times in the last two hours. Now, the screen declared, "Yr cuz OK to meet 2nite ☺."

She picked up the photograph of her and her brother David in Central Park and studied it for a long time.

Sami frowned as he tried to open his office door for the third time, juggling his coffee and newspaper in one hand and the key in the other. The lock jammed, squeaked, and finally opened. He stepped inside and his irritation evaporated. The cracked window had been replaced. He pressed the light switch. The room was instantly illuminated by a large halogen lamp, complete with a dimmer switch, and blissfully silent. The floor was clean, the bins emptied, and the dirty marks gone from the walls, which had been freshly painted. What was going on? Had the 38th floor decided to court him with new office fittings in exchange for more sympathetic coverage? And when had the work been done?

Sami had returned to his office soon after ten last night with the envelope he had taken from Roxana's bag. He planned to scan the papers, copy the digital files onto a memory stick, and e-mail them to his online backup service. He was not comfortable bringing the papers back to the UN building, but he could hardly hand Roxana's documents over to the nearest copy shop. Nor did he trust the nearby internet cafés. Unfortunately, the *New York Times* scanner was broken. It had been for a month, he remembered as he futilely jabbed the On button, but he had not bothered to get it fixed.

And then he remembered that at 10:30 p.m. the security guards changed shift. The night exit regulations were much stricter. He would have to pass through the security at the entrance tent to get out, empty his pockets, and possibly even his bag. The guards might even frisk him. Rather than risk an inspection, Sami decided to hide Roxana's papers in the middle of a two-hundred-page UN report and lock it in his filing cabinet. Two vodka cocktails and a beer chaser were not helping him to think clearly. It was only on the way home that he realized he could have stayed there and simply taken pictures of the papers with his digital camera. By then it was too late. He would really draw attention to himself if he went back again.

Sami sat at his desk, put his coffee down, and unfolded that day's edition of the *Times*. He had made the front page again, although still "below the fold": "Turmoil Continues at UN: A Secretary Dies; An Envoy Sent Away." The big piece he was working on would make the top half, he was sure of that, if not the splash. Sami stared at the photograph of Yael next to his story: she was huddled in a conclave with Fareed Hussein at a refugee camp in East Timor, her hair piled up behind her head in a ponytail, looking very capable.

He quickly turned the page. A story datelined Washington, DC, caught his attention: "President Freshwater Calls for Senate Hearing on Private Military Contractors." The White House wanted an inquiry into the growing role of PMCs, their legal liability, and full disclosure of all contracts with all US government agencies. Guards from Efrat Global Solutions had been accused of killing more than a dozen demonstrators in Dubai, where the company had just been hired to train the United Arab Emirates' fledgling army. EGS denied everything and promised full cooperation with the UAE's authorities. The reporter noted that the allegations came at a bad time for EGS. The intelligence world was awash with rumors that the company was about to sign the largest contract in history for providing worldwide military and security services for an as yet unknown client. EGS was founded by Menachem Stein, a former brigadier-general in the Israeli army. Stein resigned from the military under unclear circumstances almost twenty years ago, after leading a mission of undercover commandos in Nablus. A firefight had erupted in the bazaar and had left six civilians dead, including several teenagers who had been shot in the back. The Israelis claimed they had been killed by Palestinian militants. The Palestinians blamed the Israelis. No one was ever charged over the deaths.

Stein now ran one of the world's largest and most profitable private military contractors. Its website boasted that it specialized in "bringing stability to the world's most unstable areas." EGS was active in every conflict zone in the world and had just opened a new regional headquarters in Kinshasa, the capital of Congo, the article noted. Human-rights groups accused EGS operatives of a litany of crimes including smuggling, rape, torture, murder, and even running a network of secret prisons. EGS denied all the claims but refused to cooperate with human-rights investigators. Several world leaders, including President Freshwater, were now calling for international regulation of private military contractors.

The hairs rose on the back of Sami's neck. He sat back and put his feet on the desk, thinking hard. EGS. Olivia's voice mail messages. He picked up the telephone and called office management. Yuri answered. Sami thanked him for the work.

Yuri was as surly as ever. "What? No work, no, nothing was authorized for your office, Mr. Boustani."

"Are you sure? Then who put in the new light, fixed the window, and cleaned up?"

"We received nothing, no paperwork. No papers, no work," said Yuri, and hung up.

Sami put the phone down, his heart thumping, and grabbed the key to his filing cabinet.

He opened the drawer and looked for the UN report. There it was: "A Statistical Evaluation of UN Feeding Practices in Conflict Zones." He shook the document to find Roxana's papers. It was empty.

Yael picked up her laptop and opened East Side Escorts' website. It had been a long time since she had dressed to kill, she thought, so perhaps the website could give her some direction. Both men and women were displayed and diligently subdivided by category and subcategory, though all were equally stunning. There was even a "fusion" menu, and she clicked on a picture of Tina, twenty-eight. Tina was half-Japanese and half-Mexican, dressed in expensive-looking lingerie, pearls, and a pair of Christian Louboutins.

East Side was the agency of choice for visiting UN delegations. Its escorts could be taken to a gourmet restaurant or a diplomatic reception, without fear of faux pas or embarrassment. They were regularly checked for STDs and were intelligent, able to converse on politics and diplomacy as skillfully as they could disport themselves in the bedroom. Human nature being what it was, it was understood on the 38th floor, and by the P5, that visitors, especially those new in town, would want to enjoy Manhattan's many pleasures, including those of the flesh. When the inevitable query as to where they could enjoy some female company came from delegations' leaders—

whether to the UN or to the hotel concierge, who was always primed beforehand—the answer was East Side. The escorts usually visited the delegates in their hotel rooms, but East Side also ran its own "Exclusive Gentleman's Club" in a town house in the West Village.

The General Assembly in September was the agency's busiest time of the year, so much so that it closed for two weeks afterward to allow its employees to recover. Special visitors to the UN, at any time of the year, were allocated a dedicated individual escort, or even a team, depending on tastes. The escorts were given thick briefing folders on the visitor's home country and the conflicts being discussed at the UN. The clients were always impressed by their companion's knowledge of their homelands. Pillow talk usually yielded a rich harvest of intelligence, which the escorts recorded on concealed equipment and then forwarded to the Department of Political Affairs.

Over the years, as Yael had become trusted with the most sensitive of UN business, she had frequent dealings with East Side escorts. She often took the visitors to the town house in the West Village and naturally always eagerly read the transcripts of the recordings. Yael had become quite friendly with Carmen, the statuesque Argentinian matriarch who ran East Side and was a former secretary at the UN Department of Information. At first Yael had found the whole business distasteful, but after a while, setting up a night of paid-for sex with no emotional entanglements seemed positively straightforward compared to some of the deals she had arranged with warlords like Hakizimani. She sometimes found herself browsing the male section of the website herself. Carmen was grateful for Yael's discretion and for the amount of business she brought in. She had several times offered Yael a private room with one or more of her best "Caballeros." Yael had always smiled and declined.

But now Yael had finally called in the favors she had done for Carmen over the years. When the request for the "Special Executive Massage" came, as expected, from Mr. Lumumba in suite 3017 at the Millennium Plaza hotel, Carmen described in long and salacious detail the charms of Sharon Mantello, her new recruit from Newark. So Sharon it was, due at the hotel in two hours, at 8:30 p.m. Yael picked up Sharon's driver's license from the coffee table and examined her own photograph, which stared out from it.

In the meantime Yael had some work to do. She logged on to her computer, opened her browser, and shut down the anonymizing program that disguised her IP address and data trail. She booked a round-trip ticket to San Antonio on a flight departing from La Guardia at 7:30 the following morning; a seat on a Greyhound bus from the Port Authority terminal on Eighth Avenue to San Antonio at 3:45 a.m., in nine hours' time; and a business-class train ticket from Penn Station to Austin at 6:45 a.m., all in Sharon's name.

The clothes had arrived that afternoon: a black Donna Karan minidress, a matching raincoat and cap, Manolo Blahnik shoes, brown contact lenses, and Chanel tinted glasses. The dress showed her slim figure and toned legs; the raincoat gave her the look of a 1940s film star; and the cap, big enough to pile her hair up inside, and glasses added an air of mystery. Yael tried them on and stood in front of her mirror, turning from side to side. She nodded approvingly. Perhaps it was time for a fresh look. It was a shame that in four hours' time her new outfit would be in a garbage bag at the bottom of the East River.

Fourteen

The security guards eyed Yael suspiciously as she walked along the 30th-floor corridor of the Millennium Plaza. The two men wore identical well-cut black business suits, white button-down shirts, and navy neckties. Bluetooth headsets were perched on their right ears, and a small but telltale bulge distended the left armpit of their jackets. Heads of state and prime ministers visiting the UN were guarded by the Secret Service, but lower-ranking officials were protected by the Bureau of Diplomatic Security, which was part of the Department of State. These two looked familiar, Yael realized. She thought she had seen them guarding the Nigerian minister of resources just a month or so earlier, at a UN conference on aid and development.

The hotel seemed the same as ever, she thought, with its light-brown walls, dark, patterned carpet, and muted lighting—the bland comfort of five-star anonymity. Which sometimes was very pleasant indeed. Yael felt a wave of nostalgia as she walked down the corridor. Six years ago, for several months, she had spent most Thursday afternoons and early evenings here, as one half of what the French gallantly referred to as *un cinq à sept*, a love affair conducted between the hours of five and seven in the afternoon, although the liaisons had often lasted much longer. The Millennium had perhaps been a rather obvious choice for a memorably passionate affair with a UN senior staff member, but the hotel staff were discreet, the bed large and comfortable, the views spectacular, and it was just a couple of minutes from the UN headquarters.

A room-service waiter walked down the corridor toward her, pushing a large trolley covered with used plates and glasses. He was tall and handsome, with short black hair, brown eyes, and tawny skin. The waiter caught her eye and smiled flirtatiously. "Nice outfit, ma'am, if I may say so," he said as he maneuvered the trolley past her.

"You may," said Yael, reading the nametag pinned to his jacket, "Miguel."

She was still smiling, buoyed by the brief encounter, when she reached the door. The two security guards moved closer together, blocking her path. One was squat, muscular, and bald, the other tall and wiry, his blond hair cut short in an army buzz cut.

Yael looked them in the eye. "Good evening, gentlemen. East Side Escorts, for Mr. Lumumba. We are booked for 8:30 p.m.," she said, raising the pitch of her voice and altering her accent to sound like a Newark native.

The bald protection officer looked at her with open disdain. Disdain was good, thought Yael, because they had definitely met before at the aid conference. And now, with her photo circulating in the *Times*, she was relieved he did not immediately recognize her.

Yael let her coat fall open, revealing her tight-fitting mini-dress, and subtly pushed her breasts forward. "Mr. Lumumba has ordered our Special Executive Massage, so I will need around an hour."

"ID please, ma'am," the bald guard asked.

Yael gave him Sharon's driver's license. He looked at her and back at the photograph on the plastic card. Yael could sense his disapproval.

He checked the license against a list and nodded. "Ma'am, I am required to inform you that suite 3017 has temporarily been declared United Nations territory. United States law no longer applies. Once you go through the door the NYPD has no jurisdiction here. Do you understand?"

Yael smiled. "No NYPD? It's my lucky night," she said, raising her eyebrows.

The blond guard moved forward and stared at her, stony-faced. "Ma'am, if you wish to proceed, I am required to frisk you. I regret we do not have a female colleague available. If you believe any of your rights have been violated, or you have any complaints about our conduct, please take them up with the United Nations Department of Safety and Security. You can find all the necessary information on their website. Please stand here and raise your arms."

Yael did as she was told. The blond guard ran his hands up and down her arms, legs, sides, front, and back swiftly and professionally, not lingering anywhere. "Please open your bag," he said.

He rummaged in her bag and took out the heavy mobile telephone that Joe-Don had given her at Battery Park and looked at it with disdain.

"No mobiles, ma'am," he said. "No electronic equipment of any kind in Mr. Lumumba's suite. That's the rules."

"No mobile, no massage. Every escort must always have a cell phone with her, for her own security. That's East Side's rules."

The blond guard looked at her uncertainly. Yael felt his hesitation and growing sense that she looked familiar. She needed to take control and fast. She moved closer. "Mr. Lumumba is going to be very pissed if he does not get his massage. It's all been booked and authorized. And if he is pissed, the people who sent you here will be even more pissed. Mr. Lumumba is a VIP. Otherwise you would not be here. And you have the paperwork."

Yael stepped even closer and took the handset back. "Do I look dangerous? I guess if you are really worried, you could come in and keep an eye on us. If you like."

The guard snapped: "One hour, ma'am."

Yael walked down a narrow corridor and turned right into the suite, her heart thumping so loudly she was sure it was audible. Hakizimani was standing by the window facing First Avenue, looking out over nighttime Manhattan. He was dressed in a hotel robe and speaking in rapid Kinyarwanda on his mobile telephone.

"*Bon soir*, Professor," said Yael.

Najwa al-Sameera walked into Sami's office, took in the sight of the bureau chief on his knees and surrounded by scattered papers, and shook her head disapprovingly.

"*Habibi*, what are you doing here so late? It's after 8:30. And how can you work in this chaos?"

Sami looked up from the contents of his filing cabinet and desk drawers spread out over the floor. The envelope was definitely gone. And it had definitely been hidden in the UN report. What an idiot he was. Idiots could not help being stupid, but he was not stupid. He was worse than that. He was an amateur. He knew he could not handle alcohol. Instead of having bright ideas with a head full of vodka and beer he should have gone to bed. He looked up to see Najwa standing over him, holding a slim leather portfolio with a Louis Vuitton clasp.

"The door was open. I hope you don't mind," she said, putting the folder on his desk.

He stood up and shook his head. "No, not at all." Najwa was a distraction but a welcome one. The search, he knew, was futile.

Najwa looked around the room with interest. "Fresh paint, new light, clean walls. So that's what they were doing. " She stood with her hands on her hips and looked thoughtful. "Ah-ha! I can see the headline: 'From Triumph to Triumph: Fareed Hussein Saves the World'."

"Sure. A paint job. That's all it takes," Sami replied drily. He paused. "That's what who was doing?" he asked, remembering his conversation with Yuri, the building manager.

"The maintenance guys I saw in here last night."

"Close the door, Najwa," he said, alert now.

"You want to be alone with me? What about Foxy Roxy?"

Sami could not help smiling. "Roxana is busy with her boyfriend."

Najwa nodded. "Yes, she is. I could have told you that, before you started buying her cocktails at Grad. Did you learn anything interesting?"

"How do you know about that?" Sami demanded.

Najwa raised her sculpted eyebrows. "Do you give me *your* sources, *habibi*?"

Sammy shook his head. Najwa stepped closer and looked him up and down. "But now she has your whole life story, which you just *had* to share, as she stared at you with her big, baby-blue eyes, totally entranced by your wit and sophistication."

"Not all of it," he said feebly.

"Enough, I am sure. Foxy Roxy moves fast. Don't worry, you are not the first and won't be the last to fall for her charms. I am sure her boyfriend will be out of the picture in a month once the Romanian Information Service has everything it needs from him. Maybe you can try again then."

"I don't think so."

Najwa put her hand on Sami's arm. "*Habibi*, next time you are missing Yael and want some female company you know where I am. I will even buy you a drink." She sat in Sami's chair and made herself comfortable. "Don't worry. I did not come here to torment you. I had quite an exciting evening myself yesterday."

Sami nodded. "The maintenance men."

"I was working late on a package about the Year of Africa. Just after eleven o'clock I saw these guys going in and out of your office. I came in to take a look. They were fitting the new lamp and window. But they were unfriendly and working extremely quickly, not at the usual UN pace. Something did not feel right. They asked me what I wanted. I said I was a colleague of yours, and had left something in there. Your filing cabinet was open. One of them was holding a blue envelope," she said, enjoying Sami's now rapt attention.

Najwa paused and took her buzzing iPhone out of her trouser pocket. She slowly flicked through the menu, a faint smile playing on her face.

"Najwa, did I read e-mails when you wanted the Goma memo?" asked Sami indignantly.

"No. I'm sorry. How rude of me." She smiled and put the handset away. "Where was I? Oh yes, they asked me what I had forgotten? 'That,' I said, pointing at the envelope. At first they did not want to give it to me. They said it was theirs. I said it was mine. This went on for a while."

"And then?" demanded Sami.

"I took their picture with my iPhone. I told them I would find out their names and make them famous. On Al-Jazeera, Osama bin Laden's favorite channel."

"Where is it?" demanded Sami, relief coursing through him.

Najwa looked at the portfolio on his desk.

Sami tried to grab it but Najwa swept it out of his grasp. "Are we sharing?" she asked.

Sami nodded.

"Then open it," she said, handing Sami the portfolio.

Yael watched the emotions play over Hakizimani's face: puzzlement, suspicion, recognition, and pleasure. He put his mobile phone down and smiled widely. "It really is you."

Joe-Don's instructions sounded in Yael's head: take and keep control of the situation and set the pace. Just imagine you are holding one of your negotiations. Keep the subject relaxed, let him feel he is running things. Then get what you need and make your move. Quickly.

Yael took her cap off, shaking her hair loose over her shoulders. "Yes, it is. I hope you are not disappointed."

Hakizimani shook his head. "No, no, of course not," he said enthusiastically. "It's just that I was expecting . . . someone else."

"That's me. The UN runs all sorts of agencies, Professor."

"So I see," he replied, looking at her appreciatively.

"Aren't you going to offer me a drink?" Yael asked. She could hear his mind trying to process the situation: What was she doing there? What did she want and what did she have to offer? And was she really going to have sex with him?

Hakizimani nodded. "Of course. What would you like?"

"A glass of dry white wine."

Yael sat down on the sofa, letting her dress ride a little way up her legs, and placed her handbag on the floor. She looked around the suite as Hakizimani stood at the minibar on the other side of the room and opened a small bottle of wine. The lounge was comfortable and spacious, around thirty feet by twenty, and smelled of furniture polish and air-conditioning. The dark-blue patterned carpet toned in with lighter blue walls, and abstract art hung on the walls.

The modern sofa, also blue, sat in the center of the room. There was a coffee table, writing desk, a chair, and a fireplace. Double doors with wood and glass panels led through to the bedroom. A bottle of Johnnie Walker Gold Label stood on the coffee table next to an ice bucket and four crystal glasses, together with a box of pills.

Hakizimani sat next to her and handed her the glass of wine. "Should I get dressed?" he asked, clearly preferring not to.

Yael looked at him, assessing how much of his bare skin was exposed. Hakizimani's neck was uncovered and his dressing gown was open halfway almost down to his navel. His legs were also bare. Thankfully she could see the top edge of a pair of boxer shorts.

She moved slightly closer and shook her head. "No, I don't think so."

Hakizimani raised his glass. "*À votre santé.*"

Yael clinked her drink against his. "And to yours. *Sans* volcanoes. I'm sorry I had to leave town so quickly."

"*Oui.* The earth moved, but not for us. At least not yet," he said, laughing as he rested his hand on Yael's leg.

She gently lifted it off. "No, not yet."

Hakizimani sat up, affronted, a man unused to having his advances rebuffed. "What exactly is the purpose of your visit, Ms. Azoulay? The *New York Times* and CNN say that you have been sacked in disgrace. All the necessary arrangements with the UN have been made. I see no role for you as an intermediary at this stage."

Yael smiled, her voice conciliatory. "Professor, please call me Yael. And don't believe everything you see on television or read in the newspapers. It suits us for the moment for people to believe that I have been fired. But I am here on behalf of the secretary-general, just as I was in Goma. Obviously I could not arrive at the hotel in a UN helicopter, or a car with little blue flags over the headlights. Now that you are in New York on such a sensitive mission," she continued, sipping her wine, her tongue touching the rim of the wineglass, "we need to be discreet. We may have to meet quite often. And I am glad about that. But let's not rush things." She was pleased to see that her hand remained steady.

The subtle promise worked, and she felt Hakizimani calming, his wounded pride now mollified. Now it was her turn to seize the moment.

"Professor, we also have some unfinished business," she said, holding his gaze.

"What?" he asked, his voice wary.

"The SG wants to talk more about the terms."

"What terms?"

"The five hundred," said Yael confidently, her heart speeding up. The five hundred people that you and your friends at the UN plan to kill, she thought, her fury fueling her courage.

Hakizimani's face darkened. He put his glass down and sat up straight, flirtatiousness gone. "*No.* No, no, and no. I was warned about this. The real negotiations with the UN start once the deal is done, not before. That's what everyone told me. Now it seems they were right. This is typical. The five hundred are the spark. Everything flows from that. Everything. Years of work and planning."

He looked at her quizzically. "You did not object in Goma. Why is it a problem now?"

Because I didn't know anything about it, thought Yael. Suddenly she knew what to do.

"There is a change of plan, Professor. It cannot happen. The SG and the P5 insist."

Hakizimani stiffened and he stared at her. Yael tensed, feeling his anger rise, half-expecting him to hurl the whisky or a glass across the room, or even at her. She felt the familiar churning in her stomach. The worldly Sorbonne graduate had vanished, replaced by the Butcher of Kigali. Dealing with men like Hakizimani was like walking blindfolded through a minefield. Instinct was her only guide.

Yael had rarely been roughed up or directly threatened on a mission. There was no need. Even with Joe-Don nearby, the promise of deadly violence was always lingering in the background. Like Hakizimani, the warlords—whether in Baghdad, Gaza, or Kabul—were often sophisticated, educated men. She had once had a long conversation with a Taliban leader in Helmand Province about the use of Twitter as a means of spreading fundamentalist Islamic messages. He was an enthusiastic advocate and had proudly showed her his doctorate from MIT. Two minutes later an aide appeared and whispered in his ear. The Taliban leader's face turned cold and his eyes became distant. Yael followed him outside. A skinny frightened man in his early twenties with a straggly beard had been thrown out of the back of a truck. He lay in the dust, whimpering. The Taliban leader knelt on the ground next to him, stroking his hair and reassuring him. He beckoned Yael back inside. The fusillade of shots sounded soon after.

Yael knew the danger signs: Hakizimani sat silent and still, the muscles around his mouth tight. His eyes had turned dull, as though covered by a fine film. She knew he would kill her, here and now, without a second's hesitation, if she impeded his plans. She gripped the wineglass tightly, ready to smash it against the table edge if he moved against her.

Hakizimani spoke slowly and carefully: "You tell your SG this. If he starts altering the terms now, I will personally ensure that our communications during 1994 and subsequent years are leaked to the press. My soldiers have the guns and the UN uniforms. They attack the Tutsi camp at dawn local time." He looked at his watch. "Which is in about two hours."

Fifteen

Sami put on his jacket and placed the envelope in the inside pocket.

Najwa stared at him indignantly. "You said you would—"

Sami put his finger to his mouth, shook his head, and gestured at the walls and the ceiling. Understanding dawned on her face.

"—buy me a drink to say thank you," she smoothly continued.

"Sure," said Sami. "Cocktails at Grad? I'll call and book a table for nine-thirty. That should give us enough time."

"Where else? Just let me get my coat."

Sami and Najwa walked down the gloomy corridor to the Al-Jazeera bureau, passing the *Times* of London's office on the way. Jonathan Beaufort's workplace was even smaller than Sami's, presumably because of the steady stream of powerful stories he produced. Beaufort's investigations into the Oil for Food Program—exposing the endemic corruption of the

Iraqi aid scam that was supposed to feed the Iraqi population and had greatly enriched many UN officials along the way—had caused fury on the 38th floor. Several members of the US Congress had used his coverage to argue for a massive cut in the US contribution to the UN's budget, although the money still flowed as steadily as ever. Beaufort's work also resulted in several of Fareed Hussein's aides now serving lengthy prison sentences. Somehow the SG himself had managed to survive, discarding his protégés like a combine harvester spewing chaff.

The *Times* of London bureau lacked any kind of window, even a cracked one, and the British reporter usually kept his door open to let some air in—and to keep an eye on passing traffic. He poked his head out when he heard their footsteps and greeted Sami and Najwa, barely able to control his curiosity. What were the *New York Times* and Al-Jazeera up to?

Sami said hi and no more, and steered Najwa toward her workplace, his hand firmly on her arm, feeling Beaufort's eyes on them.

The gray metal door opened onto another world: Al-Jazeera's suite was spacious, light, and comfortable, spread over three rooms in the corner of the building, with a panoramic view of the East River. The black and chrome furniture was sleek and modern, the computer monitors slim, state-of-the art LED models. A high-tech brushed-steel coffee machine hissed and gurgled in the corner, scenting the air with the smell of roasting beans and a long, comfortable-looking leather sofa ran the length of one wall. The shelf above Najwa's desk was crowded with awards, including two gold statuettes from the New York and Berlin television festivals for her undercover report about trafficked women and children brought from Africa to work in American brothels.

Sami was reassured to see that Najwa's desk was as chaotic as his: covered in an avalanche of papers and filming schedules. He declined her offer of coffee and greeted her colleagues. Unusual for a UN media operation, not only was Al-Jazeera's researcher female, but so were the film editor, camera operator, and producer.

"My offer is still open, *habibi*," Najwa said. The producer, a lively Spaniard named Maria, looked up and raised her eyebrows with interest. "To work here, Maria. That's all," Najwa said, laughing. "We have so much empty space and poor Sami's office is tiny."

Maria nodded sagely, as though she were well used to the mercurial ways of her star correspondent, before returning to her work.

Sami looked around enviously at the space, light, and comfort of the Al-Jazeera setup. He shook his head regretfully. "I still don't think it would work."

"No? But, *habibi*, we make such a good team," Najwa replied, taking his arm and walking over to the editing suite, where she closed the door firmly behind them. Even that room was three times the space of his cubbyhole, Sami noted. Najwa leaned back against a desk and held out her hand expectantly, her tight skirt and fitted blouse showcasing her bust and hips. The warm air carried the scent of her perfume. Sami tried not to stare as he handed her the envelope.

Najwa smiled, enjoying the effect she was having on him, and took out two sheets of paper that she read rapidly. "Travel arrangements. Plane tickets. Hotel bookings. Pickup times." She looked disappointed. "So what?"

"TV journalists," said Sami shaking his head. "Read it more slowly. Fareed Hussein is flying to Geneva tonight for discussions on the launch of the Year of Africa."

Najwa shrugged. "Well, hold the front page. 'UN Secretary-General Goes to UN Office in Geneva' is hardly news."

"Look who else is traveling."

Najwa read the papers again. "Charles Bonnet. Bonnet is the UN special representative for the Great Lakes Region. Of course he would be there."

"How is Bonnet traveling?"

"Swiss Air. Business class. From JFK. Tomorrow."

"OK, that's something. Why aren't they traveling together? Take a look where the SG's plane is leaving from."

Najwa looked down at the paper. "Teterboro Airport. Where is that?"

"Bergen County."

Najwa shook her head. "Never heard of it. Is that near Manhattan?"

Sami laughed. "Bergen County, New Jersey. On the other side of the Hudson River."

She pouted. "Thanks very much for the geography lesson, Sami, but what has this got to do with anything?"

Sami sat at the desk and moved a slider up and down on the sound-mix panel. "A friend of mine works at Teterboro Airport."

Najwa picked his hand up and removed it. "Don't touch. And your friend says?"

"That I might be interested in a Bombardier Global Express, registration D–7430."

"And are we?"

Sami nodded, wryly noting the change of pronoun. "Very."

"Why?"

"Because it is registered in Berlin and owned by KZX Avionics Limited."

Najwa looked at him with new interest. "Well, now. And where is D–7430 going?

"Geneva, tonight at nine. With just two passengers."

"*Mabrouk, habibi*. Fareed Hussein and?"

"His new best friend: Reinhardt Daintner."

She smiled brightly. "Geneva is very pretty at this time of year. And such good shopping. When do we leave?"

"Tomorrow. On the same Swissair flight as Bonnet," said Sami when his telephone trilled.

It was Jonathan Beaufort: "Even though you are being such a secretive bastard, I thought you might like to know that the Rwandan ambassador is holding an emergency press conference."

"Thanks, Jonathan. Where and when?" asked Sami.

"On the sidewalk on First Avenue. By the flags. Now."

Hakizimani picked up his glass and sipped his whisky. "Of course, we will not exceed the agreed number of casualties," he said, once again the very picture of reasonableness.

Yael's mind was racing. The sound file. Olivia's letter. Reinhardt Daintner on CNN, describing "the biggest single aid project in history." The nightmare scenario was completely correct. Hakizimani's men, dressed in UN uniforms, would kill five hundred people at the Goma camp. There would be chaos, uproar, calls for international intervention. The news channels would show endless footage of bloody peacekeepers' berets left on piles of corpses. KZX and the Bonnet Group would use the massacre to take control of Eastern Congo, with the support of the UN, under the guise of security and stability. Quentin Braithwaite would be disgraced, the DPKO purged. Eastern Congo would be a colony in all but name. Eventually, of course, the news would come out that Hutu militiamen had carried out the massacre, but by then the damage would have been done.

This was her doing. She had negotiated this deal. Hakizimani was in New York thanks to her. And the Goma massacre was just the beginning, Hakizimani had said. What else was to follow? What had she set in motion? She felt physically sick.

Yael showed nothing of her inner turmoil as she spoke. "Professor, I am only the messenger. Please don't get angry with me."

She looked at her wine, wrinkled her nose, and put her glass down. "Could I have a different drink please? This is too dry for me. Some of your whisky, perhaps?"

Hakizimani picked up the bottle of Johnnie Walker. Yael reached into her handbag and took out the black, old-fashioned mobile telephone. She ran her thumb down the side, searching for the switch. Her hands were steady, but running with sweat.

The telephone slid out of her palm and crashed down on the table. She reached for it, but Hakizimani was faster.

He picked it up and looked at it curiously, turning it over in his hand. "This must be ten years old at least. And it's so heavy. Is that the best the UN can do?"

Yael smiled, her heart racing. "I know, it's ridiculous. But my iPhone is broken and it's the only secure handset that the UN's communications people could supply at short notice. Actually I want to switch it off. So we can enjoy our drinks in peace," she said, gently taking the handset from Hakizimani's palm, her fingers brushing against his hand. Several of the buttons had been forced into the keypad by the drop, she noted with alarm. Would it still work?

He nodded, poured her a generous measure of whisky, and placed it front of her on the table. Yael thanked him and ran her thumb down the side of the phone. She pressed a button three times and moved next to him on the sofa, her leg resting against his.

"I am sorry if I upset you, Professor. Just let me switch this stupid thing off and put it away," she murmured, feeling him stir with anticipation. "How about some music?"

Hakizimani reached for a remote control and pressed a button. Jacques Brel's rich baritone filled the room. He picked up his drink with one hand and rested the other on her leg. This time she did not remove it. She smiled and slid right next to him, her thigh pressing hard against him. He turned to kiss her.

She moved her face toward his, her left hand lifting and opening his dressing gown. He closed his eyes and sighed as the heavy robe fell away from his skin. She pulled his boxer shorts up toward his groin, feeling him swell under her touch. His sigh became a moan.

Yael swiftly jabbed the handset's antenna into his upper thigh. She twisted and pushed it hard against his skin for several seconds. The telephone buzzed and shook. Hakizimani's eyes bulged, the veins on his neck turned rigid as steel tubes, and he groaned loudly. The whisky glass fell into his lap and rolled onto the floor.

Charles Bonnet stood up from his chair, stepped away from his desk, wiped his damp forehead with a silk handkerchief, and zipped up his fly. Still breathing heavily, he glanced at the corner of his office as he gently cupped his still-tender genitals in his hand and sighed with pleasure. The bathroom door was closed but he could hear the sound of running water and coughing. He poured himself a large cognac from the bottle of Remy Martin XO on his desk and sipped it contemplatively before he walked across the room.

He opened the door. A slim young Asian woman was bent over the white marble washbasin, spitting repeatedly into the water swirling around the drain.

"Would you like a drink?" he asked, raising his glass to her.

She looked up and stared at him with contempt as she dried her face on a hand towel. "You are finished here," she said. "I will report you. I will tell the *New York Times*."

Bonnet leaned against the doorpost, admiring her black, silken hair and trim figure. "I doubt you really want to do that. No force was involved. It would be your word against mine," he said with the kind of confidence born of long experience. "A lonely middle-aged bureaucrat, far from home, working late to better the world, seduced by a manipulative little minx, using everything she has got to advance her career. East meets West, East takes everything it can get, once again. A sad, but so familiar story."

He stroked her hair, ignoring her shudders. She brushed his hand off, balled up the hand towel, and threw it into the wastebasket.

Bonnet sighed regretfully as he checked his tie in the bathroom mirror. "And even if they did believe your ludicrous allegations, *ma chère* Thanh, I fear that your brother in Hanoi would have to wait a very long time for his French visa and residence permit." He shook his head, walked over to his desk, and picked up a bulky report on African peacekeeping, flicking slowly through the pages. "You know how cautious French bureaucrats are. The paperwork moves at a snail's pace. If it moves at all. And if there is the merest hint of scandal . . . "

He put the papers down and poured himself some more cognac. "Of course, if those French bureaucrats do finally get off their pampered backsides, they can bring a whole new set of problems. The health inspectors, for example, in the 19th arrondissement. They might decide to take an interest in your parents' restaurant. Mekong, I think it's called? Once they start, the whole creaking machine lurches into action: tax, immigration, and who knows where it will end? Perhaps in the departure lounge of Charles de Gaulle, waiting for the next plane to Saigon."

Bonnet shook his head. "That would really be a disaster. Anyway, we can talk more at dinner about how we can help each other, can't we?" he said.

Thanh wiped her eyes, crying softly.

"At dinner, I said," his voice cold and commanding.

Thanh nodded, her head bowed.

"*Ah, bon*. There is nothing to cry about. I will let you know the time and place. You will be free?" he asked, lifting her chin up.

"Yes," she muttered.

"We will have a cordial and friendly conversation? Without threats or sulking? A pleasant meal and perhaps a nightcap to follow?"

"Yes. I look forward to it, Monsieur Bonnet," she said in a monotone.

He smiled and patted her cheek. "See, it's not so difficult after all."

The telephone on Bonnet's desk rang and he pressed the speakerphone button.

"Daintner," the speaker announced.

Flustered at the surprise call, Bonnet nervously asked him to wait, just for a minute. Daintner hung up without answering. Bonnet opened the door of his office. Daintner was standing outside. He wished Thanh a good evening, taking in her disheveled appearance and red eyes. He looked at Bonnet with disgust.

Bonnet ushered him inside as she left. Neither man noticed the tiny wire that reached from the flower in her lapel into the top pocket on the inside of her jacket.

"I was, just, er, interviewing for a new research assistant," Bonnet blustered.

Daintner shook his head and held the bridge of his nose for a couple of seconds, with his eyes closed, his face grim. He turned, grabbed Bonnet's lapels, and slammed him against the wall. The Frenchman was bulkier and more powerful but offered no resistance.

"Do you have the faintest idea of what is at stake here?" Daintner demanded. He grabbed Bonnet's genitals with one hand and twisted hard, his thumb digging up into Bonnet's perineum.

Bonnet's knees gave way. He twisted in agony and turned white. "Please, I beg you," he stuttered and panted.

"I asked you a question," said Daintner, forcing Bonnet against the wall to stop him from collapsing.

Bonnet nodded frantically. "Yes, yes, I do. I am sorry. Please," he replied, as sweat erupted across his face.

"Then learn to control yourself. Especially in the office. Or call East Side Escorts."

Bonnet nodded frantically. "*Oui, oui.* I apologize. It won't happen again."

Daintner removed his hand, sat down, and poured himself a mineral water. Bonnet staggered to his chair, his face still contorted with pain.

"We have two problems," said Daintner.

Bonnet moved to pour himself some more cognac. Daintner shook his head and passed him the mineral water. "Thank you," said Bonnet, drinking deeply. "What kind of problems?"

"The Yael Azoulay kind. And the *New York Times* kind."

Sixteen

The duct tape was exactly where Joe-Don had promised Yael it would be: on the right-hand side of the bed, under the mattress. Hakizimani lay on his side in the lounge, gagged with a hand towel, his hands bound together behind his back and taped to his ankles. His breathing was ragged but slowly stabilized. He groaned softly as he opened his eyes and blinked.

Yael crouched on the floor next to him, the handset in her hands. "It will take you a good hour to recover full movement. If you move, shout, or try to attack me, I will use it again. So soon after the last charge, death will be instantaneous. Nod if you understand me."

Hakizimani moved his head slowly, staring at the black device.

Yael said, "I am going to take off your gag."

Hakizimani's eyes opened wide to show his agreement. Yael took the cloth from his mouth.

"What do you want?" he asked, panting, his forehead covered in sweat.

"Firstly, to show you something," said Yael, as she reached into her handbag. She ripped the lining open, took out a photograph, kneeled down, and held it in front of his head.

"Who is he?" asked Hakizimani.

"David Weiss."

Hakizimani looked puzzled. "Nice-looking boy."

Yael felt a lump rise in her throat and her stomach turn over. "He was."

"Who is the girl on his shoulders?"

Yael said nothing, just stared at him.

He looked at the photograph, at Yael, and back at the photograph. Recognition dawned in Hakizimani's eyes. "What has this got to do with me?"

"You killed him."

"I've never met him."

Yael breathed slowly and deeply, forcing herself to keep calm. "You or your militiamen. It makes no difference. He was one of the nine UN workers murdered at the Belgian Mission School."

Hakizimani wriggled and tried to get more comfortable. "I told you, that was the Tutsis. The Belgian Mission School massacre had nothing to do with us."

"Don't lie to me anymore. David Weiss was my *brother.* He was twenty-four. The UN was his first job," she said, her voice thick with anguish.

He looked up at her. "Weiss?"

"We each took our grandmothers' maiden names."

Hakizimani watched her warily. Yael sensed that he was calculating that her personal involvement was clouding her judgment, and so was weakening her. Which could give him an opportunity. She needed to take control of the situation. Immediately. She opened the dressing gown around Hakizimani's neck, and ran her finger down his throat to his upper chest, feeling the clammy sheen of moisture on his skin.

"Sweat is a great conductor," Yael said. She switched the handset back on and held it a centimeter from his neck.

Hakizimani jerked back and tried to crawl away. "Yael, I am very sorry for your loss. I had no idea. Really. But ask your boss why New York did not reply to their calls for help. Ask him where the peacekeepers were. If I killed your brother, Fareed Hussein was my accomplice."

How true, thought Yael, although she could hardly start agreeing with him. "He is not my boss anymore. You were right. I have been fired."

Yael felt Hakizimani's mind race as he processed this. If she was not working for the UN, then she was there on a personal mission. And he had killed, or authorized the killing of, her brother. Not only was this personal, he was completely at her mercy.

"You said that the five hundred were just the trigger. The trigger for what?" Yael asked.

Hakizimani smiled confidently. "You cannot imagine. It will make what we achieved in 1994 look like a picnic. It cannot be stopped by me, you, or anyone else. So do as you wish. My fate is irrelevant."

A knock sounded on the door.

Yael reached over to the coffee table and picked up the picture of Hakizimani's daughters. "I found this in your wallet."

She picked up a cigarette lighter and lit it, holding the photograph near the flame. "The trigger for what," she asked again.

Hakizimani's bravado collapsed. "Please, no, don't—it's my only picture."

A faint smell of chemical burning carried through the room. The three girls stared at her, smiling, from behind the plastic covering. She tried to ignore her rising feeling of self-disgust.

The knock on the door sounded louder.

Yael moved the lighter closer to a corner of the photograph. The plastic began to turn black and melt. "Why did you have them killed? You sacrificed your own family so you could wipe out the Tutsis. What kind of man are you?"

Hakizimani's face twisted in anguish, and his body sagged against the restraints. She felt the grief and misery course through him. "Stop, please. That I will tell you. Please. Just put the photograph down."

Yael did as he asked, barely able to disguise her relief.

Hakizimani's eyes welled up and he blinked the tears away. "The French secret service put the bomb in the car. I was supposed to discover it so we could show it to the media and blame the Tutsi terrorists. The French said later it was a terrible mistake. They were very sorry but somehow the wrong instructions were sent to the bomb-maker. It was live. After that, I did not care about anything anymore. Are you going to kill me? Then get it over with."

Yes, I am, Yael wanted to answer. Every minute when we were in Goma I imagined this scene. The man who had taken so many lives, and my brother's, finally, helpless and begging for his own. Except Hakizimani was not playing his role.

Staring at him trussed up in front of her like a chicken, powerless, mourning his daughters, snot running from his nose, she felt her resolve dissolving like ice in a warm bath. She had come here ready to kill him, but what good would it do? David would still be dead. So would everyone else who had died at his hands and those of his henchmen. She needed to find out more. Then lives would be saved, not taken.

Hakizimani sensed her hesitation. He seemed to recover some of his strength as he spoke. "Do it, Yael. The first one is always the most difficult."

Is it, is it really, she thought furiously, suddenly back in Kandahar.

Hakizimani looked up at her. "Avenge your brother. Nobody will blame you. Pull the trigger—I have thought about doing it myself so many times. But I do not have the courage. *Do it.*"

She shook her head. "What is the UN connection?" she asked, her voice calm and insistent.

The Rwandan smiled cynically. "Work it out yourself. Why did the UN send you to Goma to negotiate with me? Because of coltan. Why are KZX and the UN setting up the first corporate-sponsored International Development Zone in Goma? Because of coltan. The UN gives it legitimacy. Who can question KZX and the Bonnet Group's motives now? Nobody. Fareed Hussein is the perfect alibi."

"What does the UN get?"

Hakizimani laughed out loud. "Do I really need to spell it out? There is a global recession. America pays twenty-five percent of the UN budget. Congress wants to cut that in half.

Moscow, Beijing, Delhi—they are all suffering from UN fatigue. So what the UN gets is *money.* Public money—for fancy institutes in Geneva and charities to rescue child miners. Private money in envelopes. Much more. It's a tiny price to pay for a blue flag flying over the entrance of every coltan mine. But businesses need stability, and for that KZX and the Bonnet Group need to take control of the territory and its resources. And how do we do that in Africa?"

"By starting wars."

Hakizimani nodded. "Exactly."

"Where and when?"

"Soon. I don't know the details. I am just a small cog in a very large machine. But it will be directed from the UN headquarters."

Yael's eyes widened. "In New York?" she asked.

"Of course not. There are too many journalists poking around the UN in New York. Why do you think they have set up the development institute in Geneva? It's inside the UN headquarters, but it's autonomous with no oversight mechanism. Who cares about those endless meetings in Switzerland? Nobody. They call it the Geneva option. Now *do it.*"

The knocking was now so loud it could no longer be ignored. Yael put the photograph down and briefly touched the handset to Hakizimani's neck. She had lied about the device's potency: a quick charge should not kill him.

He jerked back, a faint smile on his face, exhaled softly, and passed out. She swiftly unzipped her dress, walked down the corridor to the door, and slowly opened it. The two security guards stood on the other side, their eyes opening wide as they saw her standing naked.

"Can I help you, gentlemen?" she asked, her hands on her hips, as though she were a waitress waiting for an order.

The shorter guard turned bright red and spoke first, unable to meet her gaze. "Ma'am, our orders are to check on Mr. Hakizimani every fifteen minutes."

"I can assure you, Mr. Hakizimani is fine. Very fine indeed. But he is irritated at being interrupted." Yael paused, her voice conciliatory. "Of course, I understand you gentlemen also have a job to do. Why don't you let me get mine done and then I will be out of here?"

The two guards looked at each other. The senior one looked her up and down and nodded. "Fifteen minutes, ma'am." He closed the door.

Florence Munyakarana, the Rwandan ambassador to the UN, was tall, slim, and poised. Her long hair was tied back with a red and yellow headscarf. She was elegantly dressed in a matching *mushanana*—a long, flowing skirt and sari-like scarf draped over her right shoulder, the strong colors bright against her dark skin. She stood on the sidewalk on First Avenue, under the row of flags, waiting patiently as the scrum of journalists in front of her fell into some kind of order.

The television crews were at the front, their lights illuminating the nighttime scene. Najwa and CNN reporter Roger Richardson were in the center and flanked by Russia Today, Reuters, France 24, the BBC, and several African channels. The print and radio journalists lined up behind them. Sami stood to the side, next to Jonathan Beaufort, who gave him a knowing, amused look. Journalistic etiquette dictated that Sami now owed him a favor, and there was no doubt that Beaufort would soon call it in.

The Rwandan ambassador spoke in clear, French-accented English over the roar of the evening traffic as it turned the corner from 42nd Street. "Firstly, please excuse me for summoning you at this time in the evening. Thank you all so much for coming. The building behind us has hundreds of rooms, but I have just been told by the secretary-general's office that none are available for us to hold this press conference, so here we are standing outside in the wind. I know you would rather be at home or somewhere having dinner and so would I. But I would not call you out if this was not a matter of the utmost seriousness."

She paused. "One of life . . . and . . . death," she said, carefully enunciating each syllable.

The journalists fell silent. The television reporters looked back and forth from Munyakarana to their camera operators, nervously checking they were getting the footage. The radio reporters held their microphones out and forward as though they were about to take part in a duel, their faces set in concentration. The newspaper and news agency correspondents scribbled rapidly in their notebooks.

A strong breeze blew in from the East River as Munyakarana spoke, ruffling her *mushanana*, and she held the wide strip of cloth down as it flapped back and forth on her shoulder. "The Rwandan government is calling for emergency reinforcements of UN peacekeepers to be immediately deployed to the Goma refugee camp. We have credible information that some kind of atrocity is planned to take place there, possibly in the next few hours. This cannot be allowed to happen. Peacekeepers must be deployed *immediately.*"

The journalists moved closer and began to shout questions, their voices drowned out as a bus lurched around the corner from 42nd Street and pulled up at the nearby stop. The ambassador held her hand up and gestured at the vehicle as the passengers boarded and stepped down onto the sidewalk, several of them watching the spectacle with interest.

"What kind of atrocity?" asked Najwa, moving her microphone toward the ambassador as the vehicle departed. "Where did you get this information?"

Munyakarana smiled. "As a diplomat, I represent the policy of my government. That is all I am authorized to talk about. My government's policy, I repeat, is to call for urgent reinforcements of the UN battalion in Congo, to be deployed to the Goma refugee camp and protect its inhabitants, many of whom, as you know, are Tutsis, who fled the genocide in 1994. Genocide can never be allowed to happen again. And we fear it is about to."

Jonathan Beaufort looked at Sami, his eyes wide with the schoolboy excitement of a reporter on a major breaking story. "Did I hear right? Rwandan ambassador calls for UN peacekeepers to reinforce a Tutsi refugee camp to prevent a rerun of 1994 genocide in the next few hours?"

Sami nodded tersely, focused on the ambassador. "'Demands' is better."

Beaufort scrawled in his notebook. "You're right."

"Ambassador, why?" shouted Roger Richardson, "These are very serious charges. On what evidence do you think a massacre could take place?"

Munyakarana nodded. "I'm unable to say where this information came from—I am sure as journalists you understand the need to protect your sources. But we, the Rwandan government, believe it to be accurate and reliable or we would not have called you here. We have a credible warning that a mass atrocity is planned at the Goma camp in the next few hours. Should any refugees there be hurt or lose their lives, the Rwandan government—and the world—will hold the United Nations and, especially, its current leadership, responsible for any death or injuries. I repeat. We will hold the current leadership of the United Nations personally responsible for any casualties. I don't need to remind you all that the International Criminal Court has ruled that those who have prior knowledge of a planned atrocity, but who fail to take steps to prevent it, will be charged, together with the actual perpetrators. Thank you. That's all. I think you have your story."

A chorus of questions erupted—what atrocity, who would carry it out, when would it happen—all of which the ambassador ignored as she stepped down. The journalists immediately began calling their editors and comparing notes.

Seventeen

Around the corner from the security guards and out of sight, Joe-Don sat on the comfortable sofa that the hotel had thoughtfully provided for its guests. He was wearing a black tennis shirt, shorts, and tennis shoes, with an Adidas sports bag at his feet. Joe-Don had booked into room 3034, several doors away. So what could be more natural than waiting here for his tennis partner before they took the elevator together to their game on the hotel's court on the 48th floor? Nothing, as long as the wait was not too long, he thought, recalling the Mossad assassination of Mahmoud al-Mabhouh, a senior Hamas operative, at the Al Bustan hotel in Dubai. The surveillance-camera footage, which showed the Mossad agents sitting in their tennis gear for hours in the lobby and entering the hotel bathrooms before emerging in amateurish disguise, was available all over the Internet, posted by a furious Dubai police force, and viewed by hundreds of thousands. The Israelis were all helpfully circled in red for easier identification. The whole operation was now used by intelligence services as an object lesson in how not to carry out a stealth assassination.

Joe-Don looked at up at the dark glass bump under the ceiling that housed the surveillance camera. Joe-Don had called in several major favors to take care of that. "Quasar," a hacker whom Joe-Don had once recruited to target a Middle East bank that Al-Qaeda was using to launder UN development funds, had disabled the hotel's CCTV system five minutes earlier, just before Joe-Don stepped into the lobby. The hotel security manager, an old colleague of Joe-Don's from his time in Central America, had agreed, reluctantly, on an outage to last a maximum of twenty minutes. Joe-Don checked his watch: 8:45 p.m. Yael had another fifteen minutes. A tall, curly-haired room-service waiter walked by, pushing his cart. Joe-Don checked his name badge: Miguel. The two men exchanged an almost imperceptible glance of recognition.

Hakizimani lay still on his side, his eyes wide open and unmoving. A large damp patch spread out around his hips through his robe and onto the carpet. Yael shook him, gently at first, then harder. He did not move. She emptied the water jug over his head. He still did not respond. She stood for several seconds watching his chest, willing it in vain to rise and fall. She dipped her finger in the water and held it over his nose. No air moved over her wet skin. She looked around, trying to quell the panic rising inside her. She grabbed the box of pills on the coffee table and read the label: Digitalis, printed in large letters over a stylized picture of a human heart. She swallowed hard. *Shit.* Now what? She had got what she wanted, or what she thought she did. She looked at Hakizimani. His skin had already turned waxy, his face gray and hollow. She did not feel guilty at all. But now she needed to get out, immediately, and ten minutes earlier than they had planned.

Yael quickly dressed, grabbed the photograph of Hakizimani's daughters, wiped it clean, and placed it in his shirt pocket, paused, then took it out again and put it in her bag together with the photograph of her and David in Central Park. She grabbed her cell phone and rapidly pressed the redial button twice as she had been instructed. It was half-jammed into the keyboard and stuck after the first push. She heard a key move in the door. She had locked it and wedged a chair at an angle under the door handle. That was more than enough to deter a casual intruder but she doubted her defense would last more than a few seconds against the two guards. There were several loud thumps then the door creaked and began to splinter.

She pressed the redial button again: nothing. Her heart was racing wildly now. She jabbed repeatedly at the touch pad but the button would not move. Something smashed into the door again. Yael ran down the corridor to the door. She stood behind it with the bottle of whisky in her right hand, the black handset in her left. But where the hell was Joe-Don? And why had the knocking suddenly stopped?

Mitchell Gardiner leaned into the bend and opened the throttle as the BMW motorbike took the curve with solid, Teutonic confidence. His heart was racing with excitement—and not just from the thrill he always got of gunning the 750cc engine and feeling the bike's power beneath him. He had just completed his first freelance job as a photographer for the most famous newspaper in the world. He could already see the credit under the photograph: "Mitchell Gardiner for the *New York Times*." Perhaps he would get it framed. The bathroom would be the best place for it, he thought. That would show a suitable mix of pride and self-deprecation.

It had been a good six weeks since he had shown his portfolio to the picture editor at the *New York Times*, at Sami Boustani's suggestion. Sami was a cool guy, and he was looking forward to buying him a beer tonight to say thanks for the introduction. Perhaps they would use the photograph with one of Sami's stories, so maybe their celebration could be a mutual one. The picture editor had been pleasant but noncommittal, telling him that budget cuts meant she was using fewer freelancers, although she liked his work and would keep his details on file. Mitchell had heard all this before and never expected to hear from her again.

But how wrong he had been; his first assignment came out of the blue at 9:00 this evening, just as he was about to sit down and watch the football game. His wife, Suzanne, was already in bed, half-asleep, but he did not want to wake her with his excitement. She needed all the sleep she could get. He had even agreed over dinner—reluctantly, but with a twinge of pride at his newfound sense of responsibility—to sell the BMW and buy a car instead. His wife's argument, that there was no room for a baby seat, was unanswerable.

The job itself was straightforward: a night paparazzi shoot. Mitchell had to get pictures of two men boarding a private jet, without being seen, and pictures of the jet with the registration numbers. The airplane would be parked on a small, distant runway, in a corner of the airport that was visible from the road. Sami's friend had told him the best place to hide himself.

It was a cool, dry night as he set out, and the road was almost empty. Teterboro Airport was just over ten miles from Manhattan. Mitchell looked at the speedometer and eased back on the throttle: sixty miles an hour was a little fast for Redneck Avenue, the road that led from the airport through South Hackensack and onto the New Jersey Turnpike. He had not told Suzanne where he was going, just that he needed to go out on a job. She had touched his face sleepily and told him to drive carefully. He had kissed her warm, swelling stomach in return. He would stop by the corner store run by the Korean family on his way home and buy her a large bunch of flowers. She couldn't drink alcohol, but they had to mark this evening with something.

Mitchell had parked his motorcycle behind some trees and set up his gear there, hidden by their trunks. He could not use a flash, but a slow exposure with a tripod to steady the long lens worked fine. He had checked the shots in the camera's back panel. An Indian man, whom he recognized as Fareed Hussein, and a tall, thin European with very pale blond hair. What was the UN secretary-general doing taking off from there at night with a white—very white—guy in a gray suit? It seemed like a great story. Mitchell guessed he would find out the details soon enough. His job was to take and deliver the pictures. He was so excited that he had even tried to e-mail the best shot to Sami, but the cell phone reception was terrible and the signal kept breaking. Mitchell had no idea if the file had gone through or not.

Mitchell smiled again as he thought of Suzanne slumbering peacefully in their bed. There was nothing he loved to do more in the world than to slide in next to her and feel her wrap herself around him. Every yard behind was one nearer home, he told himself. Mitchell looked ahead as the road curved around again. A couple more miles and he'd be on the New Jersey Turnpike, then the George Washington Bridge, down through Manhattan with a quick stop for a drink with Sami, and onto the Brooklyn Bridge on his way home.

He watched the taillights of the car that had just turned out in front of him and pulled back slightly to give it space. The vehicle, a Toyota Land Cruiser with tinted windows, was keeping a steady fifty-five miles an hour, five miles an hour over the limit—not enough to get the police's attention, but, annoyingly, not enough to pull ahead.

The car in front of him slowed suddenly, its brake lights glowing red. Mitchell looked at the road, part of which had turned black, his excitement rapidly turning to alarm. The Land Cruiser was leaking oil. A lot of oil.

Joe-Don loitered on the corner of the corridor, checking his watch, opening and closing the Adidas bag—even though it was empty—and shaking his head, for all intents and purposes a keen tennis player who was exasperated by the tardiness of his partner. He touched the tiny earpiece inside his right ear. No signal yet. Alerted by the sound of the security guards' first knocks on the door of suite 3017, he had wandered around the corner and watched from a distance as they questioned Yael. It was all over in a few seconds, she stepped back inside, and the two guards took up their position again, he saw with relief. She was OK—for now. He looked at his watch: 8:50. Time was getting very tight. The cameras would switch on again in ten minutes.

But now he watched in alarm as the blond guard took out his mobile telephone and showed it to his partner, a look of surprise on his face. Joe-Don touched his right ear again. Still nothing. What was she doing? The shorter guard inserted the key card into the lock and pushed the door. It did not move. The guard turned to his colleague and shook his head. Both men stepped back and kicked the door so hard Joe-Don could hear the wood splinter.

He sprinted down the corridor, a tiny gas canister in his hand, loudly shouting for help. Miguel ran alongside him, this time without his trolley, his apron flapping.

They stopped in front of the door, breathless and panicky. The two guards stopped kicking the door and turned toward them, first puzzled, then angry.

"Who the fuck are you? What do you want?" demanded the blond guard.

"Please, come quickly. Someone has had a heart attack by the elevator. You're hotel security? You have medical training?" said Joe-Don, speaking rapidly, his eyes wide in alarm, surreptitiously taking in the state of the door.

"I called the hotel doctor, but he needs help now," said Miguel.

The guards looked at each other. Joe-Don glanced at the blond guard's smartphone. The screen showed Yael's face. He sprayed both men in the face with the gas canister. They lunged at him in fury and he jumped back. The blond guard clenched and raised his fist as both men suddenly lurched forward, their mouths wide open, and crumpled onto the floor.

Joe-Don knocked on the door: three short knocks in rapid succession followed by two more. It opened immediately. Yael said, "You took your time."

Sami sat in a wooden booth in a far corner in the back room of the bar, waiting for Mitchell Gardiner. It was just after 10:00 p.m. They were due to meet at Zone, a trendy microbrewery on the corner of Avenue A and East 7th Street, anytime between 10:00 and midnight. Zone was crowded with enough East Village hipsters to make it difficult to eavesdrop but was quiet enough to talk. Baba Maal played softly in the background, and the smell of spicy cooking wafted from the kitchen. He watched a thin blond girl with six rings in her left ear walk by, holding hands with a statuesque African woman. The bar was a short walk from his apartment, but was not his local. In fact, he realized, as he gloomily nursed a bottle of Zone's own dark beer and picked listlessly at his "mini-mezze"—hummus, tehina, falafel and tabbouleh—he did not even have a local, where the bar staff knew who he was.

But Sami did have a story. He opened the browser on his smartphone. His article was already on the website: "Refugees in Danger, Warns Rwandan Ambassador; Repeat of 1994 Genocide Feared." Soon after the press conference, Henrik Schneidermann had issued a bland statement reaffirming the UN's commitment to human rights and the Year of Africa. The ambassador's claims would be properly investigated, he promised. But Sami knew that behind the scenes the SG had immediately ordered the DPKO into action. Sami's peacekeeping contacts told him that Quentin Braithwaite had already redeployed a battalion of UN troops from their base up-country to Goma, dispatching them in a fleet of attack helicopters. The Congolese ambassador, Rose Yundala—Hakim Yundala's younger sister—had been furious, and had issued a statement denouncing the Rwandan ambassador for what she called "unwanted, unwarranted, and unprecedented interference in Congo's internal affairs."

The camp was now surrounded by armored personnel carriers and a ring of UN checkpoints. Braithwaite himself was flying to Goma tomorrow morning to supervise the reinforcements. Florence Munyakarana was all over the news bulletins as well, leading on the BBC and CNN, he saw, as he flicked through their websites. Whatever had been planned at Goma was now postponed for a long time, if not canceled, he thought. Sami read through his story again: Munyakarana really had said that if anyone was killed at Goma, Rwanda would hold the current leadership of the UN responsible. She had even issued a not-very-veiled threat to take Fareed Hussein to the International Criminal Court if any lives were lost. She must be very certain of her ground. The street-side press conference was unprecedented. In UN terms, this was a declaration of war. On one side, the humanitarians and the DPKO. On the other, the secretary-general's office, and, presumably, Erin Rembaugh and the DPA.

It was a straightforward news story, but his editors were now pressing hard for the longer, investigative piece. So what did he have exactly? The known knowns, as Donald Rumsfeld would say, were his research into Africa Child Rescue and its connections with KZX, the Bonnet Group, and Zeinab Hussein; the promotion of Hakim Yundala, the Congolese former minister of interior; and the SG's mysterious trip to Geneva in a KZX private plane.

The known unknowns were much more numerous: how Olivia had died; if she had been murdered, who had killed her and why; the significance of the messages left on her voice mail; who was the source for the claims of an attack on the refugee camp at Goma; who would want to attack it and why; and many more. The SG's trip from Teterboro Airport was especially intriguing. Why was he flying on a KZX plane when he had his own? Mitchell had promised to call him as soon as he had the pictures. Where was he? Sami's phone beeped several times. He looked down at the handset. A large data file was being sent. Would he accept? He pressed yes.

The greasy smear was now a puddle and getting wider by the second. Mitchell dropped back a gear, eased the throttle back, and tried keep control, but the motorbike began to slide underneath him. The slick reached halfway across the road. He tried to steer into the skid but the bike flew out between his legs, flipped over to the side, and slid into the nearby ditch, its rear wheel spinning uselessly as the engine screamed in protest. Mitchell slammed onto the asphalt, rolling over and over as he skidded across the road.

He came to a stop in a ditch. He lay there for several seconds, then tried to sit up, but an agonizing pain lanced through his knee and up his back. He looked at his leg, twisted underneath him at an unnatural angle. The pain was excruciating. Mitchell reached for his telephone, his hand shaking, when he saw that the Land Cruiser had stopped just ahead of him. A man was walking toward him. He would help, he was sure. Mitchell looked up hopefully as something smashed into his helmet and everything went black.

Geneva

Eighteen

Yael handed her passport to the woman sitting on the other side of the shabby, brown wooden desk. She flicked slowly through the pages with interest. "Costa Rica," she said, looking at Yael's photograph and then back at her. "I've never been there. I hear it's beautiful."

Yael nodded. "You should. It is. We have everything: beaches, mountains, rain forests, jungle, wildlife."

"So, Claudia Lopez, why did you leave paradise to come and work as a cleaner in Geneva?" she asked, looking at Yael quizzically.

"Paradise is now run by drug cartels. There are much better opportunities here. And much fewer gunmen. I am interested in international development. There are lots of NGOs and aid organizations here. Eventually I want to get a job with one. But for now cleaning seems a good way to start earning some money."

The owner and manager of Tip-Top Office Services was an imposing bottle-blonde, a Serb somewhere in her late fifties, wearing light and skillfully applied makeup. She had a husky voice, cured by decades of smoking, high Slavic cheekbones, and penetrating green eyes under frameless half-moon glasses. Yael could see that Jasna had once been beautiful, and she was still striking. The firm's office was a small room behind a *tabac* on the Rue Pradier, in the backstreets near Geneva's central train station. In addition to Jasna's desk, it contained three creaking chairs; a computer with an old-fashioned monitor, an ancient keyboard and mouse; and a battered metal filing cabinet. The walls were once white but had darkened with age. The room smelled of coffee, cigarettes, and Chanel No. 5, which Jasna wore in abundance. Several white cigarette ends lay in a large glass ashtray, each ringed in pink lipstick.

"Of course you do, *draga*, darling. Everybody wants to work for an NGO. Is that why you came to me? Because of my contracts?"

"Partly. And also because I heard you pay decently, and on time."

Jasna nodded, pleased to hear about her reputation. She picked up a packet of king-size Vogue cigarettes and offered it to Yael. "It's true. I do pay on time. Perhaps we can find something for you. But it's a big jump from cleaning a desk to sitting behind one. For that you need connections. And they are very hard to get."

Yael took one of the long white cigarettes, nodding sagely. "How did you make yours?"

Jasna slid an ashtray across the table and lit Yael's cigarette before inhaling deeply on her own. "Someone helped me. A long time ago," she said, looking into the distance. "You have experience cleaning?" she asked, suddenly businesslike. "We do need more staff. I have just been offered a contract for a new . . . "—she paused and rummaged on her desk, picking up a letter with a large imposing letterhead—" . . . institute. The UN-KZX Institute for International Development. Sounds very grand, doesn't it? It seems we don't have enough development institutes in Geneva," she said ironically.

Yael looked around while Jasna spoke. The office's only decorations were a poster of Lake Geneva, a calendar with a picture of puppies for each month, and a mirror behind Jasna's chair. A framed photograph stood on each corner of her desk, among the piles of paperwork, newspapers, and thick manila files. The headquarters of Tip-Top Office Services reminded Yael of the office of every Balkan official she had ever dealt with. The real question was, how had this mom-and-pop ramshackle-looking operation ever won any lucrative cleaning contracts at the UN? In Yael's experience that demanded either a substantial bribe, high-level contacts, or usually, both. Of course, it was theoretically possible that Jasna simply did not waste company money on fancy office furniture and fittings, just made sure to undercut the competition's bids. Theoretically.

Jasna continued reading: "It's a corporate joint venture with the UN—the first. Fareed Hussein himself is coming to the opening with all the big ambassadors: German, French, American, Chinese, and lots from Africa. The guest of honor will be Desiree Yundala, the wife of Hakim Yundala, the head of the UN's security department. Says here that Mrs. Yundala was recently appointed the head of the Year of Africa Protocol and Preparation Committee. So you see, *draga*, if you want a nice job at the UN, you need to marry someone important," Jasna said, smiling as she peered over the top of her glasses.

"The institute was originally supposed to be in a new building, but now they say the building is not ready yet, so the institute will work out of an annex at the Palais des Nations, the UN headquarters here. They want an early-morning shift, Monday to Friday, starting at 6:00 a.m. You will have to get up early, so you won't have much time for a social life. Or a boyfriend. You are a pretty girl. You do have a boyfriend, Claudia?"

There were no points for shyness where Jasna came from, especially from the womenfolk, and Yael answered confidently. "No. Do you?"

Jasna laughed—a deep, throaty sound that came from somewhere deep inside—and sat back, more relaxed now. Yael could feel her becoming more sympathetic. Yael leaned forward and held Jasna's eye. "I am not scared of hard work, Jasna. I tidied up after my brothers and sisters at home. I helped my mother. I know which end of a mop to hold."

"That's more than my husband ever did."

Yael decided she liked this woman. "Did?"

Jasna rolled her eyes, but Yael sensed the pain behind the bravado. "We came here in 1991 when the war started. I worked to build up the business but he refused to clean. It was woman's work, he said. A man's work, it turned out, was drinking with his cronies, smoking, and watching the war on Serbian television. After six months he went back to Belgrade. To fight for our homeland, he said, against the Ustasha in

Croatia. But even that wasn't enough for him. Or maybe I wasn't. Once that war was over, he went again, to fight the Mujahideen in Bosnia."

Jasna shook her head. "He was a fool. I never saw him again. Still, I can manage without a husband." She picked up the photograph nearest her and swallowed hard. "But he took my son with him to Bosnia."

Yael felt Jasna's grief radiate through the room. She looked at her questioningly.

Jasna shook her head, almost imperceptibly. She put the picture down and handed Yael's passport back to her, her hand shaking slightly as she fought to steady her voice. "And you? Student?"

Yael nodded. "Community college in New York. I want to take some more courses here. Maybe do a degree in economics."

"Like my daughter. She is a lecturer in economics at the NYU," said Jasna proudly, showing Yael the second photograph, one of a younger version of Jasna.

Yael caught sight of herself in the mirror behind Jasna's desk. Her auburn hair was now black, cut short and spiky; her eyes were dark brown, thanks to tinted contact lenses; and her skin was the color of light coffee, courtesy of a fifty-euro bottle of fake tan. Dressed in black jeans, blue sweater, tennis shoes, and a padded denim jacket, she looked like any of the many thousands of young internationals in Geneva. The ten-euro half-diopter reading glasses made her appear almost intellectual, she thought, although she still started with surprise each morning when she looked in the mirror.

Claudia Lopez had passed easily through immigration at Charles de Gaulle Airport two days ago, and there was no reason why she should not have. Claudia's passport was genuine, recently issued for a woman two years younger than Yael, although a thousand dollars handed across a desk by an old friend of Joe-Don's had ensured that Costa Rican officialdom had not yet caught up with the fact that Ms. Lopez had been killed in a car crash a year ago. Yael did not enjoy traveling under the name of a dead person, or mimicking her appearance, but recognized that she had little choice. She and Joe-Don had stayed overnight in Paris at a dingy hotel in Belleville, and the following morning he had purchased a well-used Peugeot 303 in cash for two thousand euros. They drove straight through the French-Swiss border, where, because it was lunchtime, there was not a guard in sight, just as Joe-Don had predicted.

Joe-Don had used the five-hour journey to give Yael a detailed tutorial in living off the grid. They would pay for everything with cash and never use debit cards, credit cards, or ATMs. (When Yael had asked where they would get the money, he had smiled knowingly, telling her not to worry about it.) They would keep Internet communications to the bare minimum, using both public terminals in different Internet cafés and TOR, a free anonymizing software that disguised their IP addresses, making them untraceable. They would communicate via pay phones or through text messages sent on disposable, prepaid cell phones. They would throw away the phones every couple of days, would stay in seedy hotels where nobody asked questions, and eat in cheap cafés or from supermarkets. They would blend in, be unremarkable. The Brits, he said, called it "Going Gray." Yael had listened patiently, although she was already familiar with these precautions. The good news, he added, as they trundled along at a steady seventy miles an hour, was that gray and unremarkable did not necessarily have to mean drab. Yael did not have to look like a bag lady, Joe-Don said, handing her two thousand euros.

Geneva was stolid and Swiss, but with a strong French influence, and the city was more cosmopolitan than many knew. The older Genevois were neither friendly nor unfriendly, and well aware that the prosperity of their hometown—and prosperity was very important to them—rested largely on the internationals and their generous allowances and per diems. But the younger Swiss were open-minded and welcoming. The city was home to a vast and transitory population, many of them with large disposable incomes and time on their hands. They worked at the UN complex, the International Committee of the Red Cross, the CERN nuclear center, or the myriad aid organizations, think tanks, consultancies, and foreign diplomatic missions that added zest to the otherwise staid city.

Yael looked back at Jasna as she continued: "So with your interests and experience you would be perfect for this KZX place. Personally, I do not much like German companies. The Germans killed almost all of my family in the Belgrade air raids in 1941. But they pay well and on time too, so we cannot be choosy."

She reached under a pile of newspapers and took out that day's edition of the *Financial Times*, tapping a story on the companies' page. "This is a good opportunity for us. KZX is going to merge with the Bonnet Group, it says here. KZX wants to launch its own range of mobile telephones, tablet computers, gaming consoles, and laptops. They are talking about setting up a joint headquarters here in Geneva."

Yael silently processed this news. The Bonnet Group and KZX. The mining company and the media company. Together they would be unstoppable. They could corner the market in coltan and cut off the supplies to the competition. Nokia, Samsung, even Apple would all eventually go out of business.

Jasna looked at Yael. "I follow the news. Can you guess what I did before I came to Geneva?"

Yael shook her head. "Actress? Film star?"

Jasna smiled, pleased despite herself. "Flatterer. I was a professor of economics at Belgrade University." She looked carefully at Yael. "Claudia Lopez, you remind me of someone. Have you been to Belgrade? Have we ever met?"

Yael shook her head and thought fast. Jasna did seem familiar, but she could not place her. Yael had been to Belgrade several times in the last few years on UN business as successive Serbian governments tried to assure the world that they were doing all they could to find and arrest General Ratko Mladic, then the world's most-wanted war criminal. Yael was sure she had not met Jasna among the procession of slick-suited functionaries with American accents and university degrees that Serbian governments produced to show the West that the country was on the right track.

Yael had also briefly visited the Serbian capital in early 1994 with her brother, David, when she was sixteen, while he worked for the UN refugee organization. And then she remembered that David had been severely disciplined for using UN vehicles to move Serbs stranded in newly independent Croatia across the front lines back to Serbia. What was the name of the town where they had been? Osijek. Yes, that was it. A grim place, freezing cold and frightening, where everyone had taken cover underground from the shellfire. The entire hospital had been moved into the basement. She remembered crying because the streets were full of dead dogs.

Jasna gave her a searching look, picked up a thick file, and weighed it in her hand. "This is all the paperwork we had to organize for one employee, and she is from Stockholm and has a work permit. I like you, Claudia, but with all respect to . . . *Costa Rica*," she said, the faintest trace of sarcasm in her voice, "if you don't have a work permit I cannot help you. You do have a Swiss work permit?"

Yael shook her head. Holders of Costa Rican passports enjoyed visa-free travel to the Schengen Area of the European Union and Switzerland. Joe-Don had supplied Claudia's passport, but a Swiss work permit was beyond his reach, he had explained. They had already taken a risk entering the country with a machine-readable passport, but had had no option. The old-style version would have required a visa and would have drawn far more attention from the French border officials at the airport. A Swiss work permit would demand extensive background checks, financial references, and questions to the Costa Rican authorities. Use your charm, Joe-Don had replied, when Yael had asked how to get around this.

Jasna shrugged and put the file down. "No work permit means no work. It's very simple."

So now what, Yael thought quickly, sensing Jasna's growing disbelief in her cover story. She had to get this job. Yael reached into her purse for her wallet. "Perhaps there is a way around this, Jasna," she said, taking out several large denomination banknotes.

Jasna put up her hand. "Please, Claudia, or whatever your name is, do not insult me. This is Switzerland, not Central America. I don't know how it works in Costa Rica, but here the boss pays the employees, not the other way around."

Yael put her wallet back in her purse, the sinking feeling growing stronger. So much for her charm. She had to get into the Institute. There was a plan B: to go into the UN building as a tourist on a guided visit and head off on her own and either break or talk her way through, but that was much more risky. The building was blanketed with CCTV cameras and security guards were everywhere. Either way, there was clearly no point staying here.

Yael stood up to go and picked up her passport. "Thank you for your time, Mrs. Jovanovic. It has been a pleasure to meet you," she said politely, offering Jasna her hand.

"Sit down, please," said Jasna, her voice tinged with amusement. She picked up her cigarette, drew on it, exhaled slowly, and regarded Yael thoughtfully as the smoke swirled around her. "There is one other option," she said.

"What?" asked Yael warily.

Jasna leaned back and gave Yael a piercing but not unfriendly look. She opened the drawer in her desk and took out a bottle of clear liquid and two small glasses and poured a generous measure into each.

Jasna handed one to Yael as she sat back down, and the two women clinked glasses. “It’s *slivovitz*. Home-distilled. Don’t tell the Swiss customs authorities. *Ziveli*,” said Jasna, looking Yael in the eye as she knocked the drink back in one gulp.

“*Ziveli*,” said Yael, doing the same. Anyone who did not make and hold eye contact while making a toast was regarded with deep suspicion in the Balkans. The alcohol coursed through her, the plums first caressing her palate, then delivering a sharp, fruity kick. “Thank you. That was excellent,” she said appreciatively, as she put her empty glass down.

Jasna nodded knowingly. “Like your pronunciation. Especially for someone who has never been to Belgrade. Now, Claudia, why don’t you tell me who you really are and what you want with KZX and the United Nations.”

Nineteen

Joe-Don squirmed on the deep padded-leather armchair, trying, without success, to get comfortable. He was wearing his only suit, which he hated: a navy double-breasted one from the 1990s. Its shoulders kept riding up around his neck. His necktie was too tight, or perhaps the collar of his shirt was too small. His trousers were cutting into his waist. The dark-blond wig and mustache were starting to itch, and the padding around his stomach was becoming heavy and uncomfortable. The heavy, old-fashioned tortoiseshell frame of his eyeglasses was pressing on the bridge of his nose.

But Joe-Don's outfit was not the only cause of his irritation: he had been waiting in the overheated reception room of Banque Bernard et Fils' managing director for more than twenty-five minutes. He was usually ushered straight to his deposit box. But today the receptionist in the lobby had checked his name against a list and asked him to go upstairs to see "Monsieur Director."

This was not good news, he knew. He could feel a thin rivulet of sweat running down his back and knew that if he took his jacket off there would be two large damp patches on his shirt under his armpits. He looked around and tried to control his annoyance. The room embodied the understated good taste on which BBF prided itself. The walls were lined with dark, polished wooden panels on the lower half, topped with silk crimson wallpaper. A small, original Picasso drawing was tastefully illuminated under a narrow, brass lamp. The room smelled faintly of cigars, coffee, and another aroma, something papery and fresh. At first Joe-Don could not place it. Then he realized it was the smell of money itself.

Monsieur Director's assistant, a tall young man in his twenties with dark-blond hair, even remembered how he took his coffee: black with sugar. He also brought him a tray of newspapers and magazines to read while he waited. Joe-Don flicked through that week's edition of the *Economist*, which carried a lengthy report on the turmoil at the UN. Fareed Hussein's position was looking increasingly shaky, it opined, especially if the UN's own police force did not come up with a proper report on the death of Olivia de Souza. And there were still many questions to be asked about the role of the "mysterious Ms. Azoulay," her relationship with Hussein, and the whereabouts of Jean-Pierre Hakizimani, the Rwandan warlord for whom she had apparently brokered a deal. Many questions indeed, thought Joe, smiling to himself.

Joe-Don and Miguel had quickly dragged the two unconscious security guards into suite 3017 and tied their hands and legs with duct tape. Yael had removed the SIM cards from their mobile telephones, flushed the cell phones down the toilet, and ripped out the cords from the room's telephones. The two men began to stir until Joe-Don gave them a longer burst from the gas spray. That put them under again for another twenty minutes. Joe-Don, Miguel, and Yael had taken the service elevator down to the kitchen, where their departure through the hotel's back entrance—with Miguel's jacket draped over Yael's head—had caused little interest. Stars and VIPs were often ushered through to avoid paparazzi gathering at the front of the hotel.

From there they walked briskly to a parking lot on 44th Street where Joe-Don had left a newly purchased twelve-year-old Ford Focus. They drove through the night, staying away from interstate highways, to Vermont and the Canadian border. They crossed over on a narrow, rarely patrolled dirt road at dawn. They left the car in a parking lot in Montreal, from where they had flown to Paris.

Joe-Don put the magazine down and looked at his watch again: 4:30 p.m. There was still no sign of the manager, although Monsieur Bernard himself had confirmed their appointment for 4:00 p.m. Perhaps there was a legitimate reason for the delay, Joe-Don told himself. He had chosen BBF, after all, for its legendary discretion. Despite the rigorous new international laws controlling the flow of capital and finance, it was understood in numerous capitals, not least Berne, that the world's decision makers still needed a bank that would take deposits, cash or transfer, without too many—in fact, without any—questions being asked. Joe-Don had selected BBF, which was two hundred years old and one of the less well-known, family-run firms, for that role, which it had accepted gladly and fulfilled with enthusiasm. A small but steady percentage of CIA operational cash, written off as "miscellaneous expenses" over twenty years and never enough to draw the attention of the bean-counters at Langley, now added up to a substantial sum for Mr. Wilson Smith.

Joe-Don stood up, walked over to the window, and watched a motorcyclist weave in and out of the early rush-hour traffic, a sleek procession of Mercedeses and BMWs. The sky was heavy and overcast, and a light rain spattered the window. Unlike many of the more famous Swiss banks, BBF was not headquartered downtown on the quayside of Lake Geneva, or in an imposing steel and glass building in the shopping and business quarter at Geneva's historic heart. Instead BBF conducted its business from an anonymous apartment house on the Rue de Montbrillant, a busy and unremarkable thoroughfare in the north of the city. BBF was so discreet that it did not even have a nameplate on its door, which doubtless breached Geneva's municipal codes on numerous counts. BBF used only three of the five floors, and the other two, Joe-Don knew, were rented to companies that did not exist, to prevent any curious neighbors noting its clients.

BBF's down-market neighbors included a cheap—by Geneva standards—Chinese restaurant, a bicycle repair shop, and a gas station. But the street was a short walk from the Palais des Nations, the former League of Nations building that now housed the UN's European headquarters. Rue de Montbrillant also ended at the headquarters of the UN High Commissioner for Refugees, whose entrance was easily visible from the BBF window. Joe-Don was idly watching the comings and goings when a face grabbed his attention. He looked familiar. Was it him? Yes, it was—Brad DeWayne, a political adviser, temporarily reassigned from the State Department to Erin Rembaugh, the head of the UN's Department of Political Affairs. Joe-Don would recognize DeWayne's shiny, bald head, large ears, and purposeful lope anywhere. What was he doing in Geneva?

The door opened and Joe-Don looked up expectantly as Henri Bernard walked in. In his late sixties, Bernard's tall figure was dressed in a perfectly cut gray suit, white shirt, and striped red tie. His silver hair and pink skin were freshly barbered and smelled of No. 74 Victorian Lime Cologne, which he had couriered every week from St. James's in London. Bernard was the embodiment of elegant prosperity.

"Monsieur Smith, my sincere apologies for the delay," the banker said, as he opened the door to his office.

Joe-Don said nothing, picked up his messenger bag, and followed Bernard into his room, where a much larger Picasso was mounted on the wall behind his desk. Bernard's desk was empty apart from a humidor and a penholder. He reached into a drawer and took out a slim leather folder. "You have everything you need. Some more coffee perhaps?"

Joe-Don shook his head. "You are late. I have been sitting in your reception room for thirty-five minutes. I am not here for a social call. I need €100,000 in cash from my account. Now. Not more coffee."

Bernard looked at Joe-Don with a pained expression on his face. It was hard to tell which offended him more: Joe-

Don's dated suit and rumpled necktie or his brusqueness. The banker opened the folder, drew out a sheet of paper, and slowly drew in air between his polished and whitened teeth. "We have a slight problem," he said, his face radiating regret that anyone, or anything, could ever cause inconvenience to a client of BBF.

Joe-Don said nothing, allowing Bernard's discomfort to build until he felt obliged to elaborate. The banker pursed his lips and slowly exhaled. "As you know, Monsieur . . . Smith," he said, his voice openly doubtful, "since 9/11 we have been obliged to adhere to extremely strict new rules on international transfers and to thoroughly check the provenance of new deposits, especially those in cash. Your deposits," he continued, briefly glancing down, "of €452,761 and twenty-six cents have all been in cash. We need to know how you came into possession of these funds."

Joe-Don spoke calmly. "Technically you are obliged to do that, yes, but we both know that in reality you are not. And you don't. Which is why so many governments and other agencies make such use of your services, and why Bank Bernard et Fils' pretax profits last year were more than six hundred million Swiss francs."

Bernard's mask of amiability evaporated and his smile vanished. "I have no idea where you get that absurd, and, I might say, highly offensive allegation from. We are a registered financial institution and subject to international and Swiss banking regulations."

Joe-Don looked at the banker with disdain. "I get that idea from the four-page secret protocol, a copy of which is in my possession, that you signed with the US Department of Justice, the European Commission, and Fareed Hussein's office, guaranteeing Bank Bernard et Fils' immunity in perpetuity against any legal, civil, or criminal measures by any UN member state, citizen, or instrument of any such state, for any transaction or financial arrangement entered into by the bank or any one of its subsidiaries or personnel."

Bernard sat back in his chair, an ironic smile playing on his face. "If—*if*—such a document existed, it would still not help with your case. The board has decided it is unable to release your requested funds, indeed any of your funds deposited here, until you can prove to our satisfaction that these monies were legitimately earned, and indeed have been declared to the US tax authorities. Is that a problem, Monsieur . . . Smith?"

Joe-Don thought quickly. The monies themselves were not an issue. He was confident that the sleek banker was about to crumple like a cheese soufflé. But these sudden "difficulties" with his account showed that his moves had been anticipated. Which doubtless explained the delay. And which also meant that Bank Bernard had doubtless alerted the authorities to his presence. Time to speed things up.

"For me, no. But for you, yes." Joe-Don reached into his bag and handed Bernard a ten-by-twelve color photograph.

The banker flushed, blinked rapidly, but soon recovered his composure. "What is the meaning of this?"

"Rough trade, I think our British friends call it. The photograph shows you having dinner in the bank's private dining room with Vadim Todorov."

Bernard shook his head. "I would expect something more sophisticated from you, Monsieur Smith or whatever your name is. Our bank is well known for its philanthropic activities. We sponsor a youth charity to help the young homeless. We provide them with accommodation, work, and the chance of a new life. I took an interest in Vadim's case."

"A great interest. As this photograph shows."

Bernard sat back. "So? My private life is my own affair. I suggest you leave this office now, before I call the security department, " he said, reaching for his telephone.

Joe-Don put his hand over Bernard's. "I note your advice, Mr. Bernard. But before you do that perhaps you should take a look at these," he said, handing him two more photographs.

The banker stared at the pictures and turned white.

"Vadim Todorov was fifteen years old. He was a runaway from an orphanage in Varna, Bulgaria. He lived in the train station and turned tricks to get money for glue or drugs. He had no friends or contacts here. He trusted you absolutely. You showed him a world he had no idea existed. And here he is, dead on a slab," said Joe-Don, his voice cold and hard. "He died of a drug overdose. Cocaine. The postmortem showed he had also suffered severe internal injuries."

Bernard began to shake. "You cannot connect this to me."

Joe-Don looked at him with disgust. "Your DNA was found inside him. Your friend the minister of the interior had the pathologist's report filed away and the police investigation stopped."

He reached over to the humidor and selected a cigar. He

tapped it on the table, took out a pocketknife, and sliced the end off before lighting it with a battered Zippo.

"Prove it," said Bernard, his defiance rapidly evaporating.

Joe-Don puffed on the cigar until the tip glowed red, reached into his jacket pocket, and handed Bernard several folded sheets of paper. "Vadim Todorov's autopsy results and the police report on his death. There are copies on my computer and numerous others. An e-mail containing these documents, and BBF's four-page immunity memo, will be sent to Reuters, the Associated Press, and Bloomberg in thirty minutes if you don't do as I ask. And don't get any smart-ass ideas. I personally need to enter a code to stop the e-mails being sent," he said, blowing a cloud of fragrant smoke over the banker.

Joe-Don shook his head regretfully as Bernard frantically scanned the papers. "Bank Bernard et Fils. A Geneva institution. Two hundred years of history, discretion, and tradition down the drain, just because you like slapping teenage boys around. And consider the bank's clients. They *really* won't appreciate the publicity."

He examined the end of the cigar with interest. "This is very good. Cuban?"

Bernard put the sheets down, his eyes blazing with hatred. "What do you want?"

"I told you. My money. And for you to make a telephone call."

"To whom?"

"To the minister of the interior. You will tell him to stand down the police officers in your reception area, the helicopter circling overhead, and the snipers on the roofs nearby. You will tell him that there has been a misunderstanding, that Monsieur Smith is carrying out an important and highly confidential mission for the United Nations that has been cleared by the Security Council at the highest level, that the standard protocols apply, and that you had been notified of this through the usual channels, but regretfully failed to inform the Swiss government. The fault is entirely yours. And FYI, be aware that if anything should happen to me or any of my close associates—*ever*—the police and autopsy reports and the bank's immunity memo will be released to the news agencies."

Bernard wiped his face with a monogrammed handkerchief. "Understood. But if the minister does not believe me?"

Joe-Don looked at his watch. "Twenty-eight minutes, and counting."

Twenty

Yael sat in the half-lotus position on her rolled-out sleeping bag on the floor, watching the early evening news on the small television in the corner of the room. She had just come back from dumping two garbage bags in the municipal bins in a nearby park. The trash had been carefully sorted, packed into biodegradable sacks, and sealed. One contained paper sandwich wrappers, used napkins, and pizza boxes; the other carried plastic food containers, disposable cutlery, and cups. Yael had taken great care in sorting the trash, partly because she had nothing else to do, partly because of Geneva's incredibly anal municipal regulations governing garbage disposal, but mainly because "Going Gray," she had learned, meant eating a lot of junk and prepackaged food, using throwaway utensils, and sleeping in a sleeping bag rather than using the hotel bed, so as not to leave any DNA traces on the sheets. It also meant drinking straight from the can, like the warm, flat Coca-Cola in her hand.

It had all seemed very over-the-top to her at first, like something from a Jason Bourne film. They were in Geneva, not undercover in Gaza. But these measures were absolutely necessary, Joe-Don had explained, his voice deadly serious. Yael had, whether wittingly or not, taken a man's life, fled the country, crossed the border into Canada illegally, and traveled across the Atlantic on a dead woman's passport. All sorts of people would want to talk to her now, and they would not be friendly conversations. There were no guarantees that they would not be tracked down, but their best protection was what he called a "layered defense," taking every precaution possible, so that even if one of them slipped up, it would not spell disaster.

She finished the last of the Coca-Cola, put the can down on the bedside cupboard, and sat with her head in her hands, wondering how her life had come to this. Last month she had a fantastic career at the UN, brokering the behind-the-scenes deals that kept the wheels of diplomacy and business rolling. Ambassadors, government officials, even front organizations for the world's terrorist groups would all take her calls. She lived in a beautiful apartment on the Upper West Side with picture windows over the Hudson River. There was even the prospect of romance with Sami. And now? Who knew how this was going to end?

Room 506 at the Hotel Imperial looked out on a concrete wall at the back of the main train station. The twin beds both sagged in the middle, the floor was scuffed beige linoleum, and the walls were covered in a dark-green flock wallpaper with several large grease stains. The television volume control was stuck at barely audible and a naked lightbulb swung from the ceiling. The en-suite bathroom did not seem to have been properly cleaned for months and emitted a dank, musty smell.

The rhythmic banging on the ceiling from the room upstairs had started again, increasing her gloomy mood. She was also worried about her conversation with Jasna Jovanovic. Yael had stuck doggedly to her story, insisting that she was Claudia Lopez. Just as she stood up to leave for the second time, the atmosphere suddenly changed. Jasna had told her to be at the main entrance to the Palais des Nations at 5:45 tomorrow morning. "We will see how you do," she had said, smiling gnomically.

Despite the no-smoking sign, the room reeked of stale cigarettes. Yael grabbed her pack of Marlboro Lights and lit one. The tobacco tasted sour and dry in her mouth. She switched channels on the television, exhaling loudly in exasperation at what she saw on CNN. That woman was there again, outlining all the new security measures at the Goma camp. Yael reached sideways without looking and stubbed out the cigarette on the empty Coca-Cola can on the nightstand. The cigarette broke in half, and the can slipped sideways and rolled down the back of the nightstand. Yael switched channels to the BBC. No escape there, nor at Euronews, France 24, Russia Today, or even Al-Jazeera. She was everywhere. The last time Yael had looked, Roxana Voiculescu was Henrik Schneidermann's deputy, and destined to always remain so. Schneidermann, Yael had heard, was determined that Roxana would never get anywhere near the media. But here she was, in Goma, briefing CNN. And quite well, Yael had to admit. Roxana certainly had more screen presence than the boring Belgian.

Yet bizarrely, there was no news, anywhere, of Hakizimani. It was as though the Rwandan warlord had never existed, and certainly had not been staying at suite 3017. But someone must have organized the cleanup operation at the Millennium Hotel—a person, or an agency, it now seemed, with enough clout to shut any inquiries down, presumably under the useful catchall of "national security."

Her situation, she knew, was entirely of her own making. Joe-Don had warned her, repeatedly, and at great length, that her plan for Hakizimani was extremely risky, with potentially grave and life-changing consequences. And now she had to live with those consequences. She missed New York, she missed her apartment, she missed Zabar's, she missed Bertrand and his scarves. She even realized, to her surprise, that she missed Fareed Hussein. She would far rather be sitting in his office listening to his sanctimonious nonsense than in this awful room.

Yael picked up yesterday's *International Herald Tribune*, which had Sami's story on the front page. She read it again, marveling at the quotes from the Rwandan ambassador. Yael had failed in her plan to tell Sami about the planned massacre of the five hundred people at the Goma camp. But it didn't matter. Someone else had leaked it, prompting the street-corner press conference, which, she thought, was a masterstroke. But who? Yael tapped her finger thoughtfully on Sami's byline. Perhaps she had been too tough with Sami. He was only doing his job. He was smart and funny, kind and fun, and she knew that he was attracted to her. Some decent clothes and a proper haircut and he would look quite handsome, she thought.

Yael watched a cockroach scamper up the side of the wall. She hit it with her shoe. The bug tumbled down to the floor and wandered in circles, its legs no longer working properly, white gunk oozing from its cracked carapace. An image of Jean-Pierre Hakizimani flashed into her mind, his arms and legs bound together, trying to squirm away across the carpet as she brought the handset near to his neck. The anguish on his face as she played the flame of the cigarette lighter over the slowly melting photograph of his daughters.

Had she really wanted to kill Hakizimani? The truth was, she didn't know. She certainly wanted to confront him, to show him the human face of one of his victims. One part of her wanted revenge—swift, brutal, and biblical. Another was horrified at the idea. She had planned for both outcomes, and events had taken their course. She took the singed picture of Hakizimani's daughters from her wallet and smoothed it down. Three happy, smiling young faces stared back at her. She suddenly felt near to tears.

The familiar feeling of self-disgust rose within her. What did she think she was doing? Did she really think she could stop whatever horror was planned in central Africa? How could she when she didn't fully know what it was? She looked at the floor plans of the Palais des Nations, spread out over the bed. The UN-KZX Institute for International Development was located in the old part of the building, near the offices that decades ago housed the League of Nations. It was a diabolically brilliant idea: the world's biggest humanitarian organization giving a moral imprimatur to the world's largest corporation. She had to get in, find the proof of what was planned, get out, and then blow it open—all to prevent a war which, according to Hakizimani, would make the 1994 genocide look like a trial run and would result in a "blue flag over every coltan mine."

This was no time for self-pity. Yael closed her eyes and transported herself to Jaffa beach. She came back calm and determined. The cockroach was still staggering around on the floor. She raised her shoe again and brought it down hard.

The KZX boardroom took up most of the 6th floor of a carefully restored eighteenth-century building on the corner of Rue des Alpes and the Quai du Mont-Blanc. Four large windows faced Lake Geneva, where one of several KZX corporate yachts was moored nearby. One wall of the room was covered with six flat-screen television monitors, another with posters for KZX's new and numerous development initiatives and a large, autographed photograph of Fareed Hussein. The centerpiece of the room was a newly restored Biedermeier table, the lacquer so shiny that the room's chandelier shimmered on its surface. A large bowl of fresh fruit sat in the center of the table, together with a tray of canapés from the kitchen of the nearby Beau Rivage hotel, crystal decanters of water, and silver jugs of tea and coffee, which sat on a heated plate. Three people sat at the table, but the refreshments were untouched.

They were waiting for the tall man standing at the window with his back to them. He watched the clouds over Mont Blanc on the other side of the lake, lost in thought for several seconds, tapping the newspaper against the window. He turned around and addressed Charles Bonnet.

"We have a problem, Monsieur Bonnet," he said. "A large problem, and one, I fear, entirely of your making," he continued as he handed the Frenchman the newspaper. Reinhardt Daintner sounded calm and relaxed, his studied mid-Atlantic accent now replaced by the singsong lilt and long vowels of his home city, Vienna.

"I— I—" Bonnet stuttered. He looked down at the paper and back at Daintner.

Daintner gestured at the newspaper. "Monsieur Bonnet, please, kindly share with us the results of your handiwork."

Bonnet reached for the decanter to pour himself a glass of water, but Daintner moved his hand aside. "I asked you to read, not to drink."

Bonnet scratched violently at his neck, sending a small puff of face powder onto his jacket shoulders. He looked around the table for support. Erin Rembaugh stared right through him as though he were not there, then glanced downward, taking a sudden interest in her nails, which were raw and bitten. The second man at the table picked up a file of papers in front of him and began to leaf through them.

The Frenchman picked up the news section of the *New York Times*. The front-page lead headline proclaimed: "*Times* Photographer Found Severely Injured in New Jersey: Foul Play Suspected."

Bonnet swallowed nervously and began to read: "Mitchell Gardiner, a freelance photographer, was found unconscious last night on Redneck Avenue in New Jersey, suffering from severe head injuries and a broken leg. Mr. Gardiner, 28, was on his first assignment for the *New York Times* when his motorcycle appears to have hit an oil slick, and he lost control of it. The crash is likely connected to a theft, as Mr. Gardiner's cameras could not be found at the crash site. Police officers said that the injuries were inflicted by a blow from a blunt instrument that almost split his helmet in two. Mr. Mitchell is now in a coma at Mt. Sinai Medical Center in New York City. New Jersey police say they have launched an investigation into attempted murder."

Rembaugh shook her head and loudly muttered, "Amateur."

"Thank you, that will do," said Daintner. He looked at Bonnet. "You were tasked with a very simple operation. To get Gardiner's cameras."

"We have them," said the Frenchman.

Daintner's nostrils flared and his face turned beet red. "But we don't have his telephone and we also have a potential murder investigation," he shouted, slamming his hand down on the table. "Thanks to your total incompetence. Your instructions were to crash the bike and take his gear. Knock him out if need be. But not to try and kill him. Now we will have the police crawling all over this disaster."

Daintner turned to Erin Rembaugh. "And you, madame? What am I paying you and your colleagues for? How do you explain the press conference on 42nd Street? The Rwandan ambassador herself, announcing to the whole world the plan for Goma. You understand the consequences for you all if there are any more mistakes like this? We have a leak. It's your job to plug it. And Azoulay—how did she manage to kill Hakizimani and escape? I want her caught. *Now.*"

Rembaugh leaned forward, her tone conciliatory, her hands in the air, palms out in supplication. "Reinhardt, I understand your anger and frustration. But these are temporary setbacks. The injuries of the photographer are regrettable," she continued, looking at Bonnet, "but in the grand scheme of things, inconsequential. There is nothing to link any of this to KZX and our plan for the Goma Development Zone. Nothing at all. In fact, we can turn this to our advantage. The press conference played right into our hands. The Goma camp is now completely surrounded by UN peacekeepers. The UN has shown itself to be responsive, focused, and proactive. Nobody can doubt our commitment to protecting the camp's residents—and building them a better future in the Development Zone. It is a perfect alibi."

Daintner looked doubtful. Rembaugh picked up a remote control on the table. "May I?" she asked, her voice deferential. Daintner nodded. She pressed a button and all six screens came to life. "I took the liberty of arranging for the CNN lunchtime news to be recorded."

The screen showed Mick Dickson, a veteran CNN war correspondent, standing at the gate of the Goma camp. Dickson looked relaxed, and was dressed in T-shirt and chinos. Two white UN armored personnel carriers were parked on either side of the entrance. Swedish peacekeepers wearing wraparound sunglasses manned the two heavy machine guns on top of each vehicle, scanning the horizon. UN attack helicopters took off and landed in the distance, disgorging more peacekeepers. Walls of sandbags protected the outer perimeter. Long concrete blocks were laid in a zigzag pattern on the approach road, forcing approaching vehicles to slow down. A line of cars was backed up as the peacekeepers inspected every car.

Dickson was interviewing a UN official, an attractive young woman with long, light-brown hair, dressed in a notably close-fitting safari jacket. He asked, "What can you tell us about the unprecedented claims yesterday by the Rwandan ambassador that a massacre was about to take place here?"

She smiled knowingly. "I think what's important, Mick, is that the UN acted immediately, even though the secretary-general and the Security Council were not presented with any evidence at all. As soon as Ambassador Munyakarana raised her concerns, the secretary-general ordered the department of peacekeeping to deploy reinforcements. As you can see," she said, gesturing at the armored vehicles, sandbags, checkpoints, and helicopters, "Goma is now the best protected refugee camp in the world."

She paused while three open-topped trucks, each carrying twenty Nigerian peacekeepers, drove slowly up the entrance road and through the gate, sending up clouds of dust. Dickson asked, "How will all this affect the planned UN-KZX Goma Development Zone?"

"Not at all, Mick. Everything is going ahead on schedule. The UN and KZX will be working extremely closely. Once we have both assessed the actual threat level, we plan for KZX's security department to coordinate fully with our peacekeepers, and then gradually assume more responsibilities. Always, of course, under our direction and in full consultation with the Congolese government."

The correspondent nodded and the camera moved toward

him. "Thank you. That was Roxana Voiculescu, spokeswoman for the UN. We also have Hakim Yundala, the head of the UN's Department of Safety and Security, here. Mr. Yundala, you have just arrived, I understand."

Yundala nodded. "That's right. I came straight out here, as soon as I heard that there was a potential threat. The refugees of course come first, but we must also be mindful of the many UN staff we have deployed here. Their safety is my responsibility."

Yundala gestured at the scene around him. "I think you can see that the Goma camp is now probably one of the safest places on earth. Nobody—nobody—can doubt our commitment to keeping it secure."

Rembaugh pressed a button and the screens turned black. She handed Daintner a sheet of paper. "I have prepared this press release. It can go out immediately if you approve it."

He scanned the paper and read out loud. "KZX welcomes the renewed commitment of the UN to the first UN–private sector development zone, announces a donation of one million euros to further improve the camp infrastructure, calls for the world's major corporations to follow its lead in building a vital new strategic partnership between the public and private sector, blah, blah. Very good. Send it."

He looked up at Rembaugh. "Where is Fareed Hussein?" he demanded.

"Six doors away, in his suite at the Hotel Beau Rivage, giving his speech for the opening of our institute a final polish."

Daintner nodded and turned to the second man at the table. He was in his midsixties, still slim, tanned, and fit-looking. He had a military bearing, close-cropped steel-gray hair, and deep lines around his eyes, one of which was blue and the other brown. He had sat silently throughout the exchange as he watched and noted the ebb and flow of power around the table.

Daintner asked, “General, what do you think?”

Menachem Stein reached for the coffee and poured himself a cup. “The incident with the photographer was poorly handled, but in any project as complicated as ours there will be mishaps along the way,” he said, with the trace of an Israeli accent in his American-inflected English.

He paused as he carefully selected six different canapés from the trays on the table. “The key point is to keep unexpected events and their consequences under control. And Erin has handled the press conference very well. That event came as a surprise to all of us, and shows we have a leak somewhere. That needs to be dealt with. But in the short term she has turned a potential disaster to our advantage by allying the DPA with Braithwaite and the DPKO and supporting the reinforcements. It was excellent work,” he continued, turning to Rembaugh, who, to everyone’s silent amazement, blushed and looked down.

“Hakim Yundala is also useful. We do need some African faces in front of the cameras. But the important thing is that we do not respond to events, but continue to set the pace and the agenda. We have to accelerate now and seize the initiative back. If everyone agrees, we go to level two tomorrow. Everything is in place in the field. I leave tonight,” Stein said, reaching for a sliver of smoked salmon on toast, garnished with Beluga caviar, and eating it in one bite.

Reinhardt Daintner nodded first, the others quickly following his lead.

Twenty-One

As soon as he left the bank, Joe-Don spotted the watcher: a male, in his forties, sallow-skinned, with short brown hair, sharp cheekbones, and a pencil mustache. He was wearing a white shirt and fawn trench coat. He stood in front of the nearby Chinese restaurant, reading the menu as though he were considering eating there, but was also subtly scanning the street in the reflection of the glass. The man, Joe-Don realized after a few seconds, looked familiar. He had seen him several times in the US UN mission on First Avenue. He was making no effort to hide, indeed seemed to want Joe-Don to notice him. So he must be a messenger.

But any conversation would have to take place on Joe-Don's terms. He slung his bag over his shoulder and checked the holster in the small of his back: the Glock 30 pistol was secure in its custom-made leather holder.

He walked over to a taxi dropping off its passengers at the UNHCR headquarters, and slid in behind the driver, telling him to take him to the Place Jean-Marteau. The driver, a thankfully taciturn Genevoise, weaved skillfully through the back streets, avoiding the jam along the Avenue France. Twelve minutes later he deposited Joe-Don at a small, triangular piazza looking out onto the Quai Wilson, the main road running alongside the lake, which was crowded with rush-hour traffic. It was a very Swiss public space: each point of the triangle was delineated by a low, perfectly sculpted hedge and manicured lawns radiating out from a circle, in the center of which stood a bust of the writer Monsieur Marteau. There was not a piece of litter, cigarette butt, or scrawl of graffiti in sight.

Joe-Don sat down on one of the pristine green benches, holding the Glock in his coat pocket in his right hand, and looked out over the water. The Jet d'Eau, the city's landmark fountain, suddenly erupted, shooting water more than a hundred meters into the air. An enormous, white two-deck yacht with a two-man helicopter on its upper deck cruised past, its wake sending ripples that almost reached the shore. The sun was setting, the sky blazed orange behind the mountains on the other side of the lake, and the water shimmered indigo and purple. The breeze was fresh and pleasant, and he could feel the warmth of the day as it faded. A scene, he thought, of perfect tranquillity. Perhaps he would retire here soon. He would sail his boat, count his money, give some away, go walking in the mountains. He could even set up his own think tank: The Institute for How the World Really Works.

Three minutes later a taxi pulled over on the other side of the square. The man in the fawn trench coat got out, casually walked over to where Joe-Don was sitting on the bench, and sat down next to him.

Joe-Don lifted his hand and gently pressed the muzzle of the Glock through his coat against the man's left side. He asked, "How many more of you are there?"

The man smiled and looked straight ahead, his voice calm. "None."

Joe-Don pushed the gun hard against him, twisting the muzzle.

He stopped smiling and gasped in pain. "Really. Nobody. We want to talk. That's all. Why do you think you and the girl are still alive?"

Joe-Don looked him in the eye. "How do I know you?"

"Patrick Whiteman. Deputy chief of research at the US UN mission. Started a month ago. You know my boss, Chuck O'Connor."

"Nice cover, Patrick. For?"

"Langley."

Joe-Don spoke low and urgently. "Tell them to back off. Leave us alone. Or the *New York Times* will be running a series on the CIA's black-ops squad running wild in Manhattan, killing UN secretaries."

Whiteman shook his head. "No, no, you've got it all wrong. We are not killing anybody in New York. Not this time. They sent me to watch your back. I'm on your side."

"Prove it," said Joe-Don.

Whiteman spoke confidently. "Wilson Smith and Claudia Lopez are staying in room 506 at the Hotel Imperial on Place des Grottes, above a Turkish kebab house, up the hill, a few blocks from the central train station. The owner sits in the lobby wearing a white vest, feeding his pit bull prime cuts of meat, and watching sports on the large and very loud flat-screen television. The hotel smells of cleaning fluid, stale grease from the kebab shop, and cigarette smoke. You have a twin bedroom with an en-suite grimy bathroom paid for in cash, for a week, in advance. Fifteen hundred Swiss francs, plus another thousand to not produce your passports."

Whiteman's account was completely accurate. Joe-Don moved the gun back but kept it resting against Whiteman's side.

The CIA man breathed out in relief. He leaned back and opened his raincoat to make himself more comfortable. "Thanks."

Joe-Don said, "Keep still. Who killed Olivia de Souza?"

Whiteman shrugged. "We don't know for certain. It's pointing to someone in-house. Someone who knew her and who had a plausible reason to be in the building at seven in the morning."

"So who are you protecting us from?"

Whiteman turned to Joe-Don as he spoke. "State Department intelligence. Erin Rembaugh, their in-house UN expert, is running the operation. And they don't care about you. You can keep your money. They will double it if you go away or kill you if you get in the way. But they want the girl. She's screwing up all their plans."

"Do they know where we are?"

He shook his head. "No. But you don't have much longer. A few hours maybe, until they find you. If we can, they can. Very good wig, by the way."

Joe-Don watched the rush-hour traffic for several seconds before he spoke. A blond woman drove by in a red BMW convertible with its roof down, her hair flying in the breeze. "All this excitement over a dead Rwandan warlord?"

Whiteman laughed. "Of course not. Yael did the world a favor."

"Then what is this really about?"

"Marc Rosenheim."

"The secretary of state? What is he doing?"

"Bringing down President Freshwater. Or trying to."

"Why?"

"The usual reason. Money."

"And Langley is going to stop him?"

Whiteman smiled. "No. You are."

"And what if I don't want to?"

"It's a special request from the new director. She really hopes you can help us out on this. She's a Freshwater appointee, as you know. A woman director of the CIA," said Whiteman, shaking his head in wonder. "She wants a clean sweep. No more skeletons in the closet. Freedom of information, apologies for special renditions, the works. Her husband is from Honduras, so she's *very* interested in Central America. Especially the 1980s."

Joe-Don said nothing. He watched the traffic on the Quai Wilson. It had stopped moving.

Whiteman shook his head. "Bad times. Very bad. Madame Director is thinking about declassifying a new tranche of documents. They make pretty gruesome reading. The things we did . . ."

Joe-Don stiffened almost imperceptibly. Whiteman turned to him, confident now. "We were wondering . . . did you ever testify to the Truth and Reconciliation Commission in Guatemala about your time there?"

Joe-Don exhaled slowly. "OK." He jammed the gun into Whiteman's side again. "But why is Rosenheim moving now?"

"*Ow.* Do you have to keep doing that?" Whiteman asked, as if Joe-Don had just broken wind in public. "So President Freshwater won't be able to intervene."

"Where?"

He looked at Joe-Don as though he were a simpleton. "Congo. You really don't know what is going to happen there?"

"Tell me," demanded Joe-Don.

Whiteman opened his mouth to answer but suddenly jerked backward, and the front of his shirt turned crimson.

Sami and Najwa sat on the lakeside terrace bar of the Beau Rivage hotel talking quietly. It was a balmy autumn dusk that showcased the city at its best: the lights of the yachts glimmered like fireflies, the water rippled like gray silk, young couples strolled arm in arm over the bridge, and the apartment blocks and five-star hotels gleamed invitingly. But Sami took no pleasure in the surroundings. He had arrived that morning, having lost a day while he argued with the foreign editors about the cost of the trip. Eventually they had authorized it. He was jet-lagged and tired. He had barely slept on the airplane, seated in coach between a loud American businessman and his family, including a six-month-old baby that had cried most of the way. At least he had managed to finish the longer, investigative feature that he had promised his editors. Najwa had arrived a day earlier and had traveled business class, so she was rested and raring to go. She was staying at the Beau Rivage, and he was booked into a drab business hotel on the other side of the bridge.

But Sami's malaise was more than just travel fatigue. He had felt increasingly unsettled over the last couple of days. He had the feeling that things had been moved around in his apartment, but it was always so untidy he could not be sure. An old contact of his, a former political counselor at the US mission to the UN, had called him yesterday out of the blue. They had not spoken for at least five years, but the diplomat was full of bonhomie, insisting that he take Sami for a steak dinner at his club and catch up on all the news. Sami had declined, saying he was traveling for the next few days and had let slip that he was going to Geneva. That was probably a mistake, although if the government really wanted to know his movements it would be easy enough to find out. Sometimes he felt like he was being watched.

Last night, as Sami left his building and stepped up to the car that would take him to JFK, the hairs had actually stood up on the back of his neck. There was nothing concrete, just intuition. Or paranoia. Or both—someone had certainly removed Fareed Hussein's itinerary from his locked desk drawer. And someone had organized extensive repairs to his office. As Henry Kissinger said, "The presence of paranoia does not disprove the existence of plots." Yuri had telephoned him yesterday morning. It was the politest conversation Sami had ever had with the UN's building manager. Yuri had apologized profusely about the misunderstanding, which he blamed on the confusion after the tragedy on the 38th floor—it seemed all the paperwork had indeed been authorized for his office renovation.

There was more. Sami realized that he missed Yael: their coffees, her personal e-mails that somehow made him feel like he meant something to her, and the way that her hair fell into her eyes. He kept replaying in his head their last encounter on the steps of the UN entrance on First Avenue. Maybe he should have told her the e-mail address of whoever had sent him her Goma memo. It wasn't like he knew the actual person. It could have been anybody. Why had he been so self-righteous? He could still hear Yael whispering in his ear, "Don't ever call me again." He had tried several times, and he had also written to her Gmail address. Her mobile was not just switched off but was registered as unavailable. She did not reply to his messages. Where was she?

Sami's experience at the airport had further unsettled him. He had been stopped at the border control and questioned and then pulled over again by customs officers. They had turned his bags inside out and questioned him at length about his visit to Geneva. He told them the truth, or part of it, that he had come to report on the opening of the UN-KZX Institute for International Development. Still, at least he could walk and talk. He swirled his drink around the glass, his head down as he stared at the table.

Najwa put her hand on his arm. "It's not your fault, *habibi*."

Sami looked up and pushed the drink away. Nothing would shift the lump in his stomach, not even a twelve-year-old single malt on Al-Jazeera's tab. "Yes, it is. I got him the assignment. His wife is six months pregnant. What if he never wakes up? Or he's crippled? Mitchell is a freelancer. The paper is paying his medical bills for now, but he has no insurance."

Najwa signaled to the waiter for another glass of Sancerre. "Did you hit him on the head?"

Sami looked up. "No. Of course not."

"Then stop feeling sorry for yourself. Journalism is a risky business. You can feel guilty about me instead," she said, removing her hand and looking him in the eye.

Sami nervously licked his lips and looked out over the water. A tourist boat chugged across the center of the lake. He could see the revelers drinking and dancing on board, glasses in hand. Their laughter and chatter carried over the water. "Guilty about what?" he asked, innocently.

The waiter arrived and Najwa waited until he filled her glass and left. "Sami, please don't take me for a fool. Because I am not," she said, all trace of her usual flirtatiousness gone. "When were you going to give me copies of Mitchell's photographs?"

Sami reached for his whisky and took a sip. He was suddenly ravenously hungry and reached for the tray of peanuts and Japanese rice crackers on the table. Najwa moved faster and put her hand over his, gripping his fingers so he could not reach the snacks. She looked straight at him expectantly.

He nodded. "I owe you an apology," he said, his voice contrite.

"Do I get one?"

"Yes. I am sorry. Really. I should have told you."

Najwa lifted her hand from his. "You should have. We made a deal, Sami. Are we working together or not?"

Sami smiled sheepishly. "Yes. We are."

She reached for a rice cracker. "Good. Then tell me what he got."

Twenty-Two

Yael was dozing on her sleeping bag on the floor in room 506 when her mobile beeped that a text had arrived. She picked up the handset: the screen showed a blank message from an unknown number. She sat up quickly, walked to the bathroom, stuck her head under the cold tap, and rubbed herself dry with a T-shirt. She briskly gathered her and Joe-Don's toiletries and belongings, rolled up the two sleeping bags, and jammed them all into her rucksack, together with the rest of her clothes. She folded up the UN floor plans and put them inside her small shoulder bag.

In three days, Yael had accumulated an impressive wardrobe from Joe-Don's cash allowance, including a black leather jacket that she had bought that morning on sale at Balenciaga for eight hundred euros, and a long purple merino and cashmere scarf. The scarf reminded her of Bertrand. She felt a pang of nostalgia for his stall on the corner of West 81st Street and Riverside Drive. But the scarf also gave her strength, reminding her of why she was living out of this grim room.

She put on her new jacket, marveling once more at the softness of the leather, and grabbed Joe-Don's bag, a small black nylon duffel bag that he always kept packed. Claudia Lopez's passport was safe in a traveler's wallet that she wore on a thong around her neck, together with several thousand more euros in cash. Yael checked the bed and the bathroom one last time. It all looked clear to her. She locked both bags with unique, unpickable US-government-issue padlocks; put her purse on, then her rucksack; slipped her right arm through the handles of Joe-Don's bag, hoisting it onto her shoulder; and walked briskly down the five flights of narrow wooden stairs. The hotel's owner watched her walk across the lobby and turned back to the television, grunting good-bye as she left.

Yael walked at a moderate pace down Rue des Grottes, neither too fast nor too slow, past the restaurant with no name and a large sign for "Kronenbourg 1664" beer, past the Indian-owned convenience store that sold the sandwiches she and Joe-Don had been existing on, and into the Place des Grottes, a good place, she thought, for some dry-cleaning—not of clothes, but people. The Place des Grottes was a pedestrian precinct, the roads passing through it blocked off by small concrete bollards, with a retractable post in the middle in case the emergency services needed to get through. A smartly painted green and white wooden house stood on the east side—a chocolate-box piece of Switzerland that looked curiously out of place in the urban landscape—facing a shop and a café across the square. A marble fountain stood in the middle, and a stately apartment block, painted bright pink and purple, marked the northern end. Two more apartment buildings stood on the left side. A tall cylindrical advertising kiosk was covered with ragged posters and colored flyers, flapping wildly in the cold wind that was blowing in from the lake.

A good place, then, for surveillance teams to wait. Yael slowed down as she walked through the square, observing and checking. Two young mothers sat chatting on a bench facing the fountain, their children wobbling around on baby wooden bicycles with no pedals. The women seemed completely absorbed in their conversation, and anyway it was hard to follow a target and remain inconspicuous with a three-year-old in tow. A middle-aged man, tall and swarthy with a long, curved nose, was reading a Turkish newspaper and drinking coffee on the terrace of the café. Again, too conspicuous to be a watcher, she thought. A gaggle of teenagers were sitting on the edge of the fountain, laughing, smoking, and playing with their mobile telephones. Too young.

She walked to the end of the Place des Grottes, and she could see the back of the train station ahead of her, just a few hundred meters away at the end of the street, on the other side of the Place de Montbrillant. A white and blue tram rolled smoothly across her field of view. She took a sharp right turn into an open parking lot. This was a piece of Geneva most tourists did not see: the road was cracked and fissured, the tarmac spotted with poor quality repairs, the sidewalls of the buildings raw brick or concrete. An abandoned Citroën 2CV sat rusting in the corner. The walls were covered with graffiti. A row of run-down gray apartment houses overlooked the square.

Yael kept a steady pace, looking in the cars' side-view mirrors to see if she were being followed as she walked through the lot. Any serious surveillance would be carried out by a "box": one watcher behind, one at the side, and one in front, all three communicating by radio. The really skilled operators wore reversible jackets and carried eye- and sunglasses, scarves, hats, and gloves in different styles, shapes, and colors—even wigs. They would dart into shops or alleys and change along the way to throw the target off the scent.

She couldn't see anyone, but that did not mean they were not there. But there was also a simple technique to expose even the most mobile surveillance: the "choke point," also known as "channelized terrain." A choke point could be a bridge, a tunnel, or an overpass—anything that forces the flow of pedestrians, including any watchers, in one direction. Yael's was a narrow concrete stairway that was flanked on both sides by a thick wall of ivy and that led out of the run-down square into the Place de Montbrillant. She walked slowly down the stairs, holding on to the length of scaffolding that had been turned into a handrail, taking care not to slip on the damp concrete. Best of all, halfway down, the stairway turned sharp right. A choke point within a choke point.

Yael stopped at the bottom and turned around 180 degrees, swiftly glancing back. The staircase was empty. She stepped into the Place de Montbrillant. It was a wide, windswept space bisected by a busy two-lane road and tramlines. The square faced the rear of the train station, a long, low sweep of poured concrete, divided into two wide, underlit passageways. The Place de Montbrillant was dotted with detached apartment buildings, as though the builders had run out of time, or money, or both, and the wide empty spaces were used as parking lots. A large red double-decker bus that had been converted into a community information center stood in the middle of the square. Yael watched a line of schoolchildren shepherded by their teachers cross the road, then walked across to the side of the vehicle. A passerby would see her reading the notices advertising courses in French, basic literacy, and computer skills pasted in the window. In fact, she was using the window as a mirror to see if anyone had followed her.

Yael slid Joe-Don's bag off her shoulder, as though it were too heavy and she needed to take a break. She rubbed her neck and shoulders and took out her mobile telephone, scrolling through the empty contacts menu before pressing a button. She held the handset to her ear, conversing with nobody while observing the passageway and watching for anyone coming from the Place des Grottes. It all looked clear to her.

Yael waited at the traffic light until the green man appeared, crossed Rue de la Cordiere, and walked through the dark passageway into the station, past the newsagents, bakeries, and sweetshops and out to the tram stop on the Place de Cornavin. The Place de Cornavin showed a better side of Geneva: stately, well-maintained luxury boutiques and apartment buildings, bicycles neatly parked in street-side racks, spotless sidewalks without a speck of litter in sight. She waited until the number 13 tram arrived, ensuring that she was the last one to board, and stood by the door, looking at the route map. Just before the tram pulled out she shook her head in exasperation and stepped off, apologizing as hers and

Joe-Don's bags brushed against several passengers. Nobody followed her.

She then walked back across the front of the station toward the taxi line. She stepped around the front vehicle, walked a few yards, stood on the left side of the line of cars in the road, and put her and Joe-Don's bags down between her feet. There was a strict protocol—passengers waited in line in the designated area on the sidewalk and took the first available car. She stood looking at the cars, wiping her head, to all intents a bemused and tired tourist.

The taxi drivers signaled to her to join the queue of thirty or so people on the other side of the sidewalk. She knocked on a couple of windows, pretending not to understand the queuing system. The drivers shrugged and pointed at the queue again. She continued standing on the road, looking exasperated. This was a risky move because she was drawing attention to herself. But she wanted to take a random vehicle, and was gambling that one of the drivers would take pity on her. She knocked on the door of the fifth car, a black Mercedes, and a young man in his late twenties, dark-skinned, wiry, with a mustache and goatee beard got out.

He smiled, picked up Yael's bags, and ignoring the other drivers' protests, placed them in the trunk of the car. The other would-be passengers, patiently waiting in line, looked on, outraged at this breach of protocol. One lady in a tweed suit even shouted at her that she would call the police. Yael ignored her and thanked the driver profusely.

He opened the door for her, and Yael sat back gratefully in the black Mercedes. A string of green prayer beads hung from the mirror. A taxi license in the name of Ahmed Aboulafia was displayed in a plastic holder, on top of the sunshade on the driver's side.

"Where to, madame?" he asked politely.

"Do you know the Old Town?" Yael asked.

He turned and smiled with an engaging grin that crinkled the skin around his brown eyes. "Old Town, New Town, uptown, downtown, wherever you like, madame."

Yael leaned forward slightly as the car pulled away, into the traffic. "Please drive up to the Old Town and the streets around St. Peter's Cathedral. I am an architecture student and I have to prepare a presentation tomorrow. Of course I left it all until the last minute," she said, shaking her head at her poor time management. "So let's just wander around for a while, then I will get out and take some pictures, and make some notes, you wait and then we will come back," she said, reaching into her shoulder bag and handing him a twenty-franc note as they drove toward the lakeside. "If that's OK."

It was. Ahmed took the money and thanked Yael, chatting about the difficulties of life in Geneva for a North African—the police, the paperwork—as they crossed the Mont Blanc Bridge over the lake and climbed up into the Old Town toward St. Peter's Cathedral. He stopped there and Yael got out of the car, wandering around the narrow lanes and alleys, staring at the medieval buildings and scribbling in a notepad or taking pictures with her telephone camera. Each time, she took several sharp turns in succession, doubling-back on herself. She did not see the same person or vehicle twice, and the streets were almost deserted as the shops and offices closed for the day. As far as she could tell, she had not been followed.

After a half hour of meandering around the Old Town, she went back to the car, where Ahmed was reading the *Tribune de Genève.* He smiled, put the paper down, and drove back across the Mont Blanc Bridge to the Left Bank and dropped Yael at the Place des Alpes, a couple of blocks back from the lakeside. He got out of the car, opened the trunk, and handed Yael her bags. She thanked him and said goodbye, watching his car disappear into the traffic as she checked the padlocks. It was not great tradecraft to leave the bags in the trunk of an unknown taxi, but they were securely locked and contained only clothes and toiletries. It was either this or a luggage locker at the train station blanketed by CCTV. The bags were untouched.

Yael hoisted her rucksack on, slung Joe-Don's duffel bag over her shoulder, and walked through the tree-lined square onto the corner of the Rue de Zurich and the Rue de Lausanne, the main road in front of the train station, before heading through the back streets to the rendezvous point she had agreed to with Joe-Don. She thought she saw Ahmed's car again, but there were many black Mercedeses in the evening traffic and she could not be sure. She did not see him take down his taxi license and replace it with one under a different name. Nor did she see him pick up his telephone, press a number on his speed dial, and speak for some time.

Sami was about to answer Najwa when a tall man with deep-set gray eyes pulled out a chair three tables away from them and sat down. His bald head gleamed under the terrace lights, and his ears stuck out. He wore a single-breasted navy blazer, chinos, and a blue button-down shirt and looked like he had just stepped out of the metro at Foggy Bottom in Washington, DC. He picked up the menu and idly scanned the price list.

Najwa saw Sami looking at him. She was about to speak when Sami laid his hand on her arm. The bald man reached inside his pocket, glanced quickly at Sami and Najwa, looked away, and placed a smartphone on the table.

The waiter appeared. Sami heard the man ask for a "club soda." That decided it. Europeans never drank club soda.

"*Yalla, habibi*," Sami said quietly as he stood up, putting on his coat. Najwa immediately followed. They walked to the bar, where she signed for the exorbitant bill. There was a large mirror over the bar, and Sami could see the man sip his drink. He looked very annoyed.

Twenty-Three

The men came to the village again that night. Two he knew well—Baptiste, the local schoolteacher, tall and mournful, and Lucien, who helped deliver water supplies and had one eye but was still always jolly—and two he thought were Europeans. Herve did not like the Europeans. One was skinny and blond-haired with a straggly beard. He said his name was Stephan, but his smile never reached his eyes. The other one was much darker, with eyebrows like caterpillars, thick arms covered in gray hair, and a potbelly. Herve had asked the man his name in his best, most polite French, but the man had ignored him. Herve thought he was Spanish or Italian, but he had a strange, harsh accent, and the way he talked frightened Herve.

Everyone in Kimanda was scared lately. It was a settlement of five hundred or so people in eastern Congo, ten kilometers down the road from Goma, on the Rwandan border. Compared to its neighbors, Kimanda was considered rich: it had sporadic electricity, a tarmac road, and two standing taps in the square. Most of the men worked mining coltan, digging in nearby streams and sloshing out the dark yellow mud to find grains of the precious mineral. In theory, some earned as much as two hundred dollars a month, ten times the average wage of the country. In practice, they rarely kept more than half of what they mined—the militias took the rest.

And now a new force had appeared in the chaotic mix of competing armies: the East Congo Liberation Front. Most of the different factions were backed by the neighboring states. Rwanda and Uganda were the biggest meddlers, with Burundi and the Central African Republic not far behind. There was a lot of money at stake. Herve had heard a recent report on BBC Radio that Rwanda, which had no coltan mines at all, had made $250 million last year trading the mineral. Nobody knew who was behind the ECLF, but everyone had noticed that its soldiers had the best uniforms, equipment, and guns. And they got paid a hundred dollars a month. Several of his classmates had left home in the last two weeks to sign up.

There was a new ECLF checkpoint on the road to the Goma refugee camp, where Herve sometimes went to visit his relatives from Rwanda. Some of the ECLF soldiers there were Tutsis, and they shouted at him, calling him a "Hutu Genocidaire." Herve was a Hutu but he was only sixteen and had not even been born during the time of the genocide. Last time, the ECLF soldiers had pushed him around with their rifle butts and even threatened to kill him. He still had a big bruise on his back. Now there was shooting every night, echoing through the forest. The men from the village had put up two roadblocks, feeble things made of tree trunks, one on each side of the road that ran through Kimanda. They sat there drinking beer from dusk to dawn, full of alcohol-fueled bravado about how they would fight the Tutsis and finish what was started in 1994.

And then something really terrible happened: three days ago, Evelyn, one of his school friends, had been found bloodied and half-conscious in the road, with her clothes torn to shreds. She had been taken to the hospital at the UN camp and had still not come home. Herve had known Evelyn since his childhood. Sometimes at night they would sit on the schoolyard steps, on the edge of the forest. They talked for hours, her leg resting gently against his, listening to the cicadas and imagining how it would be to study in Paris. Evelyn's father was a Hutu. Hermione, her mother, was a Tutsi. Herve liked her very much. The only way out of this mess, Hermione always said, was for Hutus and Tutsis to marry each other and make a new race: the human race.

The sixty or so men of the village were gathered in the school hall, sitting cross-legged on the floor. The benches and desks had been moved to the right-hand side to clear a space. François Nodula, the mayor, sat on a chair behind a folding table—the Europeans on his left, Baptiste and Lucien on his right. François was actually the deputy mayor. Everyone knew that the real mayor was Herve's father, but he had been killed in a car accident last year. A hit-and-run, they called it. The police had come, asked a few questions, taken a few notes, and he had never heard from them again. Now Herve was the man of the house, his mother had told him, and he had to help look after her and his brother and sisters. He tried his best, although he missed his father intensely. His mother said it would get easier with time, but it did not, not really.

Herve and the other boys leaned on the wall at the back of the school hall. The building was made of raw cinder blocks and the roof of tin sheets. It was raining hard, a heavy African downpour, and the raindrops drummed on the metal. The air was wet and thick, and he could smell the forest. Herve tried to think what his father would do if he were still alive. Watch and listen, he had always told him. Gather information and think hard before you make any decision. Then even if you make the wrong one, at least you thought it through and did your best. So that is what he would do, Herve thought, suddenly feeling comforted.

He felt the weight of his digital camera in his pocket. It was his proudest possession. Kristina, a friendly Swiss aid worker at the Goma camp, gave it to him last month. He had spent hours learning how to use it. The pictures he liked the most were the ones he snapped surreptitiously. With her encouragement, he had taught himself how to hold the camera in his hand and snap street scenes and passersby without anyone noticing. Kristina said he showed real talent at this and promised to put some of his pictures on the Internet.

Nodula was speaking, introducing his "honored guests." Nodula was short, fat, and getting noticeably fatter. The whole village admired his new car, a white Toyota Land Cruiser. Herve wanted to ask him how he could afford to run it on a deputy mayor's salary of eighty dollars a month, but his mother had looked frightened when he mentioned it and absolutely forbade him from ever bringing up the subject. Tonight Nodula was even more pompous than usual. Herve noticed that he kept looking at the long wooden boxes covered in plastic wrapping from the UNHCR, the refugee agency, that were piled up on the other side of the hall. The downpour was turning into a thunderstorm now as the skies opened. The rain sounded as though there were drummers on the roof.

Stephan stood up. "Thank you, Mayor Nodula. It's good to be back here. But I bring bad news and good news for you tonight, my friends."

The men shifted nervously on the rough concrete floor. Herve slowly put his hand in his pocket and brought the camera out, shielding it with his fingers.

"Your daughter, your beautiful daughter," said Stephan, his head downcast. "I am sorry to tell you, she will not be coming home. The doctors could not save her."

An angry muttering filled the room as the men turned to each other. Herve watched as a thin man in his thirties, wearing thick black-framed glasses taped together at the bridge, howled in despair and started sobbing. It was Jean-Luc, Evelyn's father. Herve felt his eyes fill with tears, but he forced himself to put his anguish aside. There was, he knew, a reason why the men of the village had been gathered here tonight. He would mourn his friend in his own time.

Stephan walked over to Jean-Luc and laid his hand on his shoulder. "Don't cry, my good friend," he said, shaking his head. "Tears cannot bring Evelyn back. Nothing can. But we can give meaning to her sacrifice."

Nodula nodded emphatically.

Stephan continued, turning to the other men in the room. "We have to make sure that your daughters are no longer raped and murdered by the cockroaches. That is why we are here—and we have brought what you need to make sure that you can defend yourselves," he said, gesturing at the boxes at the side of the room.

Herve watched silently and slid his fingers over the camera, switching it on. Thunder suddenly exploded like shellfire, so loudly that even Stephan jumped. Herve lifted his fingers and gently pressed the shutter button. The room filled with light.

Herve felt sick with fear. He had left the flash on.

Intrigue Swirls Deeper at UN: German, French Firms Own Allied Africa Charity; Secretary-General's Wife Has Stake

By Sami Boustani

GENEVA—Africa Child Rescue, the new charity at the heart of the United Nations Year of Africa, is majority owned by a company controlled by employees of the KZX Corporation and the Bonnet Group. Zeinab Hussein, the wife of Fareed Hussein, the United Nations secretary-general, and Hakim Yundala, the head of the United Nation's internal security office, are the only minority shareholders, an investigation by the *New York Times* reveals.

Moabi Holdings Ltd. was registered in Kinshasa, the capital of Congo, last month. The firm's majority shareholders are Claude Sambala, the deputy director of KZX's Kinshasa subsidiary, and Bernard Lalola, the deputy director of the Bonnet Group's Congo operation. The two each own 35 percent while Zeinab Hussein and Hakim Yundala each have 15 percent stakes.

The web of connections linking the French and German firms together with the most senior UN officials highlights the growing power of corporate influence on the world's most powerful international body. KZX has poured millions of dollars into supporting the "Goma Development Zone" in eastern Congo, the first UN aid project to be sponsored by a corporation. Numerous senior UN officials are known to oppose the project, but Fareed Hussein has been outspoken in his support.

President Freshwater's administration and Britain have expressed strong doubts, but China and France, who are also permanent members of the Security Council, have been vocal advocates of the new partnership. "The feeling in London and the White House is that the UN and business interests should be kept separate," said one official who could not give his name because he was not authorized to speak on this subject on the record. "But Beijing and Paris think differently." Russia, the other permanent member of the Security Council, has so far stayed on the sidelines. Whatever the United States and Britain would prefer, it seems corporate interests are binding themselves ever tighter to the UN.

Meanwhile, Mitchell Gardiner, a freelance photographer working on behalf of the *New York Times*, remains in a coma. Mr. Gardiner was attacked by unknown assailants after taking a series of photographs of Mr. Hussein boarding a private airplane owned by KZX (see facing page) at Teterboro Airport, together with Reinhardt Daintner, the company's chief of corporate communications. Police have launched an investigation into attempted murder.

These are uncertain times for the UN. Earlier this week the Department of Peacekeeping Operations rushed hundreds of UN troops to the Goma refugee camp after unprecedented claims by Florence Munyakarana, the Rwandan ambassador to the United Nations, that a massacre was about to take place there. Tomorrow, Mr. Hussein is due to open the controversial new UN-KZX Institute for International Development in Geneva, which will be housed in the United Nations headquarters at the Palais des Nations.

An in-house investigation into the death of Olivia de Souza, Mr. Hussein's former secretary, is still underway and headed by Hakim Yundala, head of the UN's Department of Safety and Security. Ms. de Souza fell thirty-eight floors to her death earlier this month. The UN has refused to allow either the FBI or New York Police to investigate, although an increasing number of UN officials believe that she was murdered.

These latest revelations will further increase pressure on Mr. Hussein, whose term is due to end next summer and who is known to be seeking reelection . . .

Yael circled the paragraph about Fareed Hussein flying on KZX's private jet. Her old boss was always a sucker for luxury, she thought as she sipped her coffee. But there were still so many unanswered questions. The rest of Sami's article reported that Jean-Pierre Hakizimani, the Rwandan warlord wanted for genocide, was rumored to be in New York, but hadn't been seen. Well, she could certainly help Sami with that, especially since the article's dateline showed that Sami was in Geneva. Perhaps they would bump into each other at the opening of the UN-KZX Institute for International Development, she thought, feeling surprisingly buoyed at the prospect. Until she remembered that she was no longer Yael Azoulay.

She checked her watch: it was 9:30 p.m. She had been sitting here for two hours, waiting for Joe-Don. The last text had said, "B410," —before ten o'clock—so it could be another half hour. But there were much worse places to be than the Black Cat—especially the Hotel Imperial.

The Black Cat stood on the corner of Rue des Pâquis and Rue de Zurich in one of the seediest parts of the city. Prostitutes lingered in the doorways of the now closed luxury-goods shops, while young North African men walked up and down, whispering their lists of drugs for sale. It was not exactly threatening—the Quai de Mont-Blanc on the lakeside and the five-star hotels were just a couple of blocks away—but as a young woman on her own, Yael was glad to be inside. The bar was dark but surprisingly cozy.

The walls were painted dark red, and the wooden chairs and tables looked like assorted flea-market and junk-shop finds. Billie Holiday crooned mournfully in the background. The people-watching was excellent. The two barmaids, who, Yael noticed, were liberally helping themselves to the stock, were now also singing along. There seemed to be rooms for rent by the hour upstairs, judging by the procession of men in business suits and women in very short skirts who passed through and disappeared up the stairs.

The owner came over to Yael's table to introduce herself. She was pale and enormously fat with bright red hair. Her surprisingly slim fingers were topped with long pink nails studded with fake diamonds. She held a large balloon glass of red wine in one hand and seemed to be enjoying herself immensely.

"All on your own, *draga*?" she asked. She reminded Yael of Jasna, and not just because she had a similar deep voice and accent. "I'm Stella," she said, holding out her hand.

Yael shook hands, glancing enviously at Stella's wine. Her grip was firm and confident. "I'm Claudia. I'm waiting for some friends."

Stella nodded, several chins wobbling at once. "Welcome to the Black Cat, Claudia. Now *draga*, you let me know if you need anything," she said, and wandered off into the crowd.

Yael drank some more of her coffee. She sensed that Stella, like Jasna, did not seem entirely convinced by Yael's new identity. Yael flicked through the rest of the newspaper to keep herself occupied. A story out of Washington, DC, outlined the growing political split between President Freshwater and

Marc Rosenheim, the secretary of state. Rosenheim was the guest of honor at the launch of "America First," a new isolationist lobbying organization that was supposedly funded by a reclusive mining billionaire based in Des Moines, Iowa. The reporter quoted several government sources who said the standoff was crippling government business and could not understand why the president did not simply let Rosenheim go.

The door opened and Yael glanced up. A woman who looked like Jasna walked in, together with an older man wearing a felt hat, a long brown overcoat, dark glasses, and a white cane. Yael looked at her again, for longer. It *was* Jasna. What was she doing here? And who was the blind man? Maybe the Black Cat was the local Balkan-émigrés hangout, which seemed quite possible. The bar was getting crowded with large, ebullient men in shiny sports suits. The Boban Markovič Orchestra had replaced Billie Holiday, the *slivovitz* flowed, and the party was kicking off nicely.

Jasna waved to Stella and smiled as she guided the blind man over to Yael, with a hand on his arm. Yael jumped up, trying to cover her surprise, and pulled out a chair for him. He handed her a copy of *Genève Soir*, the city's evening newspaper.

Joe-Don said, "We have a problem."

Twenty-Four

The air split open with a loud crack of thunder, and the school hall lit up again for an instant. It was lightning, Herve realized, his knees wobbly with relief. He managed to squeeze off three more shots before he put the camera back in his trouser pocket, the sweat pouring off him.

Baptiste and Lucien started clapping and the men joined in, shouting and cheering. Nodula stood up and held up his hand for silence. "We will make sure that any true and genuine Hutu will be able to defend himself and his family when the cockroaches attack. But first, he must show his loyalty, that he knows the Hutu Ten Commandments."

Nodula was no longer nervous, but confident and in command. "Who can tell me the first commandment? The one that tells us who is a traitor? Jean-Luc? I am sure that you do not want to be a traitor. I am sure . . . my friend, that you want revenge, for your daughter."

Jean-Luc stood up, shaking as he spoke. "Anyone who marries, befriends, or employs a Tutsi is a traitor."

Stephan nodded, a smile playing on his lips, and walked over to the large wooden crates wrapped in plastic. He took out a hunting knife and slashed at the wrapping, ripping it off and throwing it aside.

He jammed the knife into the lid of the wooden crate, levered it open, and took out an AK-47 assault rifle, still shiny with grease.

Nodula started clapping again, triggering a wave of applause. "Tell me, Jean-Luc, the second Hutu commandment."

Jean-Luc looked at Stephan, then back at the deputy mayor. "Anyone makes a business partnership with a Tutsi, lends him money, or helps him with any kind of favors is a *traitor*."

Nodula nodded, satisfied. "And the third and fourth?"

Jean-Luc said, his voice stronger now. "All government positions must be majority Hutu. The armed forces must be exclusively Hutu."

Nodula clapped enthusiastically, triggering another wave of applause. Stephan levered open the ammunition box, took a banana-shaped cartridge, and handed the gun and ammunition to Jean-Luc. He swiftly clicked the cartridge into place, weighing the weapon in his hands with satisfaction.

Nodula stood up and walked over to Evelyn's father. "How do we defend ourselves, Jean-Luc?" he asked softly.

"Hutu power!" he replied.

"How do we defend ourselves?" Nodula asked again, louder.

"Hutu power!" said Jean-Luc, his voice strong and confident.

The men in the hall echoed his answer, looking at one another and nodding determinedly.

"You know what has to be done, Jean-Luc," said Stephan, his voice soft and reassuring. "You made a mistake. You married a Tutsi. That's OK. People make mistakes. We are all human. The question is how do we make amends for those mistakes? How do we prove ourselves? You must prove yourself, Jean-Luc. Prove that you are not a traitor. Purge the evil. Cleanse your family of the cockroaches."

Jean-Luc swallowed hard and gripped the AK-47 so tightly that his fingers paled. "All of them?" he asked, his voice shaking.

Stephan nodded. "Every single one."

Nodula, Lucien, and Baptiste began to rhythmically bang the table.

Jean-Luc led the chorus of "Hutu power, Hutu power," raising and lowering the gun above his head, in time with the chant.

The cry resounded around the room, rising and falling, echoing across the village and far out into the forest. The man with the bushy eyebrows smiled and sat silently, the contempt flickering on his face as the men lined up excitedly to receive their guns and ammunition. Nobody noticed as Herve slipped away.

Joe-Don and Yael were sitting in Stella's office on the first floor above the bar. The room smelled of the familiar cocktail of perfume, coffee, and cigarette smoke, but it was also exuberantly pink: the walls were dark pink, the carpet a lighter shade, and the doors a pale strawberry. Stella's fat black cat sat comfortably on Yael's lap, purring loudly. A television was switched on in the corner, tuned to the local news channel, with the volume turned down. The thumping bass of the gypsy music carried through the floorboards, together with the faint echoes of shouts and laughter. A bottle of Johnnie Walker Black Label whisky and two glasses sat on the desk, next to a thermos of coffee.

Joe-Don poured himself and Yael two small whiskies, and they clinked glasses. He took a tiny sip. Yael swallowed half the drink in one go. She closed her eyes with pleasure as the alcohol burst inside her like a warmth bomb.

Joe-Don tapped the front of the *Genève Soir*: "Slow down. That's your ration for tonight."

The newspaper's front page showed a large photograph of Joe-Don in his blond wig and glasses under the headline, "*Armé et Extrémement Dangereux*." Members of the public were not to make contact with him, but to report his whereabouts to the police immediately, the report said, with an account of how a "*hautement tueur professionelle*" had killed "*un diplomate Américain*" with a single shot in the middle of the rush hour.

Yael sat back, digesting what she had read. "My God. One shot? Why didn't they shoot at you as well?"

"I am the bait. It's you they are after."

Yael sat back, digesting this news. "Who was the American diplomat?"

"Patrick Whiteman. A gift from Langley to watch our backs. He should have had someone to watch his back. More specifically, his front."

Yael put her hand on his. "Are you OK?"

Joe-Don nodded slowly. "I'm fine." She watched as he picked up his drink and took a sip. His hand was rock-steady.

The growing sense of unease Yael had had since they arrived in Geneva now curdled into fear. Langley. Snipers. An American diplomat shot dead in broad daylight. But she and Joe-Don had been in life-threatening situations before. Yael knew not to persist; Joe-Don would share what information he thought necessary when he thought it necessary. The shooting explained why Joe-Don was dressed as an elderly blind man. But what was the Jasna connection?

"Now listen up. This is our security situation, and it is not good," Joe-Don said, his voice deadly serious, interrupting her thoughts. "We are hiding in a brothel in the red-light district of Geneva, with a hit team, the Geneva police department, and the city's media on our tail. What do you have to tell me?"

"A blue flag over every coltan mine," said Yael.

Joe-Don looked puzzled.

Yael leaned forward, her voice animated. "It's simple once you think it through. KZX and the Bonnet Group plan to merge. KZX is going into the electronics business, making mobile telephones, laptops, and tablet computers. For that they need coltan. The Bonnet Group is the biggest mining company in Africa, especially in Congo. But they need to take control of the territory—complete control. The Goma Development Zone is the pilot project. It sets a precedent and establishes a beachhead. The key point is that the UN—Hussein actually—has agreed that KZX security staff will be allowed to control the perimeters and entry and exit. Once they control the territory and access to it they control everything. It will be a KZX colony. Of course Quentin Braithwaite is completely opposed to this. So they need to get rid of him. You know about the plan for Hutus wearing UN uniforms to kill five hundred people at the Goma camp in order to discredit the DPKO. That didn't work because someone leaked it. But they will think of something else."

Joe-Don listened carefully as she spoke. "So what now?"

Yael looked down and stroked the cat. The soft warmth of the animal against her was curiously comforting. "When I was in Goma, Hakizimani asked me if I knew Menachem Stein."

Joe-Don put his glass down, completely alert now. "And you said?"

"No, of course. But this would fit his M.O. Perfectly. And Olivia wrote in her letter that Stein had been calling Fareed Hussein on his private line. I am sure that is why she was killed, because she knew that the UN was secretly working with Efrat Global Solutions. You remember what EGS did in Brazil in Amazonia?"

Joe-Don nodded. "Peaceful protests by the indigenous people against ranchers and loggers get international attention. EGS steps in to 'help'—help being weapons and basic military training. A few ranchers and loggers get shot. The federal police and the army move the indigenous people out, the loggers and ranchers move in, and Americans can still eat their hamburgers."

"Exactly. Maybe there is a similar plan for central Africa. EGS arms the Hutus against the Tutsis and the Tutsis against the Hutus. Burn some villages, kill the women and children.

Congo explodes. The UN sends peacekeepers. KZX is there to help, as a good corporate citizen," Yael said, looking down. The cat turned around on her lap so she could scratch his expansive stomach. "The deaths mount up, Fareed Hussein explains how the UN's resources are overstretched and KZX has offered to take on some security duties. Maybe even with EGS. The UN troops are redeployed to some other crisis zone. The Goma Development Zone becomes the Eastern Congo Development Zone becomes the Great Lakes Development Zone and on and on. And there you have it, a blue flag over every coltan mine."

Joe-Don sat silently for several seconds before he spoke. "Not with President Freshwater in office. If Congo becomes a bloodbath, she will push for US troops to intervene."

Yael leaned forward to take the coffee. "Which is why, I guess, there is all this talk now of impeaching her." The cat meowed indignantly and leapt off her lap. Yael had something else she wanted to ask. She had been intrigued by Joe-Don and Jasna's body language when they walked in to the bar.

Yael looked at Joe-Don and sipped her coffee. "So how do you know Jasna?"

"We met in Yugoslavia during the war," said Joe-Don, his voice bland.

Yael nodded slowly, a smile playing on her lips. "You know each other well?"

"Well enough," said Joe-Don, looking into his whisky and swirling the amber liquid around, his craggy face suddenly softening.

Yael looked at him carefully. "You are blushing. I've never seen you blush before. Well, well . . ."

He looked up at her, a mixture of nostalgia and regret in his eyes. "Love in the war zone. It happens. But she was married, and I am not the domestic type. David introduced us. He brought her and her kids across the front lines in his UN Jeep, together with two other families. You were there, in the Hotel Hyatt in Belgrade."

A memory flashed through her mind, as intense as if it had happened yesterday. She was sixteen years old and watching CNN in the hotel room when the concierge called to say her brother had arrived. She took the elevator downstairs into the wide, modern foyer with the glass front and revolving door. It was crowded with the usual mix of aid workers, journalists, UN officials, and large, watchful men who sat there all day smoking and drinking coffee. David had just pulled up in front of the hotel. His car was covered in mud and the windows were filthy. She ran out to see him. She put her finger in a small hole in the door by the driver's seat. There was another one under the window and two more over the wheel arch. One window was missing completely, apart from the jagged shards still in the door. Three women emerged from the Jeep, followed by six children and two teenagers. David climbed out of the car, another toddler in his arms. A powerful, familiar longing pulled inside her. Yes, she had been to Belgrade.

She sipped her whisky, slower this time. "And Stella?"

"She is Jasna's cousin. You know what that means in the Balkans. We are part of the family now. Stella also rents out rooms by the hour as I am sure you have noticed. The local police chief is one of her regular clients. Apparently he likes to go to bed with three or four girls at once. Must be quite a party. He is due in later. So we are unlikely to be raided, at least tonight."

Yael nodded thoughtfully. Obviously Joe-Don had helped Jasna get her cleaning contracts with the UN.

"Do you also know Stella well?" she asked lightly, her eyes dancing with amusement.

Joe-Don tried not to smile. He shook his head. "No. Now stop prying."

"OK. But, seriously, if you knew Jasna for twenty years, and you knew she would help, then why did I have to pretend to be Claudia Lopez?"

Joe-Don stared hard at her. "Because you are Claudia Lopez, and if you don't believe it nobody else will. This is as serious as it gets. A man was shot dead next to me a few hours ago by a professional sniper. A rogue unit of State Department intelligence officers are on our trail. Erin Rembaugh and Marc Rosenheim are trying to bring down President Freshwater. These people don't want to talk to you. They want to kill you. So you had better remember that—and who you are— tomorrow morning. Especially if you run into any trouble. When is your birthday, Claudia?"

"February 2, 1978."

"Mother's maiden name?"

"Gomez. Maria Gomez."

"She must miss you."

"No. She passed away five years ago. But my father, Rodrigo does, and so does my little sister, Albertine."

Joe-Don looked up at the television and turned the volume up. The reporter, an excitable brunette in her twenties, was standing in front of the manicured hedge at the Place Jean-Marteau. The square had been sealed off with police tape. Armed officers stood on each corner and sirens wailed in the background. The screen showed the same picture of Joe-Don in his dark-blond wig and tortoiseshell glasses, then switched back to the crime scene. The reporter continued breathlessly that such a murder was unprecedented in Geneva.

The report was interrupted by an urgent news flash. A picture of President Freshwater flashed up on the screen. Joe-Don immediately changed channels to CNN. The news banner along the bottom of the screen announced, "President Freshwater's husband, Jorge, killed in a skiing accident . . . more follows as it comes in . . ." The channel's White House correspondent, a veteran reporter in his sixties, was standing outside the White House talking to the camera. "All we know at this stage is that the president's husband was killed this afternoon while skiing off-piste in Aspen. It seems that there was something wrong with one of his bindings, and he lost control and hit a tree.'

Joe-Don pressed the remote control and turned the volume down. He turned to Yael. "I think we have one or two days at the most."

"And tomorrow? Where will you be?" asked Yael, anxiety gnawing inside her again.

"Not inside. But . . . around."

"Good. Can I ask you something else?"

He gave Yael a taciturn nod.

"Who is the girl in the picture?" asked Yael, softly. "The one you carry in your wallet?"

Joe-Don stared at Yael. "Have you been going through my stuff?"

Yael shook her head. "No, of course not. It fell off the nightstand at the Hotel Imperial. I picked it up and put it back."

Joe-Don closed his eyes for a couple of seconds. "Rosemary Irene Pabst. My daughter."

Yael sat silent, stunned. Joe-Don had never mentioned a daughter. She had no idea that he had ever had a family. "What? Why didn't you tell me? Where is she? I'd love to see her."

He poured himself some more whisky. "So would I. I told her mother that those initials were bad karma but she wouldn't listen." Joe-Don looked at Yael and his features softened slightly. "She was just a few years older than you."

"Was?" asked Yael, quietly.

Joe-Don stared into the distance. "Rosie was a real idealist. She lived in a village in Guatemala and worked for an aid organization that helped the peasants and villagers build cooperatives—agriculture, weaving. That kind of stuff. She called it "empowering." But not everybody wanted the peasants to be empowered. I heard from my contacts in the police and the army that an attack was planned. I warned her to get out. Repeatedly. But Rosie was stubborn. Daddy's girl, I guess. She would not listen. She said nobody would hurt an American citizen. I tried to get the police to hold off, to wait at least for a couple of days so I could get her out. They refused. So I drove there myself, through the night."

He paused and swallowed hard. Yael looked at him, the question unspoken.

Joe-Don swirled the whisky in his glass, shook his head, and put the drink down, untouched. "They came in at dawn. By helicopter. We buried her there."

Yael felt his grief fill the room, the grief and the guilt of a parent who had failed a child. And beyond that, something more—a kind of anguish.

"How did you know the army and police commanders?" asked Yael.

"Because I trained them," he said, his voice a whisper.

Twenty-Five

Azem Lusha, the proprietor of the Hotel Imperial, was fed up. His difficulties had started a couple of days ago when the man who called himself Wilson Smith had arrived with the girl, Claudia Lopez. Mr. Smith wanted to pay in cash—lots of cash—for a room with no registration. Of course it was tempting, but Lusha had said, reluctantly, that it was too risky. He could lose his license, and then where would he be? You know how the Swiss are, he explained, rules had to be followed, or there would be consequences.

Mr. Smith said there would indeed be consequences—if he did not get a room. Life would become very complicated for both Mr. Lusha and his business associates from his homeland in Kosovo, who had claimed asylum under false pretenses. Mr. Smith even knew the name of his home village. Lusha knew other men who had eyes like that and they scared him. So he took the money and kept quiet. The girl had checked out yesterday. He didn't care. The room was paid for in advance.

But now there was this second American waking him up at six o'clock in the morning with some idiotic story about a missing daughter. He was tall, so bald his head shone, and his ears stuck out. Why did these people keep bothering him? The man handed Lusha several photographs.

Lusha looked at the pictures and shook his head. Fuck his mother, what was going on here? He was running a hotel, not a missing-persons bureau. "No," he said. "Not here."

This was true, he told himself. Nobody that looked like these two had stayed here. The man had dark blond hair and big brown glasses. The girl had short black hair and trendy glasses, nothing like this one in the photograph. "Sorry, but I am very busy," he said, scratching his potbelly. "I must get the breakfast ready. And my television is broken. I must organize the repair."

The bald man reached for his wallet, pulled out a five-hundred-franc note, and laid it on the reception counter. "Take your time. Just look at the faces. The eyes, the mouths, and the noses. Ignore the hair and the clothes. Did anyone that looked like these two stay here?" The American moved the money nearer, across the counter toward Azem's fingers.

Lusha licked his lips, staring hard at the pictures. Of course it was them. And why else would this American be here with this idiotic story? "I'm not sure . . . perhaps in the upstairs room.. There was a couple there. The man was older. But I don't want to wake up the other guests so early . . ."

The American pulled out two more five-hundred-franc notes and placed them next to the rest of the money. "Could I see the room? She is our only daughter. Her mother is distraught. We really need to find her . . ."

He nodded and reached for the money, swiftly pocketing it with one hand. "Room 506," he said, handing a key to the American.

The gun barrel was pushing into the base of Herve's throat. It was cold and hard and hurt so much that it was difficult to breathe. He coughed, swallowed, and tried as best as he could not to tremble and to control his fear. The soldier holding the weapon was younger than he was, no more than twelve or thirteen. His uniform was so new it was still stiff and was hanging off his thin shoulders. His green beret, with the ECLF badge—four metal letters over a map of eastern Congo—was sliding off his head. But the boy held his AK-47 with confidence, staring down the barrel, his head tilted to the side, like an experienced marksman, unblinking. Herve had seen plenty of young fighters with eyes like his: utterly vacant.

It was just after 6:00 a.m, and the dawn mist still hung in the air like white tendrils. The birds were singing, and Herve could hear Radio Kivu playing in the soldiers' wooden hut, next to the checkpoint. It was new and freshly painted, unlike the usual ramshackle barricades that the militias set up. A fresh breeze ruffled the leaves of the palm trees at the side of the road, and he saw a lizard scamper across the red mud. Herve's fear was mixed with a terrible sadness and disappointment. They had almost made it. Herve could see the blue flag, the sandbags, and the white UN vehicles two hundred yards up the road. He could even smell the Dutch troops' morning coffee and the thin cheroots they smoked.

As soon as he left the school hall Herve had rushed home.

He had gathered his mother, Violetta; younger brother, Henri; and his little sister, Grace, and explained what he had seen. They had packed and gone straight to Evelyn's mother's house. She didn't need persuading; Hermione woke up her two young sons, and they quickly packed some clothes, their few valuables, and some fruit and water. Herve led the two women and four children out of the village and straight into the forest. The lights were still blazing in the school hall, and they could hear the men shouting and cheering. They walked through the night toward the UN camp at Goma, sticking to a path that Herve knew the coltan smugglers used. He had no intention of using the main road. They had told the children that they were having a big adventure, and they had to keep silent or they would lose the game. They had stared at him, tired and confused, half-puzzled and half-knowing that this was not a game at all. But none of them had cried or complained.

Just as they were coming out of the forest, a few hundred yards from the UN checkpoint, they had run into an ECLF patrol. The soldiers took them back to the militia checkpoint, where they were all now held at gunpoint. The checkpoint commander was a Tutsi—tall, thin, and suspicious, with two fingers missing from his left hand. He ordered the boy soldier to lower his gun and demanded Herve's and the others' papers. They produced their documents.

He idly read them and placed them in his pocket. "Well, well. Look what the new day brings. *Genocidaires*. How much money did you steal from us when you weren't killing us? Empty your bags and your pockets," he snapped.

Herve looked at his mother and Hermione. It was useless

to protest. He felt sick with fear and shame. He had done this. He had brought them to this place. He had wanted to save his and Evelyn's family. Instead he brought them into terrible danger. The two women looked resigned and placed their nylon bags on the table. Grace began to cry. The commander stroked her head, but she only cried louder. He rifled through the clothes, throwing them aside until the bag was empty and they lay in the mud. The women then opened their pockets to show they were empty.

The Tutsi commander laughed and jammed his hand between Herve's mother's legs. She gasped, her face twisting in pain. Herve moved to help her, but the boy soldier hit him with his rifle butt in his leg. Herve cried out and his leg gave way underneath him. The commander put his hand up his mother's skirt, and Herve held back tears of humiliation as he struggled to stand up. The commander rummaged around under the fabric and pulled out a rolled-up wad of bank notes. Hermione and her sons looked terrified. Two more ECLF soldiers appeared and cocked their guns, pointing them at Hermione and her sons. The two boys started trembling, and two puddles appeared at their feet.

The commander took in the scene, laughed, and put the money in his pockets. "Very nice, sister. Let's see what else you have up there," he said, taking Herve's mother's hand to lead her away. Herve caught her eye. She shook her head, her eyes imploring him not to intervene.

Grace suddenly started running up the road toward the UN checkpoint. Everyone turned to watch her, her pink flip-flops making small slapping sounds on the tarmac road. The boy soldier turned to aim at her as she drew nearer to the French peacekeepers. Herve's mother let out a howl of anguish.

The commander eased the boy soldier's gun down. "Don't waste bullets."

Several peacekeepers had now come out to see what was happening, alerted by the commotion down the road. They held cups of coffee and sandwiches, wondering what was interrupting their breakfast. Grace kept going, sprinting toward the men. Several of the peacekeepers clapped and shouted encouragement, until she ran straight into the legs of one of the UN troops. He laughed and picked up the little girl. Herve's mother started crying. Herve smiled. Whatever was about to happen to him, at least his little sister was safe.

The peacekeeper pulled something from his pocket and showed it to Grace. She nodded enthusiastically, pulled the wrapper off, and started to eat, smiling happily, the chocolate smeared across her face. The peacekeeper turned to one of the other UN troops and asked something. He shook his head decisively. The first peacekeeper saluted, hoisted Grace up onto his shoulders, and started walking back down the road—back toward the ECLF checkpoint.

Twenty-Six

Yael walked briskly along the narrow wooden walkway that ran through the Place des Nations, taking care not to slip on the wet planks. It was just after 5:35 a.m., and Geneva's international quarter was waking up under a slowly lightening gray sky and thin drizzle. She pulled her leather jacket tighter around her, huddling in her purple scarf as a gust of cold, wet wind blew across the square. Despite its grand name—inspired by the Palais des Nations, the United Nations Geneva headquarters that stood on the plaza's north side—the Place des Nations was not very impressive.

The intersection at the Avenue de France, one of the city's main traffic arteries, was surrounded by flat-fronted, 1960s-style office buildings. A bare concrete piazza and scrubby, unkempt park, which turned to a sea of mud whenever it rained, stood in the middle. Even so, this was the important real estate in Geneva, a prized address for aid and development organizations and the UN's myriad satellite organizations. Even at this hour the road was crowded with early-morning commuters, the headlights of their cars reflecting white and yellow in the oil-smeared puddles.

Yael gingerly walked past a large slab of dark gray granite that faced out onto the Avenue de France, toward the UN headquarters. "Bosna i Hercegovina 1992–1995. Srebrenica 11. Juli 1995" was painted on the front in gold letters, a mute reminder of the UN's culpability in the massacre. Yael had been there when the memorial had been unveiled. It was not much of a commemoration for the lives of eight thousand people, she had thought then and still did now. More useful, perhaps, would be a banner asking, "Where were you on that day?" with a display of the photographs of the numerous UN officials and peacekeepers, including Fareed Hussein, who had been on holiday as the Serbs pounded the UN safe area. Who did not think it necessary to return to their desks until its fall was inevitable. Who somehow had ensured that no air strikes took place against the Bosnian Serbs.

Any sense of personal responsibility for that catastrophe was in short supply, but there was no lack of the sentimental symbolism so beloved of the UN. A large-caliber howitzer stood nearby, mounted on four steel legs, slowly rusting in the damp air. The gun's barrel was twisted into a knot, and a large metal wheel was hanging off the tip. The memory of being escorted out of the UN building in New York flashed into her mind, together with the giant pistol sculpture, with its barrel twisted into a knot. Except now, she thought ironically, it seemed that the UN, or part of it, was in the weapons distribution—not abolition—business.

Another sculpture, a brown wooden chair, twelve yards

high, stood in the center of the square. One of the chair legs was snapped off two thirds of the way up to symbolize the casualties caused by land mines and cluster bombs. The Broken Chair, as it was known, was a popular site for demonstrations, especially when the UN was in session and the world's dictators came to Geneva to be courted and flattered. Even at this early hour, she saw the first demonstrators already gathering under the truncated leg. They were Iranian dissidents, many of them headscarved women. The three dozen protestors stood silently, holding large placards covered with gruesome photographs of scarred and broken limbs, the handiwork of the regime loyalists who interrogated their comrades in the basement of Tehran's Evin Prison.

Yael saw that another group was gathering on the other side of the chair, chatting with the Iranians. She crossed the road and wandered by to take a closer look. Some were European, but many were Africans, carrying banners and signs. "UN Stop Helping Coltan Plunderers," read one. "KZX Stop Pillaging Congo," read another. And a third, held by a smartly dressed young Indian woman, proclaimed, "Hypocrite Hussein: No to Goma KZX Zone." The woman looked familiar. Yes, it was Rina, the SG's daughter. Yael's life had been turned upside down and inside out, but at least some things never changed, she thought, smiling to herself as she walked past the demonstrators and crossed the Avenue de la Paix to the front of the Palais des Nations.

Yael stopped for a moment in front of the building. The Palais was as imposing as ever, far more so than the UN's New York headquarters. The Secretariat building was scruffy, dilapidated, and showed its age. The Palais was decades older but was still smart, grandiose, and far more stylish. Built in the 1930s in a mix of art deco and modernist giganticism, clad in cream-colored granite, the UN's Geneva headquarters was nearly two-thirds of a mile long. The approach road was lined on both sides by well-tended trees and rows of the member states' flags, each mounted on a steel pole, topped with polished brass. The Palais was surrounded by vast manicured gardens and parks, all open to the public. Peacocks roamed the grounds, which extended all the way to the banks of Lake Geneva. The front of the building—most of the sidewalk—was now blocked off by two rows of stand-alone fences, and Yael barely had space to stand as she peered toward the façade.

She suddenly felt an overwhelming nostalgia for her old life. She had been through here countless times, sitting next to Fareed Hussein in a long black Audi or Mercedes driven by a black-suited chauffeur, a pile of confidential briefing papers and reports from friendly intelligence agencies on her lap. Flanked by outriders at the front and back, blue flags over the headlights flapping in the wind, their motorcade would drive through the gateway, down the promenade past the trees, under the vast main archway, and into the Palais complex, escorting them straight into the company of the world's most powerful leaders. She had loved it, of course, that feeling of being on the inside track, that she was one of the select, the elite who knew how the world really worked. She admitted, to herself at least, that she missed it all very much.

And now she was back, although on a very different mission. She had considered, even discussed with Joe-Don, simply telling Sami Boustani everything she knew so far and blowing the story open. But apart from the sound file, it was mostly words, deductions, and suppositions. The recording might be enough, she guessed, to stop KZX and the Bonnet Group and bring down the SG. But even that was not certain. The sound file would be denounced as a fake, and a team of experts would be assembled to show how it was put together. Hussein and KZX would deny everything and brazen it out. And after a few days, as she herself had explained to Hakizimani, the media circus would move on.

But even if the SG did have to resign, that would not be enough for her. Someone had sent the file to her and for a reason. There were always wheels within wheels at the UN. It was quite possible, even highly likely, that she was being used in some complicated game, although for what purpose she could not fathom. So this was something she needed to do for herself. She wanted the proof of the plan for the war. And today she would get it. She had given more than a decade of her life to the UN. It would end on her terms, not theirs.

Yael flexed her hands again, trying to stop the itching in her fingertips. Joe-Don had spent half an hour that morning carefully applying the fake fingerprints, and she was strictly forbidden to scratch them. A female voice interrupted her reverie. "Your papers, please, mademoiselle." Yael turned to see a police officer holding her hand out. She was young, barely out of her teens, and skinny with straggly brown hair. An older male officer, tall and balding, stood watching nearby.

Yael reached into her jacket and handed over Claudia's passport. The policewoman flicked through it. She stared at the photograph and then back at Yael. "You are out early, mademoiselle. What is the purpose of your visit to Geneva? Why are you standing here by the entrance to the United Nations?"

"Because somewhere in that building is proof of a plot by UN and State Department officials, KZX, and the Bonnet Group to trigger a war across Africa, so that they can take over the world's supply of coltan," she had an overwhelming urge to reply. "Once I have the details I will hand them to the *New York Times* because I like its UN correspondent. I thought he liked me, but he is only interested in what information I can provide, sadly. After that you can arrest me and extradite me to New York where I killed a man, although he deserved it."

Yael smiled cordially at the policewoman. "I am a student. I just arrived and am a little jet-lagged. I woke up early and thought I would come and see the UN and go for a walk in the park. Are there really peacocks there?"

The policewoman nodded gravely and handed Yael her passport back. "Yes, a few. It's part of the city's agreement with the UN. But, mademoiselle, please be careful today. There is a big demonstration planned, and there will be many dignitaries here. The protest has been permitted, but there will be a very heavy police presence. So please keep your papers with you and stay away from any trouble. Enjoy your stay in Geneva."

Yael thanked her, and turned left along the Avenue de la Paix, following the curve of the road toward the visitors' entrance. The lights were on in the Russian mission nearby, and she watched a large Mercedes emerge from the enormous gate, its passenger invisible behind tinted windows. Jasna was waiting for her outside the visitor's entrance. This was less grand than the main gate, but the side view of the Palais' high walls was still impressive. A narrow island topped with grass stood in between the entry and exit access roads. The UN police sat in a large black and steel cubicle just behind the island, checking the papers of incoming drivers. Even at this early hour the vehicles were lined up waiting to be checked.

Jasna took Yael's arm as they walked past the cars and toward the pedestrian entrance on the side of the building. "Sleep well, *draga*?" she asked.

Yael shook her head. "No. He snores."

"I know. Like a tractor," she said, laughing as they walked inside.

Visitors to the UN building in New York had to pass through a tent. The Palais visitors' entrance still had a sense of solidity and grandeur: the foyer was wide and spacious with large windows, a high ceiling, and well-polished floor. Long blue banners spanned the length of each wall announcing the UN Year of Africa, each with the KZX logo displayed as large as the UN's own symbol. The visitors' security area stood in the center, next to an X-ray screening machine and walk-through metal detector. UN police sat inside the island, behind a pale wooden wall, checking the CCTV monitors that covered the inside and the outside of the complex.

A tall, suntanned UN policeman with carefully barbered gray hair, even features, and lively hazel eyes sat behind the reception desk in his blue uniform. His nametag, one end of which was not properly attached to the Velcro fastener on his shirt, said "Robertson." He was still a handsome man and clearly knew it as he smiled at Jasna flirtatiously.

"We're in luck," she murmured to Yael as they walked over to him.

"Hello, darling. New recruit?" the policeman asked with a strong Australian accent.

"*Draga*, where have you been? I've missed you. This is Claudia. She is going to be working with me," said Jasna as she gave him her UN pass. "I'm showing her around this morning, before it all gets too crazy."

The policeman gave Jasna's ID a cursory glance. "Yup, big day today. Now, darling, when are you going to cook me that Serbian dinner you keep promising? I've got just the bottle of Australian red to go with it," he said, still holding on to Jasna's ID and smiling at her.

Jasna smiled back and reached for her plastic pass, her eyes open wide with promise. "Soon. Very soon. I promise. Once Claudia has started work and can take some of the pressure off."

"Just tell me when and where. I will be there," said Robertson as he let go of the ID. He turned to Yael. "Where are you from, Claudia?"

"Costa Rica."

"OK, Costa Rica, your passport you give to me, the fingers of your right hand you place here," he said, sliding a small machine with a glass plate on the cover toward here.

Yael handed her passport to the policeman and placed her fingers on the glass. Her heart started thumping.

The machine clicked and flashed. The policeman moved

the machine back and looked at the results. He shook his head. The thumping became a pounding.

Robertson frowned. "This new technology. Supposed to make life easier, but just makes everything more complicated. It's showing a problem with the results. It cannot read your fingerprints and check them against the database. Dunno why."

The policeman looked up at her. "You are not a terrorist, are you, Claudia?" he asked. "Or a radical political activist or anarchist?" His voice was light and friendly, but Yael saw that his eyes were alert and his posture changed. He was sitting up straight, focused, and now watching her with interest. What was the problem?

"Michael, what a question," said Jasna before Yael had a chance to answer. "Of course not. She is a student."

The policeman looked at Yael again, clearly torn between his crush on Jasna and the machine's rejection of Yael's fingerprints. "Try to keep still. Maybe you moved."

Claudia did as he bid. She stood completely still and slowed her breathing down. The machine clicked and flashed again. The policeman looked down at the results. He nodded, satisfied. "OK, that's fine. Just one more thing. Then I can give you your pass. The SG is here today, as I am sure you know, with lots of VIPs and dignitaries. So there is an extra security check. All visitors have to undergo retinal identification. The iris scans will be checked against our database. Should only take a few minutes. If the system is working, that is. We tried it this morning and it took half an hour. So you might have to wait for a while."

Yael nodded, her stomach churning, her heart racing again. This was a disaster. A total disaster. It was over before she stepped inside the place. They knew there would be a passport and fingerprint check and had prepared for those. But Joe-Don had said nothing about a retina check. There was no way to fake a retina scan, even with her brown contact lenses. All of her biometric details were stored on the UN database. Her real identity would flash up instantly.

Robertson immediately sensed her unease. "Is there a problem, Claudia?" he asked, his voice decidedly less friendly.

Jasna leaned forward before Yael could answer. "Michael . . . we should be in and out in an hour, long before the VIPs get here. I can vouch for Claudia. The problem is that she has an appointment with the police at 9:00 a.m. to sort out her residence and work permit. You know how long they take to arrange. If she misses that it could be months before she gets another. And then I won't have anyone to help me run the company, which takes up all my time, and then I won't see my kitchen for months . . ."

The policeman gave Jasna a wry look. "I don't know, we are under strict instructions. All those VIPs . . ." he said, his voice trailing off. Yael sensed him softening.

"*Draga*, how long have we known each other?" asked Jasna, looking him in the eye and smiling promisingly.

"Years. I've lost count."

Jasna nodded regretfully. "So many wasted years. Then it is about time that we got to know each other a little better, wouldn't you say? How about Sunday," she said, pushing the end of his nametag back into place, her finger lingering on his chest.

Robertson looked at Yael, at Jasna, and back at Yael for several long seconds. “Sunday it is, darling,” he said, waving them through.

Twenty-Seven

Herve watched incredulously as the Dutch peacekeeper put Grace down. She ran to her mother, who instantly picked her up, held her as tight as she could, and started sobbing. The UN soldier was a sergeant in his midtwenties—broad-shouldered and fit-looking with blue eyes, a shaved head, and a nametag that read "Van Dijk." He shook hands enthusiastically with the Tutsi commander as they exchanged greetings.

"One of yours, I think," the peacekeeper said, gesturing at the little girl, who was watching wide-eyed from her mother's shoulder.

"That's right," said the ECLF commander as he laughed and slapped the Dutchman's back.

"Monsieur, please, can't you help us?" asked Herve.

Van Dijk looked at him as though he had asked for a loan of ten thousand euros. He shrugged. "How?"

"We were trying to get to the UN Goma camp. We are nearly there."

The peacekeeper looked Herve up and down disdainfully. He pulled out a tin of cheroots and lit up, offering one to the commander and lighting it for him. "Keep it," the Dutchman said. The Tutsi smiled appreciatively and slipped the tin into his pocket. An engine noise rumbled in the distance, deep and low.

Van Dijk turned back to Herve. "The camp is closed. Orders. No more to be admitted. Don't worry. You are in good hands here."

Herve shook his head, his voice pleading. "Please, monsieur, these men are threatening us. Can't you see?"

The peacekeeper turned, taking in the sight of Herve and Evelyn's family, surrounded by ECLF soldiers pointing their guns at them. He shrugged. "Security checks. This is a war zone," he said as the engine noise grew louder. "I told you. The camp is closed. Those are our orders."

"Monsieur, I beg you, at least take the children," Herve asked.

The Dutchman dropped the cheroot on the ground, his lips pursed in distaste. "Stop whining."

The ECLF commander gestured at Violetta and Hermione. "Do you want the women?" he asked Van Dijk.

The Dutchman shook his head. "No. Too old."

The peacekeeper turned on his feet to see two white UN armored personnel carriers speeding toward them. One parked in front of the checkpoint, juddering back and forth as it halted. The other lurched off the road and turned in a tight circle so that it was facing the checkpoint from behind, sending up clouds of red dust. A peacekeeper stood in the turret of each APC, training a heavy machine gun on the scene. The door of the first vehicle opened and a ruddy-faced, red-haired Englishman in a UN uniform jumped out.

The Dutch peacekeeper immediately snapped to attention and saluted.

Quentin Braithwaite walked over to the ECLF commander, who returned his salute. Braithwaite ignored the Dutch soldier and looked at the militiaman with contempt. The ECLF commander stared at him uncomprehendingly. What was this about? The UN had access to satellite intelligence and had its own military observers on the ground. The peacekeepers knew that the ECLF was active in the area, of course, but several packets of uncut diamonds handed to local UN commanders and a ready supply of local girls for the UN troops had so far ensured that the ECLF could operate with complete freedom.

"Do you know what a .50-caliber machine gun does to the human body?" Braithwaite asked.

The commander nodded nervously.

"Excellent, because there are two of them pointed at you as we speak," said Braithwaite, holding his hand out.

The militiaman looked right and left at the APCs. The machine gunners stared at him impassively. He reached in his pocket and handed Grace's banknotes and the families' papers to Braithwaite.

"Good start. Now your men—I won't call them soldiers—are going to surrender their weapons. Aren't they?"

"Yes," said the commander, shaking.

Braithwaite snapped: "All guns under the APC tracks."

The commander looked puzzled. "I don't understand."

"It's very simple. Your men will put all their weapons under the tracks of the armored personnel carrier."

"But then we will not be able to defend ourselves."

Braithwaite looked up at the machine gunner in the first APC. He unlocked the weapon with a loud click and chambered a round.

"No safety on the .50. Once he pulls the trigger, that's it," said Braithwaite.

"Put your guns under the APC, quickly," the commander shouted at his troops, in a vain attempt to assert some authority.

Braithwaite watched as they slid the weapons under the tracks. He nodded. "Now tell your men to pick up these good people's clothes and other possessions and hand them back."

The ECLF commander did as he was ordered. Herve and the others watched in amazement as the soldiers gave them their clothes back. Braithwaite nodded with satisfaction and then gestured to Herve and the two families to come toward him. He opened the door of the APC, standing over them as they clambered in, the children chattering excitedly.

Van Dijk looked at him inquiringly.

Braithwaite said, "Give me your pistol."

The Dutch peacekeeper looked shocked.

Braithwaite said, "Are you deaf, man?"

Van Dijk handed him his weapon, his eyes darting back and forth from Braithwaite to the UN checkpoint.

Braithwaite said, "You can walk back to base. When you get there, you will write a full report on this incident. I will read it so it will be accurate, and I will forward it to the Dutch

Ministry of Defense. The̲n you will pack your bags and take the first plane to Kinshasa. From there you will travel to The Hague. You are a disgrace to this uniform and the UN mission. Now stand still."

The Dutchman flinched, waiting for what he knew was coming. Braithwaite grabbed the epaulet above his right shoulder and yanked it hard. The fabric ripped and the strip of cloth came away in his hands. Van Dijk stared out, rigid with shame and anger. Braithwaite grabbed the epaulet on his left shoulder and pulled so hard the Dutchman almost fell forward into the dust. Braithwaite handed both strips of cloth to the peacekeeper. "You can show that to your commander. Now get going," he ordered, his voice full of contempt.

Braithwaite watched for half a minute as the Dutchman walked up the road to the UN. Braithwaite followed the families into the armored vehicle and closed the door with a loud thunk. The APC's engine coughed and emitted a large plume of exhaust fumes, and the vehicle moved forward over the guns, crushing them under its tracks like matchwood.

Sami and Najwa sat in the lobby of the Council Chamber of the Palais des Nations, flicking through the media accreditation list for that morning's joint UN-KZX Africa press conference. Clad in the same cream-colored stone as the façade of the building, the two-story-high entrance hall was airy and spacious. The sparse furnishings only accentuated the elegance of its 1930s design. "The Ascent of Man," a giant triptych bas-relief by the sculptor Eric Gill, was mounted on the wall above the glass and metal door. The morning sun had temporarily defeated the clouds, and bright light poured in through the glass ceiling; the iron frame holding the sections of glass together reflected on the smooth, polished marble floor. Najwa's camerawoman and sound engineer sat on an identical maroon leather sofa on the other side of the entrance, their heads resting against the walls, still half-asleep.

They were more than two hours early—it was not yet 7:00 a.m., and the media event was not due to start until 9:00 in the Council Chamber. Najwa had insisted on being there first so that her camera crew could position themselves in the center of the front row of cameras. Sami put the press list down and sat back, his hands behind his head, staring at the glass ceiling and thinking. The American media, indeed most of the world's, had been full of the news that President Freshwater's husband had been killed in a skiing accident. The conspiracy-minded websites were asking how such a high-profile figure could be allowed to take to the slopes with faulty bindings. The right-wing media was calling up an endless stream of experts to testify to the danger of off-piste skiing, including a former American Olympic champion who was now confined to a wheelchair after he hit a tree in Aspen, Colorado.

President Freshwater was now on compassionate leave. The United States was technically being run by the vice president, Horace Grosvenor, an ultraliberal former governor of California, who had been appointed as a sop to the party's left fringe. Most analysts agreed that he was wildly out of his depth. Marc Rosenheim, the secretary of state, was having an excellent crisis, constantly appearing on television news channels, assuring voters that the White House was in safe hands, and making pronouncements on everything from the still-soaring national debt to the latest suicide bombings in Afghanistan.

Sami suddenly remembered that he had not read the *Times* of London yet. Had Jonathan Beaufort dug up anything new? And he still owed him a favor for the tip-off for the 42nd Street press conference. Sami opened his smartphone's web browser and clicked on the *Times* app. There was indeed a story by Jonathan Beaufort, datelined New York: "Military Contractors Clash with Peacekeepers in Congo." The article reported that an armored four-by-four SUV had refused to stop at a new UN checkpoint just outside the UN camp at Goma.

Peacekeepers had opened fire on the vehicle's tires. The car had skidded off the road and crashed. Nobody had been seriously hurt, but the vehicle had been carrying hundreds of rounds of ammunition and twelve crates of new AK-47s. The driver and passengers initially claimed to be aid workers and that the weapons were for their personal protection. Documents found in the car revealed that they were working for EGS. They had been arrested by the UN troops, treated for minor injuries, and were now being held at the UN military prison outside the capital, Kinshasa. The story was sourced to "peacekeeping officials," which by UN standards was about as on the record as it got. A spokesman for EGS blamed the incident on a misunderstanding. The company had not been notified about the new checkpoint and had believed it to be manned by local militia members in stolen UN uniforms. Henrik Schneidermann, the SG's spokesman, promised that the UN would launch an inquiry into the incident.

Well done, Jonathan; that is interesting, thought Sami. But who were the "peacekeeping officials" that were talking? He turned to Najwa, who was still flicking through the media list, shaking her head.

"Are you sure we are in the right place?" she asked. "*Grazia*, *Hello!*, *Now*, OK!, *People*, *Star* magazine, and who are the 3AM Girls?"

"Gossip columnists for the *Sun* in London."

"And they are interested in the UN-KZX Goma Development Zone?"

"I doubt it."

"Then what are all these celebrity magazines doing here?"

"I don't know. But take a look at this," he said, handing Najwa his smartphone with the *Times* of London's story open on the screen.

Sami looked up just as two women walked down the lobby toward him and Najwa. One was handsome, in her fifties, blond, and smartly dressed, while the second was much younger, taller, and slimmer, with spiky black hair. She was attractive, but it was more than that. There was something about her that seemed familiar—in the way she walked or held herself, perhaps, or the set of her eyes above her nose and generous mouth. The younger woman had been watching him and Najwa, he sensed, but as soon as he looked at her she turned away.

The two women walked past him and around the sofa and stopped in front of the door to the Council Chamber. The older one pushed hard on the large bronze handle but it did not move. Sami stood up to help. They stepped back as he gave the handle a hefty push and the heavy door gave way. The blond woman thanked him, but the younger one did not say anything and seemed curiously reluctant to meet his eye. Maybe she was just shy, he thought. Sami watched them walk into the Council Chamber while the door closed behind them. He was still wondering about the encounter when Najwa gently elbowed him in the side.

"Very good story. I never liked EGS. And stop staring at girls, Sami. I told you I am going to introduce you to my cousin," she said, handing Sami back his telephone. "Now look who is here," she said enthusiastically, as a tall Englishman walked over.

Najwa stood up to kiss Jonathan Beaufort on both cheeks. A bald, tubby photographer laden down with camera bags and telephoto lenses and a skinny young black-haired woman followed him, both talking loudly on their mobile telephones.

Sami also stood up and the two men shook hands. "Good morning and welcome to the world of celebrity journalism," said Beaufort, gesturing at the two others to come over. "This is Dave, our arts photographer, and Samantha, our contemporary-culture correspondent." Samantha had a pierced nose and dreadlocks. She grinned and waved enthusiastically with one hand, still speaking on her mobile telephone. "Definitely, yeah, definitely," she said, nodding decisively. "I've spoken to her people and they say we can have ten minutes, just the two of us. No copy approval, but they want to check any direct quotes, OK? I'll tweet the headline as soon as I have it."

Dave's head was already shiny with sweat. He shook hands, nodded, smiled tensely, and started checking his equipment.

He pointed a camera with a lens the size of a small artillery shell at the front of the Council Chamber door, peered into the viewfinder, and began walking slowly backward.

"Where's *your* contemporary-culture correspondent, Sami?" Jonathan asked wryly.

"I don't know. Somewhere contemporary and cultural I guess," said Sami. He watched, fascinated, as Dave advanced toward the centerpiece of the lobby, a blue, two-meter-high Japanese porcelain vase, with a white map of the world on an indigo background.

"I told you we were in the wrong place," said Najwa.

"No, darling, we are not," said Jonathan.

He held a rolled-up copy of yesterday's *International Herald Tribune* with Sami's story on the front page. "Nice work," he said, tapping the newspaper.

"Thanks. You did a good piece on EGS. Who's talking in the DPKO?"

Jonathan looked at Sami with amusement. "Sami, my dear old mate and esteemed colleague. As far as I remember, I offered to trade leads for a copy of the Goma memo. You declined." He looked up at the ceiling and scratched his head, baffled at the ways of the world. "A *New York Times* exclusive, your very words. And I still tipped you off about the 42nd Street presser. So I think the *New York Times* account at the moment at the Beaufort sources bank has slipped into the red. But . . . I got a good run in the paper, so I'm feeling generous today. My original offer still stands: a copy of the Goma memo and lunch at the Delegates Dining Room. On you."

Sami smiled. The story had moved so far on by now it would be churlish to refuse. "It's a deal. I've got it scanned. I will e-mail it to you."

Jonathan leaned forward and whispered. "Good. You didn't hear this from me, but Quentin Braithwaite is in eastern Congo—and he is really pissed off. What . . . ?" asked Jonathan, seeing the look of alarm on Sami's face.

"I think your photographer is about to cause a diplomatic incident," he said, pointing at Dave, who was now just two feet from the priceless artifact.

Jonathan shouted at him to watch out. The photographer stopped and looked around, realization dawning on his face. He mopped his brow and held a hand up in supplication.

Jonathan laughed. "Even I could not get that one through on expenses. But we had better get our questions in early today. We are going to be seriously outnumbered."

Twenty-Eight

Yael tried to put her emotions aside as she walked into the Council Chamber. She felt curiously pleased to see familiar faces, somehow even felt reassured that Sami, Jonathan Beaufort, and Najwa were here. Their presence was a reminder that several extremely able reporters were also on the trail of KZX and the Bonnet Group. But it was a bittersweet encounter, reminding her of her old life and of her growing feelings for Sami before his story wrecked her life.

Yael stopped and looked around at the familiar surroundings. The Council Chamber was not the largest room in the Palais des Nations—that honor was held by the Assembly Hall, which could hold two thousand people. But it was an elegant and atmospheric space that retained a powerful sense of history. The dropped ceiling and the cream stone walls at the rear and the sides were lined with giant frescoes donated by the Second Spanish Republic in the 1930s. They showed the themes so beloved of the United Nations: toiling laborers, scientists, artists, and more gun barrels. A balcony curved around the width of the room. Long before Rwanda and Srebrenica, the League of Nations had struggled in this very room to save Abyssinia, as Ethiopia was then known, while the country was pounded by Mussolini's air force, its inhabitants bombed and gassed. Haile Selassie, Ethiopia's emperor himself, had come here to plead for help—in vain.

Jasna paused in the middle of the chamber, standing in front of the salmon-pink curtains that extended almost from the floor to the ceiling. She looked at Yael, interrupting her reverie. "You know those journalists outside?"

Yael smiled wryly. "In another life."

"And you want it back?"

"I don't know," said Yael. She walked over to Jasna and stood next to her, playing with the curtain. "I want to sleep in my own bed."

"With the curly-haired boy? He could be quite handsome if he smartened himself up."

Yael flushed. "Is it that obvious?"

Jasna smiled kindly. "Let's get to work."

The UN-KZX Institute for International Development was spread out over six rooms in the east wing of the Palais. During the 1930s they had housed the financial department of the League of Nations. Until recently they were home to the Geneva office of the Organizing Committee of the Week of Solidarity with Indigenous Peoples Affected by Global Warming. The committee's members had gladly agreed for themselves, their families, and their workplaces to be relocated to New York at the UN's expense to make way for the new institute.

Yael left Jasna at the elevator and walked down the corridor on her own to the director's office at the end. The plan was that Jasna, who had a good reason to be in the area this early, would wait by the elevator and cover her, pretending to check the state of the place, while she kept watch on the elevator and the nearby staircase. Meanwhile, Yael would search the office. Jasna had given her the key.

If anyone appeared, Jasna would delay him or her as long as possible with questions about cleaning and office maintenance for the new setup, and she would surreptitiously send Yael a text from her mobile phone in her coat pocket. Yael would immediately leave. Even if the institute's staff came in as early as 8:00 a.m.—which in her experience with the UN was highly unlikely—Yael should have well over an hour to find the evidence. And most of them would probably be at the press conference, basking in the media limelight, not in their offices.

That was the theory, assuming she was in the right city to start with. Yael could still hear Hakizimani's answer when she had asked him if the war plan would be directed from the UN's New York headquarters. "Of course not," he had sneered. "Why do you think they have set up the development institute? There are too many journalists poking around the UN in New York, but who cares about those endless meetings in Switzerland? Nobody."

He could have been lying, Yael supposed, but it was unlikely. She could spot liars, and she remembered the pleasure he had taken in telling her what he knew. Something as secret and complicated as this, involving the UN secretary-general, the DPA, KZX, the Bonnet Group, and, she guessed, Efrat Global Solutions, must be set out in detail somewhere. Probably only three or four people would be cleared to see the master plan. But it had to exist, because otherwise it would be impossible to coordinate so many different actors spread across three continents on a precise timetable. The plan would almost certainly not be on a networked computer or a machine with access to the Internet. It might be on an encrypted document stored on an "air-gapped"—stand-alone—machine, or a data stick. It was also possible that it did not even exist in electronic form because any digital version would be a security risk. Maybe there would only be a hard copy on paper.

The rest of her life hinged on the next hour, she realized. If she brought out the evidence of the conspiracy, she would be a heroine. If she did not and were caught, she would be arrested and extradited back to New York to stand trial for the murder of Hakizimani—not to mention all the other stuff about traveling on a dead woman's passport—and would spend the rest of her life in prison. She felt the walls of the corridor closing in on her as she walked toward the director's office. The voice in her head was back. It spoke each time she went on a mission. Incredulous and laughing at her arrogance, it was talking now, a familiar monologue. Look at you, it said: a wastrel, hardly any friends, estranged from your mother, cut off from your father, no man, no children, a nomad who doesn't even know what country to call home, an orphan in all but name. Who are you to think you can do *anything*?

She knew not to argue back. Instead she stopped for a moment and leaned back against the wall, emptying her mind, clenching and unclenching her fists, and slowing her breathing. The voice grew tired and small and then faded away.

Yael slipped the key in the office lock. She took the key out and carefully pushed the dark, heavy wood panel. The door smoothly opened and she gingerly looked inside. It was a large and elegant office, the kind of workplace she would like to have herself, with a highly polished wooden floor and huge windows looking out on the park and Lake Geneva. A Persian silk carpet with an intricate peacock pattern hung on the wall. The office had obviously been newly decorated. It smelled of paint and coffee from the machine bubbling in the corner.

A tall, well-built man with a soldier's posture was standing at the window with his back to her, reading a document. He turned around and looked Yael up and down.

"Bonjour, mademoiselle. I am the director here. How can I help you?" asked Charles Bonnet.

Yael betrayed nothing of the shock she felt at the sight of the Frenchman. Not only was the office not empty, but its sole occupant was someone with whom she had worked for years, someone who knew her face, voice, and mannerisms. But she also knew Bonnet. She smiled engagingly, holding his gaze. Under his *savoir-faire* she sensed suspicion, alarm, defensiveness, and strong sexual interest.

She was wearing slim-cut jeans, knee-high boots, and a tight black polo shirt under her new leather jacket, and she could feel his eyes roaming up and down her body. Yael slowly walked toward him, breathing in, making sure to raise her breasts as she pointed at his desk. It was a heavy, old-fashioned wooden thing that doubtless dated back to the League of Nations itself, with two small chests of drawers on either side and a large green square of baize in the middle. The desk was empty apart from a legal pad and a brass penholder filled with pens emblazoned with the KZX and UN logos.

Yael pointed at the penholder and gestured at the notepad as if to say, "May I?"

Bonnet frowned at first, then nodded, watching her now with amusement and growing interest, she sensed. Whatever this was about, she imagined him thinking, she was no threat.

Yael wrote on the paper:

My name is Claudia Lopez. I work for Tip-Top Office Services. We clean this part of the Palais. This is a beautiful office. You must be very important. I am mute. Sorry.

Yael handed the note to Bonnet. He quickly read it and smiled at her with the grin that he imagined was boyishly charming. For a moment she almost wished she were back in the DPKO operations room, refusing yet another dinner invitation. Another part of her was quelling her rising fear that Bonnet would recognize her. But the only thing that could give her away was her voice. People saw what they wanted to: the trick, as any magician could tell you, was to keep the audience plausibly diverted. The silk handkerchiefs that materialized from behind an ear, the coin in a palm—they had either been there all the time or hidden in plain view. As long as Bonnet was interested in Claudia Lopez, and he seemed to be, Yael Azoulay should be safe. But how was she going to get the war plan now? And where was it?

Bonnet walked around behind his desk and sat down.

He put the document he was holding on the green baize square. Yael quickly read the heading: "Report on the Panel of Experts on the Illegal Exploitation of Natural Resources and Other Forms of Wealth of the Democratic Republic of Congo." It was the document that she had read on the airplane from Paris to Kinshasa when she had flown out to meet Hakizimani. Bonnet saw her glance at the report. He put it in the right-hand drawer of his desk and turned the key in the lock. He then slid the paper on which Yael had written toward him, took out a pen and wrote, *There is no need to apologize. Would you like some coffee?*

Yael down sat on the edge of his desk, pulled the paper toward her, and wrote, *I can hear fine. You can talk to me, but I cannot reply. And yes please.*

Bonnet walked over to the coffee machine and poured two cups. He walked back toward her, holding a cup of coffee balanced on a saucer in each hand, and smiled at her.

"I am sorry we don't have any British builder's tea," he said.

Twenty-Nine

Every seat in the Council Chamber was taken, and the journalists were two or three deep in the balcony. Najwa and her Al-Jazeera crew had secured a place in the center of the front row, but they were surrounded by Fashion TV, MTV, and a crew from the Trevor Johnson show at CNN. The other serious news channels had been banished to the back rows and the side of the hall. Sami and Jonathan sat two rows back, next to a feature writer from Italian *Vogue* who was utterly absorbed in texting her friends.

A giant banner emblazoned with "UN Year of Africa" and the UN and KZX logos stretched along the wall behind them. Many of the reporters were opening a small wooden box stamped "sustainable hardwood" that had been placed on every journalist's seat. In addition to brochures and press releases about the UN-KZX institute, it contained a silver UN-KZX pen, an iPhone 5, a signed DVD of Lucy Tremlett's film about Queen Elizabeth I, a Tag Heuer watch—also marked with the UN-KZX logo, albeit more discreetly—and two signed copies of Fareed Hussein's memoir, *My Journey for Peace*.

Henrik Schneidermann had appeared half an hour before the conference started and asked for all questions to be submitted in writing. He then handed out a long and detailed form that had been specially printed for the occasion—a departure from the usual UN practice. The celebrity reporters complied. The vociferous protests of the specialist UN correspondents had been ignored. Sami, Jonathan, Najwa, and several others had briefly discussed a boycott of the event, until it was clear that nothing would make Schneidermann happier.

They and their colleagues had submitted detailed questions about events in Goma and the web of connections between KZX, the Bonnet Group, and the UN. There was particular interest in Jonathan Beaufort's story in the *Times* of London about the EGS contractors.

Jonathan handed the forms to Schneidermann. He flicked through them and added them to his folder, ostentatiously putting them at the bottom of the pile.

The spokesman looked at the reporters, barely able to keep the triumph out of his eyes. "I will forward your questions to the SG. But as you can see, this is a very crowded event, and we will give priority to reporters who are new to the UN."

"And who have absolutely no idea what to ask," snapped Najwa.

Yael stepped forward and kicked Bonnet's right wrist as hard as she could. The cup and saucer flew into the air, showering his face, neck, and chest with the scalding liquid. He dropped the cup in his left hand. It smashed into pieces on the wooden floor, hurling coffee up the side of the desk, drenching his shoes and trousers. The Frenchman yelped in pain, frantically rubbing his face and shaking his feet. He lunged at her, the front of his white shirt now wet and brown.

Yael stepped aside and grabbed Bonnet's right arm, using his momentum to pull him forward and spin him sideways. He swung wildly at her with his left hand, but she dodged it and slammed him into the edge of the desk. She stepped back and punched him hard in the side of his neck. He doubled over and she briskly banged his forehead down on the baize. There was a loud thud and the Frenchman collapsed, sliding down the front of the desk onto the floor.

Yael bent down and put him in the recovery position. She checked his throat was clear, took off his necktie, tied his wrists behind his back, and walked over to the window. A thick cord was hanging down the sides of the heavy old-fashioned curtains. She yanked hard and they came away in her hand.

She walked back to Bonnet. He was pale but breathing regularly. She bound his wrists with one curtain cord and his ankles with the other and quickly went through his pockets and found his mobile telephone. She took out the SIM card, slipped it into her jeans, dropped the handset into the coffee jug, and ripped the desk telephone cable out of the wall.

She locked the door, paused for a second, and checked her mobile telephone, the heavy old-fashioned handset that she had brought from Geneva. No alarm had sounded, and nothing from Jasna. But clearly she did not have long.

The key was still in the office drawer. She opened it, took out the document Bonnet had been holding, and read the top page again. Why had he locked this away? The UN report on the exploitation of Congo's natural resources was unclassified and freely available on the Internet. Anyone could download it.

She put the report on top of the desk and rummaged though the contents of the drawer: a brochure for an escort agency, leaflets for several of Geneva's Michelin-starred restaurants, an advertisement for a spa hotel on the French border promising "luxury, discretion, and rooms available for the afternoon," a leasing agreement for a Mercedes V8 convertible, and a photograph of Bonnet with his African wife and their two very photogenic children.

The sight of Bonnet's family triggered a pang of guilt. She leaned under the desk and checked the Frenchman. He was awake and moaning softly, looking around, trying to understand what had happened to him. He tried to sit up but gave up and sank back down to the floor.

Bonnet's eyes followed Yael as she stood up and walked over to the coffee machine. She could use the telephone that Joe-Don had given her to threaten Bonnet, but what if he also had a heart condition? She did not want another death on her conscience. Instead she picked up the coffee jug and stood over him.

"How did you know?" she asked.

"I didn't. I guessed. But I knew you would turn up sooner or later. And there is a small hole on your right upper earlobe where your earring used to be. Plus, cleaners do not usually wear Balenciaga leather jackets."

"Where is the plan?" she asked.

Bonnet coughed and tried to speak. "Plan for what? There is no plan. Only what you see here. An aid and development institute."

"I will try again. Where is the plan?" she said, letting the coffee drip out onto the floor.

Bonnet shook his head, his eyes wide with anger and, she sensed, an undercurrent of nervousness, and not just because he was lying prone and scalded. "You are going to spend the rest of your life in prison, *ma chère* Yael. I always said that your conscience would be the end of you. Why can't you just do your job, like everyone else?"

"It's not me who is going to prison. You are, for murdering Olivia."

The Frenchman looked outraged. He shifted position, trying to get more comfortable. "I did not kill her. Why would I do that?"

"Because she knew about Efrat Global Solutions and Menachem Stein. You, the SG, and Erin Rembaugh are secretly working with the world's biggest private army to take over eastern Congo."

Bonnet shrugged. "So what if we are? I did not kill Olivia. I have never killed a woman in my life."

He was telling the truth, Yael sensed. "But you don't mind if thousands of women and children die along the way to help the Bonnet Group's profits?"

Bonnet laughed cynically. "Please spare me your sanctimonious moralizing, Yael. You are no better than me. How many murderers and warlords have you helped stay in power when the P5 and Fareed Hussein told you to? How many bags full of dollars and euros have you arranged to be delivered for the 'greater good'? What is the difference between EGS, an army for sale, and member states sending their peacekeepers to further their political and economic interests? None whatsoever. At least EGS is open about what it does. Five million people have died in Congo. It is the world's worst humanitarian catastrophe, with no sign of ending. How many troops has President Freshwater sent to Goma and Kinshasa? Tell me, how many?"

Yael did not reply.

Bonnet said, "Exactly. Not one. They are all in Iraq and Afghanistan, securing oil supplies and gas pipelines. We are doing exactly the same as everyone else. The only difference is that we are better organized."

She sat down nearby, out of reach if he lunged at her, still holding the coffee jug. "Where is the plan?"

Bonnet said nothing.

Yael steeled herself, forcing herself to think of what was now at stake in the room. "Tell me where the plan is. Or I will empty this over you."

Bonnet coughed again. "There . . . is . . . no . . . plan."

She knew he was lying. She poured some of the coffee on the floor. It crept toward Bonnet, steam rising.

"I don't know what you are talking about," he said, his eyes darting to the UN report on the desk. And then she realized. Like the magician's handkerchief, it was hidden in plain sight.

Yael put the coffee jug back in the machine, then knelt down and checked the bindings on his hands and wrists. "Your first instinct once I leave will be to raise the alarm. Don't."

"Why not?"

"Because if I am not where I want to be at 9:30 a.m., a sound file of your encounter in your office with Thanh will be e-mailed to the entire UN press corps. Even by your standards that was a new low, threatening her family. Thanh is a friend of mine. I gave her the recorder."

Bonnet's face twisted in anger. "*Salope*," he spat.

Yael smiled. "I'm in good company then."

She turned and opened the door to leave.

A handsome Indian man with his hair gathered in a folded-back ponytail stood in the corridor, flanked by two heavyset, shaven-headed men in black suits.

"Hello, Yael," said Mahesh Kapoor.

Fareed Hussein sat behind the long table in the front of the Council Chamber, flanked by Lucy Tremlett and Reinhardt Daintner, looking very satisfied at the rows of journalists and camera crews. Hussein had given a short speech, praising what he called the "new partnership in business and development that would be a model for the world." Reinhardt Daintner said a few words, essentially repeating the same thing. Lucy Tremlett spoke passionately and articulately about her childhood on a council estate in south London ruled by violent gangs, and how education had showed her a new world. Education, she said, was the key to everything, so she was especially pleased to announce that the UN-KZX institute would be offering a hundred university scholarships to students from the developing world.

Because of the size of the room, any journalist wanting to ask a question needed a microphone. The desk microphones had been switched off, and there was one only cordless one for the press, controlled by Schneidermann. So far, almost every question had been directed at Lucy Tremlett, mostly about her film and acting career and relationship with Hobo. Schneidermann had studiously ignored the New York press corps and their colleagues, the UN reporters based in Geneva. He was bouncing around like a jack-in-the-box, clearly having the time of his life, dealing with journalists most of whom had no interest in politics. Eventually he allowed an African journalist, sitting toward the back, to ask a question. Najwa directed her camerawoman to turn around and film her.

The reporter was young, female, and determined not to be awed. "My name is Françoise Makimbo and I work for Central African News. Firstly, I would like to say that instead of buying us these expensive gifts—or perhaps I should say trying to buy us *with* them—it would have been far better to spend the money on grassroots aid and development. I will be donating mine to charity." She held up the box and paused as applause rippled around the room.

Schneidermann frowned and shook his head. "What is your question?" he asked. "We are very tightly scheduled here and do not have time for comments. Only questions, please."

Françoise nodded. "My question is what is the secretary-general's reaction to the report in the *New York Times* that his wife, Zeinab, has shares in Maobi Holdings, the company in Kinshasa that is managing the finances for the Year of Africa? And does he have any financial interest in this company?"

Schneidermann walked over to Fareed Hussein and whispered in his ear. The SG nodded. Schneidermann said, "We cannot comment on unsubstantiated articles. We are investigating these claims and will issue a statement once we are in possession of the facts."

Sami and Jonathan looked at each other with an expression of weary familiarity. Beaufort then watched in exasperation as Schneidermann handed the microphone for the second time to his colleague Samantha, the contemporary-culture correspondent, who was sitting one row ahead of him. Samantha had started to ask Lucy Tremlett what her plans were for her next role. Jonathan stood up and walked over and took the microphone from her. She looked surprised but deferred to him, as the senior correspondent.

Jonathan said, "Can the secretary-general confirm the presence of Efrat Global Solutions in and around the Goma region? Can he tell us what he knows about their activities, and can he outline to us what measures the Department of Peacekeeping Operations is taking to secure the area against illegal arms distribution?"

Fareed Hussein looked puzzled and shrugged. Jonathan looked at the microphone and tapped it. Nothing. It had been switched off. Nobody had heard his question. He put the microphone down and repeated his question, cupping his hands and shouting as loudly as he could. The fashion and celebrity journalists looked at each other and began muttering angrily. The African journalists clapped.

Sami stood up. "This is ridiculous," he declared as loudly as he could.

Jonathan shouted again. "Mr. Secretary-General, can you please answer the question," he demanded as the door to the chamber opened. The room erupted as Hobo walked in.

Thirty

Yael closed her eyes and concentrated as hard as she could, summoning the memories with every one of her senses: the hotel's crisp cotton bedsheets smooth against her back, the pillow firm under her bottom, the taste of the champagne chilling in the ice bucket, the sound of his voice whispering in her ear, the smell of his lemon cologne.

The door opened and Mahesh Kapoor walked in. The storage room in the basement was small and empty. The walls and floor were bare gray concrete. One narrow, high window looked out onto the sidewalk. Yael sat in the middle, her ankles tied to a chair with nylon ropes, her hands bound behind her.

Kapoor walked over to her and slowly stroked her head—a familiar heavy, black, old-fashioned cell phone in his hand. "Yael, Yael. What are we to do with you? And this?" he said, his voice full of regret, picking up a strand of her hair. "You know I always loved your long hair."

Yael said, "It will grow back."

Kapoor shook his head sadly. "I don't think so. Not this time."

"Where is Jasna?"

Kapoor smiled. "In a better place than you are."

Yael's eyes opened wide in alarm. "You didn't—"

"Of course not," Kapoor interrupted, frowning. She is being questioned by the UN police, after which she will be handed over to the Swiss authorities."

"And Olivia?" She looked straight at him. "Why did you kill her?"

He stepped back, puzzled. "I didn't kill her. I don't know what you are talking about."

Yael wriggled on the chair, moving her hands. She felt the rope around her right wrist slip slightly. "Olivia was my friend. She was so happy to have met someone. She was already half in love with you. And what a horrible way to die."

Kapoor looked genuinely confused. "I really don't know what you mean. The preliminary findings of the UN investigation point toward suicide. She was lonely, she had no family, she knew that big changes were coming at the SG's office, and she would probably not be part of them. It was true that we had met a couple of times for dinner. But that was for work. She built a fantasy around that. It was very sad."

He walked back to the chair and lifted Yael's chin with the antenna of the cell phone. Yael flinched. "Don't worry. It's not switched on. Yet. But if there is a killer in this room, I don't think it's me."

"What are you talking about?" asked Yael as she carefully slid her wrists back and forth. She could feel the rope slackening further. If she could bend her index finger and squeeze it under the knot she might be able to undo it.

"Kandahar," Kapoor said confidently. "And Sharif Iqbal, your translator."

Yael willed herself to be strong now. Her personal life and her past *did not matter.* Getting out of here with what she had learned *did.* Because Kapoor knew exactly what he was doing. They had discussed what happened in Kandahar for hours in the bedroom of the UN Millennium Hotel, over and over again. He knew every detail: that one night, cold, lonely, and frightened in a village controlled by the Taliban, Yael had climbed into Sharif's tent and into his sleeping bag. Sharif had immediately fallen in love with her, announced their forthcoming wedding to his family, and had started making preparations until Yael had gently explained that she could not marry him.

Sharif had been devastated. His father was furious. Sharif had begged her to go through with the ceremony just for form's sake, and then she could go back to Kabul or New York or wherever she wanted and they need never see each other again. She could still see him—his eyes as green as emeralds, glistening with tears—pleading with her to spare him and his family the humiliation. She only had to pretend for an evening.

Just one evening, for the sake of his and the family's honor. "Then, Miss Yael, you will be free," she could still hear him saying. "Miss Yael, I am begging you, do not do this to us. You will be gone soon, but we have to live here."

That was six years ago, when she was full of certainty, self-righteousness, and politically correct ideas about women's rights and the need to modernize Afghanistan. She refused to go through with the wedding, although she easily could have. Sharif disappeared and she and Joe-Don returned to Kandahar. There, several days later, one of her contacts in the Taliban told her that Sharif had gone through the martyrdom ceremony and had planned to target the bazaar just before Friday prayers, when the Old City would be the most crowded.

Yael looked Kapoor in the eye. "I didn't kill Sharif."

He held her gaze. "No, you did not. You didn't have the courage to pull the trigger. But you arranged it."

"Yes, I did. I told the people who needed to know that he was wired with enough explosives to blow half the bazaar sky high. I told them where and when he would approach the city. There was no other way. I saved dozens of lives."

Kapoor walked nearer to her. "None of which would ever have been at risk if you had not seduced a naïve young man with no experience with women at all, let alone Western ones. Just because you were lonely and scared. You used your status and your power for your own selfish pleasure with no thought of how it would turn his life upside down."

Kapoor was completely correct. "I know. And there is not a day goes by that I don't think about that and live with the consequences."

"And then you took a life, didn't you? One growing inside you."

She forced herself to feel no emotions. "Yes, I did that as well. Sharif's child."

Her right index finger was almost free. "But I have never pushed anyone off a balcony thirty-eight floors up."

"And neither have I."

"Heshi . . . can I ask you a personal question?" Yael held his gaze, her eyes wide with curiosity, her mouth slightly open. He nodded.

"Did you . . . like Olivia?"

He shrugged. "She was quite interesting company, but she was nothing much to look at. Even with all the money she spent on clothes." He walked around to the back of the chair and yanked the ropes much tighter. "Sorry. A good try though."

Yael grabbed his fingers. "But you did like me, Heshi, when we were together. Didn't you? It was not just an office thing? It meant something?" she said, rubbing her fingers up and down against his.

He squeezed her hand, let it go, and stood at her side, gently stroking her neck. "Yael, what a question. Of course it did. I will always treasure our time together. It will be the most wonderful memorial of you—although, unfortunately, a private one."

His fingers were warm and dry on her neck as they slid up and down, caressing her skin behind her ear, where she loved to be touched. Yael closed her eyes and sighed, willing herself back into the double room at the Millennium Hotel, and her excited anticipation as she readied herself for him.

She opened her eyes. Her breath was thick in her throat now, her nipples stiffening against her shirt. Mahesh was staring at the outlines of her breasts, straining against the soft fabric. "Look what you are doing to me. Heshi . . . please. Kiss me. Kiss me like you used to," she pleaded, her voice thick and husky.

Yael willed Kapoor closer, sensing his arousal. She opened her mouth wider, breathing faster, her tongue between her lips, feeling the wetness between her legs. She leaned toward him, her face raised in supplication. "Heshi, please, nobody made me come like you did . . ."

Kapoor smiled as though the compliment was no less than his due and moved his head toward hers.

The fashion and celebrity journalists jumped out of their seats and ran toward the front as Hobo walked in, wearing a long purple African robe and a matching turban. He shook hands with Fareed Hussein and Reinhardt Daintner and kissed Lucy Tremlett on both cheeks. Tremlett walked around the front desk and stood next to Hobo, and held his hand. The room erupted in a blaze of camera flashes as dozens of photographers and television camera crews surged forward, elbowing each other out of the way.

The first mud bomb hit Henrik Schneidermann on the side of the head. He looked puzzled, shocked, then fearful to discover that he was drenched with thick yellow sludge. The second smacked into Fareed Hussein's shoulder, and the third landed on the desk in front of Reinhardt Daintner, covering his gray silk suit with muck.

Sami and Jonathan turned to look up at the balcony, from where the bombs were coming. The African journalists were not just journalists, it seemed. They lowered a long banner: "Stop the Coltan Plundering: African Resources for African People."

There were a dozen of them leaning over the balcony shouting and raining down projectiles. The camera crews and photographers turned simultaneously and directed their lenses toward the upper floor. Hussein and Daintner cowered under the table. Hobo and Lucy Tremlett rushed toward the door. As they opened it a mud bomb exploded over their heads, spattering them with the thick goo.

Sami and Jonathan looked up toward the balcony. A pretty young Indian woman held a megaphone, shouting, "If you want coltan, then here it is. Dig it out like the miners do."

She took careful aim at Fareed Hussein and lobbed a mud bomb under the table. It hit a leg and burst over the secretary-general. UN police officers were now rushing into the Council Chamber and the balcony.

Sami and Jonathan watched as two UN policemen grabbed the young woman and frog-marched her away.

Sami turned to Jonathan. "Isn't she . . ."

Jonathan nodded. "She certainly is."

They both grinned and high-fived. "*Story.*"

Thirty-One

Yael jerked backed and slammed her forehead into the bridge of Kapoor's nose. She felt the bone splinter with a loud crack. He collapsed on the floor, blood gushing from his nostrils, the black handset tumbling from his hands. He sat up, spat out a gout of blood, wiped his nose with the back of his sleeve, and scrabbled for the handset.

Yael twisted herself sideways and flipped the chair over, landing on top of him. The chair sank into his stomach and knocked the breath out of him. His hand was under her face and she turned her head to the side, took the flesh in her mouth, and bit as hard as she could until her teeth pierced his skin.

He screamed in agony and tried to push her away. She slid off his prone body and hit the floor, gasping in pain as the weight of her body forced the chair legs onto her limbs.

Kapoor grabbed the handset and stood up, fumbling with the buttons. He walked toward her, swaying on his feet, blood running from his nose to his mouth to his shirt.

He raised the handset like a dagger, the prong pointing at her face.

The door opened.

Yael heard a muffled pop.

Kapoor flew back against the wall and slid to the floor.

His face was contorted in pain, and there was more blood, this time streaming between his fingers, which were clamped to his leg. The handset fell to the floor.

Yael felt the chair rising as she was righted.

The gunman kneeled on the floor behind her and untied her hands and legs. He took her arm and led her toward the door.

"Thanks. But what about . . ." she asked, turning toward Kapoor, who was now shivering and turning gray, his teeth chattering.

The gunman smiled dismissively. "Low-caliber flesh wound. We have already called an ambulance."

"Please, just check him. We will be in a lot of trouble if he dies. And I need to get the blood back in my hands and feet before I can walk," said Yael, wiggling her feet and rubbing her legs as the waves of pins and needles coursed through her limbs.

She moved nearer the black handset, which was lying on the floor.

The gunman sighed and walked over to Kapoor. He looked him up and down and rummaged in his pocket. He took out an army-issue field dressing, ripped the cover off, lifted Kapoor's hand from his wound, placed the dressing against the bullet, and put Kapoor's hand back on it. "Keep pressing.

You'll live. Lots of blood but no real danger. Like I said, help is already on its way."

He turned to Yael. "We really need to get out of here. Joe-Don is waiting."

He walked to the door, Yael following behind him. It was funny the things you noticed in these situations, she thought. The gunman was completely bald and she had never seen anyone whose ears stuck out as much as his.

Yael sat back in the battered Peugeot sedan as it cruised along the Avenue de France down to the Quai Wilson. They had left the Palais des Nations by an obscure delivery entrance that she had not known existed, but other than that, everything looked normal. The Iranian and African demonstrators were still gathered under the broken chair, the fountains on the Place des Nations were spraying merrily, the sky was gray and overcast, and it had started to rain. So much had happened that it was hard to believe that it was still only noon.

There were three of them in the car: the driver and the bald man in the front, Yael in the back. They would take her down to the Jetée des Pâquis, the bald man explained. The Jetée stretched out into the lake from the Quai Wilson, not far from the Place Jean-Marteau. Yael watched the thin drizzle run down the car windows. The Place Jean-Marteau where someone had shot the man sitting next to Joe-Don with a sniper rifle, she thought, her unease growing. The bald man turned around as he talked to her, all smiles and reassurance. A boat would be waiting for her at the end of the *jetée*, by the lighthouse, he explained. It would pick her up and take her to a safe house on the other side of the lake, where Joe-Don was waiting. His breath smelled sour, of coffee and stale tobacco.

It was not exactly the plan she had agreed to with Joe-Don. He said he would be waiting somewhere on the Place des Nations and that she should call him as soon as she was out of the building. They were supposed to go to the Jetée des Pâquis together, where *he* would have a boat ready. He was supposed to take her to the safe house, not meet her there. But the best-laid plans never worked out precisely as they should. Neither of them had factored in Charles Bonnet or Mahesh Kapoor.

She looked through the car window at the lake as they turned onto the Quai Wilson. The right side of the road was lined with grandiose apartment blocks and shops. A wide cycle and pedestrian path reached from the left edge of the road to the lakeside, which was protected by a low wall. A thick mist rose above the water, spilling out onto the road. The gray art nouveau streetlights that were spread along the shore suddenly lit up. Many of the cars now had their headlights on as well. A motorcyclist on a red Yamaha trail bike drove in the middle of the road, a hundred yards behind them, keeping pace with the flow of traffic. The rain was falling harder now but everything looked normal.

But who was this bald guy? He had rescued her, certainly, and he knew the rendezvous point. Yet Joe-Don had not mentioned him at all, and they had spent hours going over the plan and its permutations. And where was Joe-Don? Yael slid nearer the door, rubbing her wrists and ankles, feigning exhaustion.

She could see the Jetée des Pâquis in the distance, a long and thin spit curving out into the water. Down the middle ran a concrete path to the white tower at the tip overlooking the lake. The mist was quite thick now, and the car kept a steady pace with the traffic. Yael slowly pulled on the door handle. It was locked. Could mean something, could mean nothing. It was quite an old car, old enough not to have childproof locks. She watched the windshield wipers swish back and forth. The skies suddenly opened, unleashing a torrent of water, sloshing over the sidewalk, the road, and across the windshield.

"Where is Joe-Don?" she asked the bald man.

"I told you, he is waiting for us in the safe house. On the other side of the lake," he replied, turning around again. He smiled as he spoke but his deep-set gray eyes were expressionless.

She took out her mobile telephone. The bald man shook his head.

"No mobile calls, please. For your own security," he said, turning around and holding out his hand for her handset, his shoulder holster hanging from his left armpit.

Yael suddenly knew she was in extreme danger. Her left hand curled around the stun-gun handset in her coat pocket. She pressed the button on the side to set the charge.

She sat back, braced herself against the car seat, and kicked the driver in the back of his head as hard as she could.

He flew forward, and his face smashed into the steering wheel. The Peugeot skidded across the center of the road into the oncoming traffic, its tires screeching in protest. It smashed into an oncoming BMW, sent it flying across the road, and spun around 360 degrees, triggering a cacophony of outraged honking. The force of the impact threw Yael backward hard against the seat. The Peugeot's windows shattered, raining glass shards down on her.

The bald man smashed against the right-side passenger window frame, bounced off the windshield, and slammed back into his seat. He shook his head, blinked several times, and reached for his gun.

Yael jumped forward and jabbed him in the neck with the stun gun. He roared in pain and fury, but the prong slipped against his shirt as the car continued sliding across the road.

He reared up and aimed a left hook at her head. She grabbed his wrist, pulled him toward her, and tried to punch him in the throat, but her fist only glanced off his neck.

The car bumped over the step that divided the road from the lakeside cycle path.

The bald man lunged at her again. She dodged sideways.

The car hit a tree, spun around again, skidded over the sodden sidewalk, slammed into the low stone wall at the edge of the lake, and finally stopped.

Yael felt her head smash into the door frame, and the world went black for several seconds. She opened her eyes and the bald man was reaching for her.

She pushed back and kicked him in the face, breaking his nose. He fell backward, blood trickling from his nostrils.

She yanked on the door handle and kicked the door with all her strength. It still would not open. She climbed through the shattered window, ignoring the pain as the slivers of broken glass ripped her clothes and cut into her skin.

Yael stumbled out of the car and sprinted across the sidewalk onto the *jetée*. It was several meters wide, flanked on one side by rocks and on the other by small boats that bobbed in the water. A metal balustrade ran down the middle. The sky had turned the color of gunmetal, the rain was pouring, and the wind was blowing in hard from the lake.

Yael was drenched in seconds as the wet gusts hit her. Sirens sounded in the distance. The concrete was wet and slippery underfoot. Her left leg slid out from under her, but she grabbed the metal handrail and rapidly corrected herself.

The bald man ran after her. She weaved from side to side, her breath raw in her throat, as the crack of the bullets echoed over the water. Her sodden clothes clung to her, slowing her down as she ran along the *jetée*, rock chips flying all around her.

The sirens wailed louder, and now she could hear the sound of a motorcycle engine. A few yards ahead was a staircase, one side of a short bridge that rose over the lake for ten meters or so. She ran up the stairs, taking three at a time, and dashed along the concrete and back down the stairs on the other side. She stepped off the side of the *jetée*. The water was only a meter deep but it was freezing, burning into her cuts and wounds with a cold fire.

Yael crouched under the bridge, shivering violently as she searched for a loose rock.

The bald man ran down the stairs. She looked up as he stopped in front of her and scanned the *jetée* ahead. Her hand closed around a large, smooth stone.

She jumped back onto the path behind him and slammed the rock into the side of his head. He pitched forward instantly, swinging his gun around as he fell. He fired several times.

Yael leapt sideways as the bullets smashed into the walkway. Suddenly she spun around as though lifted by a giant hand and landed facedown on the path, scraping her face along the rough concrete. The adrenaline was pumping so hard she was oblivious to the bullet that had hit her.

The bald man got up and staggered toward her, blood gushing from the cut in the side of his head and from his shattered nose. He wiped his face and raised the gun again.

Yael jumped to the right, grabbed the gun barrel, and yanked it sideways. The bullets hammered into the concrete, bouncing in every direction, sending a fresh spray of rock chips against her legs.

Yael whirled around and punched him in the throat.

He slammed his fist into her shoulder. She collapsed.

She fell to the floor, slid backward along the wet concrete, and kicked him as hard as she could in the back of his knee. He went down on top of her.

They rolled off the *jetée* into the water. He landed under her.

She sat up, clamped his pelvis between her legs, and forced his head down with both hands, ignoring the freezing cold and the agony consuming the whole left side of her body.

The water erupted around them. His feet thrashed and an arm reached for her, flailed wildly, and fell back.

The fury surged through her and her breathing turned harsh and ragged. She was sitting on David's shoulders, laughing as he strode through Central Park, and her fingers were steel talons.

A foot broke the surface, kicked up, and then sank.

She raised her head to the sky, taking in great gulps of air, the rain pouring down her face, the blood seeping red then pink from her shoulder as it ran down her arm into the water. Her legs were a vise.

The churning slowed. She felt her fingers digging into his flesh, his hands grasping at her clothes, gripping her jacket, and then falling away. The bald man kicked once, twice, feeble twitches now. The water calmed and became still.

Yael let go. She stood up and staggered out of the lake to see the motorcyclist maneuver his red Yamaha down the steps. The rider jumped off at the bottom, ignoring the spinning wheels and screaming engine.

He took in the sight of Yael: sodden, bloodied, wild-eyed. Police sirens howled loudly nearby. A helicopter flew low overhead, its blades sending waves across the water.

The bald man floated facedown in the lake. A crimson pool spread out at Yael's feet. She looked at her hands, staring at her fingers as though they belonged to someone else. She shivered violently and her legs began to shake.

Joe-Don took off his helmet and walked toward her.

"You took your time," said Yael—and passed out.

Thirty-Two

UN to Hold Inquiry into Links with KZX and Bonnet Group; Senior Official Charged with Murder; Marc Rosenheim Arrested

By Sami Boustani and Najwa al-Sameera (Special to the New York Times)

NEW YORK—Fareed Hussein, the secretary-general of the United Nations, yesterday announced a wide-ranging inquiry into the role of UN peacekeepers and other officials in Congo and the collapse of the much-heralded UN-KZX Goma Development Zone in the east of the war-torn country. The investigation will focus on the role of the German corporation and its former business partner, the Paris-based Bonnet Group. The two firms are accused of planning a regional ethnic war that would allow them to take control of the region's supply of coltan, a mineral vital for mobile telephones and computers. Several senior UN officials are implicated in the conspiracy, said officials inside the organization.

Mr. Hussein announced at a press conference that the new probe, to be headed by Quentin Braithwaite, the head of peacekeeping, would be the most rigorous in the international organization's history. "We will leave no stone unturned in our determination to find out how the United Nations, the very embodiment of the world's humanitarian ideals, could have been hijacked by two multinational corporations for their own aims. This was an act of unprecedented cynicism and can never be repeated." Recent events in and around Goma only highlighted the need for the Year of Africa, Mr. Hussein said, although its launch had been postponed for some time to give the international organization enough time to reassess its priorities and capabilities.

Mr. Hussein's distancing of the UN from the German corporation and the Bonnet Group is an abrupt turnaround. As recently as last week, speaking at a press conference in Geneva, Mr. Hussein was an outspoken advocate of what he called "a new and necessary partnership between the UN and international corporations, one heralding the start of a new era in aid and development work, combining the UN's humanitarian expertise with KZX's business knowhow." The press conference descended into chaos after activists, including Mr. Hussein's daughter Rina, pelted the podium with mud bombs filled with the river sludge that contains coltan.

The fate of the development zone was sealed after

the discovery of a document that appears to reveal a detailed and long-term plan to ignite an ethnic conflict across central Africa. The plan involved renegade UN and State Department officials, together with KZX, the Bonnet Group, and Efrat Global Solutions, the world's largest private military contractor, distributing weapons to politically volatile areas. Company officials would then either carry out atrocities themselves or encourage locals to, thus triggering a cycle of war and revenge. The fighting would then prompt the deployment of UN peacekeepers, working in concert with KZX security staff. Once the region had stabilized, the UN troops would be withdrawn, leaving KZX in control of the mineral-rich areas.

The detailed plan was inside a publicly available UN report on the exploitation of Congo's resources but concealed through a technique known as "digital steganography." Steganography involves the covert embedding of extra data on digital files such as photographs, sound files, or documents. The data is invisible but can be recovered with a password. The technique is increasingly popular because it does not demand encryption, which acts as a red flag and can bring the attention of the authorities. The war plan for Africa was embedded in a PDF document.

Photographs taken in the village of Kimanda, ten kilometers from Goma, obtained by the *New York Times*, show Stephan Mannheim, a senior KZX official, and Shlomo Ben-Ami, a former colonel in the

Israeli army, handing out weapons to local men. Colonel Ben-Ami is a director of Efrat Global Solutions, which is owned by Menachem Stein, also a former Israeli military man. The firm could not be reached for comment, and a spokesman did not return calls left on his voice mail.

Reinhardt Daintner, head of communications at KZX, said in a written statement, "KZX is one of the world's most socially responsible companies. We are shocked and saddened to hear of the involvement of Mr. Mannheim in these recent events and emphasize that he was acting in a private capacity. We deeply regret the cancellation of the Goma Development Zone project, which we still believe offers a pioneering model that can take corporate social responsibility to a new level."

British actress Lucy Tremlett and musician Hobo, who were both closely associated with the Goma Development Zone plan, could not be reached for comment.

Despite his formerly strong support for the KZX development zone project, Mr. Hussein is almost certain to survive the scandal, say diplomats. The secretary-general's four-year term ends in six months but is likely to be extended to a second term. There is little support among the Permanent Five members of the Security Council for replacing him. "Hussein is a known quantity, and that is the most important thing for us," said one official who is not permitted to speak on this topic on the record. The official hinted that Mr. Hussein's personal involvement with KZX and the Bonnet Group, which has not yet been fully clarified, could give the superpowers useful leverage over him.

Yael read to the end of the lengthy article and then put the newspaper down, feeling annoyed and unsettled. Not because of Sami's revelations about the KZX-UN-EGS conspiracy, all of which, by now, she knew. What else were he and Najwa sharing apart from a byline? Especially when she saw a mention near the article flagging an hour-long investigative documentary, now in production and airing later that month on Al-Jazeera: "Dying for Coltan: How the UN Was Almost Hijacked," presented by Najwa and coproduced by Sami.

The rest of Sami's article detailed how the arrests were coming thick and fast. UN officials were leaking that Olivia had been killed because she had discovered the links between the DPA and Efrat Global Solutions. An employee of EGS had inadvertently left a message on Olivia's voice mail. Mahesh Kapoor had been charged with her murder. Hussein had canceled his diplomatic immunity. Judges had refused bail because he was considered a flight risk. Marc Rosenheim was being held in custody while federal prosecutors decided whether to charge him with treason, abuse of office, corruption, or all three. So was Charles Bonnet, who was facing several years in prison for aggravated sexual assault. The tape of his threats to Thanh Ly was already circulating on the Internet. Hakim Yundala had resigned as head of the UN's security office and returned to Kinshasa. He had been taken off the airplane in handcuffs and was charged with the murder of numerous Congolese activists and journalists. His sister had been sacked as Congo's ambassador to the UN and had returned home to face charges of corruption and embezzlement. Zeinab Hussein, the SG's wife, had returned home to her relatives in Karachi, suffering from stress.

Talks were underway with Columbia University for the Olivia de Souza Chair in Development Studies. An offer of endowment from KZX and the Bonnet Group had been regretfully declined. Erin Rembaugh had been killed in a hit-and-run outside her townhouse in Greenwich, Connecticut. Police were looking for the driver, but there were no leads. Mitchell Gardiner, the photographer who had been attacked after taking pictures of Fareed Hussein at Teterboro Airport, was recovering steadily and had been offered a staff position at the paper.

Yael looked around the reception area. Her shoulder was aching, a dull pain that pulsed up and down her left side. The bullet, a .22-caliber, had ricocheted off the walkway and lodged in her shoulder muscle without hitting any arteries or major nerves. Had the bald man used a .45-caliber it would have been a different story. Yael had stayed in hospital for a week, before traveling back to New York. Her shoulder was bandaged up, and she faced several months of physiotherapy. No Budokan for a while—that was certain.

So now what? The last time she was on the 38th floor, she had been taken by the bony-faced Frenchwoman to a hot and airless room down an obscure corridor.

This time she was waiting in the VIP reception lounge: an enormous and comfortable room with new modern furniture, pastel-shaded walls decorated with photographs of African wildlife, jugs of iced water, fresh orange juice, bagels, cookies, and a shiny chrome and black coffee machine in the corner that could supply a branch of Starbucks. All very nice, but what did Hussein want with her? Yael could still see him snapping the pencil in his hands just before she left, as she thought then, never to step foot inside the building again. Still, she had a couple of questions she wanted to ask him. He was unlikely to answer either of them, she thought, but however he responded would tell her something.

The door opened and Hussein's new diary secretary walked in. She was a tall and buxom African woman, wearing traditional dress—a long green and gold fitted skirt, a top, and a headdress—and had a dazzling smile. She ushered Yael into Hussein's office and closed the door.

The secretary-general was standing at the window, looking out onto the East River. Autumn was sliding into winter, and the sky was gray and overcast. He turned around and walked over to greet Yael. His eyes shone; he had put on several pounds and positively radiated health and energy. His stoop had gone, she noticed, as had all the KZX posters, although the signed photograph of Lucy Tremlett was still there.

"How are you, my dear Yael," Hussein asked, his voice warm and sincere. "I was so sorry to hear about the events in Geneva. Are you recovering well? Are the doctors looking after you properly?"

Yael nodded warily.

Hussein continued: "I very much missed you and your

counsel during these tumultuous days." He smiled mischievously. "Although I understand that you also played a most important role in ensuring the good guys won in the end. And I do like your new hair. Very stylish."

Yael had to stop herself from responding in kind. Hussein was charm itself, utterly confident, she sensed, as though he had recently suffered a debilitating fever, but was now calm, rested, and well on the road to recovery. He gently took her arm and guided her to the leather sofa in the corner of the room where he sat down next to her.

"Would you like some tea or coffee? Or perhaps something stronger? It's almost lunchtime," he said, glancing at his watch. "We have plenty of time."

Yael shook her head. "No, thanks. I'm fine. Where's Yvette Dubois?"

Hussein inclined his head sheepishly, like a schoolboy caught stealing biscuits. "Working for the French Forestry Commission. But we are not here to talk about her."

"Then why are we here?" she asked, her voice businesslike.

Hussein smiled benignly at her. "Yael, I have some excellent news for you, which gives me great personal pleasure to impart. You may remember that when we last met I said that an internal review was examining your recent work for us."

Yael sat back and looked at Hussein in wonder. He was as friendly as if they had just met that morning in the UN staff canteen. Her wrecked career, the betrayal, the threats, the extreme danger she had been in, being shot—it seemed none of this had happened. And if it had, then it no longer mattered.

She said, "What I remember is a lot of false accusations,

smears, and talk about dangerous non-state actors with long arms—and snapping pencils."

Hussein continued smiling and talking as though Yael had not said anything. "Yael, I am thrilled to tell you that the internal review has cleared you of all those unwarranted allegations. I am also assured by people who know about these things that there will not be any charges or difficulties resulting from recent . . . *events*, thanks to your status as a UN employee, which brings diplomatic immunity. I cannot tell you how pleased I am about this. You must know that whatever transpired, I never lost my faith in you."

Suddenly everything was clear. She was so surprised that for a moment she could not speak.

Hussein pounced, sensing her confusion. He stood up and helped her up, taking her arm. "Come with me, please, Yael. I have something to show you."

Hussein led her through his office and down the corridor. The walls were lined with UN staff and officials. As soon as they saw Yael they started clapping, slowly at first, then in a wave of applause. Several actually cheered and shouted, "Welcome back!"

She felt completely overwhelmed and to her annoyance, her eyes prickled with tears. Hussein handed her a silk handkerchief.

The SG led her into a sizable office four doors from his, much larger than her old workplace. The room was light and airy with windows overlooking the East River. A three-seater sofa filled one corner, a mahogany art-deco desk and chair another. Her peacekeeper's beret and mug stood on a shelf. A large new cork pin board took up part of one wall. A ten-by-twelve photograph, framed in silver, stood on the desk. It was a picture of David, standing in front of his white UN Jeep on the front line in Eastern Slavonia during the Croatian war.

Hussein held both her hands in his and looked her in the eye. "Please believe me, Yael. I really had no idea that he was your brother. David was a very brave young man. Whatever you decide, I very much hope you accept this from me."

Yael felt her eyes mist up again. "Thank you. Thank you very much."

"With your permission we would also like to endow a scholarship in your brother's name for young Africans who wish to study in Europe or the United States. We have a very strong candidate in this young man," Hussein said, showing her a photograph of a smiling, intelligent-looking African teenager. "His name is Herve Mapunga. He took the photographs of the guns being distributed in Kimanda. He wants to be a journalist. I think he will be a good one, don't you?"

Yael nodded, suddenly unable to speak. She swallowed hard and walked over to the door. She shut it quietly, closed her eyes, and breathed slowly and deeply for several seconds, centering herself before she spoke. "Joe-Don?"

Hussein inclined his head graciously. "Of course."

"Jasna?"

"Her contract at the UN has been extended another five years and now covers the whole east wing of the Palais. She has just taken on twenty more employees, including several Congolese refugees who, together with their families, have just received their Swiss residency papers. Whatever you decide, you may consider that as my gift to you."

The SG turned to leave and Yael held up her hand. “Wait, please. There’s something I want to ask you. If you want me to come back, I need to know.”

Hussein nodded. “Ask.”

“It was you, wasn’t it?”

Hussein looked puzzled but willing to be helpful. “My dear Yael, what was me? I am not sure what you mean.”

“The sound file I received. You were there, at the meeting with Rembaugh and the others. I heard your voice. You knew what was planned in Goma. You sent me the sound file. And then you warned Ambassador Munyakarana that something terrible was planned.”

She watched him carefully and saw something flicker in his eye for an instant. Something almost like relief, she sensed. And then it was gone. Hussein smiled warmly, shaking his head as though dealing with a much-loved, very bright, but impetuous younger relative.

He took her hand in his again. “Let me know your decision. Take as long as you like,” he said as he left the room, closing the door gently behind him.

Yael sat down at the desk and stayed there for a long time, staring at the picture of her brother. She wiped her eyes, walked over to the shelf, put on her peacekeeper’s beret, and stood by the window for a while, watching the river traffic. A passenger ferry glided out of the East 34th Street terminal, chugging slowly toward Queens, honking cheerfully. A garbage scow moved upriver, and the seagulls swirled and dived. Everything looked exactly the same as the day she left.

Yael reached inside her wallet and took out a worn photograph, covered in plastic and singed in one corner. She pinned it in the center of the corkboard and touched it with her index finger before sitting back down at her desk.

For the first time that day she smiled. She picked up the telephone and asked the building switchboard for the *New York Times* bureau.

It rang and rang and she was about to hang up when someone answered.

"*New York Times*," said Sami.

She swiveled around and leaned back with her feet on the desk. "Hello. It's me."

"Hello you," he said coolly, trying to cover his surprise.

"Long time, no speak," said Yael.

"Just following instructions."

She tried not to laugh. "And the ones you got from coltan@gmail.com."

"Oh. Was that e-mail from you?"

"Let's just say I know what it contained. That was a great article today. Well done. Anyway, I have a question for you. Two, actually."

"I'm listening," Sami replied, and now she could sense him smiling.

"Are you free tonight?" she asked, spinning the blue beret on her finger.

"Yeees," he said warily. "Why?"

"Good. Where are you are taking me for dinner?"